TO YIELD A DREAM

Also by Oxford Stroud

Marbles

Writing Prose That Makes A Difference

TO YIELD A DREAM

A NOVEL

OXFORD STROUD

NewSouth Books
Montgomery

NewSouth Books
P.O. Box 1588
Montgomery, AL 36102

 Published in the United States by NewSouth Books, a division of NewSouth, Inc., Montgomery, Alabama.

Library of Congress Cataloging-in-Publication Data

ISBN 1-58838-099-8

Design by Randall Williams
Printed in the United States of America

DEDICATED TO MY CHILDREN:

LAWRENCE
LYNNE
ROBERT
PHILIP
LAURA

TO WHOM I YIELD MY DREAM . . .

If we shadows have offended,
Think but this, and all is mended,
That you have but slumber'd here,
While these visions did appear.
And this weak and idle theme,
No more yielding but a dream.

PUCK, *A Midsummer-Night's Dream*

Part I

The Crossing

I

The Umbilicus

SEVENTEEN AND FREED at last from the academy! A poor cadet with enough demerits to warrant a stockade, I had nevertheless graduated at the head of my class. Always ready to plunge into the unknown, I, with my grandfather's blessing, had vowed to escort my mother home alone. At the time of this crossing to the island I could not have known that the great storm was already deep in its beginnings or that the wily Spencer would appear. I would miss Rowdy, my quaint roommate, and Zacharias, the old black caretaker at the academy. But this crossing was a clean and final break.

So for the moment I gave myself freely to the groaning motion of the ancient ferry called the *Umbilicus.* Upon the bow of the old barge, jetting my chin into the spray like an eager Christopher Columbus, I stood between my anxious terrier and my mother's winged casket. The casket wings were my own creation, but they were small, unpretentious wings, unangelic in design, light sky blue, and swept back jet-like into the fuselage of the coffin.

It was early morning, and the choppy Gulf facing me, thankfully, was broad enough to embrace my restless spirit. Except for me, my aging fox terrier, and my solemn mother, only the ferry captain and his mate were aboard the *Umbilicus.*

With the aid of The Admiral—my invincible grandfather—and the five hundred confidential dollars with which he had enlisted the ferry captain, I was determined to make this special crossing alone.

"Jody, if you must stand so close up on the bow, please put your life preserver on."

It was Captain Zeorge. Every summer between sessions at the academy I had ridden the ferry boat with him to and from the mainland. He hung a life vest on my shoulder. At his arrival my terrier leapt up on the casket and sat down.

Coming slowly to myself . . .

"Oh—yes sir."

Captain Zeorge was a little heavier now but wore the same white, short-billed cap with gold stitched-in anchor and the same khaki jacket with the third brass button missing.

"And don't you reckon it's rude to let your dog to be setting on your mama?"

"Zip," I said and his ears popped up.

"Ah yes, Sergeant Zip of the academy," he said to the dog. "I see your spotted butt ain't grown a bit." He stooped over to flip Zip's sausage-long tail.

"I cut it off when he was a pup," I said. "A little dog with a long tail don't balance out."

"So you've said," Captain Zeorge recalled. "It's sad about your mama crashing on her way to Albuquerque." The inquisitive Zeorge was examining the blue casket wings.

"Yes, sir," I said. "She sang opera. Singing was like flying to her. She was an aviatrix too." I loved the word *aviatrix* as it applied to my mother. I loved the sharp X on the end of it. "We flew with her all over the country to hear her sing. Her voice was like flying over the mountain tops. She won't mind Zip being here." I sat down on the foot of Mother's mahogany coffin and tapped my fingers on the lid. "She'd recognize the cadence of his claws clicking here." I tapped the coffin lid again.

Through the morning fog, I could see the outline of the island.

When I stood up Captain Zeorge said, "I see you've put on some man-size since last summer and 'bout outgrown your big ear."

The awkward ear had been my everlasting burden, something I couldn't walk around or run away from. To make my ear even more notable it had a dimple in its crest. As a boy I had learned to turn my head slightly when in conversation, except when speaking to The Admiral or to the commandant at the academy.

"It's heredity," I explained.

"Ah yes, so you've said."

I wondered if Captain Zeorge knew of my larger problem, a pain too intrusive to turn away from and too pervasive to bury in the secrecy of Mother's casket.

"I hear your hermit uncle had a big ear too."

"Yes sir," I said.

"Is he still holed up in his basement?"

"I reckon so," I said.

When Zip sat down I punched him up again.

"Your funny uncle was a Golden Gloves champ. What's he so afraid of?"

Nothing was funny about my Uncle Minos. He had become a trouble to my dreams.

"We don't know exactly," I said.

"You ever *seen* him? Up close?"

"Only his back and shadow through his cellar window."

"They say after his fight with the Mobile sailor at Inn Lafayette he don't look at nobody. Not even . . . even his . . . his own *woman*."

"Wife!" I corrected. "Venoria. Her name is Venoria!"

Captain Zeorge meant no disrespect, but his way of saying *woman* implied a commonness in my remarkable aunt that was offensive to me. Sensing I was a bit stung he hung his head in brief repentance and said, "Now it's a real shame about your famous mama, even if she never came back to sing for us."

As a budding soprano my mother had blessed the island church with her abundant voice and greatly aroused the heart of the young Reverend Millsap.

"It wasn't her fault she never came back," I said. I wondered if Captain Zeorge knew why.

"Ah, yes . . . Now, I'm to remind you and the dog that The Admiral will meet you at the pier with the hearse and the pretty art girl. You are to be at the Holy chapel by 10, at the Church of the Holy Sepulcher by 10:30, and at graveside by 11. Got that?"

"Yes sir," I said. The Captain made a big smile.

"You ought to be able to tell time pretty good after The Admiral built his big clock on the face of the old fort."

"Yes, sir," I said.

The clock was one of a kind, a gift conceived by my grandfather, designed and installed at great expense by engineers and horologists from Zurich. You could tell time from the sky. Driven by an engine powerful enough for a Ferris wheel and as quiet as a snail, it was a huge time machine twenty-six paces across with Generals Lee and Grant mounted life-size in bronze on their steeds and each on either hand in perpetual pursuit.

Captain Zeorge backed away thoughtfully from the casket and propped his hands on his hips.

The pretty art girl the captain mentioned would be Jo Anne.

She was something of a prodigy who came into our family as a stepchild by Gloria, her petite and attractive mother. A freelance artist with a religious flair, Gloria, to her great convenience—but not without tenderness—had anchored my Uncle Claude in marriage. I lived with them during the summers. Dear, sweet, unassuming Uncle Claude—Mother's gentle brother whose natural life was fishing and whose immediate and enduring joy was the spirited Jo Anne—was lured, hooked, and landed by this nimble angler before he knew what happened. I know now that if Gloria was the hook, Jo Anne was the bait that caught him.

Even then Jo Anne was a child artist of unusual talent and had gained professional attention for her unique re-creation of fish and other aquatic creatures. But now the time had come to lay her talent on the line, to subject her art to the most discriminating critics and place it in competition with that of our most prominent artists.

Mother and The Admiral had visited me often at the academy. Jo Anne never. But with recent postcards she had dribbled to me certain drops of family news that otherwise would have come to me by slow leakage or not at all: that The Admiral each Christmas had sent a thousand dollars to my commandant "for Rowdy's special needs," that my hermit uncle had taken to wearing a grotesque mask to hide his eyes, and that The Admiral had recently purchased from the Thirteenth Duke of Chesterton the 1955 royal *Emerald Rolls Royce* for two hundred thousand dollars—"for your dear departed grandmother—for their REUNION," Jo Anne had emphasized.

One postcard was pure riddle. It said: A Civil War Likeness = *now your new abode.*

Lately, in characteristically cool diction, Jo Anne passed to me the painful urgency of her impending art contest where she would be judged with the nation's best. And to my distress, she would include *Bull Bluegill*, a special painting she had labored long upon, just for me. And, as always, she inquired about my sad roommate, Rowdy.

More recently Jo Anne had sent me a head-and-shoulder snapshot of herself smiling back inquisitively into the camera. Even from the photograph, I was amazed at her transformation since last summer.

"Now put the life preserver on," Captain Zeorge said. "This is a special trip and The Admiral don't give me five hundred bucks for nothing."

"I'll just keep it on my shoulder 'til we get there," I said.

"And if it's all the same to you I'd just as soon you not let Zip to be sitting on your mama—a matter of manners, you know," the Captain said and walked away.

"Yes sir," I said.

So here was I—rescued from the academy by my mother's death—facing the four-mile blade of island that had become my home. From the air, Hurricane looked like a Russian saber: its butt the massive Civil War fortress with its generals locked in time; its mid-mark the fabulous Ark; and at its tip The Admiral's lighthouse leaning toward the Gulf of Mexico.

What was it . . . ?

An irregularity had appeared on Mother's casket.

I stooped to see.

It was Spencer.

I had not expected to see the garrulous insect so soon, certainly not before I got to Hurricane. During my terms at the academy on the mainland, Spencer had never left my mind, but he had always remained on the island. This time, for some reason, he had ventured to meet me halfway.

He was sitting on the brass handle above the left blue casket wing. With his thin legs crossed and his brow raised expectantly, Spencer was manipulating a straw in his impressive jaws. As if impatient, but with an inquiring gaze, he held his familiar eye to mine for a moment, then, in no great haste, crawled around the corner of the coffin.

When I got to my knees to confirm his identity, he had disappeared.

2

Spencer the Ant

My first open encounter with Spencer was during the summer of my first stay on the island. Mother was on a grand tour in Europe.

This was also my first encounter with Jo Anne. We played a game she called SKY–SPY which cast me at once into keen competition. In daytime her game was a contest of finding in bundles of cumulus clouds the forms of animals and monsters and, at night, the faces of famous men in random chips of bark and leaves held up to the moon. Her instant perception was intimidating. She knew instinctively the difference *and* connection between seeing and seeing into. Being of a military academy, I welcomed her competition.

The Admiral had supplied me with an arsenal of books that fortified me—though not poor Rowdy—against not only the armies of ignorance but also the narrow arrogance of the academy. I was a voracious reader. The academy had drilled into me the academic fundamentals with thin slices of Homer and Cicero and a splash of Latin grammar. But my main passion was to be a roving naturalist, to live in the clear and clean state of Arizona—sun, sand, mountains, sky—and seek into the secrets of the universe.

Leagues ahead of my classmates at the academy, I was a lousy soldier. It pleased me most that I was the best swimmer of our institution. I could swim the entire distance around our official lake without a puff and go again. I welcomed all competition. My fear of water was zero. The colder and deeper the water, the quicker and stronger my stroke.

And I could outfish them all, including the commandant—all except old Zachariah, our black custodian and gorgeous band leader who at parade shone like a peacock in the sun. At lakeside angling he had no peer. Before each cast, he never failed to spit on his hook and mumble up a mini-prayer. His fishing was of and for quality, not quantity. He measured his young musicians by this same scale. "Music," he said, "is God's way of sortin' out the noise." Many wealthy parents had tried to buy their tone-deaf sons into the band, but they had failed.

Zack called his angling technique *skimpy-fishing*: the lightest possible tackle for the most available fish, the smallest number of worms or crickets for the most prudent catch—and all for the Glory Moment. To Zack, the Glory Moment was that special thrill of energy that burst forth when the line pulls, tightens, then sings, and the fish breaks water—that glittering instant when you and fish are one, transfixed, united between two worlds. "It's then, *click*!" says Zack. "That's when God takes yo' picture."

It was true. Since that first time when the great bream broke water, leaping like a shattered rainbow, the zing of it flashed over me like lightning. All this I told the wide-eyed Jo Anne. She promised on the spot to paint me a picture of the magnificent fish and my Glory Moment.

So now with such skills as Zachariah had imparted to me, I hoped to prove myself on Hurricane.

I never intended to be a show-off but simply to please The

Admiral and my gentle Uncle Claude who was a deep sea expert at the fishing art. But after a spell of close company with Jo Anne, I itched to squelch this precocious, ruddy-faced female puppy whose every pore oozed conceit and whose every breath upon me was the warm green of poison ivy.

"Bubba Jody the big ear," she nailed me. "With a nitch in it," she added, referring to the dimple at its crest.

Looking back now, I suppose my abrupt domestic intrusion brought Jo Anne front and center to protect her own turf. But if her insolence kindled in me immediate rage, it often brought along soft edges of restraint.

Of my fishing skills she said, "Claude wouldn't use you or your bobtail dog for cut bait." She looked at me straight and didn't bat an eye. Yet for my mother, Jo Anne had only praise. The Admiral had purchased for Jo Anne recordings of my mother's operas and the most expensive machinery to play them on. She said, sincerely, "If your mother's tongue were brushes she could paint the *Mona Lisa* and *Olympia* blindfolded." That was the self-confident, self-educated Jo Anne in pigtails speaking of Leonardo de Vinci and Manet. Even with my adolescent eye I could sense in her paintings something of the deep and mysterious, especially in her fish *Flounder.* At first sight it tickled me. Then, unless I looked away, it saddened me and, finally, made me mad. Jo Anne had painted the flat fish as true to nature as she could, even to its oddly squashed head. But she had angled its eyes in a puzzling feature that evoked, at the same moment, both pity and humor. It was a look that nailed me between a smile and a tear and which always stirred up in me a little revolution: When the tear won I hated the smile and when the smile won I hated the tear. Jo Anne's fish always won, and I ended up angry with myself.

Of my nebulous father Jo Anne cracked me sidewise with

"You're a no-daddy cadet brat." This struck the sore core of my soul, for which I bashed her nose and sent blood everywhere, for which that night she packed my big ear with kitchen-warm peanut butter, and for which the next day Gloria shut Jo Anne in her room with St. Matthew's gospel and The Sermon on the Mount and sent me crunching up the beach to spend a cooling off with The Admiral in his lighthouse. Except for her lovable Claude, Jo Anne was as daddyless as I was. There was one important difference; her father was not only dead, he was accounted for.

Afterward to enhance my prestige on the island and to dim God's sunshine on the precious Jo Anne, I—with the encouragement of The Admiral and my amused Uncle Claude—invented a freshwater fish-fetcher.

Claude scratched his chin. "A *freshwater fish-fetcher*! It's got a real catchy name, ain't it?" he smiled.

Gloria shook her head.

Jo Anne looked at my contraption and said, "Fish'll ride bicycles before they bite that."

My invention was an ingenious apparatus of one day's contemplation. Its vital parts were a string, an air-tight gallon bucket, some sinker rocks inside, and a soft sounding alarm clock on loan from Jo Anne. I promised her a live bull bluegill to paint from. She abhorred dead fish and worked mainly from specimens in the aquarium on the mainland or from her many-pictured fish books. "A fish out of water is sad," she said, "like a bird with a broken wing."

My theory was that once the fetcher was assembled and sunk in The Admiral's lake, the alarm—set exactly for the *Almanac's* Sunday sunrise at 5:29 A.M.—would purr away, luring curious fish from their sleepy deeps to the softened vibrations of my clock call. Then, using old Zack's spiritual attunement and holding my mouth just right, I would bait up, spit on my hook, and cast out for the catch. Adhering to Zack's "skimpy fishing," I had corralled only six crickets in a penny match box with air holes punched in. Simplicity was the common denominator of my theory.

The Admiral endorsed my invention and promised aid in securing patent rights to protect whatever fortune might fall our way. He even contributed a scar-faced Big Ben, an ancient time machine of doubtful reliance but one which enlarged my project from a one-bucket to a two-bucket enterprise. I set the Big Ben to perform thirty seconds after Jo Anne's softer alarm. In dry runs I checked out the double duty fish-fetcher twice. It worked. Each time the clocks sounded off, Zip's ears pricked up.

At 4:45 A.M. Sunday I was ready. As promised The Admiral flashed G-O-O-D L-U-C-K in Morse Code from the lighthouse. A full moon sifted through the clouds. I synchronized my wristwatch with the clock buckets. It was ten minutes by bike to The Admiral's lake and thirty-three minutes more before the sunrise alarms were set to go. Jo Anne and Gloria got up to see me off. I was astride my bike, balancing from toe to toe to stay upright—my spinning rod strapped on the handlebars, Zip riding piggy-back with his front paws across my shoulders and his back claws under my belt, the double-bucket fish-fetcher dangling about my neck, and my flashlight tied forward on the crown of my straw sun hat.

Claude was still asleep.

"You look like something the cat threw up," Jo Anne said. She was carrying Cleopatra, her black and white jigsaw-colored cat.

I already understood from Gloria that fishing on Sunday would be permitted, but missing church on Sunday—never! With calculated regularity, Uncle Claude did not attend church at all. Last night Gloria said to me loud enough for Claude's appreciation, "On Hurricane we catch *God* on Sunday."

"All this to drown two clocks," Jo Anne snubbed, giving me and Zip the once-over.

"So?—" I intimated.

"So here." she handed me the crickets in the match box. I had forgotten them. I blew into the air holes.

"So they can breath," I said.

Jo Anne put her lips to my ear. "Bring a big boy bream home *alive* and I'll catch him again on canvas," she teased. She leaned so close to me that Cleopatra spat and took a swipe at Zip's nose.

"You be back by church time," Gloria warned, "10:45 at the Holy Sepulcher. Remember, on Hurricane we catch God on Sunday!"

I clicked my flashlight on and pushed off.

I HAD NOT seen the Church of the Holy Sepulcher in quite this light before. I could see its oval outline in the predawn. The church had been something of an experience for me. It was a mammoth structure in the form of a great whale. It reminded me of Jonah and his big fish. Gloria called it Leviathan. The Admiral called it Moby Dick. Claude called it "one more whale of a damn church." It was a profitable tourist attraction whose mysterious donor had never been disclosed. But to me, being fatherless and already having heard disturbing whispers about the Reverend Millsap and my mother, I had the feeling of being swallowed up in guilt when I entered the eerie sanctuary.

Zip growled when we passed close to Venoria's WHY NOT SHOP where Uncle Minos had entombed himself. I turned my head at an angle that shot the flashlight beam through his cellar window. I wondered if it startled him, if the shock of it wheeled his warped body around to face the light. I pictured, too, his seizing the intangible beam and reeling me back into his darkness. I quickly turned my head and fixed the spotlight on the yellow line down the middle of the blacktop. When I stopped, the moon slipped out of the clouds.

In the semi-darkness The Admiral's lake was larger than I expected. Zip leapt from my back to make his reconnaissance. Across the neck of a little peninsula, a pine had fallen. On the other side of the old tree, near a perfect nook of moon blue water, I lay down my spinning rod and put the crickets under a clump of cool grass. Then I unslung the double-bucket fish-fetcher and flung it carefully into the floating circle of the moon. When the ripples receded, I returned to the fallen tree to await the remaining ticking off of time and to see how my invention might fare.

It was 5:17.

The fallen tree was short and thick, an old timer, a survivor of storms. But now laid down and tender with age, the old log was suffocating into the earth. Soft and warm, it had become a burrow for chipmunks, grubs, ants, and woodsawyer beetles. Over the lake the arch of dawn was forming. I sat down and rested my head back into the cushion of the old pine, and yawned . . .

—when I became aware of a presence behind me. I turned around to find an endless train of large amber ants traveling down the spine of the great trunk. I hopped over their highway and knelt down to get a horizontal view of the procession. The column moved along in orderly fashion, each trooper translucent in the rising sun. Some carried a stem or loaf of food. Others bore what looked like rice-sized pillowcases of milk or plasma. To the side by the stub of an old branch stood an official ant the size of my thumb. In my library of nature books The Admiral had given me I had never seen its like—an intense and regal insect who, with delicate antennae, passed precise instructions to each traveler on his way. He proudly breasted a flamboyant thorax slick as shellac and a transparent abdomen as clear as polished agate. What he was communicating to his subordinates I had no way of knowing, but his message was dispatched with urgency and authority as he moved the procession along in sustained formation.

Amazed, I was about to speak—

"If you *please*," the ant said, "remain silent lest you utter something painfully ridiculous or totally beyond the bounds of comprehension." He held up a slender finger and the procession stopped.

"I was—" I began.

But the ant continued.

"I'm sure the brave crickets you soon intend to sacrifice will applaud your fishless generosity and welcome their early release."

"I was—" I began again—

"Yes, yes, I know. You were about to say how astonished you are, but I assure you that your eyes are much too large and round to see anything distinctly." The ant's voice was an articulate, melodic alto, but firm and resolute.

"I can see you," I said, not wanting to lose the wonder of the moment.

"Well that is practically nothing at all," the ant said. "Your eyes were created too far from the ground to see anything with precision."

"Well then," I said, trying to hold my own, "your eyes are created too close to the ground to even see the end of the log you're on. How far do you think you can see?"

"I can see the sun," the ant declared.

I knew from my books the sun was ninety-three million miles away and that its light took some time to get here. "I can too," I said. "It took the sun seven minutes to get here this morning."

"Actually it's seven point seven, but my, my, how bright you are!" the ant said. When he held up a finger, the procession started again and another less imposing official took his place. The engaging ant now drew within a hand's breadth of my nose, shifted his mandicles into a menacing grin, and clicked his jaws. "It's true," he said in a carefully modulated tone. "As most creatures in our uncertain realm, we ants do see but dimly. Even I, impressed by your altitude, can barely see at this distance your lopsided ear and your moon-shaped eyes which are a sure sign that you are unbalanced and almost totally blind."

Not wanting to contradict the arrogant insect or to interrupt the procession again, I kept silent and continued to watch the ants appearing on the log from nowhere and disappearing off its distant end. The ant resumed:

"You human colossi have forgotten that your eye is to see *through*, not to see *with*." I hadn't the slightest idea what he was talking about. But he seemed sincere and said, "If you see only what you are looking at, you're half blind. Look," he invited, stretching out his bulbous lower part in the early sunlight. I moved my head an inch closer. "Closer," the ant urged, reclining and pointing an anxious finger to his abdomen. "I shan't bite you," he said and shifted his metallic jaws into a fierce smile.

"Ants don't *bite*," I corrected. "They sting."

"My, what intelligence," the ant said, adjusting to his already awkward position. "Well, I shan't *sting* you," he continued, still pointing to his belly. "Closer, closer," he instructed.

At this range, the ant's head looked like a bead of glazed butterscotch and his eyes like pocked moons.

"Promise?" I asked.

"Great Jupiter!" the ant complained, "I'm much too earthly wise for such adolescent nonsense. Where do you think I've been all these eons?" He paused and looked up at my nose, "You should know very well that if I stung you I'd vanish on the spot, and although death is nothing to me—nothing!—I'm of no mind to depart this morning. Besides, I'm not sure you are worth the trouble—Can you see the sun?"

"Of course," I said. Already the sun was a glowing ball of orange floating over The Admiral's lake. I was still on my knees looking over the log.

"Here," the ant said, pointing impatiently to his honey clear abdomen, "put your eye right here." The ant wanted me to look through his belly. I was so close now that my breath ruffled the sparse hairs on the ant's body.

"Up, up close," the ant insisted. "Look through me here."

I put my eye flush up to his belly as if to a microscope.

"Now," he said, "look at the sun."

"I'm trying." Suddenly a blinding glare flashed up before me.

"Don't look *at* my belly!" the ant cried. "Look *through* it."

"I'm trying, I'm trying," I said.

"What do you see?"

"A little coil of string that's pointing down toward the bottom of your belly."

"You silly dunce, that's my entrails and my anus. You are looking at the wrong thing."

"And there's a little dark glob making its way toward your tail end."

"Great god of gravity!" the ant cried. "That's a cracker crumb I ate last night. A clumsy fisherman dropped it in the grass. I've got to eat you know. But you are still looking at the wrong thing. Don't look at my entrails. Look at the sun!"

When I focused my eye beyond the cracker crumb and into the full force of light, suddenly the sun spread out beyond its perimeter and enriched an infinite horizon with golden radiance. It seemed as if the whole universe had opened up. I was stunned, filled with rapture. I could hardly breathe.

"See?" the ant said.

"Yes!" I sighed.

"That's the wholeworld in a single beholdment," he said.

"Yes." I could believe it.

"See the wholeworld ocean below?"

"Yes," I whispered.

"It's very beautiful, but dangerous out there. No one can ever cross it," the ant said.

"I can. If I had time," I said.

"Yes, yes, yes. I suppose you could." The ant took a deep breath and held it as you do for an x-ray. "Don't move now. Don't move or you will lose your vision of the sun," the ant said. "Can you still see the wholeworld ocean?"

"Yes," I said. "I can see all the way to the other side."

"Of course you can't," the ant said, clicking his jaws. "There you go again with your moon pie eyes. The best you scissors-shaped invalids can do is to see everything in flat circles, boxes, or straight lines curved or snipped off—which is no fault of your own," the ant conceded. "I fear at their wit's end your best philosophers resolve themselves in weary circles."

Most of this went over my head, but the ant had a point. Through the honey clear belly of the insect, The Admiral's lake was transformed from a flat morning gray into a endless, rippling amber with silver whitecaps licking up from the surface and slipping back into the evolving diamond light of the deep. I had never beheld such beauty. It was like seeing all the varied lights of the world through the perfect symmetry of a jewel.

"Tell me," the ant asked, "where is the sun now?"

"Everywhere," I answered honestly.

"Splendid! Now what do you see in the cloud above?"

"A great heavy face, frowning—no, smiling."

"Don't say what or who it is. Don't kill it with a name or it will go away."

A brown blob was sinking down slowly toward the right side of my eye.

"That's the same dumb cracker crumb," the ant said. "Don't look at it or you will go blind again."

"How do I not look at what I'm looking at?" I asked.

"It's not easy," the ant said. I refocused my eye as if looking into the distance.

On the rim of the wholeworld golden ocean with its endless silver lips, Zip was a Zebra galloping through perpendicular shadows and across the ocean shore of a tropical infinity.

"Now," the ant continued, "where are you in the midst of it all?" He had answered his own question.

"Right in the middle," I said, for at that moment I was at the center of all I saw, and all I saw came right through the middle of my eye.

"Enough," the ant said and with chilly fingers pushed my cheek away. "Any more of such sustained seeing is sure to drive you crazy or strike you stone blind forever." He carefully synchronized his antennae and relaxed his stern expression to one of confidential seriousness and said:

"Now, if you please, I would have you call me Spencer because that is my name. I detest last names, initials, Roman numerals, and all such useless appendices and superfluous gobbledygook—superficial attachments all. I need know you only as Jody—J-O-D-Y. If I, a mere ant, may detect the very essence of your character immediately, labeled by four letters only, then all other letters in your language will not improve you. Unfortunately, I am unique, probably a blundering, immutable mutation, but otherwise quite an ordinary ant."

For reasons I have never been able to explain, I was not unsettled by Spencer's actual presence or his all too human behavior. In fact I am convinced to this day that his uninvited appearance would have been more incredible if he had happened to me in a dream.

"You *are* a bit large for an ant," I agreed.

"You might say so. I grant that my size is an embarrassment, a handicap, perhaps even a danger to myself; but it has not diminished my powers of penetration. And," he added with military acuteness, "any flop-eared jackass ought to know that fish don't *come* to an alarm; they *flee* from it. Sound travels more soundly in water."

True. How had I forgotten this? I set the clock alarms again to ring. They did, I suppose, even if sunrise had long gone. I baited up, spat upon the astonished cricket, cast out, mumbled up a mini prayer, and waited. And waited. Would the silent water keep my fishing flaws a secret?

I wondered what The Admiral would say about a patent now. I thought of Zachariah and his standards of perfection. However, my invention *did* work; it was the fish that got the message wrong. And I was thinking ahead, of fishing at night with live lightning bugs. Even after fireflies die, their lights stay on.

Zip trotted back from his tropical paradise, panting, smiling, his tongue palpitating like a slice of wet ham. The sun was high, too late for church. I gathered up my gear, put on my flashlight hat, and set the remaining crickets free.

In an alto cadence that sounded much like my Aunt Gloria's: "And don't forget to catch God on Sunday," Spencer chanted from the log, waving a green leaf.

Zip leapt up, put his hind feet behind my belt and his paws across my shoulders. We peddled up the hot blacktop.

When I cycled by the Church of the Holy Sepulcher, Jo Anne and Gloria were following the organ music into the benevolent mouth of the ecclesiastical whale.

At home Claude was crawling like a slow lobster under the web of a shrimp net, examining its threads against the sky. At my arrival he cocked up an elbow to block the sun. I was standing barefooted and fishless before him with the clock buckets dangling about my neck. He read my face.

"You mean—" he squinted and said in serious voice, "You mean with all that fish-fetching stuff you didn't catch God or nothing?"

"Not a nibblin' thing," I confessed.

3

The I-SPY game

I NEVER REALLY hated the academy. In all truth the academy was a comfortable place. It was just different from Hurricane. The academy was a square place that you could measure and be measured by. The island allowed for no such exactness or regularity. I can hardly imagine, for instance, conceiving of my I-SPY in a dormitory at the academy. More naturally my game happened on the island in The Admiral's lighthouse. And it happened in close proximity to The Admiral's Rock Garden, a seemingly random but in fact purposeful collection of rocks that reminded my grandfather of old ideas he might forget. At the time I had not become familiar with the stones and felt it none of my business to inquire further into their purpose or arrangement.

Although separated from my grandfather by half a century and two world wars—seas of experience and continents of knowledge—I had, with my wireless at the academy, kept close company with the old sage. The older The Admiral became the closer he gravitated toward me, as if he were moving back to recover something lost. Although he could play back his past with the accuracy of an old movie, he found himself now with a poor grasp of the slippery present falling all around him. But in my time we had formed a bond that bridged the years between us. Spending half his long life as a merchant seaman, The Admiral had been everywhere, seen everything, done everything. He had rambled wide, gambled big, won big, invested wisely. He was rich, rich, rich. The only islander richer was the famous Johnny Revelation. The Admiral was old but ageless, frugal not selfish, generous but secretive, proud not pompous. He owned the whole tropical east shank of Hurricane and leased half of that to Hollywood for movies. Having oceans of leisure, he had read with relish every word that washed his way. But forgetting nothing of his old past and having so small a vessel to keep afloat his varied cargo of knowledge, he felt himself forever sinking. "Great godamighty, Jody boy!" he would cry into the microphone, his voice crackling over the gulf, "We are sinking, sinking into the quicksand of our own stupidity!"

It was probably true, as Spencer hinted, that my invention of I-SPY was a spin-off of The Admiral's Rock Garden—if one could call my game an invention at all. I have come to suspect that most inventions merely happen rather than being "thought up." A great idea may be mainly a matter of holding the assembly of the mind in a proper attitude of reception rather than consciously throwing the articulate machinery of reason into motion and grinding out a desired result.

I suspect also that my I-SPY game sprang more intimately from Jo Anne's simple SKY-SPY we played as youngsters. But it's impossible to say exactly when or where a thing starts happening.

It was mid-June. The academy was closed except for a few summer numskulls and, of course, Rowdy whose wealthy parents had abandoned him. A note from the exacting Zachariah simply said:

Dear Esquire Cadet Jody of Hurricane:

It is with a heart of Thanksgiving to Your generous Admiral and with Hope that You may soon return as I write of Cadet Rowdy who walks these Vacant halls and Weeps at night to keep His warm tears a secret from the searching eyes of His comrades and to quench His own hot dreams of a father whose voice falls short of hearing and of His cruel mother whose arms are forever empty of Him.

Yours in Military Courtesy and with a Salute from our Commandant of Unbending Steel and Your Cadet Captain Custodian and Band Master of the Academy,

Zachariah

With a sob, Jo Anne handed the note back to me.

My heart, too, ached for Rowdy. Fortunately, Rowdy wasn't rowdy; he wasn't even quite smart enough to know how dumb he was. He had clung to my shirt sleeve as I left him to Zachariah in front of Stonewall Jackson Hall. He had stood at attention with the old black man and had given me a slow and forlorn salute.

At the time, Mother was on tour from Madrid to Rio de Janeiro to San Diego and then to Montreal. On one brief Alabama appearance Zip and I flew with her from Mobile to Memphis and back. Dozens of times after take-off I had flown the Aeolian Harp—a name bestowed on the silver ship by The Admiral. On this flight into Mobile, Mother had followed my hands, touch-for-touch, on the dual controls; and I brought us down without a bobble.

By now on Hurricane, I was feeling my way into the psyche of the island, but my flying experience gave me a hands-on confidence, a self-reliance that was unnecessary at the academy. This was especially true when I was fishing the Gulf with Claude.

Sweet, methodical Uncle Claude, who knew the waters of the Gulf as surely as the king mackerel or the ever-surveying porpoise, Claude taught me tricks of bigger fishing, of navigation, and how to bite back seasickness by sheer grit. On short jaunts Jo Anne often came along to recover specimens from the Gulf to satisfy her passion for painting. Fish out of water were a pain to her, so Claude had fixed on deck a double-decker bunk-sized tank with glass windows and circulating sea water so she might study her subjects alive. One specimen she had studied intently for hours before returning it to the gulf. It was a diamond-shaped stingray. She had later depicted the graceful fish arched in a swift turn, flashing a wing of its enamel-white underside and the poisonous barb of its tail curled back in self defense. The remarkable thing about the picture was—even if you knew nothing of the creature—that this was a female ray. It was also clear that this particular ray was neither in immediate danger nor pursued. It were as if this aqua queen of diamonds had been startled by the artist, caught in shameless surprise. And this was exactly what Jo Anne had intended.

Jo Anne was Gloria's high ambition and Gloria would press her daughter's talent to the limit. I had learned to endure, maybe to love, my snappy aunt even though she was jealous of my mother. It was an artistically concealed vanity, but I could detect it all the same and have since believed that a great many artists, those laboring in the same or in neighboring vineyards, secretly despise each other and regret praise heaped on anyone save themselves.

For my part, The Admiral's permanence came pure and uncontaminated. His life had been too diverse, too romantic and rare for summation, and yet to me The Admiral—like his lighthouse—was singular and immortal.

Jo Anne's genius was another thing.

We hear frequently of great prodigies, past and present: The presumptuous six-year-old, composing and pounding out complete symphonies or the grade school sprout briefing college profs on the theory of equations. But prodigies of the graphic arts? These are nil or next to nonexistent. Those in the know say it's because such talents at so early an age lack the worldly experience and philosophic range to produce mature art.

Perhaps.

Early in the summer The Admiral—never to be satisfied with the ordinary—presented me with a bewildered bullfrog. The hapless croaker had only one hind leg and thus swam and hopped in unavoidable circles. The radius of his inland excursions was considerably less than the diameter of his pond, so he never got lost and always ended up right back where he began. Mr. Grumps I called him, a sure subject of interest for the incisive Jo Anne.

But it was Zip's spontaneous production that introduced me to the metaphysics of art. It all started with the simple act of Zip's eating a box of Jo Anne's crayons and the next day depositing the most exquisite turd in dogdom. Claude said it was caused by a lack of calcium in Zip's diet. I'm not sure, but to this day I still don't know who *owns* Zip's tidy bit of art. For safekeeping I placed such natural wonders on a special table in the corner of my room. The Admiral called the kaleidoscopic turd Zip's Magnificent Impression.

Jo Anne's genius never aroused in me cold revenge or hot jealousy. Nothing like that. But she nourished in me a crippled kind of rage, an urge to smack her and run but lacking the legs to get away. After all, she had descended into my family by proper marriage, crawled into it by way of her pretty and gifted mother. Jo Anne was becoming a painful attraction, a whetstone honing me into a sharpness for I knew not what.

However original my new game, Jo Anne understood it at once and was more intent in playing it than in me—I, who invented the game!

My game started in a most unromantic manner. I was sitting on the commode in The Admiral's lighthouse, looking down into a linoleum floor of spots. Although my initial conception was probably as old as hieroglyphics, my game had begun. First there began to emerge from the spotted maze outlines, quite naturally, some recognizable forms and images—not all at once and not all together. It was clear from the beginning that it was impossible to achieve more than one image at a time, and even that not without effort. I discovered that from the constellation of spots I must hold my eyes in open receptivity and in unblinking concentration. Then, when the fringes of my first image began to fill out and mature, there appeared a human face! My game was born.

I-SPY I called it.

The Admiral was pleased. He saw commercial possibilities and bought an entire roll of the original linoleum that we cut into two foot squares and glued onto plywood.

"Nothing new," Jo Anne declared. "We played that game with pine chips and butterfly clouds."

But my game *was* different. Unlike clouds or chips, my game was self-contained, and the elaborately spotted squares required a broader imagination and more subtle powers of recognition.

"A baby's game," Jo Anne dubbed it, even though she was prancing to play.

"Even so," The Admiral said, "don't knock simplicity," pointing out that, like the lever, illusive simplicity can move mountains and that the hidden power of the wheel kept ancient man in eons of bondage.

On a first try at the game Uncle Claude pointed out a dolphin.

Gloria saw a dove.

The Admiral saw the face of General Lee.

I knew without debate there must be rules, but I-SPY was ultra simple to play and a cinch to care for. It was all of one part. Unbreakable. No moving parts. Nothing to crack, break, tear, fall apart, drop off, or get lost.

Moreover, each game would be a brand new experience, never repeating the same pattern, because as soon as a player removed his eyes from a new-born image it melted back into the nebulous galaxy of the whole; therefore the unique revelations one might glean from the humble board were endless. Two or more could play. All you had to do was *see* an image or picture in the constellation of varied spots, point it out, have it recognized by a judge or your adversary, then count it in your favor and so on for a set time to see how many picture-images you found. The same for your opponent. The player with the most I-SPYs won. Nothing could be simpler.

On our first game—fifteen minutes each on our own board—Jo Anne and I tied 10-10.

Here the rules ran out.

What to do?

Easy.

The Admiral puts one board between us.

"The first *I-SPY* wins," he says.

I look. Jo Anne looks.

I leave my eyes open all the way to the back of my brain.

"Zip," I announce and point into the labyrinth.

"Zip?" Jo Anne inquires, putting her face close to my finger.

"See, his short tail, right *here*," I say.

The Admiral draws in closer.

"His ears. See?" I point at Zip's head.

Jo Anne looks a question at me.

"—and his nose, and tongue. See?—he's panting," I say.

The Admiral looks at Jo Anne.

"See? It's Zip," I repeat.

"I bet you could find four-leaf clovers in an airplane," Jo Anne says.

I look at The Admiral. "It's Zip alright," I say.

"A dog—maybe," Jo Anne says.

"Zip has got mighty potbellied of late," The Admiral says and adds optimistically, "but it beats playing checkers all to hell and just might make some money."

Not so.

Not at five dollars and—coming down a dollar a notch—not at four, not at three, not at even two bucks a whack. After five days of hard sell demonstrations and dead-end sales at Aunt Venoria's WHY NOT SHOP, I-SPY was a complete flop.

On a scale of one-to-ten as a face-to-face salesman I was below zero. On the third day, to bolster our hopes—but mainly I think to prolong the adventure—The Admiral ordered from a gulf coast advertising firm a blimp airborne, as long as a football field with I-SPY letters five yards high on one side and WHY NOT SHOP on the other. It was as big as Johnny Revelation's Ark. A devotee to the late A. Conan Doyle, my grandfather specified that the large P on the I-SPY side be fixed up with a face and detective cap and a hand holding up a magnifying glass so that the eye of P was looking into the character of Y. The Admiral came dressed as Sherlock Holmes with his front-and-back detective cap and armed with a water pistol. He examined each arriving spectator through his glass and then took a pot water-shot at the blimp. The gathering crowd was enchanted. Aunt Venoria was befuddled.

"Your grandfather I think is swimming in his barrel," Venoria said. She meant *drunk*.

The Admiral's outdoor spectacle worked, but backfired. It drew the crowd. But the crowd had come mainly to get a glimpse of Minos, The Hermit of Hurricane. And then they got The Hermit mixed up with Sherlock Holmes, and the WHY NOT SHOP mixed up with I-SPY, and I-SPY mixed up with the blimp until, after awhile, the milling crowd didn't know what it was looking for.

I had a notion that my first sale would have a domino effect, that from an eager audience—after the first sale—they would all arise with great enlightenment: *Ooooooh*, they would sigh, *I see*, then gobble up all the remaining games, leaving the unsatisfied customers pleading for more on bended knees.

But when I pulled out for them an I-SPY game for sale, their faces fell, and while I explained the marvel of my game, they departed one by one. I could see their knees outside, squatting down before the basement window to get a glimpse of my uncle, the Hermit.

On Thursday Jo Anne came to see my failure.

On Friday she decided, "Uncle Minos is a jinx." She cupped the words to my ear with her hand so Venoria would not hear and pointed through the floor into the cellar. "Poor, stooped soul, he can't help himself." I'm not so sure my handsome aunt felt the same.

Venoria pulled me confidentially into her strong shoulder. She smelled of olive oil and lilac water. "I want you two should take a look." She was speaking of her husband below, whose bed she had never shared. Venoria had improvised a peep-hole into the cellar. It was a two-inch galvanized iron pipe that acted as a kind of inverted periscope. "I only now and then pretend to look at him," she said.

I put my eye to the pipe hole.

"Have ever you seen before such a blemish on the scarred face of Hurricane?" Venoria asked.

I had not. Uncle Minos was wearing blinders—not the side-floppy kind made for mules and horses—but a self-styled hooded shield that fit over his brow and eyes and stuck out from his face like a tunnel. With his massive shoulders, my uncle looked like a wounded buffalo.

Jo Anne took a look and put her hand over her eyes. "He looks like the Hunchback of Notre Dame," she shuddered.

"He is what my customers wish to see and maybe later to buy these pretty shells, but not your I-SPY game," Venoria said as she surveyed the numerous shelves and cabinets of her remarkable shop. Jo Anne had on sale an impressive array of Gulf Coast fishes painted on the inside of oyster shells. The Admiral had for sale rare rocks from every country on the planet. "All this and my very pretty empty shells from his strong hands, and I must leave him alone here below, leave him," she sobbed, "to his lonely soul."

Jo Anne was touched.

"And his lie?" I asked.

There was a silence.

From The Admiral I had heard bits and pieces of my Uncle's bloody fight with the sailor at the Inn Lafayette. But of his *lie* I had heard only lisped whispers and sifted suspicions.

On Saturday Jo Anne saved the day, not for Uncle Minos but for I-SPY. The Admiral had discharged the blimp, leaving the sky surprisingly empty. He came this morning wearing freshly pressed khaki trousers, starched white shirt, and a Panama hat. He had just started his morning cigar when a busload of traveling inmates from the Pensacola Home for the Mentally Impaired pulled up. They were a jolly bunch led by their watchful custodian and a large—not fat—lady in uniform. She had a red face and wore pale pink lipstick.

The eager pilgrims were on their weekly outing. Apparently they were indexed by number, not for any degrading purpose of regimentation but simply for personal identification so that each might proudly remember and recite his or her own name and number. There were twenty-one aboard, and this morning their accomplishment was not only in identifying themselves but also in recalling the name and number of the inmate on either side of each. Thus inmate Barbara knew her name was number seventeen; on her right, George was eighteen; on her left, sixteen was Sandra. So as the stealthy madam in uniform issued out the inmates, each disembarked with a smile and happy recitation of "I'm Johnny nine; Sammy eight; Janice ten . . ." And so on. The last inmate off was a chubby lad of thirty-five or forty. He had a problem. His name was David. He stepped off the bus and said, "I am David, twenty-one . . ." He stopped and looked around as if deserted.

"It's O.K. Davy," the guard lady said, "you're just *last* not *lost*."

Then my domino notion of sales began to click, but in a surprising way:

Jo Anne pulled the custodian aside and whispered in his ear while . . .

The Admiral handed out to each inmate a bit of his rock display—"Bixhyite on Topaz, Pyrite and Angita, Obsiclon with Lithophysae," he announced mysteriously, turning his end-to-end cap around on each pronouncement, while . . .

Venoria shared, with each and all, her husband's basement art, shell figurines natural and fantastic, shellacked and glued on tiny shingles of glass and plastic while . . .

Jo Anne—her audience well in hand—gave to each inmate an oyster shell picture of a fish she'd painted while—I took the anxious custodian to the galvanized pipe-hole for a secret peek at my hermit uncle and while . . .

Jo Anne—her eyes darting back and forth to me—was talking enthusiastically, holding up an I-SPY board, pointing and moving her fingers in a swirl as if stirring up the clogged spots—stopped, then picked out a pair of captured eyes among the inmates and, still pointing, said, "See?"

A hand went up. It was David.

"I am David, number twenty-one," the voice responded.

The guard lady kept his hand held up high. The other inmates started clapping. David had found himself in a cluster of I-SPY spots.

"It's me! it's me!" he chanted over and over, pointing into the maze. David was jubilant, and the custodian came over to celebrate the discovery.

Their time was up. Escorted by the guard lady and their cheerful leader, my incredulous customers departed with their assorted treasures and six of my I-SPYs. Amid many giggles and much fun over my speckled game, the inmates counted themselves back aboard their yellow bus. Jo Anne and I bid them all good-bye.

"You mean you *gave* my games away?" I asked in disbelief.

"They didn't have any money," Jo Anne explained.

"But—"

"And you can't play but one game at a time."

"But—"

"And you've got a whole stack of dead I-SPYs at home beside your bed."

"Dead?"

"Well—flawed."

"How can a bunch of spots be flawed?"

"Not the spots, silly. It's what they can make you do."

"Like what?"

"Like lie."

"Like great God-a-mighty—That's not the spots' fault. That's *your* fault. You've got *not* to lie."

"I don't lie," Jo Anne shot back.

"Neither do I."

"How do I know you saw Zip in the spots?"

"Because The Admiral saw Zip too and said so."

"How do I know he saw what you saw?"

"Good grief," I said. "You've got to believe somebody."

It was Aunt Venoria coming out to watch the mentally impaired pull away. She was carrying an I-SPY game.

"I must fear at my age what goblins will hop out of these spots at me." She smiled and made a face at the I-SPY board. "But I dare hope my sad husband may sometime find his own self among his own dark nooks and crannies."

"Does he feed well?" I asked as if my uncle were an animal.

"You have seen with your naked eye down through my spy tube," she said. "His shoulders are those of Hercules. But now ages since our sacred vows his eyes have not met mine."

THAT NIGHT BEFORE getting into bed I stood gazing down at the stack of my "dead" I-SPYs. My eyes were fixed on an inlet of spots in the lower quarter of the board that produced, it seemed, an outline of Minos's face; but his countenance struggling to emerge, kept receding, coming up featureless. There was, however, in this profusion of dots a movement that I had not seen upon the board before. Most of my I-SPY images had come up gradually, as if from the bottom of a pool; the form would then take a fixed shape on the surface. But this particular formation moved in a forward fashion as if it were alive.

"Alive, indeed!—all of which might go to show that your eyes are more flawed than I suspected, more flawed than your simple I-SPY game; for here am I—my indestructible, irrepressible self—right under your very nose and you have seen me not!"

Who else but Spencer. He was snuggled juxtaposed between two little islands of spots. Cross-legged, he stood up like an automatic jack, with no assistance from his hands, and brushed himself off, then walked to the I-SPY title and sat down on the hyphen. "And I dare say it's wise to try to fool your venerable grandfather."

"I did see Zip in the spots," I affirmed.

"Yes, but a very foggy Zip."

"I didn't expect to find you here," I said, pointing at the game he was sitting on.

"Of course you didn't. I would be completely worthless if I were not a surprise. Surprise is always a reminder that there is something you don't know. In fact I often surprise myself to find myself in your company."

"Are you playing a game with *me* ?" I asked. This tickled Spencer.

"You might say so," he chuckled. "But all games are flawed or they wouldn't be any fun to play."

"I can't picture you as ever having much fun."

How could I have known that this would touch such a sensitive nerve in the ant?

" 'Tis more true than not," he said, looking down at his slim arms. "Except for brief interludes of sweet peace, the course of my natural existence has been a desperate game—not your kind of fun. Our great exhilaration—especially for our Queens and bold

Warriors, even for every member of our most remote colony—has been our relentless pursuit of self preservation and the perpetuation of our noble race. We are fearless and merciless in the destruction of our adversaries, satisfied only with the utter annihilation of our enemies. And for all such dedication and sacrifice, we vanish without glory or remorse."

Spencer's brief oration left me speechless. I was impressed by his baroque rhetoric and wondered if my mother had ever taken company with the meticulous ant.

"Of course she has," Spencer answered before I could ask. "Our ancient talents coincide with the first rumblings of the earth and with the wind that first hummed through the early shingles of this world."

"Did you know Mother when she was a—"

"Girl?"

"Yes. About—"

"About Jo Anne's age?"

"Yes."

"And you would like to know when love first entered your mother's heart and for whom?"

"If you please," I said, assuming Spencer's decorum and trying to hide my desperate need to know the answer.

"Very well—answer me a question."

"Shoot," I said.

Spencer tucked in his chin and looked out of the tops of his eyes like a professor.

"Where does an acorn start happening?" he asked.

At the academy I had learned to give snappy answers. "In the stem, the very tip end of it," I said quickly.

Spencer waited.

I thought: *the branch, the trunk, the roots, the earth* . . . I could tell where this was going. Spencer was watching me carefully.

"Ah me!" Spencer sighed. "You with all your store of natural knowledge. Have you not entered that marvelous chamber, both linear and cylindrical, where I with my naked sensors, have taken the pulse of the universe and felt the acorn's vital juices unite with the sun?"

"*Between the bark and pith wood! The sap. The leaf.* Photosynthesis!" I exclaimed. I loved this word. I knew my science. But Spencer had not answered my question. He was paying me no attention at all. He was walking back to the middle of the I-SPY board.

"I did see Zip," I said.

"Are you sure your eyes didn't put him there?" he said.

Someone was approaching my door. It was Jo Anne. I could tell by her footsteps. I watched the door knob. The footsteps stopped. When I looked back at the I-SPY board, Spencer had disappeared into the spots.

"Spencer . . ." I whispered. "Spencer . . ."

"Who is Spencer?" Jo Anne wanted to know.

It was only after I returned to the academy that I learned from The Admiral that the Florida Department for the Handicapped had ordered two hundred I-SPY games.

"Two hundred!" I shouted into the microphone. Static electricity was crackling over the gulf. "That's a thousand dollars!"

"Quite right," The Admiral affirmed. "The best damn therapy since your mother's silver voice or the velvet of a lady's lips . . ." Grandfather was chuckling to himself. "The inmates taught the director and the psychiatrists how to play our game! See our civilization . . . sinking! . . . sinking . . ." he cried into the mike.

I couldn't tell now whether The Admiral was laughing or weeping.

The next day I got a watercolor picture from Jo Anne of two $500 bills.

"P.S.," she had written at the bottom of the picture money, "One of these is mine. After all—I 'sold' the inmates on your I-SPY game."

This was true.

"P.S. 2," she added. "I'm sending Rowdy a game."

I wondered that I had not thought of Rowdy as a player.

4

The Ark

After I-SPY, at the unlucky age of thirteen, Jo Anne was in love with Johnny Revelation. I could tell by her eyes when I spoke his name.

First I simply read his note. The second time I savored it, absorbed it word by word, then put it under my pillow and lay back to meditate over its message. The holy script had come from Johnny Revelation, an answer to my postcard message about the lost ruby rhinestone that had fallen from his blouse. During an enthusiastic gathering and holy hullabaloo on the mainland, I had driven with the curious commandant to the great occasion. The stone had fallen loose from Johnny's dazzling jacket and trickled into the audience. I saved the jewel from the dangerous dance floor and kept it safe in my possession. The commandant thought I ought to keep it in his lock box in the main office. Zachariah said I should give it back to the fleecing Jesus at once or risk an evil spell that could spin me off to hell. Rowdy had found Johnny's likeness in his I-SPY board and reckoned the red stone so powerful that if he swallowed it he might finally learn to swim or maybe even walk on water.

Jo Anne slipped into my room that night and said, "Please take me with you to see Johnny. PLEASE."

The note was written by the very hand of the famous evangelist who had recently set the South aglow with his lithe, musical body and who in soulful voice now covered Dixie like the dew. Shimmering Johnny had cut Jesus rock records in gold and platinum and recorded commercial tapes that, if unrolled, would reach the moon.

Gloria said that with his lascivious hips and long golden hair Johnny Revelation was a sin and shame unto this world, that he was on a lustful train headed straight for hell. From the pulpit Reverend Millsap damned him, "the blonde satyr of Babylon." The Admiral said we all had a lot of "Johnny" in us and ought to shape it up before it blew our minds. He added that if Johnny did not exactly enhance the *holy* spirit, he at least energized procreation, pointing out that after each Easter week-long song fest on Hurricane there was, nine months later, a baby boom from Mobile to Pensacola.

Claude said starving alligators would spit Johnny out.

Spencer was mum on the flaming evangelist but said the blood-red ruby was the sign of war.

It was the ruby rhinestone that set me in motion.

Now from the evangelist, prompted by my postcard, his note read:

> Jody of Hurricane come alone to me with the ruby rhinestone. Be at The Ark 3 P.M., June 14.
>
> Johnny Revelation

Jo Anne held the stone in her palm as if it were the liquid blood of Jesus Christ and said, "His signature is worth a million dollars."

When I allowed it was my Christian duty to return the lost gem to its rightful owner, Gloria said, "Well—maybe—" That Jo Anne might come along—"Absolutely not!"

I was eager for the imminent mission and wore my scrolled and colored cowboy boots, clean blue jeans, and a longsleeve white shirt. I had the ruby rhinestone wrapped in one of The Admiral's large silk handkerchiefs and stuffed into my shirt pocket. I mounted my bicycle. Zip rode piggy-back, and we were off to The Ark where that night—as on many nights before—with his luscious Nola Rose, Johnny Revelation with his holy loaves of rolling sound would nourish the multitude. It was a warm and steady ride. I passed Inn Lafayette and Venoria's WHY NOT SHOP where Uncle Minos breathed alone in his cellar. Reverend Millsap standing in the mouth of his mammoth church acknowledged me with a vacant wave. Already the citizens of Hurricane had come to know Zip and me together, saying, "Here come Jody and Zip on the bicycle," or "Here come Zip and Jody on the bicycle." In the distance across the dunes and stunted oaks I could see the lofty main mast of The Ark, and fluttering on a flag staff JOHNNY REVELATION in white and red—a sign of passion and purity. Or so The Admiral said.

Zip's whiskers were in my ear. Pedaling nearer, I was surprised to find—as if it had materialized from the clouds above and settled near The Ark—the world-famous Rainbow Carnival with its cluster of many-colored tents breathing in the southern breeze. Clever, winsome Johnny was sure to prosper from such close proximity to the famous show. Or had the roving carnival leeched itself to Johnny's even more famous sand-docked Ark?

Zip's claws were digging into my backbone. I turned off the blacktop and onto a sandy lane where we stopped in the shade of a sweetgum tree. Zip hit the sand. We were halfway between The Ark and the carnival. I leaned my bike against the tree. Zip looked back to see if I was coming. The walk to Johnny's shrine was but a few short dunes away. As a challenge to entrance, Johnny had neither ramp nor evident paths to the pleasure of his Ark, only sand.

The Ark was indeed a masterwork of nautical likeness. It was designed and crafted by shipwrights from Sweden and Nova Scotia and ready for the sea. Its location in this barren region had enhanced rather than hindered its popularity. The vessel's very isolation had assured that Johnny's pilgrims be either those of means or those sufficiently inspired to make the pilgrimage, or both. It is true that The Ark was used for a variety of entertainment; but when Johnny was on Hurricane, The Ark was his alone. The Ark was his axis, and the universe here and hereabouts revolved around Johnny and the stunning Nola Rose. The main entrance to The Ark, suited to its design, was a banistered gangplank from the sea of sand to the main deck. I walked aboard and tapped on the great door with the butt of my pocket knife. Zip sat. There were footsteps in the belly of the ship. As Johnny Revelation had required, I arrived precisely at 3 P.M. The door swung open.

"I am Hano the Navigator," said the blue-bearded custodian. He had a black patch sling over one eye and a no-joke smile. The big man wore a snow-white uniform with chin-high collar and a master seaman's cap scrolled in gold. He looked at his wristwatch. "I assume you to be Jody?" he asked.

"Yes sir," I said. "Mr. Johnny said for me to be here at 3 o'clock sharp with his lost ruby rhinestone."

"Yes," the Navigator said, "but you were to come alone."

"I am alone," I said. "Zip's not really *any*body. He's my dog," which, I knew, was nearly a complete falsehood. Zip was a dog, of course; but he was most noticeably a part of my being here. Also Zip certainly knew his name and he wasn't without a body.

"Inseparable," the Navigator advised.

"I reckon you could say so," I said.

Zip slipped through the big man's ankles and was inside.

With entrance now gained, Zip and I followed the one-eyed Navigator who was saying, "The Master wants you to know that for finding and returning the prodigal stone you are to receive—personally—a full dress rehearsal performance, plus a spiritual reward that you shall *never* forget." The big man turned around and stopped me with his eye. "The rhinestone is not a rhinestone; it is a ruby. But, nevermind; because it came from The Master's coat, it is *priceless.*"

"I'd be much obliged just to shake Johnny's hand and see Miss Nola Rose and give the ruby back for nothing." I said.

I wished that Jo Anne had come along. Not only did I feel on the verge of a rare occasion, one that Jo Anne herself would relish; but there was about her presence a contagious strength that magnified my own. I knew I was invited here alone. But how could the incomparable evangelist, who attracted throngs, have refused Jo Anne, one who loved him so spontaneously? Yet here Zip was, securely aboard, Zip who didn't give a pig's poot for godly songs or a good golly damn for the whole glorious Ark.

A hollow knock echoed through the ballroom. Zip trotted to the huge oak door, sniffed, sat down, and pleasantly contemplated the brass knob. Had Jo Anne followed me on her bike? The Navigator was on top of the situation at once.

"We don't care who you are," he said to the crack in the door, "this is a most private affair," and slammed the big door.

"She's my sister," I supplied when the Navigator returned. Zip was still watching the door.

"You're *both* liars," he growled. "This little wench is got curly red hair and yours is straight and fine as flax. What do you take me for, some kind of idiot? Don't you know the Master has made *special* time for you? That this is for your *special* pleasure? Don't you *know* Johnny Revelation don't give a tinker's damn about one measly ruby or the whole Hope Diamond? It's the collection that counts. The assembly! The many! The magnitude!!" the big man cried. His voice was so loud it frightened Zip back to me. "Do you want to pay attention here and now or take your little red rock and go? We don't really need the puny stone you know."

By silence I conceded.

"Now, that's better. Follow me," the Navigator said.

He led me to within whispering distance of a circular, lighted stage to the fore of the ballroom and set me down at a long glass table. The table top and legs, chairs and all, were made of pure crystal. I would hardly have seen them except for the Navigator's guiding hand and for the azure-orange sunlight captured in the fixed angles and arcs of the transparent furniture. I felt as if I were seated in front of an intangible rectangle and upon a cushion of air. Above the stage was an oval opening through the poop deck to the sky. In the dim underlight Zip bumped his nose on an invisible table leg and staunchly refused to jump up in the doubtful chair until I laid a tangible hand in its glass bottom.

When the Navigator disappeared to fetch Johnny and Nola Rose, professional hands swarmed on stage to fix the scene. From watching Johnny's TV performances, I recognized this particular stage set. This was to be a dramatic enactment of The First Commandment which had made millions of dollars both home and abroad and to audiences both secular and religious. In the forefront, a head high glass shaft of incandescent light with a bulbous crown was set erect, over which was suspended an ebony guitar with a lavender vein of pulsing light in its cavity. Above this and fixed in the background was a fluid red Christian cross with bubbles constantly arising from within.

As my grandfather had pronounced before, Johnny's evangelistic powers were as ancient as they were unique, which helped explain the performer's enormous following. Blending sermon into song and embodying both in dance was Johnny's Holy Trinity. It had first inspired and entranced cubic miles of southern souls from Galveston to Savannah, from Memphis to Mobile. The union of sermon-song-dance was Johnny's key. He could unlock the most puritanical heart, release the most imprisoned conscience, and send weary inhibitions scampering away in shame.

Johnny's musicians *never* appeared on stage with him. All sound was pretaped and piped in, save for Johnny's soulful voice which was the very essence of release and spiritual transcendence. And finally Nola Rose, wrapped in Johnny's body, was the silent, moving dynamo infusing into the mass of dancers a centripetal spirit, creating a spectacular, singular creature of bodies and motion, moving in unison across the great ballroom.

Johnny's last two video albums—*The Golden Ladder* and *The Pit*—had outsold all other comparable performances on this side of the Atlantic. *The Golden Ladder* was a unit of ten song-dance-sermons on the Ten Commandments (fifteen minutes each), and *The Pit*, likewise, was a series of dramatic episodes on the seven deadly sins, each performance synchronized in dance. Johnny, on the tube or in his live productions, paled all competition into insignificance.

Zip had fallen asleep in the glass chair. I unfolded the silk handkerchief from my shirt pocket and laid the ruby rhinestone on the glass table. The dark formation at the starboard fore of the Ark was the Navigator, Johnny Revelation, and Nola Rose. They were moving in my direction. The stage lights came on, partially dimming my vision. The Navigator stepped forward.

"As you must know," the Navigator said, "Master Revelation never *speaks* to anyone. He communicates solely by song and body."

I did not know this.

The perpendicular shaft of light on the stage softened the glare. I could see that the bearded Navigator was balancing on his fingertips a silver tray with a clear pitcher of pink refreshment chilled to a frostiness, and a crystal goblet. The Navigator nimbly set the goblet and pink ade before me, the cool liquid releasing tiny bubbles that arose and winked upon the surface.

"Compliments from our Magnificence," the Navigator said, then cupped his hand and whispered in my ear, "Listen, you little redneck wart, you read them instructions on the pitcher or I'll pinch your knotty head off." Glancing sideways I could see the dark cavity behind his eye patch. The big man backed off with a wicked grin. "And where'd you get that big ear?"

I was shocked at the Navigator's sudden change in manner and speech. The big man had been drinking and proceeded whispering at me with breath acrid enough to curl my hair. "We don't want no trouble to screw up our act on The Ark. Now drink up, you hear?" The Navigator had a tight grip on my neck and pushed my face close up to the label on the pitcher.

"I don't drink," I protested. The label read: *Zero Cider—One cup equals minus ten pounds.* It was handwritten in red ink and signed *Johnny Revelation.*

The Navigator was back in my ear.

"It's nonalcoholic, boy. You just got to be real careful of that stuff, you hear?"

"Yes, sir. I will," I agreed. Although the Navigator's voice seemed a shift in character, this second voice conveyed a sense of foreboding. The Navigator snapped to attention before his Master Johnny and continued as if speaking from memory to an invisible audience.

"We welcome and honor young Jody for his rare honesty and loyalty and pray he may be inspired by our hospitality."

The Navigator stepped to one side, eclipsing Nola Rose: There stood Johnny Revelation.

Tall, tanned Johnny, blonde and gleaming, was too much for me to behold in a single glance. Johnny's features were sharp. His eyes brown. His lips pink. A quick smile revealed a row of perfect teeth as pure as aspirin. He wore a white high-collar naval officer's dress blouse studded with myriad rubies, brass buttons down the front, and shoulder boards of gold. From the waist down he wore black tights like a Spanish dancer's and alabaster knee-high patent leather boots as slick as cream. Yes, I could believe that Jo Anne was in love with Johnny.

With the dramatic gesture of a mime, Johnny picked the lone ruby from the glass table and snapped it back into its vacant slot on his chest. "The lost has been found," said the Navigator. Immediately, in the firmament of the white blouse, all the red stones lit up electrically. Johnny shone like a Christmas tree. Zip became alert and sat up in his glass chair.

From a loudspeaker in the back, a trumpet sounded, followed by drums tapering off towards a distant flute on a high note. Gracefully, Johnny bowed, kissed my hand, and poured a portion of the pink ade into the crystal goblet; then he and the Navigator stepped aside. There stood Nola Rose. I had another sip of cider.

And yes, ah Jesus, Nola *was* a rose, her powdered-pollened face nestled down in a collar blossom of crimson pedals, and her lips scarlet red. As in a pagan play her limber arms and voluptuous trunk were prickly green and undulating as she breathed and her dancing slippers like pointed roots as dark as earth. She, too, bent tenderly to kiss my fingers and poured another portion of the pink elixir into my goblet.

It was the queerest of queer feelings. I was feeling not lightheaded but lightbodied.

Zip hopped down from the glass chair and clicked across the teakwood floor to inspect the ballroom door. Had it been Jo Anne?

I reread the inscription on the Zero Cider: *One cup equals minus ten pounds. No matter*, I thought, *I weigh at least a hundred and twenty-five.*

The Navigator was right. The twinkling drink was not alcoholic. I knew that much. In fact it tasted sundae sweet, like Aunt Gloria's pink lemonade. I lifted the goblet to my lips and tossed off its contents like a sailor.

Johnny's performance would dramatize The First Commandment from *The Golden Ladder* and was entitled "Thou Shalt Have No Other Gods Before Me."

Once before, I had seen this notorious act on the tube, but now with my naked eye I could watch Johnny and Nola Rose with greater attention and absorption. Johnny's performance was spun into a marvelous coordination of organ chords, drums, flutes, and mounting sermon words as these two luscious bodies moved toward each other—Nola Rose starting on the right from the shaft of light and the suspended guitar, and Johnny starting from an equal distance to the left of the incandescent shaft, his head below the effervescent blood red cross.

I poured myself another portion of cider and slipped the moistened label into my shirt pocket.

With raised hand signaling silence—and eyes shot up toward heaven—the evangelist and the sure-footed Nola Rose glided smoothly into motion, the organ notes pealing off softly with a deep drum rhythm arising from the bowels of the Ark and then, trembling, delicate high flute notes entering as if on the shaft of light from the oval of sky above the poop deck. Then came Johnny Revelation's voice, surprisingly deep and melodious, flowing like warm honey upon the narcotic concussion of the drums—

> Out of a flaming tree
> The Lord thy God hath said . . .

Johnny moved in a ever-tightening spiral around the incandescent shaft and then in closer toward Nola Rose—

> Jehovah is my name
> Or all alive be dead.

Nola now in voluptuous motion, in an ever-widening counter spiral, urged herself toward Johnny Revelation and the shaft of light. The organ tones increased in tempo and intensity, pursued by ever more dominating drums.

Beholding Nola Rose in motion electrified me and sent through my body impulses beyond my means of measuring. When a glance of hers sliced by, I drained my goblet.

"Listen you little shrimp, you be careful. I told you we don't want no flaws from you." It was The Navigator again. He thumped my funny ear. Whatever the big man had been drinking, it was not Zero Cider.

I had lightened considerably since my first sip of the twinkling mixture; my rump definitely felt less weighty in the glass chair. But the cider, I was sure, was harmless. It gave a pleasant sensation, nothing to be considered wicked. *Besides*, I told myself again, *this morning I weighed at least a hundred and twenty-five.*

In spirals and counter spirals, dazzling Johnny in his twinkling blouse, and Nola Rose, weaving and fluctuating her green limbs, approached each other. They would finally embrace climactically at sermon's end under the pulsating guitar and beside the shaft of light. I had begun to sweat. In a grand gesture, Johnny bent backwards, his hair touching the floor, stretching his tights to an extreme, then straightening up.

> No other gods shalt thou behold
> No other gods to see . . .

My eyes burned. I poured myself another splash of cider.

Zip had vanished. No matter. Dogs have a way of finding themselves. The dance sped up its pace. The sermon was approaching its apex.

> No other gods shall have a name
> No other god to see
> No other gods shall have a name
> But me, but me . . .

I remembered that the climax of this performance was both violent and enchanting, as if one were at once falling into the cone of a fiery volcano and at the same time being lifted up on its golden plumes. This was much different from seeing it on TV, as different as listening to the story of a dream and being in the dream itself.

I wondered if it had been Jo Anne at the door.

With hips in furious acceleration Johnny and Nola Rose spun closer and closer around and toward the incandescent column. Above, in the cavity of the dark guitar, the pulse of the purple vein increased. Then blending in with the sounding drums and distant flute came Johnny's voice—

> The Lord thy God now speaks again
> The Lord thy God hath said
> Marvelous is my holy name
> Or all alive be dead . . .

In a dizzy swirl before the lighted shaft, Johnny and Nola Rose flowed into each other, Nola wrapped in Johnny's body, the organ sounds retreating, Johnny and Nola Rose undulating together to the dwindling drums. I, forgetting my goblet, had a swig from the cider pitcher, and Johnny's voice again—

> All lie dead
> No other gods to see
> All lie dead
> All lie dead
> But me, but me . . .

Then Nola Rose fell face down at Johnny's feet. I was stunned to be so close to such enormous energy and yet had not the slightest idea of what was happening to me.

Johnny, behind the lighted shaft, his ruby coat aglow, held up his hands in benediction. All motion froze—except that I could see Nola Rose breathing, her bosom rising and falling to the muffled drums.

The center disc of the stage, by mechanical means, began descending into the body of the Ark.

I could imagine the throng of dancers tonight and forever, young and older, following Johnny into ecstasy. But why? Was it because of what Johnny and Nola Rose were doing? Was it the dance? Was it something inside me? Was it the Zero Cider? Or was it a power far outside or deep inside that could move the nightly throng like the moving of the moon?

The hymnal organ sounds died slowly with the fading of the light. A rumbling drum was barely beating now. As Johnny Revelation, still erect, was drawn gradually downward into darkness, his last words arose like a prophecy—

> No other gods
> No other gods to see
> All lie dead
> but me, but me, but me.

5

The Rainbow Carnival

Was it I who was moving? Or was it The Ark sinking beneath me? I reached for the cider again, but it was too late. Both goblet and pitcher were beyond my grasp. I was floating upward from my glass table toward the oval of sky above the poop deck. A young girl—Jo Anne?— was peering down at me. Could she have seen—heard—Johnny's whole show from this awkward angle and elevation? I knew I was suspended. I was pleasantly aware that I weighed less than nothing at all. Which, at first, caused me no alarm. I closed my eyes in ecstasy and allowed myself to ascend toward the blue in the sky-hatch while my lightness enfolded me like feathers floating in a dream.

It was the Navigator's booming voice that rattled back my senses.

"Haaaaaaaa ha ha ha," the baritone voice bounced around in the vacant ballroom below. The Navigator was looking up at me and smiling with his rubbery lips. "You lopsided little shrimp! I told you so!" Oddly the barroom mariner seemed pleased that his warnings were coming to pass. I wondered: *Is the Navigator wearing a mask? Is his black-patched eye a fake?*

Looking down where Johnny Revelation had performed, I watched the center disk of the stage arise mechanically and snap back into place, leaving the stage as empty as it was when I arrived. But my weightlessness now became no smiling matter. Already I had risen to a height too great to fall without injury; and with the increasing elevation, my fingers could find nothing to grasp but air.

Nor had I latitudinal or longitudinal control over my direction. The grinning Navigator was receding into the shadows, and the perimeter of the sky-hatch was too wide to lay hands upon. The young girl—I caught but a glimpse—made a grab for my shirttail but missed.

When I emerged through the oval opening, a fierce sun blasted my eyes. A hot breeze pushed me across the poop deck and toward the prow of The Ark. Gravity had little claim on my body. If I weighed a hundred and twenty-five pounds this morning, at the moment I weighed less than no Jody at all. Cut off from earth, I was floating bolt upright over the stern rail of The Ark and toward the Rainbow Carnival.

A familiar voice—Was it Jo Anne's? The little lady was running down the gangplank and out into the dunes.

Zip . . .

It was as if the thought had created the fact: It *was* Zip.

The terrier had caught wind of my helplessness and was making a spirited sprint toward me. With a whistle and a snap of my fingers, I brought my body buddy into the air and over the rail and squarely down upon my shoulders. Zip, panting mightily, fixed his hind paws under the rear of my belt and his front paws aside my cheeks, just as if we were riding our bicycle.

But Zip made a comfortable difference. With his added weight, he had arrested my ascent so that we were now sailing at a sustained altitude—although a dangerous distance from the earth—toward the colorful carnival below, not more than a football field away. The girl was running below, looking up and over her shoulder.

To my joy, with each of Zip's barks, our altitude decreased; but with each descent came a dangerous acceleration, and at such a speed and angle that sent Zip and me—not like a guided rocket—but like a tumbling bundle of confusion plummeting toward a cluster of colored tents below. In the plunge, the bewildered Zip squeezed his barks into yips and then into a long, pitiful whine . . .

Before I could catch my breath to scream, Zip and I came ripping through the top of a red and white tent where a lot of firecracking sounds were happening.

Luckily the sturdy tent canvas had saved us from a fatal fall, and I was gratified that the rupture through the top was barely noticeable. But I was a bit giddy. When I stood up to brush myself off, a long, bright backboard faced me. It read: *The Gallery—Best Marksman Wins Prize.* I turned around.

The popping sounds had not been firecrackers; they were real .22 rifles and the red and white tent was not a side show but a shooting gallery. With a final yip, Zip bucked his ears and scooted under the back canvas, leaving me weaving uncertainly in the middle of the target area in front of a chain of circulating, tiny steel ducks. There was no way, of course, that the eager shooters with their busy rifles could have known that I was not a special target dropped in at a supreme moment for their trigger-happy pleasure. And how could I flee to the right or to the left when the intent marksmen, and women, were still cracking away on both sides of me at the circulating ducks?

At any rate, upon my surprising entrance, the rifle firing gradually ceased and all eyes gathered upon me. Then, as if on cue, the proprietor, chewing a black cigar, directed: "Our new attraction—our real Achilles who can never fall 'til you nip his funny ear."

"Nip his funny ear!" prompted a buxom mama, across whose bosom large T-shirt letters said: *Love Them Mountains.*

"Yeah," cried her rambunctious kid, bringing his rifle to aim and searching down the barrel first for my eyes and then for my outstanding ear.

Now all rifle muzzles rose, in unison, looking at me, my fatal ear, with their tubular B-B eyes. What else could I do—wobbly as I was—but go up and down, doing deep knee bends to keep their aims amiss before they all started shooting again. And start shooting again they did, and all at once and all with automatic loads and all—the lousy shots—cracking away at me. I dared not weave my head from side-to-side lest I surely catch their wayward bullets; so up and down behind the bar I went, faster and faster . . . until my legs grew weary and my head groggy until . . .

Plip, a bullet nicked my funny ear and out hopped a tat of blood onto my shirt.

"I got 'im! I got 'im," cried Mama's boy. "I clipped his funny ear and made him bleed! I win! I win!" The boy muscled his rifle over his head in victory. He was wearing a T-shirt that said *Buckle up with Jesus.* The mother was proud of her son and jumped up and down, making her big titties bounce.

I was trembling. "Help! Help!" I cried, trying to attract the young victor's eyes, to persuade him to put his weapon down; but the glad youngster was too thrilled with himself to pay attention.

For a moment I thought I saw Jo Anne's face, but it quickly faded into the featureless crowd.

Outside in the carnival air, Zip was barking and I fled through the split curtain where Zip's voice had come from . . .

IN MY RECENT fall, I had failed to notice that all the tents of the Rainbow Carnival were arranged in a giant donut—an ingenious stratagem to keep the customers paying and enclosed, circulating until each had paid fare for all shows. Unfortunately I had entered from an odd angle and thus had no knowledge of or access to the outer Entrance-Exit. And so I found myself midway inside another tent already filled with people; I was on stage between the professional performers and a captive audience.

Amid light applause I was greeted by a living angel if I ever saw one, which I had not. She was a humming bird of lightness, had slender white-stockinged legs, wore Peter Pan slippers and a ballerina's white cupcake skirt that suspended her airy delicacy as if in a tiny parachute. She would make all Bible-bound cherubs fall from their fluffy clouds. Around her shoulders hung a silken rainbow.

The little princess was poised aloft on the platform end of a tight wire, clasping a banana in one hand. An impatient monkey in a red, white, and blue uniform fidgeted expectantly at the other end of the wire. Midway below was an oinking seal balancing a red ball on his intelligent snout. Unlike the shooting gallery from which I had just escaped, this *was* a sideshow; and the applause I received enlisted me at once, by popular appeal, into the ongoing performance.

As well as anyone in the audience, I understood that I had been cast into a balancing act and that—never mind my choice in the matter—mine was to be the leading role. With the sustained and spirited applause and with my now acknowledged participation, the nimble princess, in one graceful motion, spiraled down the steel platform pole, handed me the banana, and placed the silken rainbow around my shoulders. With her mellow breath she whispered instructions in my ear. Then she plopped her hands on her knees, pooched her rump and puckered her lips toward mine. I kissed her lightly on her lips.

The tightwire act sounded simple enough: I was to climb the steel pole, mount the platform, and wait for the drums. At the rumble of the drums, I was to meet the monkey midway on the wire, hand the banana to the chimp who would peel and eat the fruit. Climax. Then each—I and the monk, still maintaining balance—was to return to his end of the wire. End of act. Monkey wins.

Impossible. But I had a thought, smiled to myself, and whispered in the angel's ear. She smiled too and brushed a warm kiss on my cheek.

A piece of cake, I thought. I would alter the act in my favor and lure the silly chimp all the way across the wire to get the banana, then eat it myself. I win.

But once aloft and above the accommodating crowd, I had failed to reckon upon my competitors in the drama. The slender princess, who should have been jealous and angry at her removal from the act, happily egged me on, one foot out onto the neck of the thin wire. The impulsive monkey on the opposite platform, who should have been bemused and confused at his new and inferior partner, was infuriated. The monk screeched, balled up his fists at me, and shook his head so violently that his jaws rattled. And as I tried both feet on the trembling wire, the docile seal quit his ball and started clapping his flippers and chiding me, "Go, yuorta; go, yuorta . . ."

I wished now for another sip of Zero Cider, for at this moment I had grown as heavy as iron. But the crowd's encouragement and the smiling aerialist lifted my spirits and urged me farther out into uncertain space toward the enraged monkey. The expert chimp had already launched himself confidently upon the wire and was bullying me, daring me, flipping his fingers at me in a come-along fashion.

To my surprise, I discovered that by pressing my rubber boot heels into the tightwire and by thrusting one arm out in space and holding the banana outstretched in the other that I could maintain at least an awkward equilibrium. That was, until Zip burst in upon the scene. The cocky terrier appeared out of nowhere and at once found dispute with the happy seal who had gone back to balancing his ball—all of which sent the monkey into a frothing rage so that he swung down, hands and feet upon the wire and begun shaking it so furiously that I lost my balance completely and came tumbling down on the soft seal, the bouncing ball, Zip, and all.

The great commotion sent Zip yipping into a gray tunnel at the side of the tent while the audience tumbled in laughter. Pitifully, on my all fours, I looked up at the white-stockinged angel who was doubled up in derision. To the delight of the audience, she pointed down at me.

"Bow wow wow," she barked and laughed until purple veins bulged on her dainty neck. I had fallen butt down on the silken rainbow. In the rollicking roar of the audience, the grimacing monkey loped over and, flicking his pink gums in erratic screams, picked up the banana, ate the fruit, and handed me the peel. Then the chimp did a triumphant back flip and bit a circle on my thigh.

After my shameful performance, I knew that I was the *monkey.* So I, in glum humiliation, cast the peel far into the crowd. I thought it was Jo Anne's hands that went up for it. But I couldn't tell for sure.

To make my getaway, I hurried into the slanting tunnel where Zip had disappeared . . .

Once through the mouth of the tunnel, I found myself propelled downward as if entering the throat of a great animal. This trip, I would soon discover, was to be no sideshow, unless you considered yourself the sole actor and the sole audience *you*, yourself alone. This entertainment allowed only one venturer at a time. The course down the passageway was smooth and effortless and smelled of moist earth and oiled machinery. At the dim end of the tunnel was a steel-belted door captioned with the words *For The Time of Your Life.*

Not a sound or a sign of Zip. But curiously, while I was being pulled deeper into the warm tube, I couldn't help but notice an entrapped and frightened rabbit, our friendly and native cottontail. He was thumping his hind legs in anger, making frantic zigzags in the dingy light and flicking danger with his white tail. As I neared the admissions entrance, the steel-strapped door swept open admitting me and snapped shut. The conveyor stopped and an array of floodlights came on, illuminating the belly of the enclosure.

Never in all my days could I have dreamed of a more magnificent and awesome machine. I knew now why this carnival was so famous and had engaged the world's finest performers and engineers. Being something of an inventor myself, I—however proud—could not help but draw my breath in admiration and take a bow as if to a god. This single invention was as broad of base as a city parking lot and high enough to have ingested a circus tent of people and made the Trojan Horse look like a stick pony. At this moment I felt like a flea dropped inside the works of a grandfather clock.

There was but one way out and that was through a special channel in the middle of the machine, which I believed would be no chore but a thrilling tour of certainly the most miraculous creation I had ever beheld. It then occurred to me—quite by surprise—that the machine was in operation, quietly running with exotic ease, so smoothly that its inner action might have been going on unnoticed for ages. But the amazing thing about the machine was not alone its size—its great flywheels, pulleys, shafts, cogs, and spinning continuum—but its quiet, detached precision, its almost noiseless manipulations and murmurings as if it were a giant organism alive. Certainly this part of the carnival would be enough to so overwhelm any participant as to make any other adventure in his life anticlimactic and insipid. This gigantic machine! And all for what? I could not imagine. Unless it was, at this moment, for *me* alone. Which, of course, was ridiculous.

The walkway into the splendid creature gave me a broad and safe view into its bowels. But the passage ahead was assembled so narrowly that I had to shuttle sideways between the whining belts and wheels and, with my elbows, clutch my shirt tightly to my ribs so that the eager cogs might not snare my shirttail and reel me into oblivion.

Who had taken the time to make this marvelous machine? Was somebody up there, out there, trying to show off?

Zip! Thank God, I thought, that Zip had not nosed himself into this indecipherable hive of cogs. One mistrot and Zip would be dogburger for sure.

Then, out of the innards of this humming beauty, came a primitive scream that chilled my blood. *My God! Zip! Zip!* The cry had escaped through a complex of whizzing disks and a rhythmic ratchet action to the cadence of *swishkittymitchner zoomover—clop . . . swishkittymitchner zoomover—clop . . .*

I reckoned correctly that the scream could not have come from a jammed belt or pulley or from any impediment in so perfect an invention. The scream in fact had come from the frightened rabbit that I had glimpsed in the tunnel. I could see the terrified animal plainly now. It was pinned belly up on a conveyor belt. Overwhelmed at the quiet immensity of the machine, the petrified cottontail had ceased to cry. Its ears had been seized by two of a thousand rapidly ejecting snap clamps and its feet riveted tightly to the moving belt. The conveyor was pulling the helpless animal spread-eagle and tail first into a V-transmission of revolving gears. The rabbit's cotton tail was still flicking. I could not tell if the rabbit was a boy or a girl, but I could feel the terror in its red rabbit eyes and pitied the creature with its comic buckteeth bared in vain. The rabbit did not start screaming again until its body was drawn into the box of active gears which I supposed consumed him inch by inch completely, leaving only a pink gum, like oil dripping. I imagined the impersonal mechanism compressing the poor rodent's skull inward so that its eyeballs sprang free, until at last the rabbit's screams were absorbed in the solemn rhythm of *swishkittymitchner zoomover—clop . . . swishkittymitchner zoomover—clop . . .*

Jesus, I thought, *One could be ground back into God juice in here*!

The only remains I saw of the rabbit was its soiled cotton tail, which the machine spit out. I tucked the pitiful trophy into my pants pocket, wondering what might be the purpose of so horrid an ordeal. What had the rabbit done to deserve so bloody a treatment? One slip—I was absolutely sure—and I, Jody, would go the way of the gone bunny.

I began to feel like a worm on a fishhook—no backing up. I could see into the final dim chamber of the machine which, with its narrow constriction, was sure to be the most treacherous. The pungent fumes of the machinery apparently collected here, and the passageway was so tight I had to drop to my knees and crawl. Although at the rear of the crawlway the singing cogs and spindles were smaller and more delicate, they, like swaying cobras, were more deadly.

This was the first time I had noticed a vibration and growling inside the posterior of the machine. There was also a growing pressure in my ears, in fact a pressure upon my whole body that forced me so close to the exit aisle of the creature that a hissing spindle seized my shirt sleeve, ripped it clear of my body, and flung it to the humming gears.

Then—as if the bottom had been dropped from beneath me—I was blown out of the machine and away . . .

At first I thought I had landed in my coffin, but upon hearing muffled applause and arising on my elbows I discovered that I had fallen face up in the magic saw-through box of Duo Divisio.

The famous magician's portrait and name were emblazoned on a carpet hanging from the apex of the stage. The magician himself—red vest and black cloak—was standing by, long saw in hand. I all but panicked, wondering if this wasn't getting to be a bit too much. Good Lord! If Jo Anne was missing, Gloria would set the whole coast alert—from Gulf Shores to Biloxi—in a sweeping search, with The Admiral in charge.

Outside the boundaries of Duo Divisio's enclosure, I could hear Zip barking. More comforting—I should say invigorating—was the thought that I might have seen Jo Anne's face among the audience. Though trembling with nervous energy, I was emboldened by the hope of Jo Anne's presence and by the warm reception arising from the assembly. I also found pleasure that in bearing well my tribulations I might please The Admiral. Compared to my recent rigors inside The Beautiful Machine, the saw-box stunt would be a snap. However I did not wish that Jo Anne had seen my embarrassing balancing act. Divisio's show, as everyone knew, would be only a trick.

Two pretty girls—each taking a handle of the long saw—tiptoed front stage and took a bow. Duo Divisio pressed me easily back upon a rack midway in the body box. The girls secured my neck and ankles snugly into slots on each end. Divisio furnished a short cushioned stool for my head. Flourishing his cape and sweeping his wand, the Maestro tapped the box inside and out, top and bottom, then nodded at me and at the audience to confirm the integrity and execution of the act. The pretty girls stepped back and held the long saw over me lengthwise. One of the girls put her lips in my hair and sang out in sweet voice, "We'll be seeeeeeeing you." The other girl at my feet swayed and sang out in the same sweetness, "We'll be saaaaaaaawing you." The audience whooped at that. Duo Divisio pressed his severe face close to mine and produced a glazed smile.

"When we get *through* with you," said the wizard, "you win the prize."

I was quick to note that the magician did not say *a* prize but *the* prize. I wondered what it could be . . . Then I was almost sure it was Jo Anne calling my name. I could see nothing from the box, but the sound of her voice seemed unmistakable.

The saw for the box trick was the real article: a gleaming lumberman's six-foot cross-cut timber saw with crocodile teeth. To remove himself from fraud or false manipulation, Duo Divisio gave a hands-off gesture and made plain to all that the girls were to wield the awesome blade.

Down came the box lid. The girls strapped it tight. Duo Divisio blindfolded me, then clasped my head in his hands. When the girls set the blade in business position above my midsection, Divisio let out a mournful tone, and the crowd fell silent. There was a tightening in my throat: *Nobody out there knows who I am*, I thought. *Is Jo Anne really out there? Suppose something goes wrong? Who would ever know* . . . I was about to whistle, to call out Zip's name when the magician clamped his hand over my mouth.

The saw blade now began in earnest, first the alto of the initial ripping into the lid top, then the tenor of solid penetration, and finally the baritone of the blade biting deeper into the wooden cavity. I held my breath and sucked in my belly. As I expected, there was no painful tearing of my flesh. I did think of letting out a scream that would give my audience a thrill, set them aghast; but I feared such an antic might tremble the hands of the pretty girls and send the blade awry. There was, however, a queer sensation in my spine, a queasy pulling away from myself as if my clothes were being rent, shuffled off, and my body drifting apart in opposite directions.

The tone of the ripping saw rose quickly now from baritone back to tenor, then zing—the job was finished. The nervous rustling of the audience settled off into an expectant silence.

It's over, I thought.

However laughable the suggestion that I was cut in two and drifting apart, the notion did give me a curious sense of liberation, as if my head alone was being projected from the box and had suddenly gained prominent authority over my lower part. And however misleading the severing sensation had been, it gave me a pleasant feeling of superiority. However illusory the entire Duo Divisio affair had been, I smiled at my own cool control during it all and at the gullibility of the docile spectators whose eyes awaited my undivided return.

Through the lower lip of the blindfold I could see the sandaled feet of the pretty girls shuffling about. Maestro Duo Divisio released the blindfold. The girls unbuckled the box straps and threw open the lid.

How—I did not know—but a harness had been fastened across my chest and under my armpits. In one hoist I was lifted head high facing the spectators. At once I could feel an unnatural lightness from my waist down; then, in stark confirmation, to my right and scarcely more than an arms' length away, stood my legs and lower torso.

At the shock of seeing myself blatantly cut in two, I fainted.

But with the overpowering astonishment of the audience, I flowed back into consciousness; however, I was now utterly helpless and ridiculous, suspended without traction and struggling in the air like a beetle bug on a string. Yet by now the show had become an enormous success. The homogeneous crowd was wondrously surprised by getting exactly what it wanted, but did not expect. The viewers could actually *see* me, like a hanging beef, hacked in half. Bewildered as I was, I realized that the last of the act was yet to come.

Duo Divisio explained my restoration clearly to me and to the audience: I, by blowing my breath in one direction, could move my upper half the other way so that, if skillful in my aerodynamics, I could properly position my upper part over my lower part and thus reunite myself—in short, blow myself back together.

Feeling no pain and saturated in the glad attention of the audience, I felt no need to hurry myself back into one piece. But when I gazed down again and realized that both parts of me were stark-staring naked, the spectators burst into happy spasms of laughter which sent me into some serious huffing and puffing—all to the audience's joy, but to my grief. I had not discovered the trick of controlling my breath-puffs.

My first trial maneuver was to keep my shoulders facing the audience and then to blow to the left to push my upper part sideways to the right. It was not as difficult as I had feared. I was surprised at how so light a puff could set my whole upper part in motion. Upon this progress came scattered clapping from the crowd. By my shadows on the floor I could estimate exactly when my two halves were in close alignment. At my clever maneuvering, I caught a gleam of admiration from the maestro's eye. When my two shadows on the floor converged, I puffed a gentle breath to the left to arrest my upper part in the proper position above my torso below. The crowd, sounding off in clap-clap cadence, urged me on toward my reunion.

My final move would come from the next puff. To blow myself together, I held my neck straight back and my face straight up toward the apex of the tent. Sucking in a great gust of air—the spectators now cheering—I blew with all my might. Splat! My top and bottom parts smacked back together again!

The spectators went wild with glee and shouting. I was now fairly sure it was Jo Anne on the back row, standing and jumping up in little spurts to get her head above the crowd, hopefully too far back to see me distinctly. Although naked and embarrassed, I was humbly proud of myself and meekly thanked the audience with a bow and a smile. But in looking down I discovered why the crowd was indulging itself with such excess: I had plopped myself down together backwards. My upper half had come down forwards but leaving my lower torso and bare rump poked out at the audience like two pink cantaloupes. I could walk, of course, but my steps carried my backside forward so I was not sure which way I was going. The contagious laughter of the crowd got to me. It was my first occasion of laughing and crying at the same time. So while I stood on the stage naked and agape, through my tears the whole audience blurred into one hilarious hammock of a smile.

Then, in a fury of indignation, I snapped my shoulders around so violently that I actually jerked my whole carcass aright, leaving my rump rearward just as God had intended it.

But now, unluckily, I saw that my more private parts were

exposed to the pretty stage girls facing me, who began swaying back and forth with the mighty cross-cut saw, giggling sweetly and singing—

"I seeeeeeee you, I saaaaaaw you, I seeeeeee you, I saaaaaaw you . . ."

"Praise God," I breathed with relief. It was Zip standing beside the maestro, barking so sharply that he scooted back an inch or so with each report. Duo Divisio was graciously holding my clothes in an outstretched hand.

"The prize!" announced the famous magician as I darted by, snatching away my garments and fleeing through a slit in the satin curtains.

Zip knew the way to our bicycle.

No one in the milling carnival crowd seemed to notice naked me and my dog departing like the vapor of a dream.

I could scarcely remember scrambling back into my clothes. My shirt sleeve was gone. My boots were missing. No matter. Already my bare feet were becoming accustomed to wayward briars and the summer sands of Hurricane.

"Where are your boots?" Jo Anne asked when I pulled up on my bicycle. "And what happened to your shirt sleeve?" With brushes in hand she was in the open studio in front of her easel. Zip leapt from my back and started up the steps, then stopped short in the middle of the stairs. He looked back to me as if for instructions.

"I lost them on my way back from The Ark," I said.

"Did you give Johnny Revelation back his ruby rhinestone?" Jo Anne asked. She was sipping a glass of Gloria's pink lemonade.

"Yes," I said, wondering if Jo Anne had seen me kiss the nimble princess of the balancing act or seen me buck naked and ass backwards on Duo Divisio's stage.

"Did Johnny Revelation have on his rhinestone coat and Spanish breeches?"

"Yes. He even did a dance for me with Nola Rose."

"Goody, goody for you," she said sadly. "And where did you get that blood on your collar?" She went back to painting.

"What's Zip so scared of?" I asked. Zip was still frozen in mid-stairs, his legs atremble.

"My rabbit, I suppose," Jo Anne said.

"Your rabbit?"

"Yes, there's something Zip didn't learn at the academy."

I tipped up the stairs. It was a rabbit, a real briar patch cottontail, wide-eyed and nestled down on a sofa pillow mounted on a stack of flower pots.

"Where'd you get a rabbit?"

"In the weeds on the roadside," Jo Anne said. "He's injured and is frightened out of his poor rabbit wits. Look at his eyes. He's seeing back into something he can't understand. See? That's what I want to catch in a picture before it dies away. Can you see it?" she asked.

"Yes," I said. I was thinking of the terrified rabbit in The Beautiful Machine.

"Look," she said, lifting up the rabbit's hind end, "he's lost his tail." Yes. The rabbit's haunch was as blunt as a loaf of wheat bread.

Jo Anne picked up her brushes and was back at the easel. The rabbit hadn't moved. I was getting giddy-headed. Was I still under the influence of the Zero Cider? I felt in my shirt pocket for the cider label. It was faded and flimsy, but it was still in one piece and in Johnny's handwriting.

"What's the matter?" Jo Anne asked. "You look like a ghost."

I fished out the soiled cotton tail in my pocket and handed it to Jo Anne.

"Where did you find this?" Jo Anne was surprised.

"On my way back from The Ark."

"It's no good to him now," she said, putting another stroke on the rabbit in the picture.

"Maybe you can paint it back on," I said.

That night I sat in my bedroom looking out the window at the moonlight twinkling on the Gulf, wondering: *Was it real? Was it all real?* . . . when Spencer came riding down on the window shade. He was cradled in the finger ring, swinging gaily out by one hand like an acrobat about to alight on stage.

"Everything, my dear young sir, everything is real. Even a shadow. A dream. Otherwise it wouldn't exist," he said, tripping lightly off the ring. He began making his way, almost tiptoeing to get behind me.

"Don't look at *me*," he directed. "Look straight ahead."

But I turned to see where the ant had gone.

"Please!" Spencer requested. "How can *I* project if you are looking at me? Look at the screen!" He was talking about the window shade he had ridden down upon which did, in fact, remind me of a home movie.

"Are you concentrating?" he asked, pausing with anticipation.

"I'm trying," I said.

"Then stop *trying*. That's just the trouble. Such calculated straining squeezes out your sight and clouds the mind." Spencer then began counting slowly to himself, ". . . three . . . two . . . one . . . now—are you concentrating?"

"Yes," I said.

"Now then, LOOK," Spencer said.

The screen lighted up and there was a little girl running after a pick-up truck that was backing out a driveway.

"That's Jo Anne!" I said. "She's just a little girl. What's she running for?"

"She's running to save her doll baby. Your Uncle Claude is about to back over it."

Jo Anne was too late. The left back wheel of his pick-up smashed over her doll—I could hear its last toy scream MAAAAAA—ma! The crash flattened the doll's plastic chest, and out sprang its pretty eyeballs from their sockets.

"My God!" I cried.

"Look . . ." Spencer said, sustaining my attention.

Jo Anne was gathering her shattered doll to her breast, and awkward Claude was gathering them both, consoling them, in his long, loving arms.

"What's he saying to Jo Anne?" I asked.

"He's saying 'Dear honey bun don't cry. I'll buy you another doll. Just you be glad it ain't a *real* baby'."

Disbelief and horror filled Jo Anne's eyes.

"What's she saying to Claude?" I asked.

"She's saying, 'But it's a REAL DOLL!'"

And so it was.

While all this was seeping into my brain, Spencer had ridden up on the shade string, and crept back under the valance at the ceiling.

Before going to bed, I looked at the blue circle on my thigh where the carnival monkey bit me. I examined Duo Divisio's red seam around my belly, but I couldn't tell if the irritated impression in my flesh was evidence of my reunion or merely an itchy indention made by the sharp edge of my belt.

6

Jo Anne's Game of Likenesses

At the academy I got word from Jo Anne that she couldn't get her brushes to "feel just right" on my bull bluegill picture and that the Admiral was feeding Mr. Grumps a Kudzu concoction that promised to elevate the frog's IQ.

Also an appeasing grant to the academy from The Admiral permitted Zip and me to fly with Mother in the Aeolian Harp from Mobile to St. Louis for a one-hop performance. Jo Anne was jealous of Zip and said she'd dig up Zip's tail for a ticket if she could fly with us. Later, on a postcard she drew a picture of the ancient Greek Aeolian wind instrument, floated along a few musical notes after it, then kissed in a purple lips print and signed it—

Love,
Blueberries.

But mainly Jo Anne was worried about the woebegone Rowdy, suggesting he might learn to swim on artificial "water wings" or float without support in Utah's Great Salt Lake or in the "super density" of the Dead Sea.

There seemed to be nothing she didn't know.

This was the last summer before the storm. At my arrival on Hurricane, Jo Anne's first order of business was to show me her latest creation, *Man of* War. This was her rendition of the saintly jellyfish with no eyes at all, halo-capped and floating as innocently disguised as an iceberg. As if looking up from the deep, Jo Anne had revealed the angelic nomad in a veil of liquid light so that its deadly tentacles beckoned, wavering downward in the pale blue like a shredded rainbow.

Although Spencer had suggested that Jo Anne held a mighty force in store for me, at the time she was still little more than a titillating sparkler in my darkness. But she was drawing me ever more into the center of her attention. Whether her recent invention had originated with her childhood SKY-SPY game or later with my I-SPY or with The Admiral's everlasting rock garden, there was no way to tell. But on my arrival for the summer, it was obvious that Jo Anne had elevated my I-SPY game to high art.

She called her game *Likenesses.*

As The Admiral pointed out, her game had no commercial value. And accordingly, Jo Anne wanted no credit or courtesies on her behalf. The only reward she required was that she play her game with me, to pit her talent against mine. To assure absolute integrity of play, The Admiral would be judge.

After all these years I can now only hint at the intellectional and emotional intensity of the game. Being keenly aware of Jo Anne's special genius, I was secretly honored to be chosen as her competitor. Hers was, in fact, less a challenge and more of an invitation, a fearless generosity. Yet Jo Anne possessed such natural ability, such spontaneous imagination, that I was tempted to test her game alone, solo, rather than risk her competition.

"No!" The Admiral rebuked me, "The only game played

without opposition is in the skull orchard."

But you could hardly call *Likenesses* a game. It was more of an outdoor sport or a ballet of the mind with no audience and no wispy music in the background. There was no predetermined board or field to play on and no set shapes, lines, or numbers to contend with. This was a contest that required the whole of outdoors and all day to play. At the same time it was so simple you could miss the point of playing it. Which reminded me of Zachariah's motto for serious fishing: *The more you've got of lines and hooks, the more you get all tangled up.*

All you needed for this engagement was the big outdoors and a brown paper sack. That the sack was paper was on purpose. One must be careful that it be not wet, torn, or overloaded. And all you had to do along your chosen way was to pick up pieces of nature: a pebble, a dried leaf or lizard, a shell, a chip, a burr, or any God-made thing that matched a feeling or a figure floating around in your head—that was a *Likeness.* Drop it in your paper sack but remember what it was like. For instance if you lucked upon a spiny stick that reminded you of a witch's finger or even of her dried up soul—that was a *Likeness.* Drop it in your paper sack but remember what the stick was like.

Rarest of all was a *Perfect Likeness.* If for instance, your eye happened to hit upon the spiny stick and, *without thinking,* it became immediately a witch's finger, a union made before you could *think* about it—that was a *Perfect Likeness.* No extra points but, strangely, it reduced the chance of forgetting what the stick was like because no time-gap was left between; they had happened at once.

So you see what I mean by Jo Anne's genius. Yet all so simple.

But this was not all. She had extended the game's simplicity toward the sublime. At the end of the game, you were to arrange your best Likenesses into their most attractive pattern around your most impressive Likeness and all on the confined boundary of one white handkerchief. So there was nothing complicated about the rules. The thrill of battle was in discovering and remembering what each piece was like and finally in blending them into a harmony which could capture and hold the eye. As Jo Anne said: All the pieces are *one*.

Our contest was set for tomorrow. The Admiral would be the judge absolute. He said he understood oh so well the principles of the game and the stakes thereof but chose not to compete, only referee. He explained that his youthful moments of illumination, for the most part, had fled, leaving him only the empty hulls they came in—except, of course, his own rock garden where he kept his old insights locked in stone. I was beginning to get a glimpse of what The Admiral's rock garden was about, nor had I forgotten seeing the Wholeworld Ocean—if only for an instant—through Spencer's abdomen.

Even granting Jo Anne's keen artistic instinct for shape, light, and color, it was fairly clear that I had the natural advantage in this contest. From my own I-SPY experience I had original knowledge of her game, to say nothing of my special books and my superior knowledge of the island's geography. I was a born naturalist, and from The Admiral's aerial map I had memorized every nook and cranny of Hurricane, walked it barefooted on my own. A year older than Jo Anne, I was taller and stronger. I had acquired a tough objectivity at the academy. I could cover twice her distance in a day, gather twice her number of Likenesses. As for an honest judge, The Admiral was perfect, although his favor was likely to lean my way. Jo Anne's game, as anyone could tell, was strictly a matter of chance. Considering all the possibilities in a daily game and all the outdoor objects that lay before us on the island and of all the hundreds of thousands of thoughts and pictures that might flicker through our brains—who could possibly guess how or when or where a lucky link might come along to make a Likeness?

Even so, I humbled myself. Deep down I wished never to bruise Jo Anne's feelings, for there was behind her eyes a fragileness that I felt bound to protect, never to break. Should my collection of Likenesses exceed and outperform hers, it would be little more than an accident of nature; therefore Jo Anne, even in defeat, would have nothing to be ashamed of. I would see to that. I would accept no prize or acclaim except in praise of her new game.

I was so filled with anticipation I went to my wireless to contact The Admiral to endorse again his judgeship and to propose, for his part, a gentleness, even favor, toward Jo Anne in his final judgment. The Admiral's lighthouse with its appropriate position and elevation always provided near perfect transmission.

I jiggled with the mike, signaling for contact. "Jody, Kudzu One to lighthouse . . . Kudzu One to lighthouse . . . Do you read me? . . . Admiral . . . Do you read me? . . .

There was a scratching at the other end, and then—

"Read you, Kudzu? Of course . . . Through and through . . . . I could detect you in a monkey zoo . . . Have you been chimp-bitten lately? . . ." the ant clowned.

"Spencer?"

"Yes, 'tis I."

"What on earth—How did you—"

"Learn to operate this primitive audioscopric blunderbuss?"

"Well—yes. But—"

"Sweet Jody, one of my tender sensors is more effective than a whole battalion of your dumb computers or a squadron of your tumbling satellites . . ."

This I could no longer doubt. With Spencer wireless communication was instinctive, effortless, and transcended all barriers of time and space. There was a humming in my earphones. Spencer was fiddling with the controls on the set.

"But," he continued, "I do share your fascination for our wireless connection, although I suspect that the remarkable assembly between your tender ears is still too feeble to pick up much more than static."

"I don't have time for all of that, and leave those dials alone! Let me speak with The Admiral."

"What! Awaken The Admiral? Do you think that in our teeming cosmos you can arouse anyone you wish simply because *you* call? Who do you think you are?"

"I'm not trying to be particular," I said. "I just need to speak with The Admiral. It's important."

"You are afraid Jo Anne will beat you at her little game of similitudes!" Spencer said.

"She calls it *Likenesses* and I don't want to *beat* her," I said with some heat. "I just don't want to hurt her feelings. I want The Admiral to know that. I want him to know how I feel, that's all."

"*That* is never *all*. You keep forgetting. You and your little artist suppose *Likenesses* a new invention while, sands upon sands ago, the clever Egyptians were playing your little game with the stars and had their myriad secrets locked in pyramids. I know a great deal about pyramids," Spencer said.

I was becoming irritated with the little guru but spoke as diplomatically as possible.

"Now, if you please, let me speak to The Admiral. I outrank you here. It's getting late."

"Rank! Ha! Sergeant Zip outranks you! He outranks you in nose and ear tho', alas, you have amputated his natural balance.

And late? Time again? Are you chasing the sun? Or trying to outrun your shadow? Would you have me—Spencer!—*stick* The Admiral awake? Impossible! Have you ever stuck your finger in a fire ant hill?"

"Yes," I said.

"*Yes*, and what?"

"They covered my hand in an instant."

"Well then," Spencer said, "can you imagine the concentration of royal wrath discharged if I should suddenly *stick* The Admiral awake?"

"You wouldn't have to *stick* him. Just whisper in his ear."

"Thanks for your most generous permission . . ." There was a buzz . . .

Spencer was messing around with the dials again.

"Spencer . . . Spencer . . ." I called into the mike. There was no reply.

Spencer's admiration for The Admiral was boundless. He believed that The Admiral's lighthouse was the best designed of all human utopias. The Admiral especially liked its spiraled staircase leading to the crown. But its main attribute toward perfection was its rock conic shape and, strangely, its entire inhabitation which was the grand total of one.

There was a scratching on the microphone, a click . . . then silence.

To mull over the possibilities of Jo Anne's game of Likenesses, I ambled down to the Gulf with Zip to think. The beach was vacant except for a few gulls, some ghost crabs, and a child's sandcastle. Zip was interested in the spook crabs, the airy little scavengers that flit away weightlessly and disappear into the sand.

I was impressed with the sandcastle, especially with the knowledge and care of the young architect who undertook its intricate construction, details such as the elevated base battlement, the smoothly crafted castle walls and flying buttresses, the upper ramparts with their overhanging turrets, the parapets and gap-toothed slots along the crown for the delivery of arrows, missiles, and boiling oil. And on the top conical there was a carefully inserted Popsicle stick. The delicate edifice brought to my mind knights of old and the ageless Spencer holding forth on the glory of his interminable past; and I wondered if his ancestors had ever been anything less than perfect.

"Ah yes indeed, certainly," the ant said. "Some of my nearest kin were most deeply flawed." Spencer was standing solitary on the southern rampart of the castle, holding a flake of a shattered leaf over his heart as if it were an emblem. He then carried on at some length about a vain nation of his epoch, great ants that arose, as best I could determine, inland on the Yucatan Peninsula or in the green hills of Guatemala. Theirs was an enormous population from the original family of Formicidae, a race of fastidious invertebrates who over the eons had brought themselves to the peak of social sophistication and who, with the most rigorous breeding and selection, had sharpened their intellect to the finest edge of perfection. They had refined their metaphysic into two distinct indoctrinologies: the *Ones* and the *Zeros.* But because of a deterioration in their trails of communication, there arose a rift between them that made war inevitable.

"If they were so smart why couldn't they find a clue to their problem?" I asked.

"Alas," moaned Spencer, "prolonged peace for my kind has ever been transient and too rare a commodity to grow accustomed to. The very energies that inspire accord oft conspire against it." The ant mounted a short pedestal of sand overlooking the Gulf and from there carried forward his bit of history.

Spencer explained that the *Ones* contended that 1—however conceived, individually or collectively, qualitatively or quantitatively—was always the same inevitable 1 that pointed to infinity no matter which way the world turned or traveled into the unknown. The *Zeros* on the other hand believed that their 0, if drawn exactly, had no beginning or end and therefore stood for eternity with or without movement and without the inclusion and confusion of all other things and numbers—perfect in and of itself and able to stand irrefutable whether presented in solid form, inscribed on parchment, or entertained as a figment of the imagination.

"They fought a war over that?" I asked.

"Oh absolutely!" Spencer resounded. "Our kind was never disposed to the static state. How else do you suppose two intelligent bodies can remain sane, how prevail, when each has pressed the other to the very precipice of its wits?"

"You could just politely walk away from each other and let well enough be," I said.

"Holy holes of black destruction! No! It won't work. That would be against our very nature. Don't you see what that would mean? We would both lose face and our armies forced as cowards to retreat into a hostile earth that would reject us. We then—all and forever—would be compelled to leap into the trackless abyss of darkness never to know again the thrilling sting of battle." Spencer paused and stood tip-toe. "Confrontation!" he cried. "We must ever face the foe who would trick or trifle our life away!" Spencer turned to face me. "And yet, mind you, never in rudeness nor in seeming superior. At our best, even in the exulting glow of victory, we behave at the height of good manners and in utter disregard for selfish gain or ease."

Spencer was eager to get on with his story. He turned toward the Gulf and swept his arm as if over a rippling field ripe for battle.

"All . . . all these nameless warriors . . ." he cried out across the waves envisioning the total battlefield, "all are now ready for the inevitable clash . . . Can you see them girding up their courage?"

"Yes," I said.

Spencer was getting involved. He was going to dramatize the whole event.

"Now look, the fearless leader of the *Ones* is stepping forth," Spencer orates. "He is standing alone between our two great armies. See him? Who cannot approve of such a noble one, standing like chiseled agate in the evening sun?"

Spencer was tumbling back into his history. He looked at me, then again to the Gulf and continued:

"Now watch the dauntless *One* as he throws out his crafty challenge to the leader of *Zeros*, saying, 'Answer me, valiant brother, answer me one question only and I—master of the mightiest and most numerous warriors of this peninsula—will walk away, I and my army, and leave you in peace and ever sovereign of our nation. For your honest answer not a one of your gallant soldiers shall be slain, not a one of your helpless nurse maids shall be raped, nor a single infant from your warm nursery be stolen.'"

Spencer hiked himself aloft to the upper rampart of the sandcastle and spoke in the grandest style:

"See now the brave *One*. He walks alone in a steady stride towards the dangerous *Zeros*, who bend their forward ranks into a semi-circle to receive and hear him. Though prone to peace, the *Zeros* keep their mandibles wide, hissing and swaying to the stealthy pace of their presumptuous kin, ready at a stumble or a fall to cut the noble *One* to pieces."

Spencer pauses, then continues.

"Watch. The *Zero* leader steps out to accept the challenge with a 'Yea.' Can you hear his contentious voice rambling through the jungles?"

"Yes," I said.

"Then comes the brave *One*'s question: 'How many precious *Zeros*,' said he, 'would it take to match our glorious *One*?'

"Hear the deadly silence?" Spencer asked.

"Yes," I said.

"The mighty *One* signals to his throng of millions behind him. They then cry out 'Yea! How many? How many?'

"The silence starts again . . . Hear it, Jody? Hear it?"

"Yes," I said.

"Now watch the *Zero* leader. He steps up to his adversary, face to face, and proudly shouts back his fatal answer: 'Just *one*! Only *one*!' his vain voice echoing from hill to vale across the lush green nation. Then all his endless legions as far as the eye can see sound out with him in unison. 'Only *one*! Only *one!'* they acclaim until they hear in their throbbing ears from their own throats, on evidence from their own voices, that they are proclaiming precedence—perhaps approval—to a pagan digit that in their hearts they hold in infamy."

Spencer was working up to a climax.

"So humiliated are the *Zeros*," said Spencer, "to be tricked into heresy that in a mindless rage they fall upon the astonished *Ones* and slash them down and out like screaming reeds, rank by rank and one by one until they are done."

"Good riddance!" I cried, quickly absorbing the sense of victory.

"Wait," Spencer said, stopping his narrative. He stepped up to the top conical of the castle and took hold of the Popsicle stick to steady himself. Sadly he watched the turbid ebb and flow of the evening waves as they sliced closer to the castle walls. "But now," continued Spencer, "the glowing *Zero* in his sudden lush of power finds in his brain a bright and new idea. To himself he thinks: *The heretical* Ones, *always upright and singular in their ways—as any Formicidae could see—might easily now be bent, one by one, into perfect circles, thus uniting two conflicting views into a super truth beyond refute.*"

"Great!" I said. "No truce. No more war. A union! At least a little speck of peace."

"Hold," Spencer cautioned and continued at a slower pace. "The champion *Zero*—intoxicated now not with the joy of victory but with the fever of power and perfection—orders all his weary soldiers to collect the fallen *Ones*, corpses all, curl them into circles and stake them stack by stack around the Great Entrance of the *Zeros*."

"Ye gods!" I said.

"Yes, dear Jody. Think of such low glory for all these sickly sycophants. And shame upon their drunken leader who treats his tottering troops—each for a stinking *Zero* wreath bestowed—to a tepid sip of honey water for reward."

"Didn't they all have glory enough by now?" I asked.

"Glory enough? Never! But alas, in less time than it took for the mellowed dead to rot, the shriveling *Ones* were all used up."

"And then—" I inquired.

"And then," Spencer said, "by the waning of the moon the audacious victor proclaims himself Lord of *Zeros*. He orders his commanders, grown weak on vainglory and honey water, to sweep up their *own* exhausted, quivering comrades and devoutly to curl *them* into circles and cast *them* groaning upon the rows of growing *Zeros*."

"You mean bend their own dead ones into *Zeros*?"

"Yes," Spencer said.

"My God!" I exclaimed. Spencer's deep sentiment at such self affliction and humiliation moved me to sympathy.

"And now," Spencer labored on, clasping his arms around his thin chest, "the staggering Lord of *Zeros*, crazed and laughing hideously—whose sterile Queen now lay dead and mummied in her private cell—ordered his failing captains and couriers and engineers to collect and form eternal *Zeros* out of any scrap they could scavenge from their sordid field of battle, even trash!—putrid veins of decaying leaves and the rotting antennae of the vanquished *Ones*!"

"Gross!" I uttered. "My God how gross!"

"Yes," Spencer said, shaking his head.

"I pray God that's the end of your sorry bit of history," I said.

"Yes," Spencer said. "I am finished. Even you can sense the end."

"Yes," I said. "Your disgusting Lord of *Zeros* finally ran out of stuff to make more *Zeros*," I concluded with some satisfaction.

"No," Spencer said. "He ran out of ants."

I can't say, but somehow just knowing about this primitive battle gave me to believe that these warriors of old are not extinct, that is, if Spencer knew about them—but especially if he had, perhaps, been there.

7

Gathering Likenesses for the Battle

The morning of *Likenesses* arrived. Claude was three days out in the Gulf. For breakfast Gloria fixed hot chocolate and whole-wheat muffins with honey. We ate on the long drawing table in the studio. Cleopatra sat primly on the other end. Zip watched every trip a muffin made to my mouth.

"Your mother will be singing soon in Memphis," Gloria remarked.

"Yes."

And Jo Anne added, "She'll be singing in the role of a beautiful gypsy girl who was invisible to the only man she loved."

"Zip and I are going to Mobile to fly with her," I said.

"And me?" Jo Anne suggested.

"Maybe, but not the cat," I said.

"Cleopatra, of course not. She'd yowl herself walleyed and turn to barbwire," Jo Anne said.

"Not in an airplane you won't," Gloria said to Jo Anne. Gloria did not trust airplanes and said that the only safe airplane was one on the ground or in a picture.

On an easel in mid-room was a large sketch of a carriage tilted upward, gravestones on one side and children playing in a flowered field on the other. You are sitting in the coach behind the dark driver, looking into a bright space upward and over the horse's ears. This was to be an illustration of one of Emily Dickinson's poems for the cover of *The Christian Messenger*. The magazine had already paid Gloria five hundred dollars for the picture which was to be entitled "Eternity." Alongside the celestial carriage was a smaller project of Jo Anne's—a flashy sailfish in arc between two waves.

Jo Anne went to answer the telephone.

"It's The Admiral," Jo Anne said.

When I got up for the phone, Zip followed the muffin in my hand.

"What did he want?" Jo Anne asked when I got back.

"The Admiral said be finished finding likenesses and be at the lighthouse by five o'clock sharp or we'd turn to stone and be stuff for his rock garden."

"Your grandfather's getting where he forgets which rock goes where," Gloria said.

"It's not so bad because he forgets he forgets," Jo Anne said.

"He's got more to forget than we have," I said. "He's sailed around the world nine times and read everything since Moses."

"He's a dear, sweet, rich, rich old man," Gloria said.

"He has talked to the Dalai Lama in Tibet," Jo Anne said.

"He's got a black rock with one white dot that says nobody's perfect enough to be all bad," I said.

Gloria was interested in Jo Anne's new game. She had laid out two elbow-deep brown paper sacks to put our Likenesses in and then—of all things—lunches stuffed down in a clean pair of Claude's white socks with drawstring to sling over our shoulders. Inside each sock was a boiled egg, a peanut butter and jelly sandwich, an apple, and a small mayonnaise jar of ice tea still tinkling.

"Sock lunches?" I laughed.

"The better to guide your wayward feet my love," Gloria said and flipped my funny ear.

Jo Anne smiled and said that you could never get the stale smell out of a mayonnaise jar which made the water inside taste like *yuck*, and I said we oughtn't to eat a bite or drink a drop until our game was over.

"I won't if you won't," I said to Jo Anne.

"No!" Gloria declared. "You'd both parch dry and ants would eat you up."

A horrible little thought popped up: *Spencer—a cannibal?*

"*I* won't eat till it's over," I said.

"You'd make a good Pinocchio," Jo Anne said. She shaped her fingers into scissors and took a snip at my nose.

What Gloria did not know was that Jo Anne and I would take different routes to play the game. I would take the long way behind Venoria's WHY NOT SHOP and northeast around Johnny Revelation's Ark. Jo Anne would take the shady lane down Pirates Bayou behind Inn Lafayette to the cypress bridge at Clearwater Creek.

"Promise," Gloria said. "Meet to eat at Clearwater Creek. Look at me!" she snapped. "Promise?"

We promised.

"I like that," Jo Anne said.

"Like what?" I asked.

"*Meet* to *eat* at Clearwater *Creek*." Jo Anne smiled at the little rhyme.

"Let's go," I said.

Jo Anne wore one of my long sleeve white Sunday shirts to permit the breeze and deflect the sun, a green knee-high skirt, and a pink granny bonnet that made her look like Little Red Riding Hood. I went with no shirt, barefooted, and jeans rolled up to the calf. I knew every dune and cactus patch and fixed a wad of wet moss inside my sun-hat to keep me cool.

My first find was in a sandy dip between two dunes knobbed with tall sea grass. It was the skeleton of a spoon-sized Gulf perch. It was an excellent specimen because of its clarity and the suddenness with which it caught my eye. I was to discover that suddenness in seeing a prospect always gave a deeper penetration and thus a greater possibility for a Perfect Likeness or, at least, a more subtle Likeness of high quality. Then, too, the starkness of the little skeleton lying in the sun alone between two hips of sand gave an extra dimension of pathos to my discovery.

But it did not produce a Perfect Likeness. My eye had rested on it too long. I had to think . . . to allow my mind to mull freely over the tiny bones . . . until the Likeness finally came to me, and then right quickly: "*Neptune's Comb*," I said aloud. It was a significant find. I could sense its quality. I opened my brown sack and laid it gently on the bottom.

Which made me aware of another requirement of the game. One need be careful not to crack or break a Likeness. A broken *Neptune's Comb* would lose its quality, and if it lost its structure I was apt to forget not only what it was *like* but what it *was*. I became more aware of this danger on my next discovery.

Far down the beach Zip was frolicking with some children. I was coming up the edge of a bayou when I spotted a leafless scrub oak with a single bough with a single acorn on a single stem. Interesting. I snapped the acorn stem off, held it at arm's length, and set my mind upon it to see if it might make its way toward a conception. Frankly it was a sorry looking specimen, and I was glad Jo Anne could not see me contemplating it. At the base of my brain I could feel a sluggish response to the acorn stem, a slow floating upward like a bubble in molasses; and then, very slowly, came . . . *Uncle Claude.* Yes, it did remind me of my gangly, sunburnt uncle, but it was not a spectacular Likeness, third or fourth rate at best. However, it would be a useful family factor in my final pattern. I liked that. I figured The Admiral would like it too. I placed the Likeness carefully in the paper sack. A headless Uncle Claude would be as no Likeness at all.

There was one restraint in playing *Likenesses* that was so obvious I almost missed it. Not every interest could go in a sack. I was at the moment looking down into a gun blue bayou with its giant cypress turned in reflection upside down with a formation of pelicans in flight above. No matter how stimulating, I could not put this amazing reflection in my paper sack.

But I was beginning to catch on to the subtleties and extent—even the excitement—of Jo Anne's game. Contemplating Likenesses created a kind of growing, a gradually accumulating symmetry which you could not define or express in any one of the Likenesses but which propelled you ahead with almost fearful anticipation. I was beginning to get a sense of the range of Jo Anne's game. On the one hand it was like being inside a house with many windows, looking out; on the other it was like being outside the house of many windows, looking in. I was warming up to the contest. The sun was getting high. My competitive juices were flowing. My paper sack was filling up with Likenesses.

This was another consideration I had not taken seriously—the sack itself. To overfill the paper sack would be a hazard, and The Admiral had ruled *no pockets.* But I already had a worthy collection, perhaps enough to play two games. I started a list of them in my mind:

a crab claw = *Satan's scissors*
a dead dragonfly = *the Wright Brothers' airplane*
a fawn's jawbone = (? still thinking)

a dandelion powder-puff seed pod = *a bobcat's sneeze*

a handful of rabbit pills = *God dots* (The Admiral would get a chuckle out of this.)

a double-barrel clay dirtdobber nest = *the Devil's nostrils*

a jagged shell chip = *Abraham Lincoln*

and more—

I had done well.

But my favorite so far—one I knew my mother would appreciate—was an empty cicada hull clinging to a loblolly pine. The Likeness rushed upon me: *Silent Sound.* I carefully picked the crisp shell from the pine bark. It had come within seconds of being a Perfect Likeness. *Silent Sound* had occurred almost immediately. It was of the highest quality.

Which brought out still another richness—or was it a limitation—in Jo Anne's game: actually hearing and seeing a thing in action. How could one connect to such an intricate Likeness as *Silent Sound* unless he had *seen* the gorgeous creature, *heard* its song echoing in the night, and *known* of its long sleep in the earth before it emerged to climb the tree, to sing and fly again?

The Admiral of course would connect at once to *Silent Sound.* Spencer with his perfect pitch and memory would connect completely. Poor Jo Anne. Did she know what a cicada was? But it was not her fault that I had more experience or that she could cover less ground than I. And certainly I would take no credit for what Lady Luck had placed in my path.

But still I had not found a specimen that matched the yearning in my heart: something that would engender in me my glory moment, the exact feeling when I sprang my first frisky bull bream from the water into the light.

The sun was getting high.

To celebrate *Silent Sound* I ate my apple.

Zip was back, tongue adrip and happy to be recognized.

As we passed by on seaside, Venoria was standing on the rear deck of her WHY NOT SHOP where on Saturday afternoon from six o'clock until seven she served free beer and smoked mullet. Waving at Zip and me, with one arm on high, Venoria looked like the Statue of Liberty. She came down the back steps barefooted into the sand, held up both arms, and called out, "Zip-puppy-o." This was their practiced trick for Zip, who scampered to her, kicking up little flicks of sand, and leapt into her arms. She fingered him a single goody bit and let him down. Zip was looking up at her, awaiting another signal. Venoria spoke in her mosaic English.

"Always," she said to the dog, "you know that I keep for you a little black licorice snip that your tongue remembers."

This was their private ritual. Venoria was seldom without a ready treat for Zip. "But one goody only," she held up a finger, "for too fat a dog is fit only for crabs and catfish to eat."

I nodded yes to such discipline. The academy hadn't been for nothing.

"The open sack is what for?" she wanted to know. She looked in upon my Likenesses.

I explained.

"You may well need all your whole brain in your cranium to best our little miss," she said.

I said yes to that. To Venoria Jo Anne was the Pearl of Hurricane.

"The Admiral who loves his thinking stones sometimes calls her Coral, but pop this island open wide like an oyster and there you find our gleaming pearl who one day will paint a grand picture of me *there*," Venoria pointed at the beach. "There against the waves that will never wash me away. With her tiny brush your pretty

Anne will make the waves stand still."

It has always been a minor miracle to me how an artist with brush and paint alone can arrest a wave in motion, especially one in crest or dashed against a stony shore.

Zip was looking into the basement window of the WHY NOT SHOP. Venoria stepped between me and the dog.

"Never take a mind to go down there into his salty hell," she said.

"He's my uncle," I said. "My flesh and blood. He was Golden Gloves champion once. He'll look at me."

"He is a burden grown about my body like a shell," she said.

All I could see in the gloom of the basement was the oval shadow of my uncle's powerful shoulders.

"I'm not afraid," I said.

"Then I will have to chop off your pretty ear to hang about your pretty neck so that you best remember you oughtn't go down in there and get your pretty head pinched off." She ran her fingers through my hair and laughed out loud.

Then Zip and I moved on into the morning of Likenesses.

From the deck of her WHY NOT SHOP Venoria waved to us and called, "*Bon Voyage*."

The sun bore down. Grape jelly bled through the pores of Uncle Claude's white lunch sock. The damp moss in my straw hat had failed. It was hot, hot. My likenesses grew hot and heavy in the paper sack. I walked eastward of The Ark and across the dunes where the Beautiful Machine had been. I thought of the tailess, long gone bunny that Jo Anne had committed to canvas.

It was then I struck my morning prize—a Perfect Likeness.

I almost stepped over it. Maybe what stopped me short was its unlikely location from the shore. Or it might have been its disarming commonness. Without a thought I picked it up. It was an ordinary scallop shell, orange and blue fringed, no bigger than a silver dollar.

Still without imposing a thought upon it, I held it up to the sun. I urged no comparison. But when the sun came through the shell and lit the arch of orange and blue, the Likeness came into my brain full grown: a perfect re-creation of exactly how the bull bluegill first thrilled me as he came shimmering from water. The immediate link-up was amazing because—except for the slight rainbow of colors at the fringe—there was little other similarity between the shell and my catching the fish.

Which posed a problem. Was the Likeness believable? Would The Admiral, at his age, be able to make such a farfetched connection? If not, would he believe *me*? How far could you stretch a Likeness? This common piece of cupped calcium with its little rim of color—I could easily call it *Noah's rainbow.* That would be more of a "likeness." But it would be too obvious. Too common. And a lie!

It was getting on toward midday. Jo Anne would be waiting at Clearwater Creek bridge. Still pondering the little scallop shell—almost unconsciously—I pressed on toward Pelican's Perch where you enjoy, for a price, rare sea food that only our Gulf provided. The elite but rustic fish diner announced itself out front with a large plywood replica of the ungainly bird, under which was written in letters small enough to draw you in for business:

> What a queer bird the Pelican
> It's beak can hold more than its belly can
> He can hold in his beak enough for a week
> But we don't know how in the hellhecan.

Behind Pelican's Perch was a billboard displaying a leggy

bathing girl under the sun, holding to her lips a huge Coke streaming with cold sweat.

I took out my still cool jar of tea, chug-a-lugged it and stuck the empty back in the sock. Jo Anne was right. The tea tasted like *yuck*.

In the bend of the slough, Zip had discovered my next Likeness. He was watching it with pricked ears and looking to me to come and participate in the curiosity. It was a hermit crab, that scavenging little carpetbagger that takes up housekeeping in the cast-off shell of a mollusk. Zip had cut the vagrant off from its retreat into the brackish water. The crab was furious at the interruption, swinging its main claw out as if thumbing its nose at Zip and sulking back into its shell. The little crustacean seemed, at the moment, a very awkward prospect, if he could become a Likeness at all. In the first place I felt no immediate attraction to him; and in the second place he seemed so completely withdrawn, I couldn't imagine how he could relate to anything other than himself. Also, the crab would be an unreliable piece in my final design because, once set in place, there was no assurance the little tramp would stay put for The Admiral's final judgment. To depend on the crab's staying power would be like painting a picture with a tree in the center, only to find at the showing that the tree had walked away. What's more, dropped into the paper sack, there was no telling what havoc the crab might wreak among my other Likenesses. Murdering the little fellow just to make him still was a cruelty beyond my doing. As a practical matter such an assassination was out of the question because it was the very fact that the crab was alive that made him—however unpredictable—so interesting a candidate.

Zip started barking at his discovery and making signs of conquest now that the crab was sucked up in his curlicue. I fished out the empty tea jar, dipped in some brackish bayou water, and dropped the hermit in like a stone. To avoid complete mutilation of my soggy peanut butter and jelly sandwich, I tore off a corner for Zip and ate the rest, then stuffed the glassed-up hermit in Uncle Claude's lunch sock. It was half an hour before noon. Across the dunes I could see Jo Anne in her pink granny bonnet standing on Clearwater Creek bridge.

I ate the egg in a mouthful.

I was surprised that the hermit crab connection hadn't hit me sooner. Maybe it was because the Likeness was too close to me, so near that my imagination had not been able to bring it into focus. The hermit crab was unmistakably Uncle Minos. If ever there was a human likeness to this crustaceous recluse, Uncle Minos was it. The only difference was that Uncle Minos had not retreated *into* his house, but *under* it.

Zip got to Jo Anne before I did. She had taken off her bonnet and was sitting on Clearwater Creek Bridge, tickling her toes in the shallow stream.

"I come here a lot of times to think," she said. I sat down beside her and we swung our feet in cadence through the cool water.

You couldn't really call it a creek because it was only a freshwater spring that finally fed into The Admiral's lake.

"You have to feel deep before you paint," she said. "You've got to get on the inside of a picture before you paint it."

And you could hardly call it a bridge because it was only two cypress logs with planks nailed ladder-wise across the top.

Jo Anne looked at the sun overhead and took the apple out of her lunch sock. "Time to eat," she said. She patted my sagging lunch sock and shook her head.

"I'm a little late," I said.

"You were a little hungry," she said.

"It's easier to carry my lunch *here* than *here.*" I pointed to my stomach and then to my lunch sock.

"You broke your own rules," Jo Anne said.

"Look," I said and pointed to my stained lunch sock. "My sandwich was bleeding to death. Besides, thirty minutes don't make any difference to God."

"I'm not playing Likenesses with God," she said.

"You've eaten your sandwich too." I squeezed her slack lunch sock.

"I gave it to a dog," she said.

"A dog?"

"Yes. He was sad and hungry—and ashamed," she added with feeling. "He was ashamed even of being ashamed. I could tell by his eyes and tail. If you know how, you can read a dog by his tail," she said, pointing at my deficient Zip, and added, "if he had one."

"Bow wow for you," I said. I reached into my brown sack.

"We oughtn't to show Likenesses until we get to the lighthouse and lay them out for The Admiral," Jo Anne cautioned.

"Just for kicks," I said and held out the red-headed acorn stem.

"Claude," she said without a blink. I never ceased to be amazed at her powers of perception. But she was discouraged. She said she had been "terribly unlucky" this morning in finding Likenesses and that she was embarrassed even to attempt a final display for The Admiral.

"For cat's sake," I said. "It's only a maybe-so-maybe-no game, like shootin' craps. Who can tell how the dots will turn up? It's all luck."

"Well—" Jo Anne wondered, "Don't bet on it."

Her granny bonnet had not been perfect protection; the sun had made a pink oval of her face and roses of her cheeks. Then, as if to surprise, she reached into her Likeness sack and brought out a slick—still damp—elongated ebony soapstone with two smooth folds at the narrowed end.

"What's this?" she said, bringing the Likeness in a perpendicular line with her nose, smiling, and holding me with her eyes.

With a leap of faith, I didn't pause but bounced straight back.

"Two licorice sticks on a hot flat rock," I said.

"A black cat's front legs and paws," she supplied. She held the soft, slick stone before my face. "—You know how serene a cat sits so elegantly with her front claws neatly concealed and placed perfectly together, propping up her shoulders and her intelligent head."

It was a very good Likeness. I would not have made the connection without her description. Jo Anne took a bite of her apple. "If you don't think deep before you paint you come up with junk," she said.

"Why won't you finish my *Bull Bluegill*?" This was a task that had tested all her talents.

"I can't get his eyes to look just right," she said.

I whispered in her ear.

"Oh Jody! That would make him look kooky."

"Not if you do it right. It would be a perfect Likeness of my glory moment."

"You can stretch a Likeness too far," Jo Anne said.

"You can do it," I said.

"A bite?" she offered.

I took a bite of her apple and handed it back.

"Look," she said and held up the heel of her palm.

"What is it?"

"A sticker," she said. "Off a prickly pear."

"The barb goes in like a fish hook but won't come out," I explained.

"This one has a little stem sticking out. I can feel it with my finger." She pointed to a tiny red spot. Yes, there was a little stem.

"They have to rot out," I said.

"You can pick it out with your teeth," she said. "*See* it with your tongue, then nip it out."

It wasn't easy. With much blubbering I finally nipped it out. Jo Anne sighed and kissed the wet spot of my operation. I wondered later why Jo Anne had not thought to perform this operation on herself. She unbuttoned the top of her shirt and fanned her throat with her fingers allowing a glimpse of her gentle cleavage as she breathed. "Feel," she said, presenting her face to me. I put my hand on her forehead. It was as cool as glass. She pressed her cheek to mine. "You're hot, too," she said, pulling me to my feet, giving me the come-along down the hot plank bridge, leading me along the handrail and off onto a little peninsula of soft sand that connected to The Admiral's spring. The ample water flowed from under the roots of a large beech tree and was inaccessible to the ordinary passerby.

"My kissing tree," Jo Anne announced. "The Admiral loves privacy and for people to do pretty things."

A kissing tree.

Jo Anne was going to exchange her yucky tea for cool spring water. She snapped off a beech bough and settled it into the wet sand to support her weight.

"It's not really *quick*sand; it's *slow* sand, kind of like you," she said with some obscure intention. She scooped out a hollow in the stream bed, let it fill and clear, kissed a handful with a cheer and splashed a sample back to me. Then like a doe she bent far over and put her lips to the moving water.

My lunch sock was still slung around my neck, and the hermit crab was making rock-thumping noises in my drink jar. There came across the Gulf the grunt horn of Captain Zeorge on the *Umbilicus*. Between our paper sacks of Likenesses, Jo Anne's twice-bitten apple watched us from the log bridge.

"Let's fill up our tea jars with cool spring water," Jo Anne said. She bubbled hers full in a jiffy. "Now for yours." She held out her hand.

I did not want her to know of the hermit crab. It was far from a perfect Likeness, but I might—if I could still the little critter—use him as an arresting center piece in my formal design. The hermit Likeness was sure to strike a vital nerve in The Admiral's conscience. After all, wasn't my withdrawn uncle The Admiral's own flesh and blood?

"I'm not thirsty yet," I said.

Jo Anne stood up and slipped the fresh jar of water into her lunch sock. "You're getting shorter every day," she said and stretched out her arm to demonstrate my height. I had not noticed that I was sinking gradually into the soft sand. The bog was up to my knees. "Serves you proper for drinking all your ice tea up." I was still going slowly down. Pulling up to free one foot only sent the other deeper down. To jump was impossible. Jo Anne coolly walked away on her safety bough and stood on surer sand enjoying my predicament. Zip was assessing my sorry situation with interest. I wondered if a bark or two from my old body buddy might lift me up as a couple of barks had let us down without disaster through the carnival tent. Jo Anne solved my problem with embarrassing simplicity.

"Sit down, silly. I'll pull you out."

So I plopped down flat ass in the wet sand.

And she pulled me out with her safety branch.

But not before I came unplugged, falling forward on top of Jo Anne, entangling our shoestring lunch socks so that we were both left bound together and staring squarely at each other. The wild agitation had much abused the hermit crab. He was making frantic grinding sounds inside his glass prison.

"Thanks for the landing," Jo Anne said. "I hope you can fly your mother's Aeolian Harp better than you treat me." She put her ear to my lunch sock. "I think you just crash landed your ice tea jar," she said. "And look, your lip is bleeding." But the jar was not broken.

Before we could get untangled Jo Anne went into my lunch sock and brought up the trapped crab, now sucked back into his shell.

"He's reckless," I said. "I was afraid to turn him loose in my Likeness sack. That's why I drank up my ice tea. So I'd have a place to put him in."

"You got thirsty," Jo Anne said and untangled our sock strings.

Jo Anne shook her head. "You're going to play Likenesses with a *live* crab?" she asked.

"It's not against the rules."

"You mean against *your* rules."

"Anybody's rules. You can't have rules lying out everywhere or you won't have anywhere to play without stepping on one."

It was the first time I had noticed it. In the smooth bark of the beech tree the letters J/JA were carved. "What do they stand for?" I asked.

"Guess," Jo Anne said. "The Admiral cut them there. For me. With his pocket knife. It's my kissing tree."

"It's a plain beech, a true species—*beech* from old German, into English as *boc* or *beche*, indicating smooth gray. It's in my tree book," I said.

"How wonderful," she said .

Something was bothering Jo Anne. It was her bonnet strings.

She wanted me to tie them in a bow. She held her chin toward my face.

"A bow is nothing but a pretty knot," I said.

"I like handsome knots." She thumped my skull and "Look," she said, touching my lip, "your lip has about stopped bleeding." There was a dab of blood on her finger. "It's as good as new, just like mine." She touched a little of my red to her lips.

"I reckon it is. I don't feel a thing now." I said. I finished tying her bonnet strings and stepped back.

It was past noon. The sinkhole Jo Anne made in the spring sand had leveled over with water. Zip trotted out and plopped belly-down in the wet. Jo Anne stepped up into my face like a drill sergeant. She seemed suddenly tired. From under her granny bonnet a copper curl fell out of place. A sheen of moisture had formed on her forehead.

"You have your orders sir from the kissing tree," she said and closed her eyes.

The tree was in fact a common beech of the genus *Fagus*. But I did not wish to disappoint her or to accentuate her ignorance, so I stepped kindly around Jo Anne and kissed the unsuspecting beech.

Zip followed me back to the log bridge where I picked up my sack of Likenesses.

"See you at the lighthouse," I said across the dune. She was still standing there under the tree like a wax doll, her hands cocked on her hips. But before I was out of earshot—

"My game's not over yet," she called.

8

The Battle of Likenesses

A beech tree of the genus *Fagus*? Was I missing something? At any rate I had learned from the sky-high cypresses in the bayou and, simultaneously, from the silent formation of pelicans overhead that there were some things I could not put in a sack. But there was something here more than the possibility of mere likenesses. There was a deeper, more engaging quality I had not realized.

I had just taken a cool and shady shortcut around Inn Lafayette, through the parish cemetery behind the Church of the Holy Sepulcher, leading me to a spot where every summer I had gone with The Admiral to see my grandmother's memorial stone. It was a plain marble cross under a spreading live oak, secured in a sun dial disc of concrete. It was The Admiral's invention. The unusual thing about her cross was that, set at eye-level, it had a double horizontal arm fixed at quadrants so that at all angles you saw the complete cross; and in the shadowed and inconstant sunlight it was impossible for the dial disc to tell time at all. Acknowledging that his dearly beloved had been swept away by storm, so had The Admiral left no inscription upon this spot and had decreed that his ashes be united with his darling in the sea.

From this angle in the cemetery the great whale sanctuary seemed poised to plunge into the waves of sand. I felt a tinge of sadness for Jo Anne and her unlucky Likenesses.

A broken limb had fallen into the arms of my grandmother's cross and sunk its shank into the grass. In the triangle between the limb and marble arms a spider had woven her exquisite web, an entrapment, also, too broad and delicate to accommodate a paper sack or to suffer transportation. But more. This was a Likeness, a drama alive and in action. In the bull's eye of the lair sat her Royal Highness, magnificent in her velvet orange and black. She was on her way to a trembling moth caught in the geometry of her web.

My God, I thought in compassion. *Kill the spider. Sweep the web away!*

As quickly there was a scurry—Spencer in haste on a quadrant arm of the cross, holding out before him a pine needle as if to bar me. He stopped short of the abutment.

"Halt, Comrade!" he called. "This is no court for games. Must you not know that this is sacred soil, that noble spirits shun paper sacks and earthen tomes and elude all likenesses?"

There was something comic about the gallant ant guarding a mere memory of the dead. Too, I was impatient with this interruption.

"Me? You know nothing of death. But she," I indicated the cross, "she was my grandmother." That Spencer knew nothing of death I could not deny. He had already declared honestly he could never recall a time when he was not alive.

"Alas," Spencer said consolingly, "*was* indeed, for your grandmother is not here but with roving wind and waves far out at sea. Ask the worthy Admiral. And of your misty death, yes, I know nothing, which is no fault of mine. But of your myriad graveyards, yes, I know aplenty and have dug at length among their barren skulls. We Formicidae have no need of your fruitless orchard."

In a flickering shaft of sunlight through the leaves it was easy to see Spencer's warped foot. Though spared of death, the ant had been injured. The moth made a fluttering but futile effort to escape, and the spider crept down another rung.

"I just want to save the moth," I said.

"The moth is not yours to save," Spencer responded with a legal maneuver. "This is the spider's web. This is her domain."

"An act of kindness then," I said.

"Nonsense. You want to make your sweet self feel better. Leave her alone."

"How do you know she's a she?" I asked.

"Because lazy male arachnids weave lousy webs—none so eloquent as this." Spencer reached down and stroked an anchor string of the web. The spider froze as if touched by God. The moth hung still.

I had learned to tolerate Spencer's barbed arrogance. The spider sidled down another square. The moth had beaten the pollen from part of one wing revealing its aerodynamic intricacy.

"I suppose you'll enjoy the massacre," I said, pointing to the web.

"No. No massacre, young sir," Spencer said. "A massacre takes hate and more than two to tangle. There is no hate here. A massacre is your hot and pathetic orgy of bloody murderers goaded on by mass idiocy, fear and blind revenge. We great ants have none of that!"

"You do fight," I reminded him.

"Most assuredly we do, but our wars to prevail are splendid to behold, nobly conceived, clear-headed, and fought to the last reflex of our sinews like your courageous Carthaginians against Imperial Rome—totally vicious we are to achieve victory, magnanimous in defeat, committed not to fame and trophies but to unconditional survival without remorse or malice aforethought."

"Sounds pretty bloody to me," I said. "So what am I to make of this?" I nodded at the trembling scene before me.

"An instructive little drama," Spencer said. The ant dropped his pine needle, cracked his knuckles, and sallied forth on the cross arm as if he were director of the ensuing tragedy. "—a one-act play in which our sweet prince," Spencer pointed at the trembling moth, "is embraced, kissed to sleep, gently infused, chewed, and soon sucked upon to provide our royal lady rest and a nutritious nest to lay her tiny likenesses in."

"You make it all sound mighty pretty," I said.

"—and your noble operatic mother might well sing the main part— But no. No . . . her soaring soprano would ill fit our leggy Highness in her lair; we need a seductive contralto here."

"My, my how you do love to hear yourself," I said.

"Ah me," Spencer exhaled. "I am oft the only one who understands me, tho' I declare I utter myself not in self adoration but from a private loneliness. and I would never"—the ant faced me intently—"never would I be so gross as you, trusting your fragile likenesses to that voiceless, shell-bound hypocrite!"

Spencer was talking about the hermit crab. I was surprised at his instant agitation. "And you lied! You drank your ice tea because you were thirsty, not because you would make a safe place for your one-arm scum-sucker." But Spencer was not finished.

"The very idea!" he raved, "that you should loose a slimy scavenger upon your final artistic pattern, to allow such scum to lie in union with such speechless beauty as Silent Sound and to place him in comparison with the perfect scallop shell likeness of your glory moment. You should turn the cowardly bayou buzzard back into his polluted waters to ingest his own outspew and breathe his own infected urine. Can you hear me?" he cried as if speaking to the imprisoned crab in my lunch sock. The ant's sharp voice ricocheted like flint off the gravestones. I had seldom seen Spencer so wrought up.

At these crackling words Zip appeared, almost in panic.

When I looked up for Spencer, he was gone, the spider web empty and the web drama finished.

When I got to the lighthouse for the judging, Jo Anne was already there.

"I had to put my best Likeness in my shirt pocket," she said. She patted her breast and held up her paper bag. "It's too nice to put in here." The Admiral was looking down from the lighthouse.

"Is it alive?" I asked, thinking of my hermit crab.

"Don't be silly. Of course not. That would spoil the game."

"Not if you're smart," I said. I had found a way to fit the hermit into my pattern. "A live Likeness isn't against the rules."

"It's against the spirit of the game," Jo Anne said. "You can't make live things stand still. That's why I use paint to paint with, not crickets."

"Trees stand still," I observed.

"They can't crawl off," Jo Anne said.

"Dead rocks roll downhill," I said.

Although the hermit crab was not my favorite Likeness, in translation into Uncle Minos he would lie painfully close to The Admiral's soul and be to my advantage. I would use the scavenger crab as my centerpiece. I knew how to keep him still. My best find of course was the scallop shell, even though it would be the most difficult Likeness for me to confirm and for The Admiral to visualize. It was my perfect Likeness. It had come to me immediately, effortlessly, and had struck that vital chord in my heart. It recreated instantly the thrill of springing my first bull bream from the water. By all rights and reason of the game the scallop shell should have been my centerpiece. But it would have made my game more difficult. To say the simple shell was *like* the "Glory Moment" of my first fishing thrill would be like asking The Admiral to believe that the bare shell reminded me of Zip chasing chipmunks on the moon! So I gave up on it.

When The Admiral came down for the judging he was dressed as a circuit rider: black frock-tail coat, white high-collar shirt, string tie, and a black bowl-top hat. He had a large white silk handkerchief slung across each shoulder. Spread out, these would be the background and borders of our displays. The Admiral laid out the handkerchiefs on each end of the semicircle porch at the base of the lighthouse; but he was not to look at and approve our Likenesses until we arranged our final patterns. The Admiral in a playful, almost girlish, pose bent forward, lifted his flying-saucer hat in gesture and sailed it skillfully uptilted into a seaside breeze that brought it full circle neatly back into his hand—

"Which doesn't make me the perfect *judge*," he smiled, his mustache riding high. "The only perfect man is a dead man. But see these?" He held out his fingers and wiggled them in the air. "They haven't yet lost all their agility. Now get you out about your Likenesses before our impatient sun falls down upon all of us," he said and waved us away. But not before Jo Anne kissed The Admiral on the cheek.

I knew right away I had too many Likenesses. I poured out my collection, pushed the pile aside and placed the inert hermit crab in the middle of my handkerchief. Inert? Dead? I could not tell for sure. But I had found another legitimate Likeness to keep him quiet—Spanish moss. The Likeness of this gray mass came to me quickly, from one of The Admiral's books: Medusa's hair—Medusa, the ancient mythological beauty whose hair was turned to snakes. I doused the mossy hair with the brackish bayou water in my jar and stuffed a plug of it out of sight into the hermit's shell. It was a daring chance that Jo Anne would never dream of taking, but it was an exact likeness of my Uncle Minos who was both alive and dead. The Admiral—world traveler, a man of knowledge and broad sensitivity—could not help but see in me and in this Likeness a touch of genius.

And I knew The Admiral would approve of Neptune's Comb, especially Silent Sound of the cicada hull. He would connect at once on the Bible Likeness of the two yearling deer jawbones jawing at each other: Adam and Eve in their first argument. And the rabbit pills (God Dots) around their mouths: the first ugly words of our original parents.

With skillful deployment, I managed to gang all my specimens upon the handkerchief, except one dried shark's egg (Dracula's Pillow) that tumbled out of bounds; so I squeezed it in under a strand of Medusa's hair.

"Ladies first," The Admiral called. Which gave me the advantage of showing last. Poor Jo Anne. It was no fault of hers that better Likenesses had not presented themselves in her path or that the ones she found had not fallen well in her favor. But The Admiral would be fair.

Jo Anne was ready. She was holding her granny bonnet in front of her display as if it were the curtain to a puppet show. The Admiral was standing by, his chin on the steeple of his fingers. I moved in close. When Jo Anne stepped aside, sweeping her bonnet up and out like a magician revealing his surprise, I got a good first look.

It took my breath! The stunning beauty of her simple and deft design! It was like the wholeworld ocean I had seen through Spencer's abdomen—a complete harmony! It was so perfect a symmetry that I could focus on no one Likeness without my vision spreading throughout and diffusing into the entire pattern. By comparison, my Likenesses—my shell, burrs, bones, hermit crab, rabbit pills, and all—were a mere assemblage, a hodgepodge. Jo Anne's was—how can I say—was more like my "glory moment" of springing my original bluegill free of the water into the sun. Hers was beyond expression . . . my heart knocked. My soul slipped.

Jo Anne was now qualifying to The Admiral each and every Likeness on her handkerchief. The Admiral watched in admiration. I was barely breathing . . .

At the far end of the lighthouse porch my Likenesses lay in waiting. Even at this distance I noted a slight alteration in the pattern of my collection.

With the dedication and precision of a nun, Jo Anne continued the justification of her selections. She had not even used the superb soapstone cat paws Likeness, and her sack of rejects seemed half full. Also she had left clear and even margins of handkerchief on each side of her design and enough inlets and outlets of white throughout to give a fluid cohesion to all her Likenesses.

In Jo Anne's final pattern were an impressive walnut-sized hummingbird's nest, now barren but replenished with three tiny white symbolic pebbles, a small box turtle shell of moist sand sustaining short-stemmed blooms of a pink violet, a black-eyed Susan, a dandelion, a field daisy, a red ripe cactus pear in the middle bounded round with maple leaves tan and yellow embroidered with acorns, snips of goldenrod, all embraced with a wreath of smilax vine, and more. And for every specimen, Jo Anne supplied an explicit similarity to validating its Likeness; and to each The Admiral nodded his approval.

"Aren't your flowers alive?" I asked.

"Of course not," Jo Anne said.

"But look, they are!"

"They just *look* alive. Their heads are cut off."

My handkerchief arrangement at the other end of the lighthouse porch had developed an abnormal bulge. Was it my blurred vision or the wind?

"Your acorns aren't *dead*," I observed.

Jo Anne had now made eligible all her Likenesses except one. It was a fallen sun-cured black-and-orange-winged butterfly—a Monarch. This was her Likeness that had been too delicate to put into the paper sack. The Monarch was her centerpiece.

"But you carried the butterfly in your pocket," I said. "The Admiral said 'no pockets.'"

"You put your hermit crab in your drink jar!"

"But that's not my pocket."

The bulge in my Likenesses had become elongated.

"What does your butterfly stand for?" I asked. It was a question to both The Admiral and Jo Anne.

"It doesn't *stand* for any *thing*," Jo Anne said. "It's a butterfly. It's my centerpiece. It doesn't stand *for* the center. It *is* the center." She was emphatic.

I looked to The Admiral. "It's the rule," I said. "Everything on the handkerchief has to have a 'likeness' or the game stops."

"Don't be silly," Jo Anne said. "The center is itself. Like the butterfly, it's all directions, everywhere at once, like beauty in a picture."

The Admiral was visibly impressed with Jo Anne's symmetry of Likenesses, but he was especially pleased with her defense of the butterfly.

Still overwhelmed at the unmatched elegance of Jo Anne's design, I asked The Admiral, "Are you going to let the butterfly be fair?" I wondered about the hermit crab and the doubtful plausibility of my scallop shell.

The Admiral stepped back to contemplate me from under his clerical hat. I could tell that the handkerchief bulge at my end of the porch had caused a gathering disruption among my Likenesses. The enlargement had lengthened into a white trail with a persistent tugging toward the leading edge of the porch. It was my restless hermit. He had dislodged the plug of Medusa hair and emerged from his entrapment alarmed and enraged. I was astonished at the strength of the tiny animal. The hermit's spiraled house had caught in a thread of the silk handkerchief, and the eager creature was scrambling hell-bent on the dry planks, hauling his home and all my Likenesses straight toward the edge of the porch and catastrophe . . .

I wondered if it was too late to stop this disaster. Was this, too, not a matter of luck? A matter of random choice? How could I have known the crab would free himself? And had I not spared the crab's life? Had I not tried to arrest the little beast with a gentle wad of wet Spanish moss so, whatever the outcome or whatever the final judgment, I might stand in honest competition with the naturally talented Jo Anne?

"Yes," The Admiral said, overruling my objection to the butterfly. "The butterfly center may stand for itself. I assume," he added, "that you have a worthy center for your design."

The determined crab was now scrambling along in earnest. I watched the slow progression of my endangered Likenesses.

"You do agree on the butterfly?" The Admiral spoke conclusively, leaving little choice.

"Yes sir," I said nervously.

Even if I could stop this disaster and again rearrange my Likenesses, would it be worthwhile now that I had seen Jo Anne's design? Would it be possible to reassemble, out of this disarray, my original pattern and hazard my chances in a contest I was sure to lose?

The crash of my collection—rocks, burrs, bones, and all—was considerable.

"Great God, what's that?" The Admiral said.

Zip appeared and started barking at the rubble.

My Likenesses lay in chaos on the ground. No, Humpty Dumpty could not be put back together again. And even if he could, he'd still be Humpty Dumpty. In the crash the impertinent hermit had tugged his shell loose from the handkerchief and was scratching away to freedom, away from the destruction, but sucked back into his house at the sound of my feet. I stood over my graveyard of Likenesses with a feeling of pained relief, as if somehow I had been miraculously saved.

"Oh no!" Jo Anne wailed. "Now we'll never know who won."

The frightened scavenger that had recently been the center of my moving design—first cautiously then suddenly—regained his direction and started packing off with his shell house, making haste toward the bayou.

Zip, still interested in the hermit crab, started barking again.

Jo Anne faced me, flushed with exasperation.

At that moment, without pause or reflection, I knew two things at once: Forming Likenesses was more than luck and Jo Anne's art was no accident.

Before dark I showed my fallen Likenesses to Jo Anne and retired them to my table of natural wonders, all except the hermit who had escaped. For a reason beyond me Jo Anne supplied me with another empty mollusk shell.

"Just in case your brave hermit comes home naked," she said

and laid the shell down between the jawbones of our original parents. Then she fingered up a little pile of rabbit pills. "God Dots, the first ugly words of Adam and Eve," she said.

"Yes," I said. "The words aren't in the Bible."

"Too ugly to print?" she suggested.

"I reckon," I said.

She dropped the God Dots in my hand one by one.

"Whisper them to me," she said but walked away before the words could materialize.

That night I started up from a sullen sleep to find Spencer in a rectangle of moonlight at the foot of my bed. He was doing battle with a fierce but desperate hermit crab. "Must I defend even you from this enameled sloth?" cried the ant. It was a large crustacean in a spiraled shell as big as a pear. With his hatpin sword and a rat tail whip Spencer was driving the crab closer and closer to the precipice of the bedspread.

"Back! Back! You shrinking coward!" Spencer urged in battle cry, lashing his whip over the crab's formidable claw and holding *en garde* with the slender sword. It was in fact Spencer's shrill voice that had awakened me. To maintain his precarious equilibrium and to keep up his backward progress, the crab had to reveal at times his whole pale and misshapen body, his pitiful eyes trembling on stems, his wobbly posture on the wrinkled bed—all this, and on his first perilous night in a foreign world.

I called for Spencer's attention so that he might reason with the desperate creature, perhaps spare its life. He offered me not a glance.

"The injustice of it all!" Spencer ranted. "You and your little stinking hermit. You, Jody, have overplayed your Likeness game!" Spencer scolded, holding his whip in readiness and the hatpin toward the soft belly of the retreating crustacean. I imagined that Spencer was talking about the wad of Spanish moss I had stuffed so rudely into my hermit's shell door.

"Not that, you idiot! It's the crudity of likening your grandfather's cellar-bound son—his very flesh, bones, and secret woe, the very same blood of your dear mother—to such trash as this—and," Spencer made a thrust at the withdrawing crab, "would you force upon your aging grandfather and your celestial mother such a likeness that would vulgarize their memories and rend their souls, just so you could play your little game?"

I, wound The Admiral? Offend my mother? Never?

"And," Spencer continued, never taking his eye from the hissing adversary, "the utter absurdity, the vanity of trying to crack the cosmic seam of life, of trying to find the Perfect Likeness!"

I did not understand.

Was Spencer talking about Jo Anne's cut-stemmed Likenesses—the black-eyed Susan, the pink violet—that Jo Anne had cut from their life sources and stuck in the turtle shell of wet sand? Or was he talking about Medusa's hair and the doubtful life or death cell I had crammed my helpless hermit crab in?

Spencer went on, "You have accused your pretty rival of centering her grand Monarch and of picking country flowers, but have you ever slept with the wild cicada in her earthy womb or have you with the forked tweezers of your mind picked out the glory of one pink violet?"

Spencer was speaking again in riddles.

I wondered now—with this moonlight conflict in progress—if my vengeful little hermit had indeed come back to haunt me. Spencer was not finished.

"Or, are you trying with the feather wedge of words to crack open our final mystery?"

I had not a clue as to what Spencer was getting at. He had not given me a glance but was going right on about his fiery business. The frantic crab crawled back a fraction.

"Have you gone crazy?" I asked, becoming strictly personal with the ant.

"Silence!" Spencer commanded. "Rest back upon your easy pillow. For this victory I will have no arm but mine to assist me."

The ant was becoming winded in his aggressive attack. He stumbled a bit on his bum foot, then made a gallant stab at the soft belly of the crab. Surprisingly the crab was too quick and caught the tip of the pin sword and snipped it off as it had been a hair. Which only encouraged the aggressive ant.

"But you may get killed," I cried.

"Never!" Spencer returned, breathing in quick stints. "Death is the jumping-off place to *you* in *your* world, not mine. Death is the gaping Grand Canyon in your hop-scotch language, but . . . no fault of your own." There was a kindness in his voice, an afterthought, almost an apology as he said, "I have no choice but to use this nether word when I talk to you . . . or remain silent." With his blunted rapier Spencer made another thrust at the retreating crab, adding, "and I choose never to remain silent!"

The rectangle of moonlight had lengthened on the foot of my bed. In profile Spencer looked like a diminutive but indefatigable Quixote closing in. He inched forward, step by step, lashing his rat tail whip at the avenger's quivering eyes. Pop by pop the slow crab crept back.

"Back! Back! You slothful slug in borrowed armor!" Spencer was advancing rapidly now. The crab had reached the edge of my bed and was clinging precariously to the counterpane with only the alien and unfamiliar darkness below. Spencer would not be denied this advantage. He made a final rush.

"Off! Off!" his shrill voice cut through the moonlight. "Off the security of this tumbled rag and out into our sacred space of ages so ye may glean splinters of the stars and glut thy anemic soul with such fragments of eternity that thou are fallen from!—"

After Spencer's bombastic words had soaked into my ears, there was dead silence. Then a thump on the floor.

Part II

The Landing

9

Back to the Umbilicus

When Captain Zeorge came back to check my life vest, Zip leapt from Mother's casket and sprinted away investigating the parameters of the old barge.

"You can have this if you want," Captain Zeorge said. It was an opera clipping of Mother, a copy from a London newspaper.

"Thanks," I said.

"Why didn't she never come back to sing for us?" he asked.

I didn't answer.

"I saw The Admiral's lantern last night," Captain Zeorge said.

I was not surprised. The large prismatic eye of the old lighthouse had been removed years ago to a museum in Mobile, leaving only an empty crown from where the original beam had shone. But on certain inspirations The Admiral would insert in the cavity a common lantern that, on a clear night, could be seen by all on Hurricane. No one dared ask The Admiral its purpose, but all knew it to be a message to his lost darling in the sea. There was no doubt in my mind that my mother's death had rekindled my grandfather's memory. Captain Zeorge knew it too.

"I'm sorry," he said somberly and walked away.

Except for the unexpected Spencer appearing on Mother's

casket, my crossing to the island had gone as The Admiral and I planned. But my old nagging problem came to the fore: I *was* my mother's sin. I was aware of this personal fracture as a child, but now my illegitimacy arose visibly before me and fell like a stone upon my conscience. I suppose death in its sly way is a curtain-opener to us all; but since the fatal airplane crash, I had played the hypocrite and shamed myself in pretending privately to be sorrowful. I had seen the pictures of my mother's crumpled body thrown askew among the desert prickly pears. Although shocked by my mother's death, I was not unhappy.

More uncomfortable was the fact that never had a son loved his mother more than I. But after the crash, even after the ghastly pictures, I found myself stunned and dismayed but not downcast; bewildered, but not discouraged. True, I felt guilty because of my absence of tears. I worried keenly that I could not cry as others certainly would expect of me or why, in respect for my famous mother, I did not wish myself dead in her place. To the contrary. I was elated, inspired as if a great freedom had been granted to me. It was as though God had thrown a master switch to route me away forever from the academy. Nor was it that I hated the academy. I had friends there: the indoctrinated Zachariah, the retarded Rowdy, the compromising Commandant, and a regiment of uniformed pals. The academy, in a way, was a comfortable place; it was a routinely regular ward where I could account for every day and every day I could be accounted for. Hurricane was different; its folk and island boundary were irregular and fluid and fit no square creed or policy to judge or to be judged by. And this crossing was unlike any of my others. This crossing was special. In it there was something impending, ominous. My mission was more than a duty to bring my mother home. More than sweet revenge. It was a challenge, an opening. A liberation.

At the time it was also perfectly clear to me that Mother would have approved of my strange elation. Was it not her spirit now come alive in me? Yet there was something devilishly extravagant, almost wicked, about my new release, as if I were using my dead mother's body as an excuse for my own selfish indulgence. I could not deny this. But had she not bid me to see her *boldly* buried in our family parish plot and to seek out the mystery of my insane Uncle Minos?

Mother had given me three imperatives, two of them in a single shot while we were in flight to Atlanta: *When I die*, she said with operatic clarity, *see me boldly buried and sound out the secret of your grievous Uncle Minos.*

Later, flying into Memphis, Mother in her classic voice bid me above the cockpit sound: *Allow no pallbearers from the Holy Sepulcher to lift my body. Permit no chapel testimonials, even from The Admiral, for fear my deprivers may for a moment win cheap pleasure for my pain. With your eyes freeze their crooked lips that damned me off our island and soiled our name.*

Then she charged me with a secret I have honored to this day: that the leviathan sanctuary, the Church of the Holy Sepulcher was—in name and conception—an anonymous gift from The Admiral.

My *grievous* Uncle Minos! I would remember. See my mother *boldly* buried? I would.

So how was I to seem sad when I was not?

In the pilot house Captain Zeorge was conferring with his mate and pointing toward the island.

Hurricane came nearer now, showing its special trinity: on the left the old concrete fort with its lonesome cannons looking out and the relentless Lee and Grant still riding time; on the right, The Admiral's lighthouse with its dead eye to the sea; and in the middle

The Ark, the marvelous, the intoxicating Ark—the creation of our amazing Johnny Revelation who through song and motion still stirs eager souls together into ecstasy. And I, in returning the fallen ruby from his waistcoat, had seen the fabulous Johnny in the flesh. I had touched his hand. I had kept for months the missing jewel from his waistcoat in my sole possession. And there was Jo Anne's constant plea, "Take me with you to the Ark."

The alarming barge horn sent Zip back on top of Mother's casket. The letters above the wharf WELCOME TO HURRICANE became distinct. Standing beside the hearse on the dock were Jo Anne and The Admiral—Jo Anne waving, slender in a green shortcoat and her copper curls bouncing in the breeze. The Admiral, now more gently bent, was wearing a pinched-top forest ranger's hat. When the *Umbilicus* stopped, four men in white shirts and black ties came aboard whisking Mother's coffin away. Taking The Admiral's instructions, two guys carted off my gear. Zip followed, then paused to consider his allegiance. I came along onto the wharf. Jo Anne was standing there.

"You brought your wireless," The Admiral said without ceremony. This was not a question but an imperative. He was talking about my ham radio. During a storm The Admiral considered ordinary house radios and telephones unreliable. At the sound of The Admiral's voice, Zip's ears relaxed. When The Admiral touched the tip of Zip's nose, Zip sat.

My grandfather rested a consoling hand around the back of my neck. His eyes, a shade more recessed since I had last seen him, were still bright and direct. He straightened when I extended my hand. He wore British-styled drumstick riding breeches, lace-up knee boots, a burgundy waistcoat with coat-of-arms, and the ranger hat. On his Hollywood end of the island, my grandfather had access to a wardrobe of unlimited selections. Unlike Marine

DIs, The Admiral had the leather strap of the ranger hat drawn taut under the wattles of his chin. With his flaring eyebrows and bristling mustache he looked like a cross between a Canadian Mountie and a wild turkey gobbler.

"We're sure to get a real island-stripper this season," he said. "Always best to ride out a hurricane with a wireless. Gives you outside-inside contact, if you know what I mean."

"Yes sir," I said, "Mine is with my foot locker and other stuff." The Admiral started toward the hearse and Zip followed.

I was astonished at Jo Anne. Since last summer she had slipped into a new dimension. Her cheeky ruddiness had smoothed into cedar rose. Her face was more expansive, demanding; but still there was that playful independence of her eyes. I offered my hand.

"After all we've been through!" she teased and pecked me on the lips, then took my hand and gave me welcome with equal squeeze. It was understood that, at my pleasure, I could now live with them—Gloria and my Uncle Claude.

I had not solved Jo Anne's riddle of *a Civil War likeness as our sea-side abode.*

"Sounds like The Admiral had another brainstorm," I said.

"You'll see." Jo Anne paused, changing the subject. "I painted a picture of you, and you don't look at all like you're supposed to," she said.

"You left off my—," I pointed to my guilty ear.

"No. I did your profile. I painted you from the other side of yourself."

"Thanks," I said. At least now she took me for more than a kid.

"You can hardly notice your other ear now," Jo Anne assured me. She took my chin in her fingers and turned my head sideways. "Your big ear has shrunk considerably," she said, leaning in for a closer look.

"Maybe the other side of me grew up," I said. She was still holding to my chin.

"You know ears get grown before you do and keep growing after you stop."

"I know," I said. I had never heard of such a thing.

"By the time you're full grown nobody'll know the difference." She let go my chin and looked at me head on.

"How 'bout that," I said. I resented her expression 'full grown.' Bearing now the burden of my mother's death and the privilege of an open-ended future, I felt that I had earned license enough for adulthood.

"Did your mother have one?" An enlarged ear she meant.

"No. But Uncle Minos did. It's hereditary. It's a male thing, skips around in our family The Admiral says."

"Well," she said curving her finger over the little dimple of my suspicious ear, "then I run no risk of catching it—You've seen your Uncle Minos's ear?"

"You know I haven't. Any more than you. The Admiral says no one has really *seen* the whole Minos in years. Is he still buried down in his salt vault?"

"Yes," Jo Anne said, "like a stumbling mummy."

"Is Aunt Venoria still feeding him down there from the up-and-down food dummy?"

"Yes, but his soul is starving," Jo Anne said. She had not taken her eyes off me and I was running out of words.

"Well—" I said, thinking of the picture she had painted of me. "How was I supposed to look?"

"Like some square military brat. Cocky cap. Cup-tight collar. Brave smile. Pressed uniform. Something like that. How is Cadet Rowdy?"

"I left my uniform for him at the academy with my swimming

medal pinned on. Nobody'll room with Rowdy but me. They're afraid his dumb and ugly might rub off on them. He'll be living in the custodian's quarters now with old Zack."

"Did he ever learn to swim?"

"Not yet. He'd rather swim than be God or Johnny Revelation."

"How sad," Jo Anne said, never failing to suffer for my unlucky friend.

"His parents have thrown Rowdy away like trash," I said. "I left my uniform with him so he mightn't feel so lonesome. It's hanging up in his quarters, like a dead soldier."

"Your uniform!"

"I told Rowdy he'd grow to it," I said.

"How terribly sad."

"It's too small for me now."

"Oh Jody! Not your *uniform*! I mean poor lonesome Rowdy—Did you get the picture I sent?"

I had forgotten her photograph.

"The snapshot," she reminded.

"Yes, and you don't look exactly like Snow White."

"I'm supposed to look like Snow White?" She was miffed.

"All girls want to look like Snow White. Or Joan of Arc. Or Marilyn Monroe. Or all of them."

"I'm sorry," she said, "I'm trying not to talk about your mother. The Admiral said you two have fixed the funeral your own way." I could detect a rising tempo in her voice. "Grandfather said you wanted to be alone with your mother in the hearse and at the Holy Chapel."

"That's the way it's going to be," I said. "It's a matter of honor. We want to protect her from any more ugliness."

Had I said too much? I did not know how much Jo Anne knew

of my mother's shame, her abuse, but mainly of my stubborn pride.

"Don't go getting so selfish," Jo Anne said. "Your mother's voice belonged to the world." I knew that Jo Anne held my mother in great respect, but I was surprised that she called The Admiral *Grandfather.*

"You call him *Grandfather* now?"

"Only under my breath. I love old things that are still alive," Jo Anne said. "—if that's all right with you."

"Fine," I said.

"He calls me Pearl and sometimes Coral, when he doesn't forget. You know his funny thing about rocks. Says I'm a paradox, smooth and sharp, but hasn't found a rock to fit me yet."

"No doubt," I said. My grandfather's rock garden had always mystified, amused me; and at the moment I couldn't help but laugh a little. His collection wasn't like any garden I'd ever heard of. It was more like a little Greek oracle or a miniature Parthenon erected on the mosiac stone floor of his lighthouse where he kept his special thoughts organized and secure.

"It's his way of keeping his ideas from dying or getting lost," Jo Anne said.

"But he keeps switching them around."

"Well," Jo Anne said, "they're *his* rocks."

"Did you ever finish painting my *Bull Bluegill*?" I asked.

"You'll see," she said.

The Admiral was gesticulating instructions to the hearse men. Zip came back wagging his sausage-long tail.

"Still think it's cruel to cut a dog's tail off," Jo Anne said. "Makes him look catawampus and sawed-off."

"He don't miss what he ain't got," I said like a good redneck. "With my pocket knife and a snip and a yip I did it like that—" I grimaced and made a knife sign across my finger. Jo Anne was not impressed.

"If somebody cut your head off when you were a baby you wouldn't miss that either," she said.

"Mother gave him to me when he was no bigger'n your fist."

Jo Anne had a secret. I could tell by her eyes. "Well he's back home now because five years ago"—she wagged her finger at me—"Aunt Veronia gave Zip to *me* no bigger than a biscuit and I gave him to The Admiral to give to your mother to give to *you* at the academy. How about that?"

That was her secret. I wouldn't have believed until now that Jo Anne ever wanted to *give* me anything.

"With all that swapping about no wonder Zip's tail's so short," I said.

It was in fact The Admiral who did the amputation. He cut Zip's tail off, sopped the blood away with his handkerchief and handed the tail to the Commandant who threw it out the window. I buried it that night in the middle of the drill field.

"How'd you keep a dog at military school?" she wanted to know.

"Easy," I said. "The Admiral handed our Commandant a big fat check. The Commandant slipped it in his briefcase, winked at me, and said, 'Now what're we going to name our new mascot?' and *zipped* his briefcase shut. So *Zip* I named him on the spot. At graduation he got sergeant stripes."

At the academy I was not so lucky in rank. With my library of encyclopedias, books on natural history and astronomy, I excelled in language and the sciences but lagged in military savvy. The academy was a good place to mark time. All I ever wanted was to be a naturalist, to go to the clean state of Arizona and consort with the earth and stars.

Jo Anne aimed her finger at Zip and teased, "If you've forgotten your manners, Cleopatra will be glad to slap your whiskers."

"Your Yang-Yin kitty," I said, which was The Admiral's Chinese name for her cat, a perfect jig-saw puzzle of black and white.

"Beautiful and dangerous. A purring paradox. Yang-Yin suits her just fine. Right?"

"Right," I echoed. I wasn't sure what a paradox was and couldn't even guess at Yang-Yin.

The Admiral was back, smoking a cigar. "The van is yours now. Can you drive?" he asked. I wondered if he would now drive the Emerald Rolls or keep it locked in safety from the salty air.

"Yes," I said. "On fishing trips the Commandant always let me drive his Jeep. Said I have a feel for wheels."

"At last of age," The Admiral said.

"Yes sir."

My grandfather stooped deliberately and looked into my eyes. "I suppose you are. But now you'll ride with your mother to the Holy Chapel."

"Right, sir."

"Alone," The Admiral asserted.

"Yes sir."

"Good and proper as we planned."

"Where is Reverend Millsap?" I asked. I needed to know this. Over the years the parish parson had done nothing to quell the erosive gossip about my mother. I did not want to be isolated with this man.

"I'll attend to the Reverend," The Admiral said. He pulled smoke from his cigar and let it out in a cool line over my head. "Your mother is waiting. Her sterling voice is now quiet but, by eternal God, her bones are home to stay come hell or hurricane." I knew at once the origin of his passion: It came not only from my destroyed mother but from his own darling long ago hurled away by wind and wave without a trace.

"Yes sir. We'll see to that," I said, assuming a military bearing.

"Be off," The Admiral commanded.

I marched away wondering how, at graveside, Reverend Millsap would pray for a soul that in the flesh he once disdained. I wondered, too, in what righteous way he might condone or castigate me, the issue of my mother's shame, now that I was of age to feel the sting of it.

I cracked open the side door of the hearse to let Zip in, then crawled into the back cavity of the black Cadillac and sat down beside my mother to contemplate the huge leap I had made from the academy.

"Ha ha indeed, my courageous comrade! But I dare you face your venerable grandfather with such dishonorable derision, to laugh at his rare rock archive which bears the varied bits and chips of our very being."

Spencer was sitting on the left casket wing. Frankly, with my sudden loneliness and the weight of my mother's funeral upon me, I was relieved to see the intrusive insect.

"I thought you'd be lost by this time," I said, feeling a trifle lost myself.

"*Time*. There you go skating around on that slippery word again. By this *time*? Now *when* is that? You think your tomorrow is out *there* somewhere, in front of you. Ha! Don't you see, you are facing the wrong way! You are flying a millon miles an hour *backwards into* the future. But be assured," Spencer said, "I am always exactly where I am. I am never lost."

"If you say so," I said.

"Your tedious *Time*," Spencer emphasized, and touched a

slender finger to the casket, "is your silent mother, here." He put on a cocky expression, especially for me. "Or," he smiled, "time is nothing, nothing but a bloodless clock ticking in a tin bucket." I knew the ant was making fun of my defunct fish-fetcher of summers ago.

"I don't want to think about that any more," I said. "I was just a kid. And I wasn't laughing at The Admiral. I was laughing at his funny rock garden."

"Yes, I know. I amble often there within his oracle of stones to muse and renew my powers of penetration and extension. But it is scarcely possible to laugh at one's handiwork without insulting the hand that wrought it."

I had learned gradually the validity of The Admiral's rock garden, that the stones were a kind of personal journal, a memory bank for the old traveler, a firm and reliable way for him to record and hold fast the major truths of his life. Each rock stood for an important thought. It was, he once explained, a permanent index to those sudden and arresting insights, those epiphanies that ignite our souls so infrequently that we must do our utmost to secure each and every one of them. The stones themselves were merely the medium of recall. But to The Admiral they were concrete and indispensable evidence of something real, for, as we all know, our perishable brains and books never endure long enough to preserve forever such treasures.

"He gets dizzy sometimes," I said, "just shuffling his rocks about, trying to set them exactly right to one another. It's a funny kind of confusion."

"Confusion?" Spencer questioned. "Had you the melodious soul of your mother now spirited away, you might hear in harmony The Admiral's stones in sounds this sweet—" Spencer cradled his silken antennae in one arm as if playing a violin, then closed his eyes in ecstasy as he pulled his other arm across the sensitive threads.

"Why doesn't The Admiral just write down his rock ideas and be done with it?"

"Because a rock is less airy, more concentrated. It contains more cubic truth than words. You can walk through a cloud of words. Walk through a rock wall? Never!" Spencer was sure of this. He sat back down on the casket wing and stretched his legs.

"Suppose he forgets what his rocks mean?"

"Then the meaning is still inside the rocks."

"How can anybody get the meaning out of them if the Admiral can't remember what's inside?"

"Then you'll have to ask him before he forgets," Spencer said.

"Suppose he dies first?"

"Then the rocks are yours to figure out," Spencer said as if this was as simple as playing jacks or hopscotch.

"Suppose *I* die?" I asked, surprising myself at the possibility.

"Then the rocks are mine, as they always have been," Spencer said.

"Don't start acting like God Almighty," I objected.

"Nor, my little Caesar, was I meant to be. I merely meant to intimate that in my day I have crawled upon and around all rocks. I have known them all. Understood them?—I have not! That is another kettle of fish. Look at me!" Spencer exclaimed, standing up and stretching out his arms as if to be searched. "I admit my imperfections. Though slightly crippled—stepped on once by one of your clumsy ogres—I am one of a kind, original, bound up forever between two infinities in one ageless instant. And—pardon me—I know more of rock and quarry than your whole colony of sluggish Homo Sapiens! Do you remember the key stone in your grandfather's rock garden?"

I did. And I wanted to get in a good lick to knock Spencer down a peg. "Yes," I said, "but he is always moving it around to get it in exactly the right position."

This important stone was the Great Quartz, a hexagonal crystal as big as your wrist, that The Admiral had picked up in Arabia. It stood for a single grain of sand. Of all the rocks in The Admiral's garden, this was Spencer's favorite.

"Good," Spencer said. He cupped his hands as if holding up and looking into the great crystal stone itself. "That's how large a grain of sand is to me. Do you remember what it means?"

Spencer was trying to set me up again. I did remember but was afraid the exact words might escape me.

"Never mind that," Spencer said. "Nobody is perfect enough to be all wrong." Where had I heard this before? Yes indeed, Spencer had for sure eavesdropped on The Admiral's rock garden.

I opened my mouth for the words.

"Say them," Spencer insisted. "Ideas dissipate, die without utterance!"

My mouth was still open.

"Speak!" Spencer demanded. "The words are simple but their essence embraces temples, cathedrals of meaning."

Then I said it with slow deliberation. "The Great Quartz means, *If you can't believe in a grain of sand you've got no business trying to believe in God.*"

"Excellent well," Spencer complimented with gusto, "spoken with an exquisite peasant's plainness that even your clumsy Mr. Grumps would appreciate." I had forgotten about my crippled frog. Spencer stood up and made a little bow, chuckling at my effort to reproduce a profundity. When he laughed in this manner he sounded like a blackbird tipsy on overripe mulberries.

"Now *you* are laughing at The Admiral," I said.

"Stars forbid! Certainly not."

"Then you are laughing at me."

"Sweet Jody, please know that your simple words wash clean the channels of my hearing so we may better grasp the truth and keep our bearing."

Zip resumed his sitting position on the casket, and through the windshield of the Cadillac I could see The Admiral making final preparations with the hearse men.

"Have you ever seen my funny Uncle Minos?" I asked the ant.

"Ah—'tis a depressing descent down there," Spencer said, peering over the edge of the casket wing as if into a pit. "His walls are hewn from solid salt. Salt we need, but not to travel long upon. 'Tis hard to say you've seen a person if you cannot find his eyes."

The salt cavity, a geological phenomenon, was a drawing card for Aunt Venoria's WHY NOT SHOP. The sea-side curiosity brought in tourists, archeologists, and rock doctors from nearby schools and universities. But so was Minos a curiosity, a self-imposed slave to isolation. My grandfather had accurately called his son's dreary cellar the 'salt vault'."

"Your trapped uncle is far from funny," Spencer said, "but will soon be shocked into seeing himself when the great waves come. Now tell me why you lied to your sweet Jo Anne? You know no more about Yang-Yin than I know about fish-fetching clock buckets."

"You mean The Admiral's Chinese word—for her jig-saw colored cat?"

"Of course, of course," Spencer said impatiently, "You don't have an inkling of what 'Yang-Yin' means." I could tell he was going to instruct me. "It depicts an S inside an O," he said. With his finger he inscribed the ancient symbol in the air. "Like this," he said. With his finger he spacially inserted an S into a vacuous O and scratched around in the air. "One side white, one side black. See?" he concluded, "a perfectly clear enigma."

"No," I admitted." I can't *see* letters in air."

"Well I can," Spencer said.

I was getting a little put out. "How the Ying-Yang am I to know what Chinamen thought a thousand years ago?"

"Oh patience, patience," Spencer sighed and slapped his brow.

"I can't help being me," I said honestly—and with some finality. I didn't want to get into a word war with the insistent ant.

"Yes, yes, I know," Spencer said, withholding himself. He looked at me rather pitifully as if I were a poor excuse for any kind of serious collaboration. "It's just that in you I find so little to work with," he said with some relief, "and so little ti-i-i-ime," he teased.

I held my temper.

"Well then," Spencer said, shifting his attitude, "do you remember The Admiral's rock that launched your great success?" I thought of the spotted linoleum in the lighthouse bathroom.

"No, no. Not that. That came later."

"You mean which of The Admiral's rocks spurred my I-SPY invention?"

"Yes, of course." There was a twinkle of prompting, of assistance, in Spencer's eyes.

Then I remembered The Admiral's beautiful stone that Spencer was talking about, a Skarn in Marble. To my grandfather it was an original snapshot of Creation that he had picked up in India. It was an impressive pancake-sized formation with a pink and blue constellation of fragments swirling away from an indefinite center. In his collection, The Admiral had at times placed it close to the Great Quartz and the Donut Stone.

The Admiral and the four men in white shirts and black ties were making their way toward the hearse. "Quickly!" Spencer insisted. "Remember his *words*. The meaning. The revelation!"

I was thinking . . .

"The words! The words!" Spencer encouraged.

I was thinking.

"The soul of the stone," Spencer urged. "Its soul! Its soul!"

"I'm thinking! I'm thinking!" I said, pressing open the doors of my memory.

Then the words rushed back to me brilliantly just as The Admiral had spoken them to me, holding the Skarn stone in the palm of his hand:

All things are filled with signs, and it is a wise man who can learn one thing from another.

"An old Greek philosopher said that!" Spencer cried. "I have often made haste to follow in the dust of his sandals. The old Greeks knew everything. Everything! Even your rinky-dink I-SPY. They played the same game with the stars. With the constellations!"

Spencer was getting beside himself.

We had arrived at the Holy Chapel.

At the sound of feet approaching, Zip stood up on Mother's casket.

One of the hearse men stuck his head in the front window of the Cadillac and said, "Are you ready?" He had green eyes, slick black hair combed straight back, and a long thin nose. He looked like Woody Woodpecker.

"Yes," I said. "I'm ready."

10

To the Holy Chapel

Zip was still standing on Mother's casket. Jo Anne was running towards the hearse with words for me. Woody and the other funeral guys were putting on their dark coats. Jo Anne stuck her head inside the front window. She was nearly out of breath.

"Hurry," Jo Anne puffed. "Reverend Millsap is on his way, to ride with you and your mother to the Holy Chapel—says you must keep Zip out of the cemetery—says he wants to pray with you before the funeral."

Millsap had lied. He promised to stay out of our way. I had not expected this. In his holy profession, our minister might well have detested the begetting of bastards, perhaps detested our contagious nature, maybe detested even me; but I could not believe he would lie deliberately to The Admiral. Jo Anne's face was flushed and her damp curls clung to her cheeks.

"Millsap's to do his thing at graveside," I said. "Four minutes. That's all!"

"I know. Hurry," Jo Anne said again. "We can beat him to the Holy Chapel with your mother. We'll cut him off at the graveyard."

Jo Anne was a lifesaver. I feared Millsap. I feared what kind of advantage the Reverend, knowing of my depravity, might have over me. In what way had he *known* my mother? Through her transcendent voice? Or through her generous independence? Was this all? What had nourished his unholy ire? Enclosed with him in the hearse under his ecclesiastical scrutiny, I would be his little dung beetle in a bottle, trapped. For a fleeting instant, I thought of Rowdy alone at the academy. When Jo Anne came around to the rear of the long Cadillac to get in, Zip jumped to the floor.

I could not see Spencer but heard his rustling as of a dry leaf at the head of the coffin.

I had no intention of leaving Zip anywhere but with me. Although I was older than Zip, he was older in his own way than I was because he had less time on his clock than I had on mine; and he was, I thought, *closer to the ground.* Always at my feet. Even in classes or at drill, we were inseparable. Often when we sneaked away from the academy to camp on Waculla Creek—stirring the wrath of our Commandant—we kept close company and knew how to snuggle through the cold with nothing but an army blanket, a penny pack of matches, and a flat can of sardines.

Jo Anne crawled in the back hatch of the hearse, pulled it shut and seated herself opposite me on the other side of my mother. Woody and another guy got in and cranked up. Three of the funeral men drove away in a white company pick-up, and we followed them down the single asphalt lane of Hurricane. To the bemusement of Woody and the other guy, Zip was sitting again on top of mother's casket.

Jo Anne noticed the casket wings.

"They're my idea," I told her. "Mother always said flying was like singing. I think she'd like them."

"You're always thinking things up. But *wood* wings?"

"Red cedar," I said.

"No feathers?" she asked.

"No feathers," I admitted.

Jo Anne pursed her lips as an artist might and said, "Then you took the easy way."

"I reckon so," I said.

"Good Lord! You *screwed* them on!" she said, horrified that I should rigidify the very agents of flight.

I nodded.

"At least underground they won't *blow* off," she said and then, out of the blue: "Can I see your mother?" She took my hand and pulled our faces closer together over the casket. From costly recordings afforded by The Admiral she had listened with comprehension to Mother's voice but had never seen her.

Woody looked around with raised eyebrows. Zip stood up. Through the side window Johnny's Ark was floating on the dunes.

"No-open-casket—I know." Jo Anne spoke in a dull, mocking monotone.

That was, in fact, exactly what The Admiral had ordered and I agreed—*no open casket.*

"I don't know," I said. I really didn't. Jo Anne tightened her grip upon my hand.

"Grandfather—I mean The Admiral—won't mind me looking at her," she pleaded, "I know it. It's the pew-sitters and rumor-wrinkled old bitches he hates."

"But—"

"Please," she said, softening her eyes. She pushed Zip off the coffin and put her face close to mine. "I want to paint her picture—for The Admiral. For you. I've never seen a real live dead person before."

Woody giggled. A smile slipped up on me. Jo Anne quickly

released my hand. She was embarrassed. "That's not supposed to be funny," she said. A slight tremble touched her lips. "I mean I've never seen a dead person I've loved like that up close."

It was getting worse.

"She's family," I quickly said to Woody. "She's got a right—okay?"

"If your dog don't mind," Woody said. "The Admiral give me a hundred bucks to do just like you and him say. The morgue boss ain't got no sayso now." But Woody was nervous. Somebody was behind us.

"It's Reverend Millsap," Jo Anne said. I had seldom seen this man outside his church, out of his pulpit. He was now tailing us in his red Thunderbird, honking and waving for us to stop.

"You keep driving if you want to keep that hundred bucks," I told Woody.

Jo Anne was wiggling to get in position to see Mother. In the rear cavity of the hearse there was no room to stand up and less to maneuver. On her knees Jo Anne crawled and raised up casket-high in front of me. I could see Woody in the rear view mirror. His slick black hair was so deftly parted that the glare through the windshield split his skull right down the middle. In leaning over to unlatch and lift the coffin lid, I had to rest my chin on the crown of Jo Anne's head. I saw that the neck of her blouse lay open. Her hair smelled like crimson clover.

Reverend Millsap whipped past us in the Thunderbird and was trying to squeeze in between the hearse and the white company pick-up.

While Jo Anne looked into the casket, I lifted my eyes for a moment to glimpse Mother, then closed the lid for the last time.

Jo Anne folded her arms over her breasts and took a deep breath.

Millsap and my mother?

Jo Anne looked straight up at me, breathing in my face. "She looks like Amelia Earhart," she said.

I had seen pictures of the famous aviatrix.

"Yes, that's a fair likeness," I said, liking, too, what I was seeing of Jo Anne and feeling her sweet breath on my face.

11

Inside the Coffin

WITH THE EXCEPTION of letting Jo Anne peek into the casket, I had been able to keep Mother pretty much to myself. But I was glad Jo Anne had the last look because, although she had never seen my mother alive, she had known her as no one else on the island. Already in Jo Anne's company I was feeling less and less the bastard.

I slipped Woody a crisp ten, and on a sandy short-cut we beat Reverend Millsap to the Holy Chapel. The hearse guys rolled Mother's coffin away. Jo Anne joined The Admiral and left me for my brief watch over Mother, my nearest and dearest one whose voice had encircled the world. This sacred niche of time The Admiral had permitted me without question. At rigid attention by the Chevy van The Admiral saluted me. Jo Anne held his other hand. Zip followed Mother's coffin. I followed Zip.

Far out in the Gulf the *Umbilicus* grunted its horn, and I knew Captain Zeorge was plowing back to the mainland. From this elevation on the island I could see the extent of Hurricane: the old fort on one end with Lee and Grant astride; The Admiral's lighthouse; and, in the middle, Johnny's Ark.

In the breeze, fluttering on the main mast was the flag JOHNNY

REVELATION in white and red.

This was the first time I had entered the Holy Chapel. Set apart from the leviathan church, it was a double-duty utility divided by a wrought-iron arch—on one side a place to sell coffins and on the other a place to wait and meditate the dead. The *wait* side was an auditorium designed so that the two main aisles formed a cross with a pulpit in the crux. Behind the pulpit and at the head of the cross was a bier to elevate the casket of the deceased, later to be embellished with flowers and cards of sympathy. Because of Mother's wishes, The Admiral had disallowed flowers, plaques, or the presence of anyone save myself. So as required I sat alone on the cushioned pew of the right arm of the cross facing my mother. Softly embroidered organ music was being draped in from above. There was Zeorge's lonely barge horn again, the Gulf swallowing up the groan and leaving me dead alone. Mother's coffin was bare, except for the unpretentious wings I had devised, so modest that even The Admiral had not seen. In vain I tried to shed an honest tear.

When Zip clicked by I got up and followed him under the wrought-iron arch that dissected the Holy Chapel, paused . . . feeling displaced . . . uncertain, just standing there . . .

The uncertainty—why? I had never felt so free but never so at a loss with myself, yet not unhappy. Woody and the other hearse men were out of sight. Where was Zip? *Spencer*?

Maybe I was weary with my recent crossing, woozy from the unfamiliar motion of the Gulf. Without realizing it I had passed into the *sell* side of the Holy Chapel. This was an elongated canopy of clear plastic allowing in full light. It was the commercial department, a place for the bereaved to purchase coffins. A pleasant lady in a gray suit and white puritan collar walked by. She smiled at me and nodded as she walked, whispering syllables to herself and committing their significance to a pad in her hand. In the background behind the new caskets stretched a mural. I knew in an instant it was the hand work of my Aunt Gloria: a lush green Eden—apple tree, Eve, serpent, and all—with a saddened Adam leaving The Garden at the far end, and a smiling face of Jesus in a cloud above. The sleek coffins were aligned in their steel moorings like dainty ships, each tagged with a fitting price for its perilous voyage.

The pleasant gray lady whispering to herself passed through a door underneath the face of Jesus. In my solitude I wondered how I might induce the cagey ant into my company.

Spencer, I whispered to myself.

Directly across from the departing Adam, I—still uncertain of myself—climbed up the little ramp to the most expensive casket in the lingering fleet and peered in: *A narrow slot of pink satin emitting an odor of gardenias; midway a discreet sleeve rolled back to conceal legs and torso; and a silk pillow for a head . . .*

Was it the pink? The odor of gardenias? The mesmerizing music from above? The click of Zip's toenails on the polished tile? . . . or was it Spencer, ever alert to my crazy ways, rustling in casket folds of satin? What absurdity on my part would it take to fetch him? . . .

Then on an uplifting echo of my mother's voice, I exclaimed so strongly that my words resounded in the plastic canopy:

"She's an AVIATRIX too," I cried.

"An AVIATRIX too," the canopy repeated.

I listened to the crisp mixture of letters that cut like sharp propellers . . .

Spencer . . .

Then I stepped up and slipped into the pink cockpit, laid my head upon the silk casket pillow, and closed my eyes as if dead . . .

"Eager to wing away so soon?" Spencer crackled.

The jaunty insect was sitting coolly at the foot of the new coffin on a puffy cluster of raised words that read *Now abideth Love.* In one hand he held the pearl-headed rapier. With his top-knot antennae, his vest-tight thorax and translucent agate abdomen, the handsome ant seemed fit for all occasions. I was about to open my mouth—

"Enough! You have deceived no one but your gullible self," Spencer said and pointed his nifty needle at me. "Again you are on the verge of uttering something quite inane. *Aviatrix*! Indeed. Ha! *Like sharp propellers* . . . Ha! Ha! How embarrassingly sissy can you sound? I dare you even to murmur such lily-laced words to your bold and fearless Admiral. His immobile garden rocks speak more eloquently."

"I was—" I began.

"Yes, I know. You were fishing around to catch me! Ha! Well look." He twirled his rapier like a cheerleader. "You were about to imagine how it feels to sail away with your sweet mama to heaven or to some other absurd utopia."

"I was not," I defended myself. "And I wouldn't exactly call my mother *sweet.* I have no intention of *sailing* away anywhere or of ever going back to the academy. I've had enough of the commandant and his dull authority. I have graduated, finished, ahead of my class," I said with some pride.

"Yes, yes, I know. You young sprouts are always graduating *from* something *to* something but never get it all together. So now—our brand new Jody has become his very own neat little utopia, but—ahhhhh—I fear so deeply flawed and so worried that he is not sad precisely when he should be."

At the academy I had learned—to my surprise—what *utopia* means.

"You do know what the word means?" the ant pursued.

"Of course."

Spencer cracked a smile. "Just as I thought," he said.

"Thought what?" I asked.

"That you are still as headstrong and blind as ever."

"But utopia does mean *nowhere*," I said committing myself.

"Yes, but it can also mean *now here* or *here now* or *ne'er who* or *he worne*. Your kind become so addicted to single meanings that you scarcely get the whole picture." Spencer's expression was less a smile and more of a grimace. He pointed his blunted rapier to my ear.

"You're making fun again of my queer ear," I said.

"Well, all flesh equals out in the end, but I can see you're still unbalanced."

"Thanks a lot," I said. "Nobody notices my ear anymore."

"I do!" Spencer piped, as if through a small clarinet. "You are blaming yourself because you are a bastard. Do you suppose you have a big ear because you are a bastard or that you are a bastard because you have a big ear?"

I couldn't answer. Spencer continued.

"My, my! What vacuuity! I fear your best celestialogists have conceived of nothing better than a bulging globe searching for its center and the center ever in quest of its circumference. It is quite remarkable how, in so brief a history, your colossal colony has reached such a high plateau of ignorance."

"High enough I hope not to get stuck with a pomposity like you."

Spencer was amused. "Ah, sticks and stones may break my . . . —but it might be quite otherwise," he said. "It may be I who am stuck with you. Enough of this! Quite enough! It is my nature to cut through time and trifles, not to get encumbered in them. You remember, of course, that you are here to bury your incomparable mother *boldly* and that your unfortunate salt-walled uncle will not be present at your mother's grave. But he, your bewildered Minos," Spencer said gravely, "forget him not!"

No, I would not forget him. Mother had etched this man in my memory: the once magnificent Minos, the Golden Gloves God of Hurricane who never crushed his opponent in the ring but who, at last, picked him up from the canvas and cried at his defeat. Minos, still a man alive, a man turned monster, who, on his wedding day years ago, closed himself alone and alive in his salt-walled basement. Woven into my brain was this still living man who had become alternately to me an illusive hero and family ghost, a chameleon kinsman who sifted in and out the shadows of my mind and, at times, startled me from my dreams.

"Yes," I said. "I know. He's still buried in his basement."

"Alas, 'tis true, but seems too that you, reclining here in your cute canoe, are not quite ready for your final voyage." I had forgotten that I was in a coffin.

"I thought you'd be impressed," I said, coming to my elbows.

"Impressed? You more oft depress me. Look at you, ruddy-hued and pink cheeked! All your effulgent blood aflow. You make the sorriest sight of a corpse I've ever seen."

"I thought you might peek in on my monkish uncle, to see—"

"Spy? Never! I have means more honorable. But it will not be easy to confront your afflicted kin—to extract him or ever to flush him out! That will be a great ordeal, but not for his sake alone. By all our noble souls and all the ancient storms I've known, it will not be easy. You can count on that! And, remember too, your storm is now abrew."

I intended to interrupt, but Spencer held up a hand and went on.

"Recall, I say, the embarrassing battle of Likenesses between you and your brilliant sister; and remember well the slothful hermit crab that shocked your conscience."

"I remember, " I said. "But for the umpteenth time, the girl is not my sister."

"Ah yes. Well, just so long as you know the difference between a boy and a girl, between a girl and a beech. Of the genus Fagus! Ha! I trust that your proper instincts will not again forsake you nor that your blindness be longer than a blink."

Indeed I did remember the unruly hermit crab and how my rude Likeness of him nearly did me in.

"Great galaxies!" Spencer exclaimed. "Your hapless uncle is a symptom of your present tribe, but judge him not too swiftly." In the clustered phrase he was sitting on, Spencer fixed his pin stick securely in a crevice of *Love*, stood up, flexed his wiry arms, clicked his jaws, and said, "You have a lot to learn from your little artist. But you are here to return your mother to the earth. I know a great deal about holes-in-the-ground," Spencer said.

"I reckon you do," I said. I was vexed at Spencer's conceit. "And you can crawl back in your measly earth hole anytime you wish. I don't have time now to be mumbling and stepping over you."

Why—I could not say—but I had never been surprised that Spencer knew I was a bastard.

"Patience," Spencer complained. "Harping on time again."

"You can bug off any *time* you like," I said, not intending to be mean but merely trying to hold my own with the aggressive ant.

"Now Jody dear," crooned Spencer in his miniature alto, "if you would but incline your awkward ear toward me, you might detect my meager creeping and avoid crushing me into your too too solid earth."

Spencer poised himself acrobatically, swung to the rim of the casket, and put his face to mine as if to confirm my existence. However simultaneous our sense of presence, I wondered if the insect with his polished dome *was* a spy, or a foreign agent. Spencer was smiling down at me.

"It's my ear again. I wish you'd lay off my funny ear. You know very well it's hereditary. I can't do anything about it."

"You can hear with it," Spencer said. "Other than being like it is, there appears nothing else the matter with it except, perhaps, that the other side of your head is a trifle small. We ants have our hereditary curiosities to be sure, but in our glands, not our ears! Ha!" Spencer crackled. "We ants are all great alchemists, much greater than your moo cow Pasteur or your forensic FBI blood daubers." Then, like a gentleman—with ever so slight a limp—Spencer strode back lightly to the word cluster and propped on his slender stick.

"Well," I said, "You are unusual for an ant."

With adroit forefingers Spencer adjusted his antennae and said, ". . . which makes me one of a kind, unique! I confess that my size is an impediment, my limp an embarrassment; but my sensors are of equal dimension and perfectly synchronized—always. Look at me!" Spencer held out his arms as if crucified. "I am indestructible—a chip off the God-block! My timelessness is perpetuated by the ancient process of Cosmosis, an entity too profound and obvious for your narrow mind. I have ridden on elephants over the snowy Alps with the great Carthaginian Hannibal and from his windy sleeves and broad shoulders beheld magnificent victories. I have seen Caesar fatally punctured on his senate floor. I have watched the blood blue ink of Shakespeare's genius dry in immortal words upon the page. Although death avoids me," Spencer cried, "I have assimilated such wisdom that I may mark his fatal steps upon the face of this much abused earth."

"Like not getting stepped on again?" I needled. I sat up in the expensive casket and waggled the toe of my shoe in the ant's face.

"Quite so my brave aviator," Spencer responded with theatrical wit, rising to his full height on the clustered platitude. Twirling his pearl-headed rapier, he gave a formal bow as if to royalty and finished with "Henceforth—even though your shoe hath both eyes and tongue—in my cosmic extension I will endeavor to avoid its clumsy sole. Now," he continued with mild alarm, "crawl out of that silly coffin! Out! Out! of this dreary morgue! The weather outside is blooming toward a happening. We have a mother to bury, and here comes your pretty companion."

Jo Anne, I wondered . . .

But I did remember the hermit crab, my battle of Likenesses with Jo Anne, and kissing the dumb beech tree.

12

THE FUNERAL

WOODY LED THE other four funeral men who slowly rolled Mother from the Holy Chapel back to the Cadillac. Zip, head down, followed the casket like a sad pony. I trailed behind. If Mother's death had been a curious blessing to me, it also had been a profound shock whose repercussions were now trembling back into my conscience. Being a bastard at the academy I was a cadet; being a bastard on Hurricane I was Jody. There was a difference.

Clouds to the south were gathering. Jo Anne was waiting in the back of the hearse when they shoved Mother in.

"Millsap hasn't showed up yet," Jo Anne said.

But the preacher managed to intercept us after all.

As we approached the Church of the Holy Sepulcher, Millsap stopped the Thunderbird crosswise under the archway of the cemetery and was on foot toward the hearse. I had never seen the Reverend so completely free of his pulpit. But here he came parading with great strides like a circus Uncle Sam on stilts, flapping in the breeze, an alarming spider of a man at least six and a half feet tall with a sober Lincolnesque face and dangling hands and wrists that exceeded his coat sleeves—in fact a pleasant but pitiful sort of man.

Jo Anne ducked behind mother's casket.

"What are you hiding for?" I asked.

"I don't want him to think I have any special privileges."

"That's crazy."

"I don't want him to think I know anything . . ."

"Anything about what?"

"About him and—"

"*Him* and who?"

"About Millsap and your mother."

"What? What? What?" I cried. Again, the supposition was too sudden and remote for me to grasp.

Reverend Millsap was coming on.

"You're afraid," I said. "Sit up." I got on my knees and put my face in her curls. "For God's sake sit up!" I whispered out loud.

I didn't want to confront this man alone.

"He's all yours," Jo Anne said with calm abandon and settled down into a frog position.

"I can't talk to him now," I said to Woody.

"I've got my window rolled up," Woody said.

"Mine too," the other guy said.

"Mine too," Jo Anne echoed from the floor.

I wanted to bite her leg.

From this distance I could see that our family few had arrived in the cemetery. They were strolling among the monuments, meandering toward the service tent. The mouth doors of the leviathan church were closed.

Millsap and my mother. What could this mean?

Uncle Claude had cut short his deep sea fishing in the Gulf. He walked dutifully behind the petite Gloria. Gloria carried her short-stalked Japanese parasol with painted dragons. The Admiral was standing reverently before Grandmother's memorial cross. With his ranger hat removed and his marble hair awash in the summer sun, my grandfather was outstanding among the gravestones. I wondered if he realized he was standing in a rock garden not entirely unlike his own; I wondered if he would ever divulge his secret gift of the leviathan church; and I wondered, too, about his Great Quartz stone and the futility of believing in God if you could not believe in a grain of sand.

On a turf of green facing the Gulf stood a character I could not identify. The Admiral was headed our way.

Reverend Millsap approached the hearse, braced his hands on the hood and leaned his keen face into the windshield. He was talking earnestly and his words came muffled through the glass as if wrapped in cotton.

"What does he want?" I asked Woody.

"He wants you to shut up your dog in the hearse and pray a word of prayer with you," Woody said.

Jo Anne arose to her all fours for a peek, and Zip leapt back up on the casket.

"He's coming around to the back," Woody warned.

The rear glass was darkly tinted. All I could see of Millsap were his teeth, his clerical collar, and his white hands. The other form was The Admiral. He pulled the tall preacher aside and, after words, sent him away holding up his long arms in consent. When Millsap cranked the Thunderbird, we moved behind him into the cemetery, but stopped a good distance from the service tent. Woody got out and opened the wide back door.

"You're making me damn-well earn my hundred bucks," he said, "and you better make up your mind about that bobtail dog."

Zip hit the ground, trotting around the trunk of a monument like he had springs in his joints.

"We've got a dog problem," The Admiral said.

"Like—?" I asked.

"Like Zip," Jo Anne supplied. She was brushing wrinkles from her dress.

"He won't bark. I promise," I said.

"Not his bark," The Admiral said. "His manners."

"He'll sit when I say so," I said.

"For goodness sake," Jo Anne said, "you know how boy dogs are around trees and things."

I did. I whistled Zip up, hopped him in the hearse, and shut the door.

"Make haste," The Admiral said. "The weather's threatening."

Woody and the others were laying Mother on the rack over her grave. The Admiral, on his way to the service tent, turned and beckoned to me and Jo Anne. The service tent was under a spreading live oak. There were seven chairs on the pad. One for each of us and an empty chair for Uncle Minos. Over the wireless The Admiral and I had planned the service down to the last second.

Spencer and The Admiral had been right about the weather. Bulging biceps of dark clouds were rumbling our way. No great wind yet. For the moment the high morning sun glared down upon the flat grave stones, and gray stockings of Spanish moss swung lightly from the boughs above. The cemetery was the top spot of the island, enclosed by a dense collar of tropical shrubbery and perennial flowers devised by The Admiral, installed, kept clean, and cared for by hands from the Church of the Holy Sepulcher.

The Reverend Millsap, as instructed, stood facing us with his back to Mother's casket. He was to hold forth four minutes—no more. The funeral was set between two verses of scripture chosen by The Admiral. The first was to be spoken by me, the final verse by The Admiral.

The entire service was to last no more than nine and one-half minutes.

Reverend Millsap made a gesture, and we were seated.

As The Admiral required, he and I sat under the tent on the left, the others on the right. Jo Anne sat behind me between Gloria and Claude. Venoria sat in the rear beside Minos's empty chair. But I was wrong about the number of chairs. Instead of seven, there were eight. Beside the vacant chair there was, at the far front end, an extra chair occupied by the stranger I had seen earlier. Although he seemed vaguely familiar, I was satisfied I had never seen him before. Not that his presence was disruptive but that it was unexpected, almost presumptuous, as if an old acquaintance had turned up uninvited at your home, awaiting recognition.

A steady breeze was sweeping inland from the Gulf. Reverend Millsap held out the Bible with a long arm and smiled kindly at me. This was my cue. I stood and delivered:

In the beginning God created the Heaven and the earth . . .

And stopped.

The Admiral had told me to remain standing for as long as it took for the words to *soak in*. I reckoned thirty seconds. Too long The Admiral reasoned. By that time, he advised, the impression of such a mighty event would have begun to dissipate in shallow minds and lose the grandeur of creation. He told me to count to fifteen and sit down.

I counted to fifteen and sat down.

Now Millsap was on his own. Four minutes. He retreated to the safety of The Lord's Prayer.

Our Father which art in Heaven . . . he began.

The stranger's hair had wisps of gray. He wore wire rim glasses. He was not listening to the minister but looking introspectively across the Gulf. I held my eye on him like a magnet until I attracted his attention. There was a certain ambivalence about the man. He allowed me the slightest suggestion of a smile and resumed his gaze across the white caps. I switched my surprise to The Admiral who cut his eyes to the stranger, puffed out his cheeks, and drew his chin and neck into a question mark.

Thy will be done . . . continued Millsap.

And whose *will* had set in motion the festering enigma of Uncle Minos, a dreadful duty Mother had dropped on me? And what had Jo Anne meant *between Millsap and my mother*? Millsap's head was not bowed in prayer but his face and angular jaw were upright toward Heaven, his eyes open, his hair awash in the wind. Had this man lain with my mother? My mother's early voice was sanctified in his church and nurtured in his holy eye. Was this all? Except for song, my mother had been the silent one. Unselfish and gladly successful in pursuit of her bliss, she had left me mercifully to mine—and to my severance from the academy and now into the company of Uncle Claude and Gloria, and to the doubtful hospitality of Jo Anne.

I looked back at the empty chair: Uncle Minos the darkling. Minos the family humiliation and abomination. At this time no explanation or revelation would have been sufficient for me to understand so void a human soul. How could once so glorious and so physical a champion of the ring resolve on his wedding day never to speak or look again upon his handsome bride? There was his bloody fight with the sailor—and the rumor of a lie. That was all. And now twenty years of self-interment! Of encapsulation in his sterile salt wall basement! It is true, because of his notorious isolation, he had become a legend, yes, and a prosperous lure for tourists to Venoria's curiosity shop. The Hermit of Hurricane! But I knew little more about the inside of this man than of his empty chair beside Venoria.

Give us this day our daily bread . . .

And *bread* was the word for Venoria, whole-wheat bread—not "pretty" but handsome, not glamorous but wholesome. Her features were bold and her presence lush enough to hold all of nature in her lap. Jo Anne had not missed Venoria's elemental beauty and promised to paint her in oils facing an unruly sea. At a rumble of thunder, I looked back at Venoria. With a glance, she took me in. I relaxed and, joining the stranger for a moment, rested my eyes on the whitecaps in the Gulf. Millsap paused and looked at the volatile clouds closing in. Woody, standing behind a large concrete angel, was smoking a cigarette. I could see Zip's paws on the back pane of the hearse and knew he was barking his lungs out.

Forgive us our trespasses as we forgive . . .

Rooted in my mind were this rangy clergyman and his pious few who had trespassed on my mother's soul and now cast their wavering shadow over me.

Gentle, red-faced, rawboned Uncle Claude and his snippy Gloria were an unlikely pair. Gloria's pink sweet smile and sky blue eyes belied the tough gal beneath. From her I had learned that my greatest household asset was in sharpening Jo Anne's genius. Gloria had needed me, but not in entire selfishness; for in loving Jo Anne she had found me there. But then, as now, it seemed perfectly natural that Gloria and Claude had made no babies. Jo Anne in her spring green dress, seated between this lanky fisherman and his unlikely wife, seemed to relieve the contradiction. I glanced back. Gloria had her eyes wide open looking steadfastly down into the funeral grass. Claude smiled and nodded to me his sympathy. I wondered about sad Rowdy at the academy and about black Zachariah whose ample library consisted of *Webster's Unabridged Dictionary, The Holy Bible,* and Colonel Scott Flint's *The*

Complete Manual of Military Courtesy. Millsap, I supposed, was a one book man.

Lead us not into temptation . . .

When I looked back, Jo Anne with her quick eyes was giving the stranger the once over. Then a ludicrous image popped into my mind: Spencer, the ant, in clerical collar and assuming an ecclesiastical air, was pronouncing Zip and Cleopatra "Man and wife!" The reluctant animals were holding paws. I was father of the groom and Jo Anne was giving the bride away. I blurted out a giggle. The Admiral, thinking it a sob, put a hand on my knee. I braved another glance at Jo Anne. She wagged her head at my indiscretion, closed her eyes, then opened one at me.

But deliver us from evil . . .

The Admiral had neither bowed his head nor closed his eyes. Not because he was obstinate or irreligious but because, as he once explained, one should never close his eyes when addressing God. In the first place, he said, such a habit was rude and evasive; in the second place there was no evidence in scripture that God or Jesus or the prophets required closed eyes to make contact with Him. "Can you imagine—can you *imagine*! he repeated, "Job talking to God with his eyes shut?" I had only a Sunday school notion of Job—although I was sure Job looked something like The Admiral—but, yes, it struck me as being downright unmannerly to be talking seriously to anyone, especially to God, with my eyes closed.

For thine is the Kingdom . . .

As to his unorthodox sentiments, I knew from our varied conversations across the Gulf that The Admiral believed in God or at least in the essentials, such as knowing that he wasn't God. Otherwise why would he have secretly conceived of and donated to the denizens of Hurricane the Church of the Holy Sepulcher?

Even so, my grandfather was slowly and unceremoniously frowned out of his own church; however I recalled that his retreat was with a steady smile and unrepentant heart. His idolatry was no more than his innocent rock garden. Millsap had belabored my grandfather over the Great Quartz stone which, according to the Reverend, represented materialistic doctrine that displaced God as the prime mover of the universe. Although Millsap would not himself pronounce The Admiral an idolator, he warned his parish that the old traveler had sailed to the brink of damnation.

The power and the glory . . .

According to The Admiral's schedule, Reverend Millsap had but two minutes remaining in the service. I would listen carefully now to what he had to say of my mother and certainly what he would have the modesty to leave unsaid. *Besides her voice, what else had this man to do with my mother? Did he know the stranger?* Towering above my mother's casket, he looked down at me. I did not avoid his eyes. He would not shame me here or even intimate my depravity, not with my mother quietly at his back and I and The Admiral squarely before his face.

Forever, amen.

About my mother, Millsap began:

"On this storm-tempered isle forty years ago a lovely little soprano at the tender age of twelve was discovered and thence dubbed by her wise father 'The Pearl of Hurricane,' a real jewel of our very own who was graciously and immaculately prepared at such lofty institutions as the conservatories of Paris, of London, of Barcelona, and of New York . . ."

There was thunder and stitches of lightning.

The stranger shifted his eyes from the white caps to the clouds. I looked around. The irreverent Woody quickly enjoyed the last breath of his cigarette and with his shoe suffocated its remains in the grass. Gloria was staring sternly at Uncle Claude who sat folded in his lobster arms as if asleep. The Admiral placed a veined hand upon my knee. Jo Anne opened her eyes to look at me.

A low oval of grave clay rested between the minister and me. To hide its inevitable return to the earth, the diggers had partially covered the mound with a sheet of plastic grass. A few clay clods had rolled loose. With my shoe tip I flicked a prominent clod back towards its mound, only to see it sent back with equal velocity. In the cavity from where it came, stood Spencer, thoroughly incensed, I suppose, that he should be so ungrounded and rudely dug in upon. To emphasize his displeasure he stood in the open clay pock, jutting to me his grim chin and cocking one wrist down hard upon the hip of his abdomen. I felt that he was about to speak when again the thunder rumbled, and Millsap made haste to conclude:

". . . who not only touched our hearts with song but who held enthralled the most adoring and sophisticated audiences in Europe and America and whose voice of late was silenced on the lonesome plains of New Mexico . . ."

The stranger was now looking at me.

". . . and may our gracious Lord, the author of all utterance and song, may He—" Millsap held one hand back toward Mother and the other up with his Bible, concluding, "May He grant passage to this, your child's immortal soul."

Millsap's time was up.

It was now Grandfather's duty to seal the service. With final words, The Admiral stood.

"May the Lord Jesus Christ be with you all—amen," he said and was finished. It was only recently that I realized he had set me up with the first verse and himself with last verse of the Bible.

But now there would be no minister's consolation. No clasping of hands. No hovering. No handkerchiefs. No tears. The Admiral led us quickly away.

Woody and his hearse men, like cautious crows, stood in waiting around the concrete angel. The clod that Spencer had sent jetting onto the tent mat was smashed. Reverend Millsap, as instructed, departed the rear way, passing uneasily by my mother's casket. The stranger had vanished. Jo Anne took my hand.

"Who was the graying stranger in the wire-rimmed glasses?" she asked.

"I don't know," I said. "He looked familiar."

"Yes," Jo Anne said, tightening on my hand, "a little like you along the brow."

It was over.

"Poor Millsap," Jo Anne said.

Somehow, I too felt sorry for the tall clergyman with his Bible, his head hung forward like a little boy ambling home alone with his lunch box.

13

To the Merrimac

THE FUNERAL HAD gone well enough, but I could not fathom why I felt so keen a sympathy for the melancholy minister. Had he in his holy adoration of my mother ever laid an unwelcomed hand on her body?

"I never saw the man in my life," Gloria said of the stranger. She and Claude were sitting at either end of the center seat in the Chevy van. Although the van was now mine, I felt it improper that I should be driving. Especially today. Nor did I feel free to ask my grandfather about the expensive Rolls he had purchased from the Earl of Ipswich. I could see the lighthouse in the distance.

"Going where?" I asked, to solve Jo Anne's homecoming riddle.

"H-O-M-E," Jo Anne spelled mysteriously.

"We've moved?" I wanted to know.

"You'll see," she said. "There's always something new to see on Hurricane." Jo Anne was sitting stiffly beside me in the back seat. Zip was up front with The Admiral and Venoria.

"I'm thinking the stranger was a man of music," Venoria said. "It was by his eyes that measured the rhythm of the waves I could tell." Zip watched Venoria intently for his goody-bit.

The Admiral was driving. He started a cigar and said there was something familiar about the stranger but that at times we are strangers to ourselves and to each other and that it was this common confusion of identity that offset us all.

"Your father?" Jo Anne guessed with genuine curiosity.

—a silence.

What Jo Anne guessed, of course, was impossible. It was officially verified that my absent father—from the beginning oblivious of me—was shot down, lost, and absorbed by the jungles of Vietnam.

Gloria held that because of his wire-rimmed glasses and graying hairline that the stranger was of ecclesiastical or scientific inclinations; then said, to my distress, that she had "squared away" my new room in neat military fashion so I would "feel right at home." I wondered what she had done with my army of books and table of natural wonders.

"I never noticed the stranger atall," Claude said. "But with my own eyes shut I could see my hermit brother sittin' in that empty chair and he wasn't even there."

Jo Anne said, "I caught the stranger with my eye and fixed him right here." She pointed at her head. This was the artist speaking.

"Better there than in the skull orchard," The Admiral said. I knew he smiled because his ears moved.

Gloria agreed. She enjoyed my grandfather's approval and generosity and knew there was nothing the old salt wouldn't do for me or for her remarkable Jo Anne.

Venoria caught my eye as we let her off. She pointed at the new waist-high lettering on top of her WHY NOT SHOP?. The question mark was an addition to the sign. It was a cypress knee carved in the form of a sea horse. With her quaint husband entombed below, her curiosity shop had extended its fame from Pensacola to Biloxi, Mississippi.

"The sea horse was Jo Anne's idea," Gloria informed me, "but Minos whittled it out. Your glum uncle is slow and bumbling but he has the hands of an artist. He carved the weird creature out exactly—spine, barbs, snout—and put the question mark dot under his tail." I had seen the proud, arch-necked little sea urchins in glass aquariums, parading around like tiny stallions.

"Minos ought to know a lot about question marks," Jo Anne said. For over two summers she had been working on a portrait of the staunch Venoria.

"A sea horse is a born question mark," I added.

"My timid Minos doesn't dare his eyes upon me or even his face upon a mirror to see himself," Venoria said. When Venoria stepped out of the van she gave Zip a goody-bit from her handbag. With a wink she looked at Jo Anne. "Maybe at some time my Minos will look upon my picture and give his eyes back to me," she said.

As we passed the *Inn Lafayette* I could see The Admiral's winged eyebrows in the rear view mirror. The Admiral had told me in some sad detail about my uncle's bloody fight that wedding night at the ancient inn and, later, hinted at *the lie*. That was all I knew. Making sense of the inverted and twisted Minos was like piecing together misty sections of a worried dream.

Jo Anne was upset. She said that her art display was dangerously close at hand and that she was all atremble at her prospects of national competition, especially now, to have to stand and watch what she called her "fishy pictures" fall under the critical eye of art experts. The famous critics were Dr. Roger Scott and the popular Carlos Expondos. Dr. Scott was a retired professor emeritus of architecture from Virginia, now director of the Archives of Southern Art and History. Expondos, a flamboyant modern artist, was an enthusiastic collector of ancient Mexican artifacts and a point man for the National Enlightenment of the Arts. Dr. Scott and Carlos Expondos were to arrive next week.

"I'm beginning to feel like your Uncle Minos," Jo Anne said.

"About what?" I asked.

"About the experts. I want to burrow down. I don't even want to look at them." Tightening on my hand she pressed her tension into me.

"Did you finish my bull bluegill picture?" I asked.

"Yes. He's yours to have in your new room."

"Did you fix his eyes like I wanted?"

"You'll see," she said.

Before going back to the academy I had left Jo Anne a permanent model bull bluegill frozen lake-fresh in a block of ice. I had honed the top of the ice crystal into a perfect curve so that—wiped smooth with a damp cloth—the fish was authentic, permanently preserved, and clearly magnified.

There was tension in Jo Anne's arm and in her voice. She pulled me in closer and whispered—

"Reverend Millsap was in love with your mother," she revealed.

This was a suspicion not entirely new to me. But the sudden slash across my conscience that they might have been lovers, coming directly from Jo Anne, left me lightheaded. When I turned swiftly upon her, she put a finger to my lips.

Lightning crackled sharply, releasing a host of raindrops as large as muscadines that crashed into the windshield. In the retreating rumble I realized for the first time that I had been cut free from my predictable academy. The thunder hurried Zip across the middle seat and into my lap.

Since Mother first eased to me the knowledge of her banishment and my depravity, I had wished the island to be nibbled away by waves and ingested into the Gulf. But now that I had been thrust into open view, a legitimate illegitimate, my secret heart craved to stay the course, to weather any storm—the storm predicted by The Admiral and confirmed by Spencer—even to the vengeful moment of witnessing the pathetic Millsap fighting off the unconscious waves to come, clinging for life in the jaws of his leviathan sanctuary.

Millsap in love with my mother? Without her knowledge? Without her participation? Without her permission?

And yet I had no sound evidence to fire my hate upon this prevailing minister, except that he seemed from the beginning to be the ugly center of my mother's exile and the slow festering of her local damnation.

The rain passed as quickly as it had come. The sun popped out. The van stopped. Jo Anne slid her side door wide open—

"Home!" she announced and watched my face. Not 'til this moment did I understand the meaning of her riddle of *my new abode*, sent to me at the academy on a postcard. The old Gulf home I'd known in past summers had been whisked away as if by sky hooks. Now this!

"My God!" I uttered. "It's the Merrimac!"

True. The new beach house as nearly resembled the old Confederate thunder tub as any likeness I had ever seen. I knew at once it was a brain child of The Admiral's, a burst of his old imagination.

"A gift house from The Admiral!" Jo Anne praised. "Isn't she beautiful?" It wasn't exactly the right word. The original battleship was an awkward vessel designed not for the open sea but for sluggish, close-up bombardment. In fact it was ugly. I had pictures of the old iron-plated warship in my library. There was hardly a stitch in the whole quilt of that bloody war that I didn't know.

"She'll make a damn fool of hurricanes," The Admiral said of the land-anchored house. "All storms start far out at sea to build up their rage for us." He put his arm around Jo Anne.

Reminded of my storm-lost grandmother, I understood instantly the deep sentiments of The Admiral. From his lighthouse he lived in watchful defiance of high island winds. He thought of hurricanes as creatures alive and went out, his white hair aflare, to meet them on the beach. The Admiral had spared no expense on the construction of this triple-layered bulwark. "A cloister for my Pearl of Hurricane," he said, and patted Jo Anne on the head. Slanting up forty feet off the ground, it was studded on four corners in the island sand by barrel-sized pine piling with oak board and batten all around its tapered sides, sides stout enough to bounce off waves the force of cannon balls. The steps up to midsection were thirty solid feet of railroad crossties banistered in iron and railed lengthwise with steel beams from stem to stern. Set snugly underneath in reinforced concrete and framed upward in safety glass was a combination flower garden-art studio. Gloria and Jo Anne had a hand in this—and all with patient Claude's permission. The only other work of equal craftsmanship and endurance on the island was Johnny Revelation's incomparable Ark.

Cleopatra was stretched out flat-bellied in the up-front sunshine corner of the new studio. When Zip approached the glass, the cat arose, swelling to porcupine proportions, and made her tail into a bottle washer.

"It really looks like a pyramid with the top chopped off," Jo Anne said of the Merrimac. "Your quarters—up there." She pointed and winked. "You're in the Navy now." The four windows across topside looked like gun ports.

Zip watched Cleopatra gradually deflate. The Admiral tapped me on the rump with his walking cane and bid me inspect my new quarters alone. Jo Anne followed me halfway up the stairs. I paused to ask her about my bluegill picture—

"Did you paint the pupils of his eyes like I wanted?"

"You'll see," she said.

But first to meet my eye in the expansive wardroom was a mural that dominated the opposite wall—a lengthy scene of Jesus on the stormy Sea of Galilee, lifting His terrified disciple from the waves. Clearly it was a master-effort by Gloria to christen the advent of the Merrimac.

A floor above, my cabin quarters were truly "squared away": my scarred footlocker at the foot of a four-poster bed; roll-top desk, lamp, and captain's chair; and—a sure sign of The Admiral's attention—my nature books shelved and classified on the wall; my table of natural wonders; a walk-in closet and dog bed labeled *Sgt. Zip*; and the four gunport windows facing south from which I could see the Gulf, the Church of the Holy Sepulcher, and The Admiral's lighthouse leaning slightly out to sea.

In a crystal bowl by the bedside floated a Madonna lily blossom as big as a sun bonnet.

And yet, for all my newly acquired liberty, I could not but welcome the military neatness of my new room, its uniform simplicity, the fixed order of my faithful books, and the old familiarity of my footlocker.

"WELL, HOW NOW my courageous Jody! I shiver that you would scuttle our sandy isle and leave your lonely parson hanging from the baleful jaws of his holy whale." It was Spencer. "Are you fearful that the old fish might mistake you for a Jonah? Do you not know that a hurricane would inundate your salt-dried uncle before you might assess him truly and thus forever thwart your mother's wishes?" The impulsive ant was standing on my footlocker in the arch of letters ALABAMA MILITARY ACADEMY. In a flippant half loop, Spencer had flung around his neck a finger length silken scarf such as daring aviators used to wear. There was an odd configuration about the ant, an anatomical addition. "I have always admired," he continued, "your aeronautical heroes such as the Lone Eagle Lindbergh and the dragonfly ace Baron von Richthofen who riddled from the clouds his adversaries like brazen house flies."

I was astonished to see that Spencer's unusual shape was caused by a pair of tinseled wings that he held folded close to his sides. "Yes," Spencer said, turning around daintily as a Parisian model, "they aren't quite dry. They are an inevitable but temporary acquisition for mating, a fate which I sadly learned to avoid. They are nevertheless of rare beauty, don't you think?" Spencer lifted his wings uncertainly as if they were not quite his own.

"Yes," I allowed. "I see it is now *you* who prepares flight to the heavenly regions." I was hoping to irritate the ant and gain a little advantage over his ostentatious manner. The dinky appendages did look preposterous on the austere insect, as if he had abruptly sprouted little pancake spatulas.

"Nothing divine, I assure you," Spencer said. "But we must cherish such natural favors as they occur however frail or impertinent."

"Have you tried them out?" I asked.

"Merciful Jupiter, no! What would you have me do? Jump off the end of your footlocker and break my neck?"

"You're afraid," I said.

"Rubbish! I'm afraid only of becoming the donkey you already are. You and your alluring language are a bit habit forming, you know." Spencer was having some involuntary trouble with one of his wings which kept fluttering upward and falling into disuse.

In jest, to encourage a little verbal skirmish, I made a move as if to sweep the ant away.

"Well, at least a very young equus asinus—" Spencer softened, "an intelligent, but a very silly jackass."

"Now, please sir, how so?" I encouraged.

"By detesting the Reverend's love of your mother. So he is an ugly parson! An ecclesiastical spider! But who are you to say who should love her? Or whom she should love? Look at me," Spencer demonstrated by standing tip-toe. "You may think me beastly, but it is I alone who have heard the music of the spheres. Who could escape the charm of your mother's voice?"

"Good Lord! Me? I wasn't even born yet! How could I keep Millsap from . . ."

"There you go again getting all tangled up in time. See what a silly ass you are, trying now, beyond the womb, beyond the tomb, to inoculate your mother from another's affection? Tut tut. Would you hog your mother's love? Forbid her silver tongue to touch the world? I should be fearful now to even be your donkey's shadow."

Spencer was trying to make the wayward wing behave.

"I don't know what you're talking about," I said.

I had not expected so provocative a response, but I wanted to find out what knowledge Spencer might shed on the Reverend Millsap or on the mysterious stranger. Spencer's other wing began an embarrassing twitch which he immediately put under control of his left arm.

"Maybe you better forget about being my donkey's shadow and try out for angel," I said. "You look light enough to fly." I couldn't help but smile at the frustrated ant. And then for a bit of friendly intimidation I raised my shoe above his head and threatened, "No you, no shadow."

Spencer whipped around so quickly that his wings spread out. "No *light*, no shadows," he corrected, fingering my heel out of his way. He then stepped forth into full light and flipped his scarf another turn around his neck, "which is precisely what you wish me to be—non-existent!"

The thought startled me. He said this with such feeling—as if I had deserted him—that I spoke up quickly to repair our allegiance.

"It seems you'll be wherever you wish," I acknowledged. "I suppose you wonder why I haven't given you away, exposed you to Jo Anne or reported you to The Admiral?"

"Not at all," Spencer said calmly. "In this fickle world you will soon enough be thought a fool, and to admit conversing with an ant would remove all doubt."

That was certainly true.

"I reckon I ought to thank you for being at my mother's funeral."

"Your most humble guest," Spencer nodded. "But you need not ingratiate yourself to me. Since my short residence here, I seldom miss these grave occasions which, save for your nighttime slumber, are the most honest of your ceremonies where, except for a few soul-soothing platitudes, there is the most pleasant absence of your scathing hypocrisies. However, your nightmares are probably more true to life and, I might add, certainly more interesting."

This was too much. "You should talk!" I erupted, "a—a spindly little dirt-digging bug slinging around highfalutin' notions nobody understands. If you're so smart, who was the stranger at the funeral, the one with the graying hair and the wire-rimmed glasses? And what did Millsap have to do with my mother?"

"He loved her, you little pollywog! Fell in love with her! How could the poor ugly cleric help himself?"

Strangely, something I had said so struck Spencer that he sagged a little, and all his limbs went slack. It seemed, but for a second, that a teardrop filled his eye.

"I confess," he said, "that your lovely language—so eloquent from the poetic tongue and the pens of your famous scribes—has become an addiction to me, an impediment. Juggling such worthy words, 'tis true, has clogged my original instincts. But," he resumed his former intensity, "I deplore your barbarous reference 'bug' to *me*! I forbid its degrading application to my prevailing race or to myself while I am in your company. How can you possibly perceive the agony, the depth of my loneliness?" Spencer's other wing had started a little spasm of its own. "As to the original cosmic inheritance of your entire nation, especially your elite," the ant continued, "I fear your tangled tongue has all but beat your better instincts into submission."

Both of Spencer's wings had become more animated and seemed now in tone for flight. Moistening his fingers in the teardrop on his cheek, Spencer anointed his antennae and pulled them into close alignment.

"Like how?" I inquired about my decadent instincts.

"Like not reflecting, knowing in your better eye who the stranger was! Such abominable aim—missing a sweetly offered kiss! Missing your lovely companion's lips and kissing a dumb beech tree! How insensitive can you get?" Spencer slapped his brow in exasperation.

"I don't understand," I said. "What about Millsap? My mother?" The flurry of Spencer's wings had accelerated in my ears to the magnitude of the twin-engine swish of the Aeolian Harp.

"But how?" I insisted, wondering if I had really lost all my original senses.

Spencer made his hands into a small megaphone and broadcast

his words to be heard. "Like not de-tect-ing what at this ve-ry moment lies di-rect-ly be-hind your thick head." His voice carried in gusts over the increasing rush of his wings. The tail of his scarf got caught up in a whirl of air. The urge to look behind me stopped at my fascination with the agitated Spencer who was being energized by a force beyond his control.

"Behind—my head?" I called out. "What about the stranger? About Millsap? Did he ever—"

Spencer's words were getting chopped up in the whir of his wings. ". . . have detected . . . that . . . she—"

"I can't hear you!" I cried.

"—she . . . of course . . . has been . . . a . . . to you . . ." Spencer's words were becoming more chopped up.

"I can't hear you! I can't hear you!" I cried again.

"Well *I* can hear you! What's all this much-of-a-fuss about?" It was Jo Anne who had entered my new room. She had her arms outstretched graciously as if to hug me. "How do you like it?" she asked. She was not talking about my military room. She was talking about her painting of *Bull Bluegill* on the wall, behind me. This was what Spencer had been hinting at. This was the one important thing in my room I had failed to see.

"I-I-I like it," I claimed, without having seen, without having looked. I didn't want Jo Anne to suspect I had neglected to appreciate the supreme effort of her talents. If she had done her job, the painting—once I cast my eyes upon it—would re-create immediately and completely the original thrill, the glory moment of my first catch. It would be spontaneously—without pause or thought—a perfect Likeness.

"Do you like the way I fixed his eyes for you?" she asked. On this one artistic imperative I had given specific instructions, a trick taught to me long ago by Spencer: The pupils of the great bream's eyes were to be tiny bream created in the image of the real bull bluegill, a fish caught for the first time seeing *through* himself.

"It's the first time I've ever done anything quite like this," she admitted. Jo Anne was referring to my requirements for *Bull Bluegill*'s eyes. She was a stickler for authentic detail, and to stretch nature beyond certain limits made her uncomfortable. "Up close he looks kind of goofy," she explained. "You've got to stand back just so far to see him right."

The Madonna lily in the crystal bowl was Jo Anne's idea. She dipped her finger in the cool water and touched it to my lips.

I could hold off no longer.

I faced the picture.

This was it! Her bluegill was an astounding reproduction, a Perfect Likeness better than the one from my scallop shell of our summer contest—but with one exception. It exceeded my expectations. Jo Anne not only had caught on canvas exactly what I had experienced in God's clear air, she had reinforced and enhanced it. Her fish not only resurrected my original thrill, it refined and intensified it. It would have made old Zack at the academy glad. In her painted fish the exacting Zachariah would recognize immediately the truth of my glory moment—the shocked glare of the big bream's eyes transfixed, its bull neck bursting from water into the sun, its arched tail and its blue-orange gills flared in defiance of the tight thread and the unseen hand that held him. As old Zack had said, "When you two is bound together forever in that one second, that's when God takes yo' picture."

Bull Bluegill!

Yes, this was it—Jo Anne's masterpiece!

But his eyes were mine.

14

Bull Bluegill and Zip's Magnificent Impression

The experts were to arrive this morning to judge Jo Anne's art. Dr. Scott, via the *Umbilicus,* was to come early by state car and lodge at the Inn Lafayette. At 10:37 a.m. Carlos Expondos was to parachute in at a popular drop spot on the beach. The Admiral and I would pick up the spectacular Carlos and unite him with Dr. Scott at the old French tavern.

Jo Anne was nervous. The judging of her best aquatic art was tomorrow. When I unhung Bull Bluegill for the judging and brought him down from my room, Jo Anne and Gloria were in the morning glow of the studio discussing how to arrange the chosen five pictures for the experts. Besides *Bull Bluegill,* Jo Anne had picked *Stingray, Man of War, Flounder,* and *Mr. Grumps* for the judgment. Grumps was the one-hopper bull frog that The Admiral had given me two summers ago. I was surprised that Jo Anne, now with a scholarship and national fame in the making, had placed her portrait of the lugubrious frog in serious competition. I had nothing against my crippled amphibian, but Gloria thought him pitiful, even comic, and that his picture would dilute whatever enthusiasm the critics might have for Jo Anne's other work.

All five paintings would hang in the rear of the studio under neon lights. Of the five creatures only Grumps was still alive. Only two of Jo Anne's pictures would be chosen.

There was no doubt in my mind that *Bull Bluegill* was Jo Anne's masterpiece. And, for better or for worse, I had a hand—rather, an eye—in his creation. But now with critical judgment upon us, ownership of *Bull Bluegill* was in doubt. Jo Anne had already said: "*Bull Bluegill* is yours to have in your new room." But it was not clear whose he was if he was hanging somewhere else.

The crazy thing was I *wanted* Jo Anne to win in national competition. But now that I had seen what marvels she had accomplished with my original fish, how she had amplified and refined my glory moment, I hadn't the heart to abandon him to the unknowing public. Yet here I was hanging him in mortal danger.

Scholarship or no scholarship, Jo Anne's hundred dollar retainer from the Enlightenment had put a legal barrier between me and my endangered fish. But if inserting the tiny minnow pupils in Bull Bluegill's eyes was my invention, it was Jo Anne's hand that had set them there so perfectly.

"Hang Bull Bluegill on the right next to Mr. Grumps," I said with some authority. I hoped Gloria's theory would prevail and the critics, shying away from the ugly Grumps, would jump over *Bull Bluegill* and land their final choices on *Stingray* and *Man of War*.

"All right, all right," Gloria complained, "if you're so dead set on your begrumbled frog. But Grumps is grotesque—the rotten apple that will spoil the batch."

"Mother!" Jo Anne was irritated. She would take up for her picture of the glum frog. "Look at his face," she instructed. "Grumps knows he's got a gone hopper and knows you don't know that yet, so when you find out what he already knows about himself it makes you sympathize with him and then you realize you might have something missing too which allows him to smile at you while what you've just learned soaks in. See?" she said.

It was all as clear to me as a wad of string.

"I see all right," Gloria said, "but Grumps is a rotten apple. Critics have litmus paper for brains. Show them your one rotten picture and everything else you paint is poison."

"She's sorry for Grumps," I offered.

"I'm not *sorry* for him," Jo Anne said. "He just knows he hops in circles, which is more than a lot of folks know."

Without argument I hung *Bull Bluegill* on the far right. Jo Anne hung *Flounder* in the middle. This was her infuriating flat fish picture that nailed me between a smile and a tear. Next to *Flounder* Gloria hung her favorite, *Man of War*, the angelic nomad in a veil of liquid light with its deadly tentacles wavering in the blue.

"Now—where's *my* fish?" It was The Admiral in positive voice. He had entered from the verandah. He wore strap leather sandals, a French beret, and a cream-colored scarf tucked into the front of his shirt. Of all Jo Anne's art, we knew his favorite and on this occasion would allow him no disappointment. "Ah, here it is." He picked up the remaining picture. It was *Stingray*. He placed it first, stepped back and snapped the neon lights on. "Now see what our Hurricane Pearl has wrought!" he said with admiration. "With her magic brush and the elixir of Kudzu, even Grumps will fly. *He shall return*," The Admiral said, echoing a resolution from the famous General McArthur. A smile sent his mustache riding to the top of his cheeks.

I admired, even as a boy, all that Jo Anne had painted. There was in her art an evident thread of genius running through every curve and color, never a denial or contradiction of what the eye had seen but an extension of it into the marvelous and inexplicable.

Jo Anne had refused my plea—to paint the great manta ray. Uncle Claude agreed. The manta was much too large, she said, to squeeze onto a regular canvas, that to so reduce the huge fish would diminish his "magnificent joy" and his "natural nobility." "I'd need a whole wall for the manta," she said. She was right. Fishing far out in the Gulf stream with Claude, I had seen the friendly giants at play, broader than army blankets, weighing over a ton each and flying divinely above the rippling sands. When I described to Jo Anne how sportsmen aboard their grand yachts harpooned the grand creatures for fun, she cried.

The smaller diamond ray more suited her artistic fancy—*Stingray*. This was her agile female ray armed and arched in swift defense.

"Always our alarm is set to guard our secret," Jo Anne said, moving her body as if in concert with the fish.

The Admiral nodded his head.

"—And ever anxious of the black hound that tracks us down in the howling storm," continued The Admiral as if remembering the heart of an old poem.

I did not understand.

"And now," The Admiral said to me, "let's go gather up our art fly on the beach." He was talking about the parachuting Carlos Expondos of the Enlightenment of the Arts.

I WAS STANDING in the middle of the orange landing dot when the airplane appeared. The Admiral lit a cigar. A small crowd had gathered on the beach. When the flamboyant expert bailed out he was nothing but a flea in the blue, falling slowly at first. I was looking straight up. Then he was plummeting faster, like a dart, his chute still sealed. The gathered few gasped. There was laughter when I jumped back and away from the target spot. Then out bloomed Carlos Expondos in his red kidney-shaped parachute growing quickly more distinct and gliding serenely and surely towards the bull's eye beach marker and alighting smack in the middle of the orange dot without losing his balance or taking a step. A round of applause.

"I am Carlos Expondos of the Enlightenment," the expert announced with a fringe of foreign accent. He frowned at his wristwatch and poked out his lips in self reproach, "—and ten seconds late," he said, making light of his flawless arrival.

Expondos was thirtyish, lean, tan, and dark eyed. He had sweeping black hair that fell to one side in a careless arc over his cheek and wore an Australian bush jacket with pockets aplenty.

"I am called The Admiral," welcomed my grandfather and shook the critic's hand.

"Yes, yes," said Carlos, bundling his chute. "I have entertained your wise and instructive correspondence concerning your talented granddaughter. The photographs you provided were especially helpful, perhaps decisive. And you are—" he looked at me. I handed the expert an armload of parachute.

"Jody," I supplied.

"Jo Anne's brother," I presume.

"No kin. Just family," I said.

"You are as talented as she?" he quizzed.

"In a different direction," I said. "She's an artist."

"And you?" he asked.

"A naturalist," The Admiral answered, "but without the *Beagle* or the Galapagos."

"Yes, yes," Carlos said, huddling his chute and wrapping it with the cords. "So you know your Darwin?"

"Just a bit," I said. "I like natural things."

"Yes, yes," Carlos said, "don't we all, but I'm eager now to meet our genius of the subtle touch. I'm sure she's a natural of the first order, although I've seen only photographs of her work." He emphasized the word *photographs*. The Admiral had spared no expense to have made the finest photographs of Jo Anne's art.

"She's my Pearl of Hurricane," The Admiral said, "a young lady now; but we must not cut her away from her shell too soon."

"Oh no no, definitely not," Carlos agreed. "At her age, we must protect her from her own talent. Your gifted Pearl has that rare hummingbird's touch of enhancing mere aquatic creatures with an enigma of the deep and impenetrable. And yet," he observed, stooping under a trail of The Admiral's cigar smoke, "her tender age has so far denied her that indispensable sense of the tragic."

The tragic? I wondered.

I would drive.

Once inside the van The Admiral unsheathed a new cigar from its wrapper and passed it deliciously under his nose. Sitting in back with his parachute Mr. Expondos expressed, without apology, his disdain for the obnoxious weed, proclaiming cigarette smoke the deadliest of gases and a cigar the dragon of tobaccos. "Will you permit me," he said, "to jog along behind, at a modest rate of speed, for a 'lung of fresh air' and 'a leg of exercise'?" We would. At the first stop sign the blistering blacktop had burned Carlos out and he was back inside. "Your van has halitosis," he puffed; and with kind deliberation The Admiral started his new cigar.

"Has our ponderous Professor Scott arrived on Hurricane?" Carlos wanted to know.

"We are taking you to him this moment," The Admiral said, emitting a gorgeous plume of smoke that snaked its way back to Carlos.

"Dr. Scott's at the famous Inn Lafayette," I said.

"Then please, you need *not* make haste," Carlos said with a prickle of irritation.

I was surprised. "You don't like Professor Scott?" I asked.

"Oh yes. Yes of course. I like him like I like a visor or a coat of armor. It's just he belongs to—well, to the Dark Ages."

"Like King Arthur?" The Admiral suggested.

"Scott *is* King Arthur—without the roundtable," Carlos said.

"Like Robin Hood?" I asked.

"Yes, yes if you like. He's as obsolete as dear old Robin but not as lean, not as handsome—sluggish, loveable old bale of blubber," Carlos sighed, then scowled at the thought of his colleague.

"Inn Lafayette is where the professor is," The Admiral said, "—oldest tavern in the South, notched from cypress logs by the French in 1783. No storm has budged her since. The professor swore he'd rot in Hades before he'd sleep a night in any matchbox motel."

"That figures," Carlos said.

And I said, "The Professor said 'old inn ghosts make better company than a beach full of sun-blistered sand hogs.'"

"That figures," Carlos said.

The original heart of the old inn was the long oak bar and table room which was the scene of the embarrassing wedding fight between my Uncle Minos and the Mobile sailor. In recent years the lodging rooms multiplied and spread into a half-circle from end to end forming a great horseshoe with a cedar post portico front and center.

When we arrived in the Chevy van, Professor Scott—seated shirtless on the portico in a broad ladder-back rocker—was plenishing his tumbler from a bulbous wicker wine jug as big around as a watermelon. No mystery now why Carlos had called his colleague a bale of blubber. Bald headed and barrel-chested, the art doctor was enormous, embellished with a bush of rust-red whiskers and an oceanic belly overflowing his waistline. I was the first to take the stairs to the portico. When the professor stood up, his belt disappeared under a wave of flesh. He was barefooted and wore white knee-highs.

"I'm Jody," I said and extended my hand.

"I suspected as much," said the happy professor. "I spoke with you on the telephone. Your southern accent is still pleasantly uncorrupted." The art doc had a hefty one-stroke handshake that nearly jerked me out of my shoes.

"And this—" I turned to present The Admiral.

"This," interrupted Dr. Scott, "is your wise grandfather with whom I have conversed and corresponded and in whom I find a kindred heart."

"And this—" The Admiral began, turning to Carlos—

"This," continued the professor, "is our glamorous modern—if art can be called *modern*—art improvisator, Carlos Expondos extraordinaire, my ethereal student of recent vintage who perceives artistic genius and the boundaries of infinity in the inscription of an idiot's single black circle upon a square of white and who finds beauty in a random splash of mushy cow manure upon a backyard bed sheet."

Carlos dumped his parachute in a pile on the porch and received the professor's hand. "Splendid to see you again, honored doctor." There was intentional artifice in his greeting.

"An ill-disguised lie. You wish me dead and comfortably buried in some antique dung heap." Dr. Scott chuckled heartily, sending an undertow of mirth trembling across his belly. "But I am yet alive. Alive, my dear Carlos! I should have smothered you long ago with your own preposterous dabblings and droolings before your graduation." He raised his voice playfully. "But I am now too old for such luxuries."

"Please, wise sir, postpone your demise, for this small isle would sink to bear so heavy a loss."

The Admiral acknowledged the rivalry of these two and winked at me. I could tell theirs was a lively, not a hateful, animosity.

"A toast," gestured Dr. Scott, passing out ice tea tumblers for his burgundy. "You also, young laddie." He touched my forehead with his finger. "Your brow says you're of age. It's brain not brawn that makes the man." I was delighted he had not noticed my irregular ear. The Admiral nodded me his approval. But I remembered the irresistible Johnny Revelation and his dangerous Zero Cider. I took the glass.

Before the wine, Dr. Scott brought from his voluminous white slacks a tobacco-packed meerschaum pipe with a head engraved bowl as large as a cornbread muffin. When he got it going, he puffed a kindly ring of smoke toward Carlos. Carlos gauged its velocity and sliced it softly with a finger and a smile.

Dr. Scott then poured from his wicker jug a token draught into our tumblers. "A toast to our nimble lassie of the brush." We lifted our glasses. "I suspect," he said, "I might select—from the excellent photographs alone—*Bull Bluegill* as Jo Anne's finest work; *Stingray* her second best."

My heart faltered.

"I think I might prefer *Flounder* first; *Bull Bluegill* second," Carlos said.

My heart sank.

"You've got to see the originals first," I said in loud voice. "All of them!"

"Of course, of course," the experts said together.

And we drank.

"Our modern seer Carlos prefers the cockeyed *Flounder* because he wishes all natural things to look ridiculous," said the professor.

"Some natural things *are* ridiculous," said Carlos, gazing at the doctor's girth. I started to mention that I had helped invent *Bull Bluegill*'s eyes, but Carlos continued. "Flounders' eyes are perfectly *natural*, but Jo Anne's *Flounder* has metaphysical import, suggesting that—however awkwardly—even primitive creatures might synchronize cockeyed views."

"Horse manure!" exploded Dr. Scott. "It simply means that that's the way the fish is—flat-eyed on top and, like a lot of folks, blind to the past and everything beneath them."

Sensing the heat, The Admiral urged our glasses up again in unison. "To the irreplaceable grape," he praised, "our most reliable work of art."

"To the vine and wine," said the large doc.

"To its many tastes and times," said Carlos.

We nodded our glasses toward each other, then drank.

The toast finished, Dr. Scott replenished his glass from the wicker jug and whispered coarsely to The Admiral. The professor was worried that after the judging he might be stuck with the esoteric Carlos. No problem, The Admiral explained. At noon tomorrow a government helicopter would arrive to fly Mr. Expondos back to D.C.

Dr. Scott rolled his eyes in relief. "By air he comes. By air he goes," he said.

That night in my room, examining my collection of natural wonders, I sensed a familiar presence resting between Silent Sound and Neptune's Comb. It was Spencer seated stoically on the lid of Zip's Magnificent Impression holding across his knees his authoritative hatpin as if it were a scepter. Aware of Mr. Expondos's expertise in Mexican artifacts, I had been mustering thoughts about my terrier's colorful little turd.

"Hail Spencer on his royal throne," I chided, getting in the first word. "I see you've lost your dainty angel wings and given up to gravity."

"Well," he replied, "at least I haven't lost my mind, and I pray that a thimble full of wine has not twiddled your powers of discrimination."

"Nothing is the matter with my brain. I knew you were here before I saw you."

"I should certainly hope so. At least you have your geography right, but not yet the proper gumption to access pictures, let alone hurricanes."

"Pictures?"

"Yes. The very idea of allowing your slothful frog—a pitiable and lugubrious gastrocolic—a place beside Jo Anne's superb productions. The frog is hideous, brainless, feckless, and fit only to be recycled in the groaning bowels of volcanoes."

"I thought—" I began.

"I know what you thought. Ha! You wish you could ride comfortably in the calm eye of a hurricane so you can be safely in the middle of everything and see all without payment of the flesh, without a rending of the spirit. Rubbish! You know nothing of the terrible beauty of hurricanes or the tingling epiphany of real art. You can't even see from *here*," he pointed at my nose, "that you are *always* in the middle of everything and very likely to see nothing but what you are looking at."

"I can see you are a scatterbrain."

"Well," Spencer said, inhaling so that his thorax shone like anthracite. "I am still surprised that with your boxy brain and sky-strained eyes you have been able to see into anything at all."

"You think I'm being selfish with my Bull Bluegill picture."

"Of course. How could you be otherwise?" Spencer grimaced and clicked his jaws.

"Bull Bluegill is my invention, especially his eyes."

"Well, I assume your selfishness is as acute as your sweet competitor's—*or his*!"

"His? His who?"

"Your parachuting Expondos of course—your gadfly from the clouds. Great Galaxies! I've met his like a million times since this temporal pouch of sand peeped from the sea. Without effort I can detect his breed a hundred dunes away." Spencer shook his oblong head making his antennae bobble. "And this." He pointed to a slick silver ridge running down the middle of his abdomen. When he puffed himself out he looked like a thin Spanish conquistador wearing breast armor. "I can hear your clumsy, clod-bound ogres scrambling for treasures upon my own good earth that I have owned since—but I am not always lucky. Look," he wailed, lifting up a crooked foot. It was the first time I had seen his injury up this close. "My foot is forever bent out of shape." I leaned in for closer inspection.

"A crab can grow a new claw," I said, "so surely, dear Sir, you should be able to grow a new foot."

Spencer was in no mood for fun. "I am no crab, please!" he said indignantly. "And nourish not the notion—as some blooddobbers do—that a claw may grow a new crab." I was as close as I could get to the ant without becoming cross-eyed. Yes, the lower pod of his right leg was crooked like a bent tip of brier.

"That is close enough," Spencer warned. "We must always respect our distance. Once I let you peer through my belly for a clearer view of the whole world. That was careless of me and much much too dangerous for you, even though at the time you were young enough to absorb such seeing."

"I'm sorry about your foot. I'll try not to step on you," I offered.

"My earnest thanks," he said.

Gathering his wits and inclining his antennae downward toward Zip's colorful turd Spencer said, "Are you smart enough to catch the clever Carlos, remembering of course that brains and judgment seldom strive together?"

"You mean lie to him about Zip's Magnificent Impression?" I nodded at the small jar Spencer was sitting upon.

"Lie? Of course not."

"Trick him then?"

"Yes, yes, you silly thing—with his own game, trick the witty parachutist with Zip's pretty piece of doodoo! Zip's doodoo. Our voodoo! Ha ha haaaaa," Spencer laughed. The ant was immensely amused at himself and knocked his skinny heels gaily against the glass jar. "Let us present to our cloudistic critic the everlasting Tlehhizcalpantecuhtli, the Precious Serpent of the Aztecs!" He pronounced the elongated god's name in the most precise poetic fashion:

> Tee lee heez cal
> Pan tee
> Q butt teelee

"It's not really a relic," I admitted of the little turd.

"I know," Spencer said.

"It's not even five years old," I insisted.

"I know, I know," Spencer echoed.

"It's not even from Mexico!" I said.

"Oh great Jupiter!" Spencer exclaimed. "Everything is a piece of everywhere and is as old as the stars—unless . . . unless . . ."

15

The Gig

Dr. Scott and Mr. Expondos arrived at the Merrimac next morning in the state car. The professor recognized at once that our coastal home was a mock-up of the iron-slabbed frigate that slugged it out with the Yankee Monitor over a hundred years ago. He rattled off the history and nomenclature of the sluggish old war tub, reminding us that it took her two miles to turn around at sea. Which made me think of my crippled Mr. Grumps hopping in slow ellipsoids from and to his pond.

"Are you sure you didn't design the old Confederate galleon?" Carlos jabbed at the professor.

Gloria, impatient to make known she too was an artist, was amazed at the colossal Dr. Scott who was as massive as Henry VIII and dressed up like an ambassador. As a gift in one hand the professor carried a half gallon of burgundy; with the other, he sedately took Gloria's fingers and said, "We are delighted, my dear, for your kind permission. And this is Mr. Expondos of the Enlightenment, our guru of modern art whose perception of truth and beauty transcends all frame, form, and reference." then turning to Jo Anne, "Now you must be the talented young lady to whom we owe this pleasure."

"Yes sir," Jo Anne said, "thank you. And thank you too Mr. Expondos. From the lighthouse I watched you sail out of the blue." There was a light in Jo Anne's eyes as she beheld the graceful expert. With a finger Carlos swept a fallen arc of hair from his eye.

Still wearing his coat of many pockets, Carlos bowed politely. "And may I thank *you* too. I often fly to my art," he said.

"This is Mr. Grumps," I said, indicating my complacent bullfrog. He was sitting on the door mat of the Merrimac.

"I recognize him from the colored photos," Carlos said.

"Ah," said Dr. Scott, "the ole one-hopper."

"He hops up here when he needs a little snort of Kudzu," I said.

From a ketchup bottle I gave Grumps a gurgle of the green juice which he swallowed with great satisfaction. "His one hind hopper makes him travel in slow circles," I said.

"How can he hop straight up here from his pond if he hops in circles?" Carlos asked.

"It's the Kudzu," I explained. "It's improved his vision so he can start out wide and hit the spot."

"Perhaps our art professor could use a nip of such an expansive liquor," Carlos said.

"If he sticks to his circle he never gets lost and always gets back to his pond," I said.

"Then perhaps it is Mr. Expondos who needs a nip of your wonder juice," Dr. Scott said.

"As a matter of fact," The Admiral said, "Grumps prefers the parabola to the perfect circle. It gives him greater scope and control."

"In other words," Dr. Scott said, "like old masters of the art, the frog knows that the most rewarding contact between two points is not a straight line or a random splash of cow dung."

"And old windbags should not over inflate," Carlos returned.

"Good morning, Mr. Grumps," Dr. Scott nodded as he stepped over the frog.

"Good morning, Mr. Grumps," said Carlos, following the art doctor.

Jo Anne kissed her finger tip and with it lightly touched Grumps off on his morning circuit.

"Kudzu juice has boosted his brain power a hundred percent," Jo Anne said.

"Which gives Grumps an IQ of two," Gloria added.

"Wonderful!" Dr. Scott exclaimed, who was interested in the new beverage.

"Kudzu is indeed a wonder weed," explained The Admiral. "It grows like wildfire in the South and has about accomplished what General Sherman set out to do. It's a miraculous plant of the Orient which, properly brewed, distilled and reconstructed, promises relief for dedicated drinkers and greater longevity for all."

"God forbid," said Dr. Scott.

Midship at the top of the stairs The Admiral opened the thick oak door to the wardroom and let us in.

On a serving table Gloria had neatly centered a glass bowl of spangled snapdragons surrounded by ice tea glasses, flanked on either side by a crock of crushed ice, a pitcher of tea, sliced lemons, garden mint, cheese straws, sugar cookies, and crust-trimmed chicken salad sandwiches cut into equilateral triangles. Gloria made no overt gesture, but by eye she led all attention up and starboard to her mural on the wall. It was her most ambitious effort: a huge picture of Jesus taking the terrified Simon Peter by the hand and lifting him from the angry waves. In a quick exchange of eyes the perceptive professor knew it was the work of my Aunt Gloria.

"Marvelous! Marvelous!" said Dr. Scott. "How distinctly you

have drawn these two—quite an accomplishment in our deconstructed age. I recognized the men instantly. But Madam, you have made his face too pale and his neck too thin." He was talking not about Jesus but about the frightened apostle. "Our theologized Christians have never got it quite right about this rustic young man. Simon Peter was not old and he is and will always be a fisherman, a redneck. Never a saint! To take the glaze and sunburn from his cheeks diminishes his raw and untutored contact with God."

Gloria was not put down.

"His face is enlightened by the miracle that is happening to him," she defended.

"Madam," said Dr. Scott, "that was no miracle but a lilt of the artist's brush and the happy surprise of a harmless illusion. The Master's greatest act of divine administration was at a simple wedding, a glad *wedding* when he changed feckless water into wine, when he instilled into the insipid liquid a soul!"

With the idea of Zip's Magnificent Impression still buzzing in my mind, I pulled The Admiral over for a whisper. Jo Anne listened in.

Then I said to Carlos: "Would you like to own the rarest wonder of the ancient world?"

I took the expert by the arm and led him aside. Jo Anne was following, listening at a distance.

"Besides your remarkable Mr. Grumps," Carlos said, "what might that be—the Holy Grail? Or the Fountain of Youth?"

"It is in fact," The Admiral assisted, taking the expert's other arm and assuming an attitude of confidence, "a priceless pre-Columbian relic I once liberated from Old Mexico, a flawless artifact perhaps symbolizing the inevitable union of life and death, the eternal frolic of polarities as we find in the Yang/Yin principle in Chinese philosophy, which," The Admiral proposed, "I'm sure you are aware of."

Jo Anne had stopped and was standing in the middle of the room with her hands propped on her hips.

"Of—of course," said Carlos.

"A perfect coprolite," informed The Admiral, testing the extent of Expondos's knowledge and integrity. *Coprolite*—from The Admiral's mouth I had learned the meaning of the word: petrified turd.

"Oh yes. Y—yes, of course," stumbled Carlos.

"Now—" interrupted Dr. Scott, "a little refreshment and a toast to our mother artist of the mural on the wall and to the lifter from the dulling waters and to his happy wine, God's greatest invention since the seductive Eve. Now, a touch of red," and he uncorked the burgundy with a pop, "and thence," he continued, "to our tea and cookies and then to the studio for the judgment, which I predict will fall not elsewhere but in our lovely lady's favor." The doctor swept his massive arm toward Jo Anne.

"Do you mind if I watch you choose?" Jo Anne asked.

"Heavens no," said Scott, "so long as you keep your mouth—" he sealed his lips with a finger and smiled down into Jo Anne's face. "Once you've put your art in sum, forevermore remaineth mum."

Jo Anne was pleased with the little rhyme from the large art doctor.

I skipped the tea and cookies and hurried upstairs to my room to fetch down Zip's Magnificent Impression. Through the transom, Carlos was saying that our judgments of the day were of fleeting value in an ever changing world.

"Horse manure!" bellowed Dr. Scott. "The world spins and we spin on the world's spin or have no spin at all—no uprightness of our own. We may become dizzy—even drunk!—" arose the professor's purple voice, "but we must hold fast our old verities or go down sniffling and empty handed . . ."

I HAD NOT heard Jo Anne, but she followed me to my room. When I picked up Zip's Magnificent Impression and turned around, she was standing there looking at me, then at the small glass jar containing Zip's waxen wonder. The hundred dollar retainer check from the Enlightenment was sticking up in clear view from her breast pocket. Jo Anne was going to strike a bargain with me. She picked Zip's treasure from my hand and said:

"If you lay a claim to *Bull Bluegill*, then this," she stuck the jar in my face, "is half mine!" She put the jar behind her back.

What was she up to? This was in fact an original production that Zip had actually done, with some effort, four years ago after eating the box of Jumbo crayons. On sight Gloria turned up her nose, Jo Anne smiled, and Claude laughed outright. Zip had made no claim on his unusual creation, so I preserved the prize as mine, airtight.

"But wait," I said, "Zip's my dog."

"And these," Jo Anne said, holding out Zip's Magnificent Impression, "are *my* crayons!"

With that she stuffed the hundred dollar check from the Enlightenment into my shirt pocket.

"For what?" I asked.

"Your half of *Bull Bluegill*—eyes and all."

"Wha—" I began.

"And this," she said, kissing me on the cheek and handing me the jar, "is yours for free—to have and to hold until . . . until . . . oh, never mind," she said and swished around the doorway in such haste that left her skirt aflare.

Pondering Expondos's zeal for ancient Mayan artifacts, I tucked the Magnificent Impression under my shirt and headed for the studio where Jo Anne's paintings were in judgment—there to learn the worst: Dr. Scott had chosen *Bull Bluegill* as Jo Anne's best, *Stingray* second; Carlos had selected *Man of War* as best, *Bull Bluegill* second. Either way *Bull Bluegill*'s fate was sealed and the fish picture of my glory moment gone. I took quick conference with The Admiral.

My problem was his pleasure.

And so, each of us taking an arm of Carlos, we led him out upon the verandah.

"It's older than Columbus and scarcer than moon rock," I said, revealing my treasure.

"In fact it is more than that, especially to a connoisseur," pursued The Admiral, getting in the expert's ear. "It is—I confess—a holy icon I lifted unlawfully from an ancient Mayan tomb in El Caracal near Itza, very probably—as you can see—a religious manifestation symbolic of the god Xipe, The Flayed One, also called Youallahuana or He Who Drinks at Night."

I was amazed at The Admiral's knowledge and recall of such authentic details.

The Admiral turned aside to get a cigar going. Carlos studied Zip's colorful gastronomic creation.

"Yes, exquisite," Carlos exclaimed, taking the jar and holding it to the light. "Absolutely fantastic. So well formed and defined."

"We are fortunate to have you here to confirm what we as laymen could only suspect," The Admiral said. He fixed the jar in Carlos's hands to another angle.

"Splendid. Splendid," Carlos said. "Its colors so harmoniously diversified. Almost, we might say, in mint condition."

"But priceless," said The Admiral.

"So well preserved," said Carlos, ducking a dragon of The Admiral's smoke.

"An image of the Precious Serpent, Tlehhizcalpantecuhtli," said The Admiral, "also called the House of Dawn which I'm sure is a landmark in your memory."

"Uh—oh yes, very possibly," Carlos mumbled and pulled the jar closer to his eyes. "It resembles a beautiful old chieftain in full ceremonial array and curled back into fetal form."

"Wonderfully put," The Admiral said. "Something only a scholar could have assessed so well."

"A true work of art," said Carlos.

"And fortunate to be rescued by such a professional hand as yours and now to be placed in its proper slot of honor among its peers in antiquity." The Admiral paused. "I pray," he said, "the curse of money may not inflame the god Youallahuaana, He Who Drinks at Night. You," The Admiral looked critically at Carlos, "I trust, are not of a superstitious nature."

"Oh no. No!" Carlos said and crossed his heart.

"Good," The Admiral said. "Any mention of money to me is repugnant, but this," he pointed to the fruit jar, "belongs now to my grandson here, Jody, who you understand will honor your confidence and your care of this rare relic. As you know," The Admiral continued, "art remains its own agent and reward. Fame and fortune are but idle dust upon the windowsill of life."

I loved it when my grandfather waxed eloquent. He leaned over and chuckled me a whisper. With this he wadded through a gulf of cigar smoke and left me alone with Carlos.

"I don't care about the money," I told Carlos. I explained to him Bull Bluegill and my boyhood glory moment.

"Interesting," he said of my growing problem.

"A hundred bucks might be enough for me to buy back *Bull Bluegill* from Dr. Scott," I proposed.

Carlos pondered, looking deeply into the jar.

"It's not the money," I quickly emphasized. "To anybody else *Bull Bluegill* is just a fish picture."

Carlos was still thinking deeply and said, "Maybe just enough to tempt our dear old blubber belly."

"I'm not trying to tempt anybody," I insisted. "Without me *Bull Bluegill* can't make any sense to anybody." I plucked Zip's Magnificent Impression from Carlos's hand.

As quickly from his coat of many pockets Carlos flipped up a hundred dollar bill and jerked the fruit jar back.

"Just changed my vote to *Man of War*," he said.

I picked the money from his fingers.

"Our secret?" said he, his eyes aglow. "You'll keep our secret in the—in the thin, thin, air?" He held up his fingers and wiggled them daintily.

"Right," I agreed. "Not even Mr. Grumps will know, I swear."

I found Dr. Scott in the studio casting a final eye on Jo Anne's selected portraits.

"I hear you would have a word with me," he said. The Admiral had told the professor my *Bull Bluegill* story.

"I would," I said, knowing Jo Anne had withheld nothing from the great art doctor.

"You do make a pitiful claim for yourself," Dr. Scott said. "I understand the airy Carlos changed his *Bluegill* vote and Jo Anne bought your half of *Bull Bluegill.*"

"That's right, sir," I said. "I'd like to buy *Bull Bluegill* back for the hundred dollars you paid for him."

"That, my boy, that was a lease, not a purchase. One never *buys* art, only the picture and a piece of time to keep it in."

"Well, whatever," I said.

"That's mighty generous, but know that you may buy back only that which is strictly yours—which is *Bull Bluegill's* eyes. They *are* your idea which, I might add, are a bit freakish if you get too close." Dr. Scott pulled out his penknife and opened the blade. He set the sharp edge to *Bull Bluegill's* eyes. "I'm a doctor of sorts," he said, "but a very poor surgeon."

There was the sound of a helicopter approaching.

Dr. Scott looked at me. His eyes were brown and kind. His lips burgundy.

"Two hundred bucks for the whole fish, eyes and all," I bargained. I put the retainer check with the hundred dollar bill and held them out to the doctor.

"Two hundred bucks?" Dr. Scott said with surprise. "May I ask how you suddenly have become so wealthy?"

"You may not," I said honoring my secret with Carlos. The chopper was coming in closer. The Admiral was on the beach waving hand signals.

Dr. Scott snapped the money away from me and stuffed it with a thump into my shirt pocket.

"I've already made up my mind," the professor said with finality.

"You can change it if you wish," I offered, fearing the worst.

"Never!" he declared.

"Would you take—" I began, thinking of The Admiral whose money knew no end.

"I will take nothing!" the large art doc roared.

My heart sank.

"Nothing," he continued more gently and thumped my skull.

My God, I thought, *he wants the whole fish picture for himself.*

Dr. Scott walked to his burgundy jug and poured another glass of purple.

"I saw your 'glory moment' in an instant. Felt it in my bones! Which is payment enough for me—though I confess I suffer now quite a drought of glory moments."

The copter had settled in.

"You see," he said, "you get everything for nothing. And, frankly, I fear that in a dull museum your lively bream might spring free his hook and lose your glory moment forever."

On the beach, clutching Zip's colorful turd, Carlos was ducking under the slow copter blades and climbing into the cab. In a moment the machine lifted straight up, then tilted at a nonchalant angle and headed for D.C. I imagined Carlos catching with a finger an arc of fallen hair from his cheek and laying it carefully back into place. Zip was running around in circles in the sand, barking up at the departure. Jo Anne was waving furiously after Carlos as if her arm would fly away.

Later The Admiral picked up the winning pictures—*Stingray* and *Man of War*—and accompanied Dr. Scott to the state car.

To regain honorable right to my fish, I gave back the retainer check to Jo Anne and returned *Bull Bluegill* to my room.

Jo Anne wanted to know how I came by the hundred dollar bill.

"A hundred dollars?" she exclaimed in disbelief. "For Zip's Magnificent Impres—O! . . ." Jo Anne gasped and clamped her hand over her mouth.

The Admiral dropped by and gave Jo Anne a dollar and whispered something in her ear.

"A dollar for what?" I asked Jo Anne.

"Another box of crayons for Zip," she said.

16

The Sin of Uncle Minos

Even before Jo Anne put the finishing touches on Venoria's portrait, I—with a purpose of my own—would be present for the unveiling. Jo Anne and The Admiral were to make the special delivery tomorrow. From the first, Uncle Minos and Aunt Venoria had been an accumulating mystery to me, a dark little drama that I had not been able to piece together. As far as I had learned during my summers on the island, the only thing that Venoria and Jo Anne's mother had in common was their quaint leviathan sanctuary with God alone persisting as a shadowy bond between them. But as an artistic challenge Gloria had allowed, even encouraged, Jo Anne to paint the elusive Venoria.

Jo Anne had the retentive eye of a camera and could paint from memory. Done in more manageable and enduring oils, the portrait was a large likeness of the handsome Venoria clad in a white flowing robe and standing solitary on a sand dune with a tempestuous sea behind her. What had this bold woman to do with Uncle Minos's strange behavior? Why had Minos on his wedding day sealed himself away from the world? And why had I been manipulated away from this morbid member of my own clan?

Occasionally on bike visits to the WHY NOT SHOP I had briefly glimpsed my uncle through the opaque panes of his basement window or, more directly, through Venoria's inverted cellar periscope. But the only features I could discern of the man were an occasional flash of his anxious eyes and the wayward bobble of his hooded head as he walked.

Venoria had been—and to the islanders still was—something of a local goddess. Of native Indian, Negro, and French-Cajun blood, her roots reached back everywhere into antiquity. After the beach wedding, in celebration of her holy union with Minos, the robust Venoria swam naked across Hurricane Bay and back without pause. Upon her return, Minos, in an over-glow of wine, waded out to receive her in a blanket, kissed her wildly; then, holding up his dripping bride, he swore with loud audacity: "Any man but I who lays a hand upon this flesh will die, or forever in a salty grave I'll lie."

"Why did he ever say such a dumb thing like that?" I asked The Admiral. "Why didn't he just walk home happy with his pretty wife?"

"It's a young man's disease. He didn't know rash words can reach back and grab you by the throat."

Venoria—to Gloria's rigid discontent—had repeated her nude swim each anniversary. Gloria called it "an embarrassing vanity." My second summer on the island, I had watched with Jo Anne the annual ceremony from The Admiral's lighthouse. Last summer on the shrimper, Claude and I had followed the aging Venoria to see her safely back to shore. The event—never lewd or undignified—had become an island ritual. Even so, by order of The Admiral, newsmen with their cameras were warned to keep a modest distance from the unabashed Venoria. But after the nuptial swim years ago, Minos had never again been present on the beach to meet his love nor had he shown himself in public.

The Admiral finally told me about the baffling fight at the Inn Lafayette. After the wedding a beer-inspired merchant seaman from Mobile had laid a playful hand upon Venoria's body. To keep his word, Minos slapped the happy sailor sideways and smashed him back against the bar. That was how the fight began.

So the night before we delivered Venoria's portrait, I am lying wide awake wondering how my plot will work on Uncle Minos. Or will I be immediately and completely obliterated in an outburst of his wrath? From the half-open door a shaft of light falls across the counterpane and up against the footboard of my bed, making the likeness of a stage . . .

"I'm sure you know no more about storms than you do about directing a play, especially a tragedy." It is Spencer. He is sitting cross-legged on the bedpost, wielding a large kitchen match as if it were a baton. "You have in your innocence performed in but a single drama. As I recall you played—"

"One of the Wise Men," I supplied.

"Then you were miscast. With your hee haw ear and rectangular brain, you should have played the donkey or the bale of hay."

"I suppose that's funny?"

"Not really, but neither is your gloomy uncle. He's a sad case. Do you know why he is stuck down in his miserable basement?"

"He was honoring his heroic promise."

"Only superficially," Spencer said with his devilish grin. "It is because of his hyperepheniaplanepseudos."

"His what!? Don't go showing off to me."

"Quite a common and tragic flaw it is."

"He was drunk."

"Oh he was drunk all right, but you don't have to be drunk to say such stupid things. You can really say stupid things more eloquently when you are stone sober."

"You blame Uncle Minos because he was jealous of his handsome Venoria."

"Heavens no. How else should a young buck be? His passion for Venoria was a precious gift devoutly to be wished! But I'm sure you would know nothing of such delightful foolishness." Spencer cleared his throat formally, proceeding to make a point. "Your grandfather *saw* the fight," he prompted.

"Yes. It was a bloody brawl. He told me the whole sorry story over the wireless."

"Very well," Spencer said, hopping down from his bedpost. He folded over a bed wrinkle and seated himself professionally like a movie director on the right wing of the stage. He carefully adjusted his antennae. "O.K.," he said, "Let's take it from the top, just as you got it from The Admiral." Spencer held up his match stick and brought it down decisively.

"Action!" he said.

Act I

Scene: Jody is sitting with The Admiral at one of the barroom tables in the Inn Lafayette,witnessing the fight as his grandfather saw it twenty years ago. Venoria, a bride, is standing astonished on the balcony above the bar. She is being consoled by an older man and woman. The bartender, a small brown man, disappears into the back room. The inflamed Minos has just smashed the sailor against the bar. The sailor fakes a smile. Blood is on his teeth. They stand eyeing each other.

JODY: Why don't you stop the fight now? Minos is winning.

The Admiral: I can't. It's his fight. He's got to go all the way. Minos doesn't know his own strength.

Jody: Then Uncle Minos will have to kill him. It's his promise.

The Admiral: Not really. He'll just have to win the fight.

Jody: Suppose he doesn't? Minos has a soft heart. He's not in the ring. There are no rules. He doesn't have to go the distance.

The Admiral: He must. Otherwise he will be humiliated. He has never been defeated.

Jody: He can get killed. Look at the sailor's eyes. Who knows what the sailor will do?

The Admiral: Some things are worse than death. No dishonor is worse than to lose a fight while your love is looking on.

The sailor moves away from the bar, circling. A trained boxer, Minos whips out left jabs, then throws a fast right that splatters blood from the sailor's nose. When the sailor lifts a chair overhead, Minos dives into the sailor's belly. They go down to the floor together, knocking over chairs and tables and sliding into mugs of spilled beer. They get to their feet slowly. The sailor is backing toward the door, then halts . . .

Jody: Stop! Stop, while Minos is winning!

"Cut!" Spencer was upset. "Jody! You are revealing that your uncle did not win the fight. This is something that, as director, I must manage, not you! You are an *actor*. You are getting ahead of yourself and displacing indispensable suspense. Suspense is the very engine of action. You are jumping off your time track."

"But that's what happened. It's a fact."

"A fact, perhaps. The truth is a different thing. The truth, that's my deparment."

"You mean I've got no choice?"

"Of course, you can walk off the stage anytime you please. It's your play."

I was about to respond when Spencer turned on his sharp heel and took his seat again. He got my eye, then held the match stick over his head, wondering—"Now where were we?—"

"Action!" he called.

On the balcony, Venoria has not moved. She's still standing eagerly between the elderly couple, obviously her mother and father. The wedding party and local drinkers in the barroom form a large parenthesis around the fighters. When Minos moves aggressively again, the sailor stands pat. A smile commences at the corners of the sailor's mouth. The sailor whips out a lengthy pocket knife and flicks out the dangerous blade.

Jody: It's a switchblade. It's not fair!
The Admiral: Shhhhhh . . .

It is the sailor now who advances. Minos is backing up toward the bar. One lunge and a swish of the switchblade forces Minos to scramble onto the bar top, then to his feet. It is a contest of eye and nerve.

Jody: Uncle Mi—
The Admiral: (*puts a hand over Jody's mouth*) Shhhhh . . .

The sailor is coming on. Inch by inch Minos retreats to the inner edge of the bar. Anguish and uncertainty are in his eyes. He feels backward with one foot, testing the empty space, then, carefully, steps back, turns and falls face and arms down behind the bar.

JODY: Did he fall on purpose?
THE ADMIRAL: A misstep. He tripped.
JODY: He's getting up.

From the balcony Venoria and the elderly couple are looking down at Minos crumpled in the bar slot. To one side the wedding guests and local drinkers fold into a homogeneous crowd. Swaying with the open switchblade, the sailor stands straddle-legged, hunched forward in the middle of the bar floor. The blood from his nose has coagulated on his cheek and chin. Minos gets to his feet and starts to make his way from behind the bar into the open room.

THE ADMIRAL: He's limping.
JODY: Is he hurt? Is he play-acting?
THE ADMIRAL: It was the fall. It's his leg.
JODY: Look, he's coming out to face the sailor.
THE ADMIRAL: Yes. He must.
JODY: He dropped behind the bar head first. Is he really hurt? Is it a trick?
THE ADMIRAL: Shhhhhh . . .

Minos advances slowly toward the sailor. Minos is holding a hand on his left thigh, and his foot is crooked out at an awkward angle. The sailor stops swaying, cocked forward in readiness like a quarterback. Minos stops, drops to one knee. The two study each other while the silence ticks off between them.

JODY: It's a stand-off.

The sailor now, confidently, comes erect. He flashes the long knife. Waits. At length he folds the open switchblade back into its handle and smiles victoriously. The sailor assumes satisfaction, turns his back upon Minos and with two companions disappears through the open door of the tavern.

THE ADMIRAL: It was the fall. It's his leg. He busted his leg. He must have.

Venoria, bewildered, is staring down from the balcony. In the middle of the bar floor Minos is leaning unsteadily on one arm, as if propped up by a straw. The Admiral rests his elbows on the table and buries his head in his hands. Sorrowfully Jody puts his arm around his grandfather . . .

"Cut!"

Spencer is pleased with the scene.

"I'm getting tired of this," I said. "I don't know if I'm in the play or out of it. You may have rubbed elbows with Alexander the Great and Hannibal of the Alps, but you are a lousy play director."

"At present I'm your *only* director. And, as one who knows his holes-in-the-ground, I might add that, as an actor, you have canyons to fill. In the acting business you must see and feel what you are doing from the outside *and* the inside of yourself."

"And how, master director, am I to get outside myself?"

"Don't be so dense. That's why we are doing the play, so you can step outside yourself while you are still inside yourself."

"Oh," I murmured, trying to balance Spencer's see-saw logic.

"Now," Spencer said, pointing his match stick at me, "rest back upon your pillow. Concentrate. You cannot project unless you sink back into yourself. Think: What does your fisherman Uncle Claude speak of his doleful brother Minos?"

"Claude," I began, "doesn't talk much . . . but I remember once—"

"Action!" Spencer said.

Act II

The sun is dipping into the Gulf. Claude is bringing the shrimper in towards Hurricane Island. Jody is at the wheel. Claude is behind him with an affectionate hand on Jody's. shoulder. Jody is anticipating an eventual confrontation with Minos. He wonders when Jo Anne will finish her picture of Venoria so that he might spring the portrait on his reclusive uncle and shock him back to life.

JODY: Which do you reckon stopped the fight? Uncle Minos's leg or the sailor's switchblade?

CLAUDE: Switchblade probably. Hard to tell exactly. Like trying to tell where a hurricane starts happening.

JODY: At least Uncle Minos didn't lose.

CLAUDE: Didn't win neither.

JODY: Well, he's still alive.

CLAUDE: Not exactly. Better fall down dead in Hell than dangle on the edge.

JODY: You mean Uncle Minos holing up down in his basement?

CLAUDE: Something like that. (*With his large hand Claude turns Jody's head around and looks Jody in the eye.*) Boy, what do you want—just to *make* Minos look at *you*? (*He points to a slow V-formation of pelicans overhead.*)

JODY: Not really. I just want to see his crippled leg, see him when he looks at Jo Anne's picture of Venoria. That ought to blast his eyes open.

CLAUDE: He won't look at you or the picture neither.

JODY: How can he not look?

CLAUDE: Hard to tell exactly.

JODY: You ought to know; he's your blood brother.

CLAUDE: (*seriously*) He's your blood too. (*pointing again to the formation of pelicans*) A hulk of our own flesh hunkered down in his basement!

JODY: Has he ever been upstairs to Venoria?

CLAUDE: Not as I know of.

JODY: How's he eat?

CLAUDE: By conveyor. She cranks food down on a tray.

JODY: They say he cried when he knocked somebody out in the ring.

CLAUDE: That's what they say.

To compensate for the Gulf current, Claude points Jody starboard to the northeast tip of the island. The pelicans are disappearing in the distance.

CLAUDE: Pelicans are the ugliest and most graceful of God's creatures.

JODY: I'm going to take Jo Anne's picture of Aunt Venoria straight down to him and stick it of a sudden before his eyes. He'll look. While he's stunned, I'll look at his leg. Feel it. I want to *see* his eyes look at me!

CLAUDE: Won't work.

JODY: I'll catch his eyes.

CLAUDE: You can't make a man who won't look at you do anything.

JODY: *Catches a final glimpse of the pelicans.*

CLAUDE: You think one look's going to thaw a soul's been froze up twenty years?

JODY: (*mocking Uncle Claude*) Don't know. Hard to tell exactly.

"Cut!"

Spencer liked my mimicry of Claude and winked the shutter of his eye.

"Now who's getting in the way of the play?" I complained. "I was just fixing to ask about my uncle's leg."

"You mean you were going to ask Claude if Minos stepped off the bar accidentally on purpose?"

"Something like that. I need to know if Uncle Minos really hurt himself."

"That will be my part in the last act."

"Your part! You're not supposed to even be in the play."

"Nonsense. A director does as he must! I am perfectly capable of performing any number of functions at the same time."

"Just a minute," I said, "if I jumped off the *time* track a minute ago, you're jumping out of *place* now."

"I must function according to the inevitable proximity of my cosmic nature," Spencer argued, sweeping his hand around to the four corners of the room. "I may read your dreams and detect storms before they hatch; so permit me then my vantage view which, from your simple eye, renders your perspective not wrong but embarrassingly inadequate."

"Well," I said, "if you are going to be so brainy I might as well get out of your silly play right now. I know what I know."

"Yes," Spencer said, "I'm afraid you do."

"Well," I said, resting my head back upon my pillow, "I'm out. It's over!"

"If you wish," Spencer said, "Then you shall never see me perform on the stage or know the folly of your foolish uncle. I am thoroughly familiar with the superior techniques of Sophocles and Shakespeare and avoid the obscene excesses of your modern drama." The ant cocked one foot over an ankle and leaned back confidently upon his stick like a country squire. "Now . . . let's see . . . ," Spencer mused, "I was thinking of what really got your Uncle Minos in such an awful fix . . . your granddaddy thinks it was a busted leg; your fisherman Claude thinks it was the switchblade . . . and your Aunt Gloria . . . what does she think of—"

"Of Minos?"

"Yes."

"She hates him—guts, tongue, and toenails. Says he's a sickly coward and hypocrite. She says if Venoria wasn't so blood-mixed and moral she'd have quit him years ago to rot in his stinking cellar and never swum her hefty rump across Hurricane Bay again. Says if she was me she wouldn't waste her eyes on Minos even if he was resurrected out of his salty cellar by Jesus Christ."

"Action!" Spencer called.

Act III

Scene: The morning sun is slicing through the many panes of the studio. Aunt Gloria is standing tip-toe watering her baskets of impatiens hanging from the ceiling. Jo Anne's finished portrait of Venoria rests on a easel. Venoria's feathers remind Jody of the head on the Statue of Liberty. Jody has just fed Mr. Grumps his daily indulgence of Kudzu juice. Grumps is sitting plumply on a discarded watercolor landscape.

AUNT GLORIA: I know you are determined, but it's hopeless to look at your Uncle Minos, especially into his eyes. He is worse than dead. It would be like looking into a dry well.

JODY: Jo Anne and I have seen him through his basement window. His head bobs like he's limping. I want to see how bad his leg is. Maybe he needs a crutch or something.

AUNT GLORIA: His leg is his crutch. He's hiding behind his leg.

JODY: That's impossible.

Mr. Grumps hops off the discarded landscape and pushes himself against the glass window.

AUNT GLORIA: Jody, nosy Jody! Anything in this world is possible with you youngsters. It wasn't your uncle's leg or the switchblade that put him down in his basement. It was his blasphemous tongue. 'Til then Minos was sweet tempered, never lost a fight or ever was undone until his golden goddess inflamed him, swam naked across the bay and back again. Then, right then, on their wedding beach, Minos let his tongue slap his brains out. Some prize fighter! Have you ever heard of such outrageous vanity? And then at Inn Lafayette when the sailor stared him down, Minos went soggy inside like a drowned rat.

JODY: I want to shock him. Make him *look* at me.

AUNT GLORIA: He can't. His lie won't let him. His sin is worse than suicide. He's already dead.

JODY: I'll sneak down to him. Surprise him. He'll have to look. Jo Anne thinks I can find his eyes.

AUNT GLORIA: (*mildly exasperated*) You both are all hope and heart.

(Mr. Grumps begins thumping around the baseboard of the bay window.)

"Cut!" Spencer cried, coming to his feet and waving his match stick. "You must get that disgusting toad off the set. He is nothing more than an inarticulate glob of protoplasm and has nothing whatever to do with the action or intent of our play."

"He's not a toad," I defended. "He's a water frog. He's got a bum leg. Like Uncle Minos. Like you."

"Nonsense! Grump's hind leg is off, absent, gone, reclaimed back into the old world. But I must admit," Spencer continued, "that your spunky aunt has a point: Anything in *this* world *is* possible. But not in a play! If everything in a play were possible, nobody would believe it." Spencer became suddenly pensive. "Have you ever noticed, noble Jody, that the older your kind gets the more they look like frogs? You have to believe in the impossible."

"And if everything was possible, I'd be somewhere else instead of here listening to you and making a jackass of myself."

"Precisely," Spencer said. Mr. Grumps finds the side door to the studio cracked open and hops out in a wide arc toward his pond.

"If you keep cutting me off," I said, "this is going to be a very short play."

"Well, I'm a very short director," Spencer said, drawing himself up to full height, then, assuming a professional attitude, "I trust you will retain your aunt's impression that Minos is hiding behind his leg, for I'm sure you haven't the foggiest of what she meant."

"Don't be so sure, Mr. Smartyass." Gloria is frozen in action on the stage, and I go back into my act. With hands in pockets and chest puffed out, I start walking in thoughtful circles around my aunt.

"Wait, wait, wait!" Spencer waved his match stick at me. "You are supposed to be the innocent one, and here you are stalking around the stage like you're Sherlock Holmes. You are getting out of character. Are you listening to me?"

"You said it was all right in a play to step outside yourself."

"No. I meant it was all right to step inside the outside of yourself and outside the inside of yourself. You are stepping outside the outside of yourself, which is dramatically impossible—a fatal error!—and it makes us both look ridiculous."

"But you said we must believe in the impossible."

"Of course, but not the impossible impossible."

"You know what?" I said.

"What?" Spencer replied, leaning aristocratically on his stick.

"I think you're crazy."

"An opinion honestly dispatched and one in which I must sometimes concur. Now, if you please, let us get on with the action, before intermission."

"Intermission?"

"Yes. Before the final act we shall take a breath so that you and our talented artist may try your trick on Minos."

"Don't call it my *trick*. It's for his own good."

"Very well, your *stratagem*. After intermission we shall complete the play—if you behave yourself. But I beg of you not to commit any more anachronistic nonsense until our play is over." Spencer gave me a tired smile. "Promise?"

"I promise."

"Splendid! Now tell us what your pretty sister thinks of our Uncle Minos."

I explained again that Jo Anne was not my sister, not even kin, which made no impression on the ant who had already declared with sure authority that all humans, up close, look alike—

"Action!" Spencer called.

Act IV

Scene: *Jo Anne, wearing blue shorts and a loose polka dot blouse, is in the studio touching into Venoria's portrait a final impression. Even at a distance Jody can appreciate the Olympic harmony of*

Venoria's body. The painting is a large likeness, a yard in length. On a drawing table beside Jo Anne lies open one of Jody's books, The Great Inventors. *As Jo Anne leans toward the text for a closer view, Jody is surprised to glimpse the gentle revelation of her breasts. Jo Anne is not studying the diagrammatic inventions of the great Leonardo da Vinci but one of his famous paintings.*

JO ANNE: (*thoughtfully*) I believe people may be more interesting, after all, than fish. For instance, Venoria. And Uncle Minos. Can you believe he hasn't really *looked* at Venoria since they were married?

JODY: That's why I want to blast him with your picture. Plop it down right in front of his dead eyeballs—shock him back to life.

JO ANNE: Ummm . . . So maybe he will be able to see her again, to take her in his arms and—

JODY: But how?

JO ANNE: Ummm . . . yes . . . You'll think of something.

(Spencer quickly directs Jody to stand facing Jo Anne so the two can unite their dramatic energies.)

JODY: The dumbwaiter!

JO ANNE: Uncle Minos's food elevator?

(Spencer is nodding his head.)

JODY: Yes.

JO ANNE: You ride down on the dumbwaiter? Surprise him?

JODY: No. I'll creep downstairs into his basement. You crank Venoria's picture down to him in the food cradle. I'll pop the main light on just as it gets there. He'll have to look.

(Spencer nods again.)

JO ANNE: At my picture of Venoria?

JODY: Yes. When the picture blasts his eyes, I'll fake a fall and get a look at his leg. Feel it. I need to know.

Jo Anne: Sounds clumsy to me, dangerous.

Jody: It'll work.

Jo Anne: (*contemplating the portrait*) Venoria is so terribly beautiful. How could he ever take his eyes off her?

Jody: Maybe it'll shock them together again.

Jo Anne: Poor Uncle Minos and his sad sickness. My heart weeps to think of him.

Jody: The dumbwaiter. It'll work. It's got to. For The Admiral's sake.

Jo Anne: I don't think what caused it was the switchblade or his leg or his loose tongue.

Jody: Your mother does. She thinks Minos's tongue slapped his brains out. Led him into a lie.

Jo Anne: That's too simple.

Jody: Then what?

Jo Anne: It was Venoria's beauty. Beauty seeps into everything, even into Mr. Grumps and your Uncle Minos. It has curious ways. It's unavoidable. Mysterious. Dangerous.

Jody: Good Lord! You aren't going to blame Uncle Minos's sickness on Venoria!

Jo Anne: Not Aunt Venoria, dummy—her beauty. She can't help being beautiful. Look how marvelously proportioned she still is. (*Jo Anne pulls Jody in closer and indicates Venoria's total beauty by sweeping the palm of her hand over the entire portrait. She puts her arm around Jody's waist. Jody had watched the painting progress, mature, but there is now a slight alteration in Venoria's features. Exactly what, Jody cannot make out.*)

Jody: Just because she's beautiful is no cause for Uncle Minos to hide himself away forever. It's not manly. It embarrasses The Admiral and Uncle Claude to death and makes your Mama furious. It's like what's the matter with him is contagious.

Jo Anne: He loved Venoria. You know he did. He kept his dreadful promise and buried himself alive for her.

JODY: Some promise! He could have let the sailor cut his throat and saved himself a lot of trouble.

JO ANNE: Don't be so gruesome. He sacrificed himself for love. A shadow of love is all he's got now.

JODY: And maybe a bum leg.

JO ANNE: (*remembering a poem*) Stone walls do not a prison make.

JODY: Holy Moses! His walls aren't stone. They're solid salt. He's living a freak's life in a freak place—except for Venoria. Nobody comes to her WHY NOT SHOP but milky-legged tourists, ice cream kids, and college rock doctors. All Uncle Minos does is polish The Admiral's spare rocks and glue together kooky birds and doodads out of sea shells. The Hurricane Hermit! And you think he's a hero!

JO ANNE: A mystery. Look at what he's suffered! His sorrow! He's served his time. Tried to save face.

JODY: Some face! He wears a hood like a sick moose. His eyes won't even look at you. Not Venoria. Not anybody.

JO ANNE: Leave him his name. His honor.

JODY: Sweet Jesus!

JO ANNE: He's paid for it. A hundred times over.

JODY: *It*! (*Jody measures his words.*) What-is-IT?

JO ANNE: His sin or whatever Mother says makes him afraid.

JODY: (*timidly, looking to Spencer*) His hyperep— (*Jody is trying to remember Spencer's long word.*)

JO ANNE: His what?

JODY: Ahh—his whatever it is you're talking about—

"Cut! Cut! That will do!"

Spencer was angry. He pointed the ignition end of his match stick at me, "Never, NEVER look off stage to me for advice! It makes you look like a dunce. It shows your lack of confidence and distracts the audience. Moreover, it humiliates me." This was the first time it occurred to me that Spencer and I were the only audience.

"That long word is yours, not mine!

"You mean Minos's hyperpheniaplanepseudos?"

"Yes."

"Nevermind. I shall attend to that later." Spencer squared his thin shoulders, raised his chin confidently, and said, "I trust that you noticed the charming maturity of your pretty co-star." I was embarrassed that Spencer had caught me in my casual glimpse under Jo Anne's blouse. "I don't mean that, you silly imp. I mean her superior perception. She appreciates the complexity of our little drama and of your gloomy uncle."

"He'd be less complicated if we knew his leg was crippled."

"I suppose you'd like his whole leg rotted off."

"Sure. It'd solve all our problems."

"Very well. Let's take our intermission and, we may hope," Spencer stressed, "you will see your uncle's leg *and* his eyes tomorrow. Afterward we shall resume our drama to its final act in which, with your kind permission, I will play my humble part. But during my performance I implore you to pardon my frail voice which, however true, carries poorly in the open theater."

Standing midway between the bedposts, Spencer touched the tips of his antennae, and from his slender waist bowed a graceful bow.

Intermission

When The Admiral and I climbed into the Chevy van to make the risky art delivery, Jo Anne was already in the back with a silk shawl covering Venoria's portrait. Zip hopped in after us. I was driving.

"I told The Admiral what we're going to do with the picture," I said.

"I told Claude and Mother, too," Jo Anne added. "They don't think it'll work."

"Worth a try"—The Admiral said and lit a cigar. "And you two show that picture to Venoria first. It's her likeness, her picture, and her Minos."

"Oh pos-i-tive-ly," Jo Anne said.

I had watched Gloria with her professional fingers demonstrate to Jo Anne the finer techniques of oils, especially in creating the angry sea that lay behind Venoria; but as a matter of artistic freedom Gloria had left her daughter to the final conceptions of character and spirit.

"I hope his leg is busted up real good," I said.

Jo Anne took a last peek at Venoria. "It's our best chance," she said.

The Admiral made an O with his mouth and jawed out a smoke ring. "You best be careful in lifting up his pants leg," he warned. "In his shoulders Minos is yet a powerful man. To him you are an alien."

"He's seen me through his basement window," I said.

"But he doesn't know who you *are.*"

"Yes," Jo Anne said. She made her knuckles into a hinge. "He can crush your skull in his hands like *this,*" she said and clamped the heels of her palms together.

"Just you remember," The Admiral said, "Minos is *family.* As long as he casts a shadow, he's one of us."

I acknowledged to myself that confronting my weird uncle was more of a challenge than I had imagined. As Jo Anne had observed, people might be more interesting than fish. For me the reclusive Minos had become a consuming enigma.

Venoria met the van on the oyster hull apron of her why not shop. No slender, ill-fed modern dolly was Venoria, but a mature mahogany Amazon with flowing black hair cut high in bangs across the brow and gathered in a panther tail down her spine. She had a firm, almost masculine, neck, supple limbs, and the tight waist of a concert cello.

Zip, knowing his reward, hit the ground first in a stiff-legged sprint, then leapt; Venoria caught him in her arms and dropped into his mouth a goody-bit. "Bright good morning, little foxy," she said to the terrier, "—and to all, and to my pretty miss of the painted fish." She released Zip and kissed Jo Anne on top of her head, then stepped back from the draped picture with knowing curiosity. "What?" she exclaimed, "Am I grown now so ugly you must take a sash to hide me?"

The Admiral whispered to Venoria the secret purpose of the picture.

"I want you to see it first. It's yours," Jo Anne said.

"I will like that very much, "Venoria said, "But you must be wary of my troubled Minos."

Jo Anne handed the covered portrait to The Admiral, making sure the shawl hung free, and stepped aside. I stood beside Venoria.

Jo Anne watched Venoria's eyes, then slowly drew the veil away.

The morning sun hit the canvas, and behind the lone Venoria the painted waves came alive. It was then in the pure light that I saw Jo Anne's alteration of the portrait. It was in the face, the expression. From her once explicit lips, Venoria now wore the slightest suggestion of a smile, if you could call it that. I wondered if this sly addition had been inspired by the great da Vinci or if it was Jo Anne's invention.

No matter, Venoria had seen and liked. She smiled approvingly at the picture, held her shoulders back, and said, "Yes, maybe after all, even now, he may look at me."

I barred Zip from the WHY NOT SHOP? and snapped the screen door shut. Venoria's place smelled of sand, salt, shells, and smoked mullet. Venoria spoke on. "Beware of my lonely Minos who is an empty man and may close like the tunnel of a rolling wave upon you. Even now I ill speak his name for he has not beheld me these years since our holy vows nor have I permitted his ears a word from my mouth. Be careful in your going down upon him and beware," she said again, "for my Minos is an empty man."

The solemn essence of Venoria's voice made me swallow hard. I felt an emptiness in myself.

The Admiral fit the portrait face forward and upright in the large food cradle. One pull of the bell string would alert Minos that food was on the way; two rings announced its arrival. From Aunt Venoria I had sketched a mental picture of my uncle's vault below: eleven steps down to the landing; left turn; toilet under the stairs; work tables on the center floor; to the right, posted bed and chifferobe; to the left, toilet wall with bright lights switch; straight ahead the dumbwaiter.

"Take off your shoes," The Admiral whispered. He lifted the latch on the door.

One hand on the bell string and the other on the pull rope, Venoria stood ready beside her portrait. At a single ring as the tray creaked downward, I took a breath—as if starting under water—and in the half-light crept barefooted halfway down the stairs. At the second ring I quickly tipped down to the landing, crouched, breathing quietly, and fixed my fingers on the switch to the light bulb that hung above the mouth of the food shaft. In the square of window light, I could see the oval shoulders of Minos as he shuffled toward the dumbwaiter.

Minos was not wearing his gruesome hood. As he turned his head, his features in shadow were cast in sharp profile against the white salt wall. I had misjudged my uncle's height. The Admiral was right; Minos was a man of impressive size and power that even his sloped shoulders could not belie. And so Minos stood in shadow, leaning slightly with his back to me, facing the portrait of Venoria that had come to rest before him.

I listened to my heart.

Then flicked the bright light on, igniting the picture.

I feared a sudden reaction, a jerk of the oval shoulders or an aggressive shift of the whole body to see who was guilty of this intrusion. But, save for the slow contraction and expansion of his chest, Minos did not move. He stood transfixed before the portrait. I crept closer, close enough to hear his breath, to touch his body. Now I would bare his leg, see the blemish in his flesh—but:

Which leg to bare?

Which leg to bare?

Fearing that the rude light had exposed me too soon, I crawled forward into my uncle's shadow, wondering if Minos might turn now and let his wrath fall upon me. In the glare of the naked bulb I could see only an outline of the man, holding the face of Venoria's portrait to his chest. Then his shadow moved aside, and Minos stepped into the light.

He was neither grotesque nor infirmed as I had imagined. His sunless face was smooth and fair. His hair, self-trimmed round as a mushroom, reminded me of a monk's. His shoulders, slightly hunched, were arched and as thick and tight as concrete. And his eyes, dark and hungry, were feeding deeply into me.

"You have come to see my leg," Minos said.

I was stunned.

Still on my hands and knees I crept backwards, knowing that I was the first one in years to feed his eyes. Or had it been Jo Anne's picture of Venoria that had cracked his eyes open?

"How did you know?" I managed.

"My leg has a mind of its own. Will you now lift my trouser leg to satisfy yourself?" His voice was steady, his eyes still burning down into me. "You are Jody," he said. "Your ear betrays you." I was surprised at his visual acuteness, for my ear's discrepancy was now barely noticeable. "Are you afraid?" he asked.

"No."

"*No* what? *No* you won't lift my trouser cuff or *no* you aren't afraid?"

"No, I'm not afraid."

"Why are you trembling?"

"I'm not used to crawling around on my all fours," I said, feeling like a lost puppy.

"Did I tempt you here?"

The question baffled me.

"Answer me," he demanded.

"No sir," I said, and yet he *had* tempted me here.

"Can you see me now?" he said.

"Yes sir." I could see also in him the tiniest enlargement of his left ear and a clear resemblance of The Admiral. There was a tincture of Mother about his eyes and mouth.

"Come closer," Minos said. I rose to my knees.

"Closer," he urged.

"This is close enough. I can see from here."

"That's *not* enough. Lift up my trouser cuff." Minos tightened his lips. "Put your hands down on my leg."

My courage was slipping. I inched closer to my uncle and started to reach down.

"Not that leg," Minos warned.

"Jody!" In mild alarm Jo Anne's voice tip-toed down the stairs.

"It's the little artist," Minos said, clinging to the portrait. "I have heard her voice. She has brought her pictures to my window." I did not know this.

"She is Jo Anne," I said.

"Yes," Minos said. "You are wasting my time. Lift up my trouser cuff."

I started down again, putting my fingers on the cuff and lifting up.

"Higher," Minos said.

There was his ankle bone.

"Higher," Minos demanded.

The cavity of his pants leg slipped up as freely as if over a stick.

"Now the calf," Minos urged.

A blue vein led up to the knee.

"Higher, higher—all the way!" Minos was breathing heavily.

I lifted up until the leg was bare.

"Now, see! See it all!" Minos cried. "A leg doesn't lie!"

"Yes," I said. "Yes, I see!"

And so I could. From a withered thigh, the knee bulged like a knotted root with the flesh of the calf drawn taut like onion skin over the forebone.

"Jody!" Jo Anne called again, this time in clear alarm.

As I came slowly to my feet, Minos pointed me up the stairs. I could hardly stand. I held out my arms.

"The picture," I requested. "Jo Anne painted it for Venoria. It's hers."

"Go!" Minos commanded, clinging to the painting. His eyes followed me to the landing. He held the painting at arms length and looked at Venoria, then back to me.

I hurried away, stumbling hard upon the stairs, not once but twice. Minos was still pointing up and pressing the portrait to his chest when I closed the basement door behind me.

When Spencer appeared that night for our final act, I pulled the covers under my chin and played asleep. He emerged from under the footboard and climbed to the summit of my toes. Like a Cicero, he stretched out his arms for poise and bespoke himself in soliloquy:

"Adhering to my ancient nature, I have maintained my unique distance throughout this droll recess, but must applaud here my slumbering chum for his descent into his uncle's vault alone. His performance there, though crude and stumbling, was about as much as we could wish from a sprout so near the dangerous age of reckoning, knowing as I do the awesome storm accruing. Nor am I dismayed that he now claims capture of his uncle's eyes or disclosure of the long flawed leg. I suspect, also, that our pretty artist, with equal zeal, will own that it is she, her art, Venoria's beauty, that cracked the stubborn ice of Minos. Had I a gland or flowing duct like yours—" I could see through a slit in my eyelids that Spencer was looking directly at me—"I, too, would have shed a modest tear. Alas, your wise and weathered grandfather will be glad to know his regretful son has suffered real affliction. And your tireless Venoria is renewed in heart that her broken Minos keeps her portrait as a sign of hope. Gloria—our pious little buttress—remains unmoved, declaring death for Minos is better than his sad seclusion. And your gentle, Neanderthal Claude still clings to the switchblade fear as cause of his brother's fall."

Spencer then resumed his normal mode, slid down a valley in the counterpane, marched across my body to my ear, and said with great enlargement, "NOW!—Jody dear—I'm sad to say, you must come alert so we may finish out our little play."

"Oh—" I said. "It's—it's you."

"Don't look so surprised, my little innocent; you watched me all the while and heard my every word. How did I sound? Was, or were, the acoustics adequate? Was I not accurate and distinct?"

"Okay, I suppose. I was sleeping on one ear."

"Now remember, you cannot remain insightful in your performance if you are always preoccupied with your own vague self."

"I was thinking of Uncle Minos," I said.

"Very well. You recall that I am now to share the stage with you. I promise to be brief, very brief, on this last *leg* of our drama." Spencer made a smile. I caught the pun.

"That's a pretty ugly thing to say about my uncle," I complained. "From what I've learned I don't think we even need to finish this stupid play. I know all I need to know, and if you're so hell-bent for glory on the stage, go ahead, just say your lines. I'll listen."

"Just *say* my lines? Never!" Spencer objected. "Would you amputate my words, however few, and leave them without meaning, squirming on the stage like earthless worms? I know as well your lines. Now prepare at once not only to *say* them but to *act* them honestly from within."

"You've been spying on me!" I said as if the insect had been hiding in a socket of my mind.

"Absolutely not!" Spencer was incensed. "My constant presence makes me no spy. You overween yourself if you think I watch you all the time. Have *I* no privacy? I am not always ubiquitous." The word struggled into my brain and bogged down. "I mean I can't be awake all the time," Spencer explained. "My cosmic necessity has assigned me to you—without my consent, I might add."

"No need to go getting so all ruffled up. I'd rather just tell what I know about my Uncle Minos and be done with it," I said. "I'm getting tired."

"And miss the fun of ending?"

"I don't think I'm having much fun right now."

"Very well! We'll stop the play. I'll say nothing more and leave you to perish in your own insipid darkness."

"You're pulling that *director* stuff again."

"Certainly. They do it more profitably all the time in Hollywood and on television, although with more disastrous results. Now—turn your eyes—*there.*"

Spencer pointed his match stick between the bedposts where the open hall door cast a quadrangle of light upon the footboard of my bed.

"Action!" Spencer said.

Act V

Scene: Twenty years ago in Inn Lafayette. Although still the director, Spencer is taking part as an actor. He is sitting on a saltshaker in the middle of the bar. For effect he rolls a dime down the oaken beerway. It slows, wobbles, and, in a diminishing circle, tinkles out its dying chime against the hardwood. The old tavern is uncomfortably silent and empty. Across from himself, Spencer has positioned Jody facing the myriad liquor bottles and huge bar mirror.

SPENCER: What did your uncle do when he saw Venoria's portrait?
JODY: Nothing. He just stood there like he was made of stone.

SPENCER: He said nothing?

JODY: Nothing. Not then. But he knew I had come to see his leg.

SPENCER: Did you ask him about his leg first?

JODY: No. He just knew I wanted to see it, to see if he'd been lying.

SPENCER: Had he been?

JODY: No. I saw it. He's crippled. His knee was bulged out in a white knot and the flesh round his calf bone was as tight and dry as a drum skin.

SPENCER: Did he look at you? Into your face?

JODY: Yes. It was like he was trying to devour me with his eyes. I felt sorrow for him. I cried, a little.

SPENCER: (*The ant is impressed and tightens his jaws before proceeding.*) Do you see the big mirror across the bar, in front of you?

JODY: Yes.

SPENCER: Now watch carefully. Let's play the fight scene back.

JODY: The scene The Admiral told me about?

SPENCER: Yes. I want you to see it like it was.

JODY: The Admiral told me like it was. He wouldn't lie to me.

SPENCER: Of course he wouldn't, but he was sitting out there. (*Spencer points to a barroom table.*) I—yes I—was here. (*Spencer taps the bar, pointing with his stick.*) I saw it all, not part of it. Don't look at me! Keep your eye on the mirror. See . . . the sailor wielding the switchblade . . . Minos jumping up on the bar . . . See!

JODY: Yes.

SPENCER: Minos is backing up, backing, backing . . .

JODY: —backing up to . . . about . . . here! (*Jody points to the inside edge of the bar.*)

SPENCER: Yes.

JODY: —and slipping off . . .

SPENCER: —and falling . . .

JODY: Yes. It was an accident just as The Admiral said.

SPENCER: Don't look at me! Stand up so you can see. Keep your eye on the mirror. Look, carefully. See your uncle falling down . . . behind the bar . . . Could your grandfather have seen that?

JODY: Of course not. He can't see through oak.

SPENCER: (*The action proceeds in slow motion.*) Watch. See how your uncle falls shoulders first behind the bar, how his sturdy arms catch him, cushion him . . . let him down with ease and how he slowly rolls unhurt . . . as sound as any silver dollar ever slapped upon the bar. (*Spencer locks his eyes into Jody and nails words into Jody's brain.*) JODY, YOUR UNCLE LIED ABOUT HIS LEG.

JODY: (*There is a long silence with growing tension.*) That's a lie! I saw his leg with my own eyes! It was shrunken, pale, crooked like a bent stick. (*Jody leaves the bar stool in a fury and throws himself into a chair at one of the tables. He clinches his fist and is about to demolish an ashtray when he finds Spencer reclining there as if in a glass hammock.*) Hell spit on you, you little devil, always digging up the worst. What do you want?—want me *not* to see what I saw with my own eyes? Is that what you want?

SPENCER: You have just seen what you saw—with your own eyes.

JODY: But that was in a mirror, something done before I was ever born. How do I know it wasn't a trick?

SPENCER: I don't play tricks on you. You play tricks on yourself. I don't say that Minos is lying now. Your eyes did not deceive you. His leg *is* crippled. If you live a lie long enough, you begin to believe it; it gets to be real, deadly.

JODY: Mirrors are tricky.

SPENCER: Brainy Jody, Minos doesn't know now that he is lying! He thinks it's the truth.

JODY: You're trying to show off, to get off the hook. You're saying Minos was afraid, pretended a dead leg to hide behind.

SPENCER: Well, he didn't want to lie. Shame drove the lie into his head, and his leg began to dry up. It didn't die all at once. His leg may not be all dead yet.

Jody: You can't prove Uncle Minos lied.

Spencer: I can't prove rainbows or elephants.

Jody: Come on. You're making Uncle Minos a coward!

Spencer: *Was* a coward. That was *then*. The lie has petrified his leg. Maybe the lie hasn't reached his heart yet.

Jody: (*Bites his lip*) Damnit! Damnit! Damnit! I want to believe him! I need to!

Spencer: Would you believe his lie *for* him?

Jody: What does it matter? I'll believe what I want to. Who'll know the difference?

Spencer: (*Spencer leaps from the ashtray.*) I will, you little rascal! You'll not wiggle out of our play so easily. I am director. Desert me now and I'll shoot infernal worry at your soul and ride wild horses in your dreams.

Jody: I can't sleep thinking my uncle is a coward, trapped forever in his stinking basement.

Spencer: It took courage for him to face Venoria's portrait, to look you in the eye. Something touched his dying soul.

Jody: (*Jody reflects on the wry smile that Jo Anne had added to the portrait.*) Suppose it *was* Venoria's beauty that started it all . . . her eyes . . . her smile . . . (*Jody thinks.*)

Spencer: Or Minos's boastful mouth.

Jody: Or the sailor's switchblade.

Spencer: Or the fall.

Jody: Yes. If only for that one second of his life Minos hadn't been afraid—his fear!—he wouldn't have lied.

Spencer: You should talk! What about you—stumbling out of your uncle's basement? Many a babe has fallen down the stairs, but heady Jody, you fell *up* the stairs! (*Something in Spencer's barb, in the reflection of Venoria's painted smile, in the image of falling* up *the stairs pricks Jody's funny bone, and Jody laughs and laughs until tears flood his eyes. Spencer continues.*) I confess I am a pain in the noggin—a real joy buster. But I am glad to find you have not lost your jolly spirit or your fear of falling into your uncle's salty basement and catching his—

Jody: His hyperphe—

Spencer: (*Pronounces his long word poetically.*)

Hyper fee nee
Ah plan ee
see you dos.

Jody: Who knows what that means?

Spencer: Alas, even with its singular extension it is the very soul of brevity! Your pampered academic and epistemological socioglites are forever using black holes of tortured thought from which no light escapes. In your timely brogue the grand word means—no, I will not bring myself to corrupt it—which would sound something as awful as your squatty Grumps might croak. Now listen carefully. In its original tongue and tone it is forever beautiful to the ear, even if you hap to miss its meaning. (*With flawless eloquence Spencer again utters his elongated word. Although on a plane higher than Jody can appreciate.*) Now, my groggy Jody, how liked you that?

Jody: It sounded like a long wiggler worm with the hiccups.

Spencer: (Smiling) May the constellations preserve you!

Jody: What does it mean?

Spencer: (*Reluctantly, drawing close to Jody's ear.*) Very well, in translation, but only for you. For *us*. Promise? I can hardly bear to hear myself utter it in your inadequate brogue.

Jody: I promise.

Spencer: (*whispering*) It means *pride-deceit-lie*. (*Spencer is embar-*

rassed.) It should, however, not be so disintegrated by the tongue as this, but pronounced *whole*: *pridedeceitlie*.

JODY: (*Looking incredulously at the ant.*) Why didn't you just say so in the first place?

SPENCER: So you left your uncle's basement in a hurry?

JODY: Yes. It was an order. After all it's his basement.

SPENCER: I see. And he kept the portrait of Venoria for himself?

JODY: Yes. He pressed it to his chest like a shield.

SPENCER: Excellent! Perhaps—just perhaps—your pretty miss has chipped the chilling ice of your brooding uncle. And perhaps—just perhaps—you have rescued his dying eyes. What more in your sublime awkwardness could you wish?

JODY: (*assuming the ant's diction*) I could wish in your sublime magnificence that you take leave of me.

". . . Cut! That's a wrap." Spencer said and disappeared backstage behind the bedposts.

Part III

The Storm

17

Grumps Recycled

I wondered if Jo Anne's portrait of Venoria would have any lasting effect on Minos or if Spencer's dramatic efforts had revealed the real source of my sad uncle's plight. If our private play was for real it might be that the death in Minos's leg had not yet reached his heart. But Spencer's little drama had done nothing to account for my accumulating attraction to Jo Anne. Nor had it erased the tension of my illegitimacy or solved the mystery of the stranger at the funeral. More unsettling was Jo Anne's daring intimation that the spidery Millsap might be my father, which was of small importance to Spencer. But to me, even the shadow of such a suggestion was not only absurd but obscene.

The morning after our little theatrical, Spencer assured me—but only scatteringly—that by the meagerest employment of my innermost fibers I could discover the proper avenues to clear up these questions for once and for all. Then, in summary, tilting his head back and aligning his antennae toward me, Spencer allowed, "Such clear channels are forever present for us but are now sorely clogged by dazzling stalactites and stalagmites along the way. I know a great deal about secret caverns in the bowels of our earth." Then, in his early morning industry, the ant scurried away.

I had little doubt about the storm that both Spencer and The Admiral had forecast. Being of a certain kin, I, too, had sensed its coming. Spencer had first picked up its embryonic stirrings off the coast of Africa and later its continuation in the Sargasso Sea of the Atlantic, north of the West Indies. A week afterwards on his wireless The Admiral received positive signs from San Salvador in the Bahamas of a constricting turbulence shaping westward along the Tropic of Cancer. And four days later on my own ham set Jo Anne and I had picked up distinct code from a ham operator in Havana, reporting ". . . a b-r-o-a-d d-i-s-c t-h-r-e-a-t-e-n-i-n-g t-h-e S-t-r-a-i-t-s o-f F-l-o-r-i-d-a." The cyclone was now officially identified and was entering the Gulf of Mexico. Radio and TV were full of warnings up and down the coast from St. Petersburg to Galveston, Texas. With the new storm on the make, with Mother now laid to rest, and with my new freedom spinning in upon me, there arose a tightening in my brain. I went to the beach to think.

Seagulls were circling The Admiral's light house. A familiar shadow started over me. Quietly, from behind, Jo Anne grasped me around the chest.

"It could hit anywhere," she said of the impending storm, pressing my arms to my ribs. I took a deep breath that tightened her arms around me. Zip had come along and stood where the waves stopped on the sand.

"I know," I said. "A hurricane is batter's luck with the world throwing a wild baseball at you."

"And we're just a sand dot between Galveston and St. Petersburg," Jo Anne said, referring to our little island. Her chin was snuggled in my spine.

"It's bottled up in the Gulf now. It'll smash out somewhere," I said.

"Yes," Jo Anne said. "I want to see Johnny Revelation, in the flesh. Let's go to The Ark before it hits. Does The Ark carry sails?"

I had not thought of this, but I had seen with my own eyes that the magnificent craft had no engines.

"She's made for the sea," I said. "If the wind breaks her loose, she'll take the waves."

"Let's hope," Jo Anne said. She was breathing into the back of my neck.

"I've been aboard her. Seen her. Inside out. She's got a pilot-house and a five-foot helm wheel you can spin with a finger and a real stern rudder like a butcher's meat cleaver."

"But no power of her own," Jo Anne observed. "No direction."

She was right.

"The Ark is made of European timbers shaped by Scandinavian shipwrights that go back to the Vikings," I said.

"But, Jody, she's just for show. Anchored in the sand. She's Johnny's play pretty." Jo Anne released me, slipped her head under my arm, looked up at me. "I feel something strong coming on. Let's go to The Ark. Now. Before it's too late. You promised."

Jo Anne had seen all Johnny's TV installments of *The Golden Ladder*, the dramatization of The Ten Commandments. But there was one episode of *The Pit*—a counter series of *The Seven Deadly Sins*—that Jo Anne had not seen.

This was Johnny's furious enactment of the third deadly vice, ANGER. This shocking performance—slated now for Hurricane—was called "The Consummation of Madness." It was a rendition wherein unrestrained love proves to be the antidote for the ravages of jealousy.

Nola Rose, of course, would play the soothing solution to the passionate Johnny.

I had not forgotten my promise to Jo Anne. And I knew by the tone of Jo Anne's voice that Gloria's objection to The Ark would no longer hold.

"You're in love with Johnny Revelation," I said.

"Oh, but I do *love most* my warty Mr. Grumps!" she teased. "Just one little kiss on his froggy head and he's a prince!—and all mine!"

"You read too many fairy tales."

"Only because they're true."

"He's a fake," I said.

"Mr. Grumps?"

"No. Johnny Revelation. He's pretty but won't talk. Only sings and dances sexy dances with his luscious Nola Rose. He's afraid of something." I thought of Hano, Johnny's patch-eyed custodian. I could still see his rubbery lips and smell his fiery breath.

Johnny Revelation had recently won glowing acclaim in Oslo and Paris. He had gained international fame and was now aboard his renowned Ark, back home on Hurricane for a songfest to set in motion a sacred gathering and grand influx of warm swirling bodies and liquid souls from everywhere to be led in nightly seizures by the super-soul himself. Already hordes of pilgrims were sardined in nearby motels eager to be engrossed and ready to launch themselves into ecstasy at the master's command.

"You want to see if I can resist Johnny," Jo Anne said. I hated the way she could hit the bull's eye without even looking.

"Don't be childish," I said.

"Do you think Johnny will remember the lost ruby rhinestone you found for him?"

I didn't know. But I remembered Johnny's Zero Cider and the exotic Nola Rose. I was afraid to ask Jo Anne if she had really been present during Duo Divisio's spectacular exposure of me at the Rainbow Carnival—if she had actually seen me buck naked and bare ass on the stage. At the time, I had suffered this embarrassing event with such intensity that I feared the shock of it had blurred my memory. I wondered, too, about the beautiful underground machine and the demolished rabbit that oozed like pink oil from its teeming gears. Jo Anne started walking away.

"Johnny Revelation is dangerous!" I shot at her. Jo Anne swung around, screwing her toes into the sand.

"You're jealous," she fired back, then turned slowly and followed Zip up the beach to the Merrimac.

The Admiral had arrived in the Emerald Rolls. It was parked on the boardwalk like a jewel in the sunshine. *For their REUNION* . . . Jo Anne's words came back to me. The reunion of The Admiral and my grandmother?

When I got back to my room The Admiral was waiting for me beside my table of natural wonders. He was examining a piecrust-sized disc, holding it up to the window light. The Admiral had grown noticeably older since last summer. He wore a loose, white linen suit, black tie, and black patent leather slippers. His shoulders were broad but now coathanger thin, his neck lean and his sleeves too long.

"I'm sorry," he said, holding out the curious crust.

Then with light agility, my grandfather flicked the disc out an open window into an uplifting breeze that brought it in an elliptical arc back exactly to the hand that sent it. I was amazed at the old man's graceful precision and caught in a glimpse a deadly likeness between the dry disc and The Admiral's pale hand.

"What is it?" I asked.

"A very dead Mr. Grumps," The Admiral said, almost as if I should have known, and handed me the oddity. It was as light as air but unmistakably Mr. Grumps, as flat as a platter.

"How on—" I began.

"Run over by a truck and sun-dried flat on the blacktop. But always comes back." The Admiral smiled, holding up his hand and flexing his fingers.

"It's Grumps all right," I said. "You can tell by his one-hopper all dried up around his rump like he's been fried in a big skillet."

There was, of course, a connection between Mr. Grumps and my grandfather because The Admiral had given me the unusual frog, but the likeness in my grandfather's hand escaped me. There was a prevailing odor of salt and asphalt about the altered Grumps, his mouth now baked into an eternal smile.

"Kudzu stretched his brain too far," The Admiral advised.

"That's probably it," I agreed. "Grumps hopped out of his parabola and got cut off from his pond," I said.

"Roads are everywhere nowadays," The Admiral said. "Like soggy spiderwebs. We're all caught up in web roads."

"Yes sir," I said.

"Like long bogs of quicksand."

"Yes sir," I said.

"—and we're sinking down in them," he added.

"Yes sir," I said.

"The whole world is sinking amuck among boggy web roads."

"Yes sir," I said.

The Admiral was on a roll.

"There's no way to hop *around* a road. We're trapped!" he cried. "And sinking, sinking—"

"Exactly right sir," I said.

I held Grumps up to the window. Light sifted through the splotched hide of the flat frog, making apparent his dominant hind hopper and a splintered abstract of bones. When The Admiral stepped between Grumps and the window light, a dim profile of Grandfather's face appeared through the frog skin.

When I lowered Grumps, there was the Emerald Rolls on the boardwalk as if it had arrived from a million light years away.

"I'd hate for Jo Anne to see Grumps now," I said, shaken at the sad shape of my diminished friend. The Admiral moved out of the light.

"Do you think she'll recognize Grumps now?" I asked.

"Absolutely," The Admiral said. "With her sharp eye and a paint brush, our Pearl can see through just about anything."

But I had my doubts that she could see through Johnny Revelation. While I was arranging Mr. Grumps among my table of natural wonders, The Admiral disappeared down the stairs.

There was small creaking toward the rear of my special collection . . .

It was Spencer with fingers laced behind his head and cradled back in my neglected scallop shell. But I had not forgotten that the simple relic had once been the occasion of my swiftest and most exalted Likeness, surpassed only by Jo Anne's portrait of *Bull Bluegill.* The ant propped himself up on an elbow.

"May I express my unselfish delight that your slothful collopitus is now suspended."

"How thoughtful," I returned curtly. Which brought Spencer upright.

"I mean your frog has found an end to his fruitless circumnambulations."

"I see," I said.

"Respecting your grandfather, I must grant your lugubrious Grumps a sad nod; but I refuse to applaud his transmogrification into a dehydrated pancake."

"I shall communicate your sentiments to the frog," I said.

Spencer leaned forward to say—almost upsetting the shell—"As one more profoundly grounded and articulate, I am simply saying we should now be pleased that your inebriated Grumps may never again be required to humiliate himself in such wobbly and unproductive circles."

I was quick to jab at the ant's excesses. "Articulate! Ha! You wallow all over yourself in words. What a swell-head! Such stuckupness! At least Grumps knew where his pond was."

"Yes, yes—*was*. But I, an old alumnus of these grounds, a Formicidae, I am never *gone* but always all rolled up in *now*. I know exactly where I am, this very moment. I'm in your special scallop hull, the kernel of your heart's desire, your dearly remembered 'glory moment.'" Spencer graced himself by standing up nimbly in the cradle of the unsteady shell, barely retaining his balance by taking hold of my finger and hopping out upon the solid table top.

"Whoops," I assisted.

"My humble thanks. Pardon my bum foot . . . Now, briefly," Spencer proceeded, "let's face it. Grumps *was* ugly, still *is* ugly, and as you may observe—flat! Finished! Ready for the eager engine of the earth to reclaim him. Death is nothing," Spencer exhibited by cutting a chip out of the air with his index finger, "nothing but an empty parenthesis dropped into the infinite sigh of time."

It was then that my grandfather's pale hand and the circular crust of the dead Grumps came together in an arresting Likeness. But before I could grasp its full significance—

"Blessed sight turned inside out!" Spencer exclaimed and hurried on with, "Now we must be getting on about our business."

"Where'd you get this 'we' stuff?" I asked, provoked at the ant's presumption.

"O great balls of fire!" Spencer cried. "My dear tadpole, endure me a little while, at least until we have suffered through your blooming tempest. We yet have a storm to swallow. I would as soon miss Haley's comet—that glorious sash across the constellation of Scorpius—as miss your little breeze-to-be." The ant straightened himself and took in such a breath that made his chest glisten. "You are taking Jo Anne with you—to The Ark," he said as a foregone conclusion.

"Of course," I said. "I promised."

"Excellent well. No doubt she shall rescue you from the yearling bastard that you are."

"Rescue me?"

Spencer was examining his crooked foot. There were barefoot sounds in the hallway and a squeak of my bedroom door.

"Rescue me?" I inquired again.

"Never mind . . ." Spencer was saying. "If I told you, you would not believe me; and if you believed me, all in one gulp, you would croak, then we'd miss our little breeze completely—are you listening to me?"

"Y-yes," I said. "I'm listening . . ."

It was Jo Anne at the door. I could tell by the shadow of her ankles.

18

To the Ark

It took Jo Anne but two seconds and a brow wrinkle to assess my frog tragedy. "It's Mr. Grumps," she said instantly, expelling all doubt and explanation. She held him to the window light and turned him slowly as a wheel. "Still going in circles," she sighed and dabbed a tear from her eye. With a finger she traced his mummified lips. "Look, he's still smiling," she said. It was the same smile I had seen on her picture of the frog. And then she laid down Mr. Grumps on my table of natural wonders.

But beyond Jo Anne's zeal to see Johnny perform his shocking episode, "The Consummation of Madness," I had a powerful urge of my own to take Jo Anne to The Ark; and the ominous weather only sharpened my desire. In fact I craved a taste of the dark violence that had destroyed my grandmother, that had surprised my mother in the desert and wasted my anonymous father in the jungles of Vietnam.

The storm had brushed Key West, heightened, nudged St. Petersburg, intensified, nodded at Apalachicola, and swung clockwise in a lefthook toward Mobile. Our island folk were battening down and bracing for the big blow.

The truth was I would take Jo Anne to The Ark not just because *she* wanted to go but because *I* needed her to go with me—certainly not because I was afraid to meet the hurricane unaccompanied or to face again the formidable evangelist. Jo Anne had become as familiar and sensitive to me as gravity. Without her the whole venture would be meaningless.

"You've got a letter from the academy," Jo Anne said. The sun was at ten o'clock in an orange sky. Jo Anne was standing by the roadside mailbox holding the fluttering envelope to the light, trying to decipher its contents. I could tell from the elaborate inscription that the message was from Zachariah.

"It's from Zack," I said.

"I think something is the matter with Rowdy," Jo Anne said. She was wearing jeans, a pink blouse, tennis shoes, and a white scarf tied cowboy style around her throat. I slipped the letter in my shirt pocket to read later.

"I'm not surprised," I said.

Rowdy was trapped now in the tenth grade. At each graduation ceremony he was given what the Commandant called the *Cadet's Merit Award*, but the burden of Rowdy's achievement was that he knew his honor was a sham.

"Something seems always the matter with Rowdy," Jo Anne said.

"It's because he can't get away from being cut off," I said. "He's adrift like a spaceman chopped from his life-line."

"He's more cut off than Uncle Minos," Jo Anne said.

"Maybe not," I said.

I couldn't forget my reclusive uncle in the pit of his cellar holding the portrait of Venoria to his chest.

"I could just cry for Rowdy," Jo Anne said. "He's like a toy soldier swept under the bed."

"Better dead than lost forever," I said.

"Don't say that!" Jo Anne said.

And yet her likeness of the lost toy soldier painfully fit Rowdy. Even today I can recall Rowdy, not much more than a child, grappling with his problem: We are in the Captain's Lounge of Robert E. Lee Hall, awaiting parade. Rowdy is looking bravely at himself in the large door-length mirror, holding his narrow shoulders back and his plump chest out like a robin's. He glances aside at his reflection in another mirror on an adjacent wall that—in an avenue of diminishing images—multiplies him out of sight. Then he looks at me sadly and asks, "How far am I away?"

"Did Rowdy every learn to swim?" Jo Anne wanted to know.

"No. He's afraid to give himself up to the water, to let himself all the way down in it. You sink if you're afraid of it, if you fight it."

Patrolmen were combing the coast sides, blaring instructions to evacuate.

"Johnny's faithful are leaving Hurricane because of the storm," Jo Anne said.

In fact only a few of Johnny's devotees ever made it to Hurricane, and even fewer actually came aboard The Ark for a personal encounter with Johnny himself. As far as I knew I was the only one alive who ever got a private performance from the exhilarating evangelist.

Across the fog and the deep-breathing Gulf, heavy freighters plowing toward Mobile momentarily disappeared.

"Gloria and Claude will be wild if you're gone when the hurricane hits," I said.

"They'll know I'm with you," she said. That would not bode well for me.

"Yes, I know. And The Admiral will turn red and explode."

"Reverend Millsap says he's going to pray out the storm in his whale church," Jo Anne said. She was smiling.

This was the spectacular sanctuary that The Admiral had himself conceived and brought into being by his own secret means. Ecclesiastically it was *God's* church, but to me it was The Admiral's, from which he had been so obliquely ostracized. This was a secret I have kept to this day.

"Claude is bringing in the shrimper," I said.

The evacuation had started in earnest. Last night I listened to the *Umbilicus* loading and then groaning back and forth to the mainland. Johnny's pilgrims were defecting. Serious-faced tourists and campers were driving to the wharf, anxiously awaiting the old flat boat. Deep-sea fishermen were coming in. Midway to the mainland, Captain Zeorge sounded his barge horn.

"You think Johnny'll chicken out or stay the storm?" Jo Anne asked. It was important for her to see the famous evangelist in performance, in the flesh.

"We'll see," I said.

I got in the van. Jo Anne followed and closed her door. In the distance, fluttering on the main mast of The Ark, was JOHNNY REVELATION lettered in red.

When I cranked the motor, Jo Anne covered my hand with hers and followed my knuckles as I shifted the gears.

I had forgotten Zip!

Often I had allowed myself to be intentionally separated from my terrier, especially during dress parades at the academy or on long flights with Mother in the Aeolian Harp. But this was the first time I had actually forgotten my old body buddy. Yet I was keenly aware that on my initial mission to The Ark it was Zip who had given me a certain sense of bearing and direction.

"What happens if the Gulf crashes into Minos's basement?" Jo Anne asked.

"He'll have to come up to Venoria or drown."

"The Admiral . . ." Jo Anne wondered. "He goes out, bareheaded and fiery, to meet high winds. Does he hate hurricanes?"

"Not really," I said. "They're a challenge, a ritual, a contact. He wants to face the same fury that carried my grandmother away. He's drawn to hurricanes. There's something in them that brings him back to something he has lost forever."

"Like his rock garden?"

"Something like that," I said.

"Claude says The Admiral is going to leave you the rock garden, the lighthouse, and all when he dies."

I had no knowledge of this, but it was at this moment that the likeness of my grandfather's pale hand and his face in the frog skin came clear. Also I knew in my heart The Admiral would amply "remember" Jo Anne and that she, too, would somehow become a part of my inheritance.

We were approaching The Ark. To challenge his most diligent followers, Johnny had inlaid an embracing boardwalk around The Ark so that each pilgrim, to achieve his pleasure, was required to make his own path across the dunes to board the master craft. Jo Anne loosed the scarf from her throat, drooped it over her curls, and tied it under her chin. I stopped the van.

"Now," she said as if prepared for the Second Coming. She was smiling again.

"What are you smiling at?" I asked.

"At Reverend Millsap in his whale church," she said. "He's like Jonah in the whale."

It was a likeness too plain to miss.

"He's safe then," I said, remembering the old Bible story. "He'll be spit up on dry ground."

We laughed together at this.

"You can't blame Millsap for loving your mother," Jo Anne said soberly. "He was the Frog Prince who never got his kiss." I recalled the gangly minister, Bible in hand, slinking away alone behind my mother's casket.

"He hates me," I said.

"You?"

"Yes."

"Why?"

"Because I got born. Because I swelled up in his mind and squeezed love out. He couldn't stand—"

"It's not your fault," she said.

In Jo Anne's presence I could feel inside me the insidious octopus of illegitimacy receding.

Jo Anne was staring at The Ark.

There was a firecracker pop and a swish of rotor blades.

This was as close as Jo Anne had ever been to Johnny Revelation.

Poised on the poop deck, beating slow concussions, was a large, goose-bellied helicopter with eager crew and company hustling about.

"Oh no!" Jo Anne cried. "Johnny's leaving The Ark! He's not going to do 'The Consummation of Madness.'"

19

The Kiss

"Damnit . . . Damnit . . . Damnit . . ." It was the first time I had heard Jo Anne cuss. We had trudged across the dunes to The Ark and hurried up the gangway onto the main deck. Johnny Revelation was standing beside his goose-bellied copter between Nola Rose and Hano the patch-eyed first mate. Jo Anne was nearly out of breath. "Damnit . . . Damnit . . ." she panted.

Her words were more of a lament than an accusation. The Gulf wind had picked up a stinging rain, and the TV cameramen and soundmen and prop guys were in great haste to get away. I ducked under the swooping blades and shouted at Johnny Revelation.

"You're ratting out because of the hurricane!"

I think Hano recognized me. Jo Anne was near enough to behold her blond Johnny clad in a fluttering purple robe and to glimpse his luscious Nola Rose. I caught the glancing light in Nola's eye. The leggy dancer wore yellow split-at-the-hip shorts, her face powdered white, her wet lips dark red and as slick as glass. As Hano helped the holy two into the copter, I shouted again through the whir—

"You're chicken, Johnny Revelation. Chicken!" But the accelerating blades beat my words down.

"And you're in love with . . . in love with . . ." came Jo Anne's voice. I couldn't tell if her words were meant for me or Johnny Revelation. The heavy-bellied copter lifted, leaned toward the mainland, and wafted away.

"What? What?" I cried.

When I turned around, Jo Anne and I were standing face to face.

"You're in love with Nola Rose," she said. A lace of fine mist had formed on Jo Anne's eye lashes. She laid her arms across my shoulders and touched her nose to mine. Then pressed me back a step as if measuring my sincerity. "Aren't you?" she asked.

I had never dreamed of such a thing. But Jo Anne's directness and immediacy lifted a corner of my darkness. It was not that I hadn't noticed the bare power of Nola Rose or Jo Anne's remarkable metamorphosis since last summer; it was that I had not noticed their likeness and the shattering difference between them. Jo Anne had blossomed into maturity, and more. The shock was like running smack into a mirror of myself.

"Aren't you?" she persisted.

The helicopter was gone but still making soft concussions in the distance.

"Don't be silly," I said.

This was silly for sure because I could never really touch the one and only Nola Rose, never reach across Johnny's ever withdrawing stage.

"Aren't you?" Jo Anne softened.

"Of course not," I said. "You can never touch people like Johnny and Nola Rose. They're always—well, way out there." I pointed into the wind. "They live in a different world."

"We all live in a different world, sometimes," she said, wiping a wet curl from her eye. She backed off and took the posture of an artist at work. As if painting a picture she flicked her finger across my brow, then from my chin to cheek. "With this," she said, waving her imaginary brush like a little wand, "I can touch whoever or whatever I please—" she paused to search my eyes, then finished with, "and save our secret."

Our secret?

Jo Anne was beginning to sound like Spencer. Then I remembered *Stingray*, Jo Anne's portrait of the surprised lady ray arched in swift defense of her ancient mystery. She was talking about herself! Of all Jo Anne's portraits, *Stingray* was The Admiral's favorite and, to me, second only to *Bull Bluegill*. I wondered what latent enigma Jo Anne was withholding.

Above my head Johnny's name in red was popping on the mainmast.

"I do not think—" Jo Anne speculated, dabbing her finger upon the imaginary canvas, "—I do not think pretty Johnny would like the picture I'm painting of him now."

The wet curl was loose again, tickling her eye. I took hold of Jo Anne's wrist and thrust her finger gunpoint blank into Johnny's airy portrait and said, "BANG."

The weather prophets had warned rightly of the hurricane's rapid and violent progression. Already a gale was mounting in velocity, sucking up cliffs of vapor from the Gulf.

Still holding her wrist, I pulled Jo Anne across the main deck and into the pilot house. We had been alone together many times, but this was the first time I had been so absolutely alone *with* her. The cockpit pilot house sloughed off the stinging rain and muffled down the gale outside. Or was the sound I heard the sharp propellers of the Aeolian Harp clipping up echoes of my mother's voice? I slammed the storm door shut and turned around.

I could tell Jo Anne was going to kiss me.

How can I say?— How, at this moment, could the most inaccessible and scattered agents of my body and soul be so keenly synchronized and prone to her—she, once so foreign yet familiar, and now so new, so near to be drawn to her lips to kiss, so close, so real that I had no choice but to close with her and flow with her pure energy . . .

A whistling wind was sounding round The Ark—then a sudden shifting as if the groaning craft was being urged into the sea. From the helm came a muffled tapping as of two rocks, knocking under water. It was Spencer. The ant was inside the compass, riding bareback on the highly agitated pointer and thumping his thumb, as he was able, upon the glass facing. Unfortunately, because of the rapid rotation of the needle and the broad diameter of the instrument, the centrifugal force was such that Spencer was obliged to lap both legs over the head of the arrow to keep from being thrown disastrously into the brass casing.

Surprisingly when I opened the compass chamber and stopped the spinning pointer, the ant was immediately disgruntled, fuming about the insanity of one-way latches and accusing me of betrayal and incompetence, declaring, "You should have known that I— I who have toiled with Ulysses on the wine-dark seas and on his weary oar smote with him the sounding furrows, that I, the most prompt and eager of navigators, should be and am always *here right now*!" Spencer banged his fist down on the quivering needle. The ant was visibly drunk from his spin but persisted, "And you, you sea-legless swabby, should know—even by your most abused sensors—exactly where you are and the exact nature of your cargo. It is of no commerce whatsoever," he continued, "that you know where you are going, which is forever impossible, but it is essential that you have the wherewithal to get there."

"Well thank you and damn your weaselly eyes for sneaking

into my privacy and screwing up the compass so it won't know North from the cuckoo's nest!" I said stoutly.

"Nothing of the sort," pled Spencer. "Never would I deflect an instant of your precious bliss."

"But you have. You already have!" I insisted. "I was—" I began, sensing a constant slipping of The Ark and an elevating buoyancy. "I was—" I began again.

"Yes, yes. I know. You were kissing your pretty little artist—and still are if you would but turn your head."

I was skeptical of the ant's uncanny powers of manipulation.

"No tricks," I stipulated.

"No tricks," he said and raised his hand as witness.

So when I turned, it was true. No tricks. Jo Anne and I were there uninterrupted, embraced, breathing, our hearts in tune . . . Jo Anne . . . Jo Anne . . . her lips and mine softly together . . .

"And eclipsing time!" Spencer cried. "Ah *time*, you illusive little devil angel riding high between the eternal waves of ether and hiding beneath the carpet of the sea—Gotcha! Ah what dual miracles are accomplished by simple lips!"

I could tell by his tone that Spencer was getting a bit stretched out, and yet I could not deny that I was actually engaged in a double act of which one phase was no less real than the other and during which I could not distinguish where one left off and the other began. And it seemed true, especially in the company of Spencer, that the ant's occurrence did not exist without my presence.

"Of course, of course, of course," Spencer expanded. "Otherwise detached from me and left to your own devices you would be exiled forever in the boring country of yourself."

Sometimes, even at his flightiest, I could catch a spark of Spencer's wisdom.

"Are you finished?" I hinted.

Spencer was not finished.

"What? Do you think our connection is magic? Mere child's play? Fantasy?" Spencer continued. "Do you think you are nothing more than a wandering hulk bearing down upon the scales of life so you can weigh your wretched self? What of me?" the ant commanded. "I weigh not so much as your little toe and have labored in vain with emperors and saints over the creation of empires and the density of archangels. Are we not more than little toes and airy words? More than tumbling stones or wrinkled mountains? Great Olympus! Are we not more than mere slaves to gravity? I know a great deal about gravity," Spencer said, dismounting lightly from the compass needle.

But his bum foot faltered and, before he could right himself, the dizzy ant fell and cracked his noggin on the brass casing. The impact sent such a resounding pock across the instrument that I feared he had seriously injured himself. But when I placed my pocket comb upside the interior wall, suggesting a stairway out, Spencer bounced back with—

"Never!" he exclaimed. "I honor my given spaces, not those I might wish for, but I fear the turbulent air outside has played havoc with my synapses." The hurricane had now moved in aggressively with whipping rain around the pilot house.

"I think it was the bronco ride on the magnetic needle that jiggled your juices and probably screwed up our compass," I ventured, aiming to stay one-up on the ant.

I could not help but look back at myself. Jo Anne was whispering in my ear.

"It started happening to us before you knew about it," she was saying and put her cheek to mine.

I had no doubt that this was true.

"Didn't you ever want to kiss me?" she asked.

"It never crossed my mind," I admitted.

"Is it crossing your mind now?"

It was.

"You don't have to think about it," she said. "It's like seeing what a picture means before you paint it," she whispered and put her lips back to mine.

Our hearts were beating together. Jo Anne released the scarf from her chin . . . Jo Anne . . . her hair . . . her abundant hair . . .

I was breathing into her hair.

"Was it happening to you before you knew about it?" I asked.

"I think so," she said. "I could feel it a long time ago. Even before you came to Hurricane."

"Your kissing tree," I said, recalling The Admiral's beech tree at the spring, a tree of the genus Fagus.

"Yes," she said. "Love's not a beginning. It's something you kind of start out in the middle of even if you don't know exactly where or what it is." I could feel her lips speaking against mine. "Can you feel it happening now?" she asked.

"Yes," I said.

"Whatever love is, it's always in the middle," she said, "never on the edge of or at the end of. It's like painting a picture. There's no end to getting to the middle of it."

"I can believe that," I said.

"You can feel it better when it starts happening between us," Jo Anne said.

We put our lips together again.

Yes, as surely as grass grows in Alabama, it was happening. And it was happening between us.

But what was new about Jo Anne—I mean absolutely, inexplicably, and irrevocably new—was . . .

"Hold! Hold! Don't utter it!" Spencer cried. He was gesticulating with both arms from the open rim of the compass. "Cast not a blundering word upon it or it will perish forever!"

Spencer was standing on the top rung of my pocket comb and pointing under the helm wheel to the main deck where Zachariah's letter had fallen. Jo Anne had picked up the letter and was reading it. Her eyes were wide in disbelief. I could tell by the intensity of Spencer's expression that the ant had something momentous to say. The urgency of his message became even more apparent when he lowered his head and parted his antennae, looking me straight in the eye.

"Rowdy is dead. Drowned," he said with flat finality.

And before I could recover, added—

"I can only surmise how you might feel about such trackless intangibles, but it behooves me to speak plainly before the fact, dark and naked, knocks you down."

Rowdy dead? Dead? The thought struck me like lightning, but at a peculiar angle—not that my retarded roommate was dead, but that magisterial Death would pay attention to poor Rowdy.

And how could anybody, especially Spencer—after we had become so sensitive to each other's inner habits—be so blunt, so dispassionate in this disclosure? It was not that I doubted Spencer's word, for I had found his powers of perception far superior to my own. Zack's letter, though still sealed, had lain in clear view and within easy range of Spencer's introscopic vision, so I was satisfied that Spencer had already beheld Zack's unhappy message. I had, in fact, suspected the worst myself and assumed it my private privilege to make the announcement. The very idea that Spencer should swipe this right from me! And Spencer's cold bluntness so smacked of poor taste and timing that in disgust I slammed the face of the compass down upon the astonished ant, yet not so rudely as to jar him from his ladder. Nor did I close the glass lid too tightly.

Jo Anne had not finished reading the letter.

The storm was now moving in steadily with its fits of fury pounding against The Ark, making it groan so deeply in its timbers that it was impossible to know if it was wind pressing her across the dunes or keen waves slicing in from underneath and lifting her up upon the Gulf.

Strangely, the many-windowed canopy of the pilot house reminded me of the ant's multi-socketed global eyes; and I was, suddenly it seemed, on their underside looking up with the ant and out upon the storm. I couldn't tell if The Ark was moving or the earth moving under us. From the corner of my eye, tumbling in the slanted rain, the familiar greeting sign from the wharf vaulted by like a drunken boomerang, saying WELCOME TO HURRICANE.

"Cremated!" Jo Anne exclaimed, looking up from the letter.

—TO HURRICANE the sign flashed again.

"Cremated?" I repeated incredulously.

"Cremated," Jo Anne confirmed and handed me the letter.

It read:

> ATT: CADET JODY EMERITUS—honored graduate of the Academy and your illustrious and generous Grandfather, GREETINGS.
>
> It is with a heavy heart and countenance downcast that I instruct you of Cadet Rowdy's Death—Drowned from His Heroic effort to swim without our watch in our official lake now outlawed to our regiment for a term and henceforth hallowed in

> Rowdy's name and in remembrance of His frail body that failed Him and that was borne away from our temporal citadel here and, by order of His soulless parents, burned to cinders leaving us only your empty blouse whose presence He saluted everyday and whose tarnished buttons are now bequeathed in words by His trembling hand back to you, departing now as He must in the mist of our sad memories but rejoicing and ever happy now in the Kingdom of God.
>
> With sterm and unflinching loyalty from our Commandant, I remain your humble Scribe, Band Master, and Keeper of the Academy, Zachariah

I wondered if there was sufficient punishment for such a crime. Jo Anne, who had never seen Rowdy, had tears in her eyes.

"They burned him up so they'd never have to look at his lonely face again," I said to Jo Anne.

"—so they wouldn't have to see *themselves*," she said.

Yes. That was it—so they wouldn't have to face themselves. I cringed at the cruel, keep-a-stiff-upper-lip way I had left Rowdy entangled in his own inadequacies: stranded, standing beside the regal Zachariah, presenting me his breathless salute. Jo Anne was squeezing my hand.

"You did what you could," she said. "You were his friend. You and Zachariah. You left him your uniform and your swimming medal."

"Some comfort," I said. "I should have given him Johnny Revelation's ruby rhinestone. He thought it was the living blood of Jesus. I should have given it to him."

"Or a snort of Zero Cider," cracked Spencer, who had wedged open the glass facing of the compass. He was fanning his antennae with the palm of his hand. "And please, kind mariner—upon launching into our atmospheric dimension—permit me a puff of your unruffled cabin air to refresh my tubes. Tho' my breathing apparatus is primitive, it, like old Cosmosis, is shorn of superfluous parts and is built to last forever. Remember, I am not the least of your oxygen sucking creatures and certainly not one of your Oxy-morons! Hahaaaaa," Spencer chuckled at his ill-timed wit.

"This is no time for your foolishness," I scolded. "And I would as soon you not speak to me *now*—" cutting my words short and indicating Jo Anne's presence.

"I'm afraid," he said, "you have little choice in such matters. Unfortunately my voice is programmed for you alone, and my size allows me to hide behind your most common objects or stand concealed in their deceptive shadows."

I knew instinctively that this was true. But now that Jo Anne was in such close proximity and had grown into such charming intimacy with me, I feared she might intercept my private introspections with the ant. But as Spencer had already warned, if I were to seriously attempt to actualize even our most casual exchanges I would immediately be declared insane.

"Abolish the thought," Spencer said. "Such is not to be. You alone are on my wave-length, and any translation you might pass to your precious partner or the noble Admiral would be garbled and mean no more than the incoherent squeaking of a cabbage to a marigold or the croaking of a Grumps to the harmonious and indestructible soul of your mother."

Jo Anne was putting Zack's letter back into its envelope.

"But Jo Anne," Spencer continued, "your pretty princess of the Likenesses"—he nodded to me his approval—"*she* is the stuff that queens are made of."

"Queens?" I asked.

"I know a great deal about queens," the ant said.

20

The Introscopic Voyage

I AM RETURNING Jo Anne's kiss when the lights flicker in the wheel house. "Have we been here before?" Jo Anne whispers.

I can feel the warm moisture of her words *been here before* on my lips.

Already the shattered waves of the Gulf are coming in upon The Ark. The overhead light dims. Outside a premature darkness begins.

Except for Spencer I would not know of the sliding door that leads down a steep staircase into the ballroom of The Ark. When I reveal the opening, Jo Anne is impatient to investigate and takes my hand. The lightbulb overhead dies. Immediately the auxiliary electrical system kicks in. The bulb above revives, and the lights below go ablaze across the empty ballroom. The evangelist had neglected nothing for his safety and comfort.

Before I can restrain Jo Anne, she is down the stairs and into Johnny's holy shrine. Spencer is complaining from the compass well.

"Will you permit this ungainly goose to founder in the deep while you flitter after your pretty pleasure?"

In summers past I had maneuvered Claude's shrimper in

weather fair and foul. A hurricane will be a different matter, and I will tolerate no abrasions now from the garrulous land ant. I cannot tell if The Ark is leaning off keel or if I am losing my equilibrium. Fearing that dangerous waves are slicing in under us, I take the wheel and spin a hard left rudder.

"Hold fast!" I command.

The Ark is creaking in all her innermost joints. If angry water is under us, I have no choice but to man the wheel and steer clear the dunes, for if the craft collides and snaps, Jo Anne will be the first to catch the blast. I hold a hard left rudder.

"Ho now! Oh for the steady steering of an old mariner!" Spencer responds.

"Steady as she goes!" I call out, remembering an old movie about Captain Ahab.

"Ho! Ho!" Spencer calls back, teetering on my comb top. "The greenest swabby that ever walked a deck knows to hit a storm head on, lest we . . . whoops—" Spencer is going over backwards, until I put a finger behind him "—lest we capsize," he finishes.

"Afraid?" I ask the embarrassed ant.

"Roaring Neptune no! Fearful sailors sink. I float very well, thank you."

But the ant looks a little woozy, and I'm not sure he knows much more about navigation than his old Ulysses.

I hold a hard left rudder so we can cut a circle and not be blown out to sea.

"Pure Grump's logic," Spencer says, referring to my old frog's circular navigation.

"Grumps never got lost," I defend.

"Got lost just once, and splat!" Spencer corrects.

How do you 'head' into a storm that's going round and round? I think to myself.

"Ho! Still hold fast a hard left rudder and slip clockwise into the big wind," Spencer says with confidence.

"But we'll just be going around in what's going around?" I say.

"Absolutely," Spencer cries out above the battering storm. "And so it's impossible to get lost because we will always know exactly what we're lost in and exactly where we're lost at."

I can't tell if I'm getting dizzy from Spencer's physics or from the weaving motion of The Ark.

Jo Anne . . . Jo Anne . . . her name arises spontaneously as something tangible and fundamental in my mind.

Even today at the sacrifice of all my knowledge and collective soul, I can find no way to say *love* with complete confidence or to utter aloud the power of a single kiss. To even suggest a likeness would be a vanity and an abomination. With the storm now around me, with Jo Anne's breath and the touch of her lips upon me, my desire was to plunge forever into the swirling fray with all my life and be swept up into a soaring action beyond all expression and conclusions.

"Jo Anne!" I call out aloud.

"My, my," Spencer opines. "Such sweet, sweet ecstasy. But, I fear, without such delightful intercessions you should run amuck among your frail reckonings and all your brainy books."

Through the fingers of the banister below decks, I can still see Jo Anne standing by Johnny's glass furniture in the ballroom. This is where from Nola Rose's hand I had sipped the Zero Cider. Above was the skyhatch where I had floated free of The Ark and toward the Rainbow Carnival where Zip and I had catapulted through the canvas tent top. In muffled sound from the stage below arises an echo of Johnny Revelation's voice—

No other gods
No other gods to see
All lie dead
  But me, but me . . .

And yet I know that however awesome a hurricane, its duration is brief and I must last it out while it lives.

"There you go again, skating around on slippery time," Spencer said. "Your thoughtful grandfather with all his smart rocks should have provided another horse on the Old Fort clock for you to ride."

I hold up the palm of my hand toward Spencer which says *hush*.

I lock the helm at hard left rudder and go to the sliding door. I call Jo Anne's name again. But for the whistling of the wind outside she can not hear.

"Look," Spencer is saying.

He had climbed to the top of the comb ladder and is walking across the binnacle. He is carrying on his shoulder the injured needle from the compass. He stops and points the arrow up at the many windows of the pilot house.

"See," Spencer indicates, standing tip-toe and stretching to his full height.

I look up.

Spencer is pointing the arrow toward a certain window pane with a lavender glow around its perimeter. An intensification of the light pulls me in closer. When I wipe the condensation from the glass, I can see through the curling mist outside: There is the famous Inn Lafayette where long ago my hermit uncle had his fateful fight with the Mobile sailor and where, lately, I participated in the last sad act of Spencer's play. The double doors of the old tavern are blown open, but the place itself is standing firm against the mounting storm. There is little doubt in my mind that The

Ark has washed clear of the sand dunes and is on the move.

"Ahoy there mate!" Spencer calls from the helm box. His voice tinkles out in such a toy, unnautical manner, so artificial, that I have to smile. There is something so absolutely preposterous about my situation that I feel as if I am viewing myself through the wrong end of a telescope. And yet the novelty of the occasion sweeps me back—to summers before—into a keen appreciation of Spencer's admonition: "If you see only what you're looking at you're half blind."

"Yes, yes," Spencer says, "now you're getting the gist of it."

"None of your tricks," I remind him.

"Tricks? Moon juice! You are merely seeing *through* the shifting mist, which is quite an accomplishment for your lunar eyes. What do you expect of yourself, of me?!—to roll up your disgraced God in a slender tissue so you can smoke his divinity, breathe his divine essence into your feeble brain? Now *that* would be a 'trick' which, I might add, I would not perform upon even one of your lowest Homo Sovereigns. Now, look again—" Spencer advises.

The ant is pointing starboard to another pane in the pilot house. I can tell by his attitude that he is in an instructional mood and I am about to be informed. Such was a familiar posture at the academy with my instructors, especially our exacting Commandant when he carried his riding crop and slapped it nervously upon his thigh to extract quick answers from cadets.

"Are you paying attention?" Spencer prompts.

My desire to be with Jo Anne, to feel her breathing, is throbbing in my chest; but Spencer's intensity with the compass needle carries my eye to a lighted pane where—in the silent storm—there appears the old Confederate fort sunk in its bed of dunes. And there, upon the face of The Admiral's gigantic clock, are the noble Lee and the relentless Grant, still astride their mounts and in hot pursuit; but in the muted gale their steeds have halted—stopped at 4:30—in a gentle canter.

—*That's two hours ago,* I think.

"They should have run faster," Spencer says of the bronze war horses.

"Don't be silly," I say.

"At least your scholarly General Lee stopped when he was ahead," Spencer says. The ant is playing with words again and puts on a sardonic grin.

I check the chain lock on the wheel and go to the sliding door where I can see Jo Anne through the banister. She is standing below by the glass tables. She has one arm outstretched as if testing the validity of the transparent furniture.

"Jo Anne!" I call.

But in the engulfing sound around us, my voice is absorbed in the vastness of the ballroom.

"I can assure you," says Spencer, "That your little princess is going nowhere now, which is to say exactly nothing about nothing. I can know nothing about *nowhere.* Absolutely Nothing! But," Spencer affirms, "I know a great deal about *now here.*"

"I suppose you do," I say, stooping again to make sure of Jo Anne. Her arm is outstretched. She has not moved. And, yes, enclosed in the ribcage of The Ark, she is indeed going nowhere and could only be *now here* exactly where she is.

Then it hits me like a hammer: Gloria! Claude! The Admiral! Jo Anne is their heart of hearts. She is Gloria's finest work of art, Claude's little pet, The Admiral's pearl, and Hurricane's artist of the Isle. Should anything happen to Jo Anne I will be the scourge of the island, buzzard bait, the slime of snails. I can imagine white-hot rage emanating from Gloria, though not from Claude, a gentleness which curiously causes me a deeper pain; for Claude has never so much as raised his voice against me. And The Admiral: He has always taken my side, covered my small tracks with his great ones, taken me into his assuring confidence, cried aloud over his crackling wireless, "Great God Almighty, boy, the world is sinking up to its ass in the bogs of stupidity. We're trapped, trapped in the ever-spreading web roads . . ."

"Magnificent!" responds Spencer holding the compass needle aloft. "Such wholesome words cheer my trampled soul. The old salt yet knows his stones, knows that his rock lighthouse—composed with diligence—can yet suffer the slings and arrows of outrageous fortune, even seas and seas of troubles."

I did not know at the time that Spencer was borrowing words from our great dramatic bard. But on he goes—

"Fear not, but now, briefly," he says, "for your comfort hear this: The Admiral thinks his pretty Pearl is safe within the sturdy Merrimac with Claude and Gloria, and Claude and Gloria think their pretty genius is safe with The Admiral in his rock-bound lighthouse. Now patience!" Spencer cautions, "and look—" he says, pointing at two incandescent panes in the pilot house.

In the first frame Gloria is sitting nervously in the lamplight under her mural of Peter the Bible fisherman being lifted by his Master from the Sea of Galilee. The flickering light from the kerosene lamp makes the startled apostle come alive. By another lantern in my upper room, Claude is fidgeting with my ham radio, trying without power to activate the dead machine.

In the second frame is the lighthouse. The Admiral is placing his lantern in the crown of the old tower. "Notice," Spencer says, "how trim he has set the wick to alert his darling in the sea, for it is she alone who knows his light and slumbers with him in the endless night."

With another lantern in hand The Admiral is descending the spiral staircase to the ground floor where he goes to one knee, studying his rock garden. Moving first one stone and then another—

"He is going to make a final selection," Spencer says.

"Yes," I say. But I do not understand Spencer's troubling word *final.*

"Look," Spencer says, "He is picking up—"

"It's the Great Quartz!" I say.

"Of course," Spencer says. "His most solid thought."

"His favorite rock," I say. "It stands for a single grain of sand."

"I know," Spencer says admiringly. "Just gaze upon it! What form! What grace! How majestic! A stalagmite of the gods!!—the last word of all stones, if you can glean its meaning."

"I suppose so," I say.

Spencer looks directly at me. "It means the origin of *everything! Everything*!" he cries. "I know a great deal about origins."

"I suppose you do," I say.

The Admiral is fading out of sight, and I fear I am losing my grandfather.

"He has gone into the stone annex of the lighthouse where he keeps the Emerald Rolls," Spencer says.

"The Rolls? For what?" I ask.

Spencer casts his gaze as if into the far beyond.

"Perhaps to roll—to roll—on and on to touch again his love before he leaves. Have you so soon forgotten?" Spencer says, raising the compass needle overhead as if in triumph.

. . . *before he leaves,* I wonder.

A STORMY JOLT rocks The Ark, almost knocking Spencer off the helm box. I fall to my knees. Jo Anne is safe. I can still see her outstretched arm below. I am convinced that the tough oak hull of The Ark—regardless of the hollow and departed Johnny—is as sturdy as the *Golden Hind* that sailed the fiery Sir Frances Drake around the world.

Quickly taking hold of the wheel again I can feel an undertow and a forward tug of the Gulf. All my energies rush together into the filament of my brain—*Jo Anne*!

Spencer has moved to the edge of the bulkhead. Without effort I can perceive his strategy for catching and holding my attention: He is inviting me into his prodigious memory. The ant knows me well by now, knows my eagerness to pursue whatever mysteries pass my way. But I, too, have grown wise to the ways of the cagey ant. In his intriguing presence I know to catch myself before being conjured out of sight, beyond my powers of return. Following his familiar eye, I can already anticipate our next move . . .

I'm about to snatch away the compass arrow and do my own pointing, but Spencer aims it swiftly at a far window in the pilot house—a pane I can immediately see through with uncommon clarity. It is Veronica's WHY NOT SHOP? The ? mark and the S-H-O-P letters are blown away, leaving WHY NOT trembling in the wind. The storm is coming on with furious accumulation. Weather prophets have predicted winds of over 120 miles an hour. The coastal palms are bending into the horizontal. The funny What-a-Queer-Bird-is-the-Pelican sign sails by. The basement windows of the WHY NOT SHOP? are smashed open. My uncle's basement is flooded. Bent forward, Uncle Minos is ascending the stairs. His wet clothes adhere to his round shoulders and suck up to his withered leg. With one arm he holds to his chest Venoria's portrait. Venoria is descending the stairs. She is taking hold of his other arm, both ascending the stairs, carefully, until they stand together atop the flight. In the gray light their eyes slowly meet, in between them the painted Venoria standing before the tempestuous waves.

I am astonished. Minos has been so long in isolation I can scarcely believe anything would bring him out. "It's Jo Anne's painting!" I shout. "Her picture has done it!"

"Her art?" Spencer muses. "Perhaps, but might not the storm have played a part?"

I am about to seize the compass arrow to suspend the scene so I might speak to my fractured Uncle Minos; but Spencer flicks the pointer to another pane which reveals the cemetery: There is the quadrangle memorial cross for my grandmother, and there is a funeral tent. In the shadow of the concrete angel Woody is smoking a cigarette. I am sitting under the service tent in front of a mound of earth that now marks my mother's grave. With his back to me and facing Mother's mound of earth, Millsap stands speechless with the Bible hanging downward in his hand. To my right at the leading edge of the tent sits the familiar stranger gazing out upon the silent white caps. Spencer is right. Time is not only slippery; it is a see-saw bobbing on the sea. The Gulf is calm. The morning light rests leisurely upon the water. From behind me there is a soft crunching on the artificial tent grass. It is Jo Anne. She is wearing the same dark green dress she wore at my mother's funeral. She is coming forward, hesitantly, to greet the stranger. Perhaps to alert him? To interrogate him? She stops. I am sure from the stranger's expression that he is aware of her presence. He tilts his head toward her attentively. From my view against the Gulf the stranger is in clear profile. Even with his wire rim glasses and graying hair, I can see in him a striking resemblance to myself. I want to follow Jo Anne to get a closer look at the man, but my chair holds me like a magnet. Jo Anne makes a dainty tip-toe semicircle behind the stranger as if to catch him unaware. Then, surprisingly, she bows discreetly and very tenderly caresses the curvature of the stranger's ear. I reach back to touch the dimple in my own ear where Jo Anne's fingers are. The stranger is not alarmed nor does he move his head. Then Jo Anne whispers to him politely as if to confirm a secret. He smiles in acknowledgement, never looking up to see her face, and Jo Anne tip-toes back into the stillness behind me. Woody drops his smoldering cigarette in the grass and walks away. I try to stand but cannot.

"Of course you can't," Spencer says. "You can sit and you can stand. But you can't do both at once, at least not with your geometric brain, which is no fault of yours."

The sound of the storm has intensified.

Spencer is still standing on the boxed bulkhead but now has slung about his shoulders a thin gray shawl that makes him look like a little Moses on the mountain.

While the ant is in his introscopic mood, I wish mightily to get a glimpse of—maybe a private word with—the Reverend Millsap, our island pastor who has compounded my illegitimacy, confused my origins, and lurked among my dreams.

Thunder jars The Ark. Spencer turns starboard, holding forth the magnetic needle like a divining rod.

"I know a great deal about magnetism in the Earth," he says.

"What did Jo Anne say to the stranger?" I want to know.

"Well now," Spencer says, "shan't you have to discover that for yourself?"

Getting to my knees and keeping one hand on the wheel, I can see Jo Anne in the ballroom below. She is still standing, as if transfixed, by the glass tables.

"Jo Anne!" I call.

"She is quite all right and quite, quite *now here*," Spencer expostulates.

"Enough! Quite, quite enough!" I send back, enunciating Spencer's fastidious diction.

"Ha, ha, haaaaa. Ahoy there!" Spencer laughs with hearty companionship, flinging his hoary scarf around about his neck, then turning gravely upon me. "Quickly, quickly—" he says.

With the compass arrow he indicates a glossy pane to the fore of the pilot house. I lean forward toward the glass, wherethrough I can see very clearly the leviathan sanctuary, the Church of the Holy Sepucher.

The force of the storm is sounding in the jaw-doors of the architectural fish, making a weirdsome moan deep into the vestibule of the church. I am surprised that the bulk of such a huge mass has not been moved or shifted by the fierce gales, but I well know that the structure of the ancient mammal was designed for currents and densities deeper than my own.

"Precisely, precisely," Spencer says. "Now," he continues, "we must be exquisitely tuned for this—in perfect pitch."

"Pitch?" I question.

"Yes, in perfect spontaneous internal harmonious synchronization."

I look at the ant.

"Riding on the same sound track," Spencer simplifies.

"I see," I say.

"It is not your eyes we need now but your ears. Think of your lovely mother's voice. Can you hear her voice?"

"I think so," I say.

The hurricane has encompassed the whale church with an airy but yet very physical sound.

"Are you listening with me?" Spencer asks as we enter the sanctuary.

"I'm trying," I say.

The auditorium, pew by empty pew, is vacant save for the Reverend Millsap. He is kneeling in candlelight before the altar.

He is praying for his own wretched self, I think.

"At least he's not a deserter," Spencer says.

"He wished my mother dead, dead because of me!" I say bitterly.

"You are not listening," Spencer says.

"I can't hear him," I say. "He's just moving his lips."

"You are listening for the wrong thing," Spencer says. "You have got to hear what he is *saying.*"

I'm getting nervous in the presence of the mumbling Millsap, in the midst of such pious hypocrisy, but mainly anxious for Jo Anne. I want to be perilously close to her. I am about to cut out of this weird scene altogether when—

"Please God—!" Millsap cries out.

"Can you hear that?" Spencer asks.

"Yes," I say.

"Now listen up," Spencer says.

Millsap is praying so fervently that the veins in his neck swell out. But I can hear nothing except his sputtering.

"What's he saying?" I ask.

Spencer is peeved at my incapacity and swiftly points the compass arrow to the pastor's heart. "Any translation from his bosom here," Spencer says, "will be sorely inadequate, especially in your language."

"Good Lord!" I say. "This is no time for fiddling around."

"Well—" Spencer hesitates, falters.

For the first time I feel the ant's equal.

"Come on!" I urge. "I need to know Millsap's heart."

I think of my mother's body lying crumpled among the desert prickly pears. I think of Jo Anne standing immobile, vulnerable, by the glass tables in Johnny's ballroom, in the rumbling belly of The Ark.

"The Reverend is—" Spencer begins.

"Hurry!" I sound off. "Time is running out."

"The Reverend is asking—" Spencer begins again.

"Yes," I encourage.

"—is asking for . . ." Spencer points the arrow to me. "—for *your* forgiveness."

"*My* forgiveness?" I hear my voice wander through the sanctuary. The altar candles waver.

A fear seizes me.

Oh my God! I think, *Millsap is my* . . .

"No, no, no," Spencer intercedes with stern conviction. "You are jumping to conclusions. Millsap is *not* your father! How could you have missed so obvious a revelation?"

To the rear of the sanctuary a burst of lightning ignites the stained glass window. Millsap lifts up his thin face. Tears fall down his cheeks. In profile his sharp countenance protrudes like a hatchet in the candle light.

Spencer turns and holds the compass needle outstretched into the nervous light.

"I have," Spencer says with considerable gravity, "often received profound signals from monks, mystics, alchemists, and courageous soldiers of the cross. I confess I feel a kindred spirit with your lonesome Reverend of the Holy Sepulcher. In such souls there resides still the original stuff of our old creation, the hidden sinews and fires that flex our minds and proclaim our affinity with the stars. But, my Jody dear, you have judged this man too harshly," Spencer says with a tinge of pity. "Although his gawky form and bland affection forbade him union with your mother, how could he not have fallen in love with her lovely voice which, alas, launched his heart into sublime despair? I know a great deal about despair," the ant says.

I am as much relieved as I am shaken by Spencer's disclosure. It is immediately clear to me why Millsap wanted to "pray" with me at Mother's funeral. He didn't want to pray; he wanted to make a confession to me.

"Yes, yes. Excellent well!" Spencer exclaims. "The shattered parson has accepted you for the innocent bastard you are. Don't you see?"

I am stunned.

"The Reverend," Spencer says, "is at this moment beseeching his heavenly father to forgive him for corrupting so rare a love for your mother, for turning such a tempered passion into smoldering hate. Can you blame him? But, Jody, you will not listen to him. You will not give him audience. So who else does he have to talk to?"

"I—I see," I mumble

"Well," Spencer muses, "that remains to be *seen*. But we are not here to *see*. We are here to *hear*. Are you listening?"

"Yes," I say, beginning to tremble.

The storm outside is pounding hard upon the leviathan sanctuary. Millsap arises slowly, crosses himself, picks up a lighted candle. He proceeds down the aisle towards me. Spencer is right. Millsap is not a deserter. Of his parish, he alone has faced the hurricane. I try to catch the minister's eye as he passes, but he holds a steady gaze across the candle in his hand, letting fall upon me his lengthening shadow.

"Did you hear what the Reverend *said*?" the ant inquires of me.

I had heard but had not the courage to answer.

21

The Admiral's Solution

While I was absorbing my encounter with the Reverend Millsap, Spencer had returned to the compass well and was trying to reset the magnetic needle.

Then a quick reflection—a flash of my frail grandfather in the old tower, lighting his lantern, perhaps for the last time—burst into my mind with such force that I held to the wheel for support. In the same instant there was a rapid clatter of footsteps ascending the steel stairs from the ballroom below. When I turned around it was Jo Anne. She grabbed my hand, her expression one of surprise and alarm. I read her face instantly.

"The Admiral!" we exclaimed in one voice.

"Their reunion," Jo Anne said. "He's gone out to meet her in the hurricane."

I knew that was true.

"The lantern! It's for her," she said.

She was talking about my lost grandmother. Yes, The Admiral would do this. Jo Anne put my arms around her waist and rested her cheek on my heart. I kissed her hair.

"I'm going out for The Admiral," I said.

"I know. Was she beautiful?" Jo Anne asked.

I didn't know. "Yes," I said. I kissed the curve of her ear.

"We've got to go get him. Now!"

Here was *time* again. I wanted to hold Jo Anne still—precisely right now, inside this moment—to feel her heart and to . . .

There was an audible lift, an ebbing of the storm. Jo Anne put a finger to my lips, listening . . .

"It's the eye," I said. "We're coming into the eye of the hurricane." I kissed her finger.

"How long does an eye last?" she wanted to know.

"Depends on how fast the hurricane travels. Hurricanes slow down when they hit land," I said.

"Do they ever blink—I mean close up on you, suck you up like a giant squid?" she asked.

"No," I said. "They just finally die. But the wind spins faster on the inside of the eye. It can blow out your backbone."

"Hurry," she said. She tossed her scarf over her head, tied it tight around her cheeks; and we stepped outside the pilot house into a dull twilight.

The eye was opening.

A calm was coming on. A haze was lifting from the island. The mainway cottages and shops along the waterfront lay astonished in awkward tilts and tumbles crossed with leaning light poles in a spaghetti of wires and cables, crinkled billboards and open fissures—the whole coastline knocked silly into a long, snaggle-toothed smile. The lighthouse was visible—surprisingly near—with its bead of lantern light in the crown. There was no way to tell exactly if or how far we had traveled, but The Ark was now aground, pushed up against a solid wave of sand. The gangway hung down like a broken arm to a dune below. I tested it first by taking hold of the handrail and stepping carefully backwards. Jo Anne followed. I took her by the waist and lifted her down into the dune grass. With the lighthouse in view I was getting back my bearings.

The eye was now wide open. But it would soon be dark. We were inside a furious circle of wind and rain. The sun was dropping down outside the wall around us as the eerie calm slipped in as softly as a pillow, without a soul in sight.

Where had all the seagulls gone?

Jo Anne pushed her scarf back, releasing her red hair, as if listening to the silence. Around the rim of the whirling bowl, the scarlet of the dying sun set ablaze Jo Anne's abundant hair—her lips about to speak . . . And oh my God! Her red, red abundant hair!

"I hope we're not too late," Jo Anne said.

This was of real concern. The Admiral for all his age and frailty was absolutely fearless and dedicated to such thoughts and commitments that had sustained his life. Often on afternoons he would take walks, a dune or two from the lighthouse, to meditate the sea. I knew where to look. The wind and waves had swept the coast roads smooth with packed sand except for interrupting palms that lay flat with their balled roots popped up.

"They look like dead all-day suckers," Jo Anne said.

I picked up my pace. I was practically running now in the damp sand. I did not know how long the eye would last.

"He'll be—about there," I guessed, pointing to the left of the lighthouse. The red rim of the sun was gone. Jo Anne was breathing heavily behind me.

"How do you know he's not safe in his lighthouse?" she said. She had her fingers locked under the back of my belt. I dug in harder, pulling Jo Anne along.

"I just know," I said. "He'll not allow this personal hurricane to pass without . . ."

"—without touching his love?" Jo Anne said.

Yes, this was it.

The Admiral's lantern was clearly visible in the fading daylight.

Jo Anne saw The Admiral first—a sliver of black slumped on the beach side of the north dune. I feared the worst. My eye had missed him because I had never visualized my grandfather as being *limp* or *down* but always as erect, eyes straight forward, jaw jutting out. He was wearing a long, black weather slicker, not from the mock-up Hollywood wardrobe. This was the genuine article from his own days at sea, a squeaky old sealskin cloak that he had picked up in Nova Scotia and that always hung on back of the main door in the lighthouse. Stiff with age and lifted from its nail, it would stand alone.

The Admiral was not dead. With the old coat flung open I could see the rise and fall of his feeble breathing. I could tell by the intensity and concentration of his eyes that he recognized me. His mouth was making words without sound. I could read his lips.

Jo Anne got to her knees and put her head to his chest. "It's something about *web roads*," she said.

"I know," I said, reconstructing the movement of his lips into words, "*we're sinking in the bogs of the ever-growing web roads.*"

"And look," Jo Anne said.

It was the Great Quartz. The Admiral was clutching the profound crystal in his hand, his knuckles as white and tight as stone.

"And this," I said. It was a rope tied around The Admiral's waist. I got to my knees with Jo Anne. When I snapped the rope up from the sand it pointed to the lighthouse.

"His life-line," Jo Anne said. "his way back to the lighthouse."

This was *not* it.

"No," I said. "It was to hold him *to* the storm. It was so he wouldn't get blown away from it. It was his way to get *to* something, not to get away from it." I was absolutely sure of this. I untied the rope.

Jo Anne stood up, absorbing the scene. I knew The Admiral was now becoming a picture locked in her mind's eye, awaiting her brush and her interpretive fingers. She was seeing, even now, into a larger likeness as she conveyed, ever so lightly, a smile to me.

"He's smiling," she said, pointing to the lighthouse.

So he was.

"She has seen his lantern, and he has touched his darling in the sea," Jo Anne said.

Yes, I believed that.

Now a problem: Where to go? To the lighthouse? Or back to The Ark? Jo Anne was pointing to the lighthouse, to the lantern in the crown.

"The light is for her, not for us," she said, excluding any intrusion upon so sacred a union.

With that I picked up The Admiral and started back to The Ark. Jo Anne placed his hand with the Great Quartz on his chest and took his other hand in her own.

I was surprised at the lightness of my grandfather, yet more surprised at the weight of time and distance and soul I bore in my arms. Who was this in this old seal cloak, this gray mass who had walked the streets of old Constantinople, known of Tlehhizcalpantecuhtli the House of Dawn or Youallahuanna The Image of the Precious Serpent and one who had prayed with the Dalai Lama, entered the great Pyramid of Giza and seen and heard the seals of Nova Scotia?

The wind was returning in the opposite direction. It was almost dark.

Climbing back aboard The Ark was more difficult that I had expected. With The Admiral in my arms, I was sinking into the wet sand and dune grass. I could not raise my foot high enough to mount the shattered end of the gangway. Jo Anne moved quickly. Freeing first one arm of The Admiral and then the other, she shucked off his heavy slicker and laid it out for my support. Only then, and with an assist from Jo Anne, was I able to mount the gangway and move up to the main deck. Jo Anne opened the door to the wheelhouse, and I laid The Admiral on the pilot's bed.

The evangelist's auxiliary electrical system had failed. I touched a lighted match to the emergency lamp on the wall and to the candle by the bedside. The Admiral watched the little wick climb into flame, then closed his eyes. Jo Anne put her face down to his.

"Can you hear me, Grandfather?" she said. His shirt was torn open and, to feel his breathing, Jo Anne laid her hand in the hollow of his ribs.

This was the first time I had heard Jo Anne say *grandfather* to his face.

"Yes," The Admiral said. His eyes were closed and he was still smiling.

The returning wind suddenly blurted through the door, sucked it shut with a wham. The candle flicked.

"Is he breathing?" I asked.

Jo Anne lifted The Admiral's arms and laid them respectfully across his chest.

"Jody," she whispered with suppressed alarm. "The Great Quartz—it's gone!"

Yes, The Admiral's hand that had held the stone was empty.

"It fell outside when we took his slicker off," I said.

"It was here," she said, lifting The Admiral's hand. "I know where it fell in the dune grass." Jo Anne picked a flashlight from the wall rack.

The hurricane was back in a big way.

"Hear it?" I said. "It'll blow you away." I thought of my grandmother, The Admiral's darling, swept away before I was born.

Jo Anne made a move toward the door. I grabbed her, took her by the shoulders, and shook her until her curls flopped and her eyes were misty.

"No!" I cried. "You'll be blown away!"

I had shaken up Jo Anne's blood. Her face was flushed. Her eyes widened. Her lips were trembling and, again, her red, red abundant hair . . . I had an overwhelming urge to embrace Jo Anne totally and to pull her softly all the way into myself. The hurricane was now sounding with a vengeance.

"I know where it is in the dune grass," she said of the fallen stone. She had the flashlight in her hand. I took hold of her arm.

"The Admiral wouldn't allow you to do it," I said. "It's just a rock. He's got it all inside his head now, where it counts, where it belongs." Jo Anne's eyes brimmed.

"It's yours too," she said. "You need to have it so you can *see* what it means." My fingers fit all the way around her arm like a tourniquet.

"You're hurting my arm," Jo Anne said.

"I . . . I . . ." I began. At all times before, I had simply seen Jo Anne directly; now I was courting her eyes. And now she was listening to me, giving me her eyes.

"I love . . ."

I uttered alive the fearful word for the first time. And now I was hearing it for the first time as if it were not my own voice but an echo wandering in from the hills beyond. Yes, it was happening between us. We were now seeing into each other for the first time. And, yes, as Spencer said, I was at this moment traveling a million miles an hour backwards into the future.

When Jo Anne closed her eyes the tears fell down.

"I think he's dying," Jo Anne said.

I thought of Spencer's philosophy and wondered if death *was* nothing.

"Jody! Jody! Jody!" The Admiral cried, his voice diminishing with each effort. I rushed to my grandfather and bent over him. He was staring straight up at me, seeing not through me but around me as light sweeps around a distant obstacle and unites itself in space. He was holding his fist to his mouth as if speaking into a microphone with his voice crackling across the Gulf of Mexico.

"Hey boy," he announced cheerfully, "we're sinking, sinking in the ever growing bog of the web roads . . ."

The sound of the storm barged in. When I turned around Jo Anne was stepping out the door and onto the main deck. I was lucky that she had taken the flashlight but too late to stop her. The hurricane, spinning at a furious rate, snatched her sideways and away like a paper doll and slammed her body against the bow rail, her arms reaching outward, reeling so that the flashlight, zigzagging in the haze, glazed her face—her mouth shocked open in a silent cry, her hair slashed and streaming across her brow.

Was she screaming? Bleeding?

How can I say?

It was not alone her sudden pain that moved me out into the hurricane, not just a challenge from the ravishing gale hustling upon her, nor any courage I had learned at the academy. It was anger. It was a quick rage that flared up in me at so rude a tyrant that could suddenly possess Jo Anne's pure lightness, abuse, bend her lithe body, blast her eyes, crush her chest, bruise her soft lips that I had so recently and sweetly kissed. Great God Almighty!

But I was no match for the backlash that hit me, slammed me flat to the wet deck. Was The Ark listing? My eye caught the white disk of light in Jo Anne's hand. Was it the Gulf again under us, altering gravity? I got to my hands and knees, my butt to the howling storm. Or was it the wind urging me from behind? As I tried to stand, a blast as swift as a slingshot sent me flying headlong toward the disk of light. But in the sudden sweep I was able to catch myself on the bow rail, hold there until I crumpled down upon the heap that was Jo Anne.

In the swirling rain the beam of light lay like a blade across her face. She was warm and bleeding—no sound from her; but I could feel her breathing, faintly. I got the light and moved over her, slipped my arm under her shoulder and lifted her head in my hand. Beneath her hair a torn poster read—*The Consummation of Madness*. I put the light to her face. A wet gash on her temple ran pale red in sketchy tributaries into her eyebrows. Her eyes were closed. I put my face close to hers.

"Jo Anne," I said into the sound around us. The rain made pink puddles in her eye cups.

A chill worse than winter washed over me.

The weather prophets were right. From its inner core the hurricane had hit its maximum. No wonder The Admiral had lashed himself to the lighthouse, not to escape but to hold himself to and into the fury. No man could stand alone against it. And in this cold wind, here and now to me turned torrid, I—this sapling of myself blown flat with all my leaves stripped off—could think of nothing worse than this. So *here* and *now* was I, holding Jo Anne's head above the main deck . . . her wet streaming hair, her red, red hair warm in my hand, and I could think of nothing worse . . . unless . . . unless . . .

My only traction back to the pilot house were my fingernails and warped cracks in the wet boards beneath me. But there were quirks of nature in my favor. I could crawl; and the elliptical shape of the pilot house bent the inrushing wind flush down upon the main deck so that, rather than beating me down, it pressed me up.

My shirt was ripped open. I stuffed the flashlight, beam forward, between my belly and belt buckle. With Jo Anne in the cradle of my arm I scuttled like a lame crab across the main deck. But there was a problem: With the sounding storm whipping down head high from the wheelhouse, dare I risk the wind? Stand up to open the door?

I did. I took Jo Anne in my arms, out of the gale, and laid her alongside The Admiral on the pilot's bed.

22

Between the Devil and the Deep Blue

The bed was hardly big enough for them both—so close together The Admiral and Jo Anne. And I too stunned to cry, even if my eyes would let me. Jo Anne had shed her tears. I had seen them fall upon The Admiral's chest. And for whom? Herself? The Admiral? Or for his darling in the sea?

"Jo Anne," I whispered.

Now her tears were red. Was it the blood seeping from her brow? Or was it the black rain that had beat down upon her face?

My God . . .

Her pink eyelids were still closed and I was suspended, still standing there—I could not hear the storm.

Nor hear her breathing.

"Jo Anne . . . Jo Anne . . ." I called quietly to her.

I placed her head straight back, chin up, and parted her lips with my fingers . I had never done this before. I had never seen it done. From the academy I had only the vague pages of a manual flick by in my mind: *the blank face, the diagrammed throat, the black air passages from mouth to lungs.* The small print said: *Make a tight seal.* It also said: *Look, Listen, Feel.* It said: *Breathe not hard but long, full . . .*

I put my mouth to hers—*a tight seal.*

Now—

B r e a t h e —

Pause— 2, 3, 4

B r e a t h e —

2, 3, 4

Her chest was not moving.

"Goddamnit!" I cried.

Where did the— 2, 3, 4 come from? The manual? Or from counting cadence on the drill field?

"My God!! What's the matter, the goddamnmatter!"

Her eyelids were still closed.

There was a pulse at the base of her jaw. I lifted her shoulders and shook her fiercely.

"Breathe—goddamnit—breathe!" I commanded.

Her nose—her nose!

I had forgotten to pinch her nose closed. My breath had escaped through her nose!

An emptiness fell in upon me . . . The tree that fell in the forest with nobody around . . . Did it make a sound? If nobody saw it, did it exist?

Greatgodalmighty!

Now—

Again.

B r e a t h e —

2, 3, 4

B r e a t h e.

How many times?

2, 3, 4

Her chest was moving. Was it her breath or mine?

There was lightning and a crunch that jarred The Ark, knocking me away from Jo Anne and dumping The Admiral to the floor. Another flash and I could see the main mast snapped off with its butt cocked up across the poop deck. I hurried around to The Admiral.

I could tell by the way he lay, by the angle of his leg, by his fixed jaw, that he was gone. The wall lantern blinking across Jo Anne and The Admiral's bedside candle blinking back were sending conflicting signals. I gathered up The Admiral in my arms. He was a light as air, dead, but still smiling as I laid him down again, smiling . . . with his darling in the sea . . . and Jo Anne lying there—these two together in the dueling light.

And I, too, standing there over them . . . The storm roaring back into my head—was drawn out upon a stem of thought, so thin and brittle, that I dared not breathe to think about it. For a holy moment I let my fingers rest in the cavity of The Admiral's chest.

Jo Anne—was her chest moving or was it the pulsation from the lantern on the wall? The gash on her forehead—I had seen but not thought about. The blood had chilled, thickened and stopped in little tricklets. With a wet curl I wiped her cheek and brow, careful not to open the wound, and ripped a piece of sheet to wrap her head. A pulse was in her throat.

"Jo Anne," I said.

Her chest was slowly rising, falling.

The Ark was trembling, moving. I knew not where. I stumbled to the helm. We were still locked at hard left rudder. The compass needle was missing. In the wavering shadows I made my way back to Jo Anne and took her hand.

"Now aren't we the brave one! And such poise! Such chivalry! But I fear you are more scared *of* death than *to* death."

Spencer was sitting on the crossrail of the pilot's bed, holding the compass needle at ease across his shoulder like a veteran rifleman. I had completely forgotten him. A quiver of shame ran through me, not because I had quit the wheel or forsaken the quarrelsome insect but because I knew the ant was aware of my crab-like recovery of Jo Anne on the main deck and my poor performance at mouth-to-mouth resuscitation.

"—And just to think," he said, "The same lips that you so recently and so sweetly kissed . . ."

And yet even if—as Spencer had so often affirmed—he knew *nothing* of death, it seemed incredible that he should barge in here over the last threshold of my privacy.

"Not all all," he said with perfect candor. "If I know nothing of death—now hear me plainly my little pilgrim—I plead not guilty to being oblivious to the evacuation of life. Look there." He pointed the needle to The Admiral. "See what a noble soul is departed. Life is more easily detected by its absence than by its affirmation."

"And look," he said pointing the needle to Jo Anne. "*She* is breathing."

Now I could not move my eyes from Jo Anne. Her breath was quickening, deeper now—her pink eyelids so peacefully closed . . . Was The Admiral's smile contagious? Was Jo Anne smiling too—the same smile she had painted on our staunch Venoria's portrait that I had taken down to my morose Uncle Minos? Was her smile for real? I could not tell in the flickering light, in the howling storm.

I could say nothing.

A fear seized me.

Her *pink eyelids*—so peacefully closed that they might pale and behind them her real sight recede unprotesting into the ever silent backwaters . . . *She looks like Amelia Earhart,* Jo Anne had said of my mother; after which I had closed the casket lid forever.

My fear increased.

"Jo Anne!" I held her dripping body toward me and pressed her to my chest. I put my lips close to her mouth to feel her breathing. "O love . . . love . . . I love . . . She smelled of dark sea water. From a wet curl I intercepted a pink droplet and kissed it to her cheek.

Her eyelids trembled.

"O love . . . love . . . love—Jo Anne?" I pleaded.

"Cuckoo, quite cuckooed is she now. Knocked sideways and silly, but no harm there," Spencer said, pointing the compass arrow to the bandage on her head.

I could muster no words for the ant but was encouraged by his optimism and took some assurance in his recurring presence. It was true there was no pain or fear in Jo Anne's expression, nothing sinister in her smile. It was as if in the turmoil of the storm she had turned up a new wrinkle in her game of Likenesses and was waiting for me to catch on.

"Or perhaps it pleases her to know that you're a chip off the old block"—I knew Spencer was talking about The Admiral—"and that you, hale and courageous, met the storm undaunted."

I had not taken my eyes off Jo Anne.

"Or perhaps she smiles at your enormous eyes that failed to see so obvious and most delicate a nose through which your precious breath passed more easily *out* than *in*.

"What? What?" I cried at the outrageous ant, coming to the surface of myself. "Enough of your interruptions. Why not crawl back into your little dunce-hat hill and mumble your murky words to yourself!"

"Alas not *my* words, I assure you! 'Tis your language, not mine. Are you so long in learning that your most marvelous words, however well set together, are mere shadows? Are you, brave traveler, afraid of shadows?"

I took my eyes off Jo Anne for a moment and glared at the erudite insect. "A-N-T" I spelled out in his face—"a *mere* shadow!"

"Of course, of course," he replied. "But not *I* myself. I am no *word!* This is *I*, Spencer, the very abundant evidence you behold before you. It is *I* who cast a shadow. Not my shadow *me!*"

I had learned well that, beyond a certain point, normal discourse with the ant was impossible.

"But," Spencer continued, "I must praise your attention to our grand old guard of the lighthouse and in seeing his little lantern winking out to sea—though it seems your sleeping beauty here has spied it first."

Spencer had not finished. He was holding his arrow upward in the many-paned pilot house.

"To even see the little lantern beam in this frenzied wind and upon this hustle-clutted isle is a subtle insight indeed and one that I most earnestly applaud." Spencer swelled in pride, his thorax glistening in the lamplight. "Such supreme incision to the truth summons up in me the old joy of being sprung again from my original darkness into the dawn of early light!"

I could not answer the ant. At the moment I was balanced on a rim of fear, dreading that Jo Anne might slip back deeper into her pleasant but dangerous dream or that she should wake to find The Admiral dead.

I could no longer hear the storm. Had it swallowed itself up in its own violence? Had it, too, ceased to breathe and buried itself at sea?

"Jo Anne," I said.

She was opening her eyes.

"Jo Anne." With my hands I held her face towards mine.

Still quite out of it, she was seeing through me, opaquely, searching out my boundaries . . . now closing in. I could tell I was coming into her view, more clearly now as one draws a microscope into focus.

"Jody?" she said as if I had appeared unexpectedly in her private dream.

"I thank you. Thank you verily, verily," I said.

We were breathing together again.

I kissed the little scar of red on her bandage.

Her smile broadened. She traced the curvature of my ear with her fingers and stopped when she found the little dimple in my flesh.

"You're the stranger at the funeral," she disclosed to my great amazement.

"The stranger?" I did not understand.

Spencer was nodding his head in accord.

"Yes," she said, "the man with the wire-rimmed glasses and the graying hair."

Spencer was smiling too, inclining his arrow toward me.

"I'm Jody," I said incredulously, "just plain me, Jody!"

"You still *are*," she said. "Isn't it fantastic." She wiggled her fingertip in the little dimple on my ear. "—same as the stranger's, a perfect Likeness!" she said, rising on one elbow.

Was I losing my equilibrium again? And yet only moments ago I—through a glassy pane, a haze of storm—had seen her very fingers feel the stranger's ear.

Spencer was peering down sagaciously on me as if it mattered not a gnat how old the graveyard stranger was—a man certainly not less than thirty years my senior. And yet in profile at my mother's funeral his face, as if cast from mine, seemed very like the shadow of my own—as in a family album when you catch a certain glint of eye, a cut of jaw, a turn of lip or, in all, a sudden and unmistakable attitude and inclination of yourself.

Immediately I thought of Spencer's anachronistic metaphysics, his wild admonition that I was flying backwards into the future.

"And why," Spencer asked from above, "should I not, with my ineffable cosmic extensions, glimpse the future if you with your colossal brain can salvage only the dregs of yesterday?"

With Jo Anne's uneasy sanity lapping around me and the ant's esoteric logic eroding my common sense, I thought out loud—

"I can't *see* tomorrow or *around* corners!" I grasped Jo Anne's hand for reassurance of my present existence.

"Ha!" Spencer said, "nor can you see but one side of a tree—unless you walk around it. And that takes t-i-m-e *time*. But I assure you the other side of the tree is there."

"He's old enough to be my father," I said of the graveyard stranger.

"But he is *not* your father. Your father is dead, exhausted in the jungles of a foreign land. Enough of this! The stranger is you and you are he. Do you not know that time runs through and wraps around a tree?"

Jo Anne was watching me wistfully. She still had her fingertip in the little dimple of my ear.

"A perfect Likeness," Jo Anne said with finality.

"Ah yes, yes," Spencer continued, "we all at times tread with the great bard in our petty pace: tomorrow, tomorrow, and tomorrow—that sunny untilled vale into which we drag our brave new shadows of today. I know a great deal about shadows," the ant said.

"Are you talking to yourself?" Jo Anne asked, her eyes filled with wonder.

"Maybe so," I said. "Does your head hurt?"

She put her palm to my cheek. "You're bleeding," she said.

I did not say whose blood it was.

"It's nothing," I said.

"The Ark . . ." she said. "We were going to The Ark . . ."

"Yes," I said.

"To get there before . . ."

"Before the hurricane," I assisted.

"Johnny . . . Johnny Revelation . . ."

Jo Anne was coming around.

"The copter . . . it's lifting off . . . away . . ."

"Yes," I said.

"Johnny! He's leaving with his Nola Rose! They're not going to perform the *Consummation of Madness*!"

"That's right," I encouraged.

"O Damnit! Damnit!" she scolded.

It was all coming back to her now.

"The pilothouse, the wheel—" she exclaimed.

"Yes," I said.

She paused and observed me thoughtfully. She touched her fingertips to my lips.

"Kissing," she said. "We were kissing."

"I know," I said. "You let it start happening. I can feel it happening now between us."

"Yes," she said and closed her eyes.

I put my lips to hers. "Is it still happening?" I asked.

"Yes," she whispered.

The storm was rushing back into my mind, rocking The Ark. I stood up. Jo Anne had discovered the cloth around her brow. I stopped her hand before she could remove it. She was thinking . . .

"The lighthouse! . . . the lantern! . . ." Jo Anne recalled—

Then in quick succession—

"The Great Quartz!" she said.

"The Admiral!" she said.

It was all coming back to her.

Spencer had disappeared from the crossrail of the bed.

Without moving her eyes from me, Jo Anne took The Admiral's hand. She was looking at me but seeing The Admiral beside her. I fixed The Admiral's shirt collar neatly to his chin and straightened his face forward on the pillow.

"Is he still smiling?" she asked.

He was.

"Yes," I said. I took Jo Anne's other hand.

A calm satisfaction spread across Jo Anne's face and a softness appeared in her eyes. It was, as she had often said, like seeing into the inside of a picture before it is finished, seeing not the light on it but the light coming out of it, spreading into a broadness beyond all frame.

"His hand is cold," she said.

"I know," I said.

Lightly a smile touched the corners of her lips. A chill passed from her hand to mine. I smiled too at the hugeness of it all compacted into this little cockpit of time.

So while the storm wore on, we watched The Admiral's bedside candle quietly settle down into its tallow skirt and flicker out.

23

The Calm

In the early morning, from the pilothouse The Admiral's lantern was invisible. The compass arrow had been returned and reset and was trembling on its pivot. Except for the injured gangway and splintered main mast The Ark was whole and, as far as I could tell, still anchored in its original sand. Jo Anne had removed the bandage from her forehead. Surprisingly I could barely detect the faint pink line where the cut had been. When I threw open the pilot's hatch the sun in its old habit was riding lightly on a peaceful Gulf.

Jo Anne, remembering the Great Quartz, tripped carefully down the dangling gangway and onto the sand in search of the stone. That she could find the transparent rock at all—a clear symbolic grain of sand!—upon the tattered dune and among the coastal grass was a miracle. She stood in the hatchway examining the stone.

But The Admiral was dead, and there fell upon me an absurd problem: I did not know exactly *how* I should pick him up. This was no problem when he lay stricken on the beach or when the jolt of the main mast flung him from bed to deck. Nor did my reluctance stem from any fear or superstition of the dead. I never regarded myself as pious, but now there was something holy here, something abiding in the way my grandfather lay, something unmoving in this shuffling of events, something untouchable, fixed at the fulcrum, something sure in the never ending flux of time . . .

"The White Silence," came Spencer's muffled voice, "—a well-wrought phrase from your lusty Jack London of the great north woods." I had ceased to ponder the ant's spontaneous occurrence or his random connections. "Only once on the great Sahara have I faced the danger of such vast loneliness," Spencer continued, "and yet from the steeple of such protracted emptiness there are still the bright stars that we have always known."

So then how was I with my mere bare hands to alter The Admiral now, to even bend his knee or tilt his head and so to rend this sacred silence? Dare I brashly pick him up and crack this ancient solitude in my unpracticed arms?

"For my sake," Spencer said, his voice trailing off, "dare not lose The Admiral's stone . . ."

"Jody," Jo Anne called from the hatchway. She was holding the crystal rock up to the sun.

And so we left The Ark and walked together across the dunes, Jo Anne with the Great Quartz and I carrying my frail grandfather in my arms like a windless bagpipe.

"Old bagpipes never die," Spencer's voice sifted up to me. The ant was much amused at his bagpipe allusion, and I could hear him chuckling around in The Admiral's garments. "They only fa-a-a-de away," he concluded with a dramatic flourish. I knew he was referring to our flamboyant General Douglas MacArthur.

Beyond the boardwalk I could see the van.

The immediate shock of what lay before me was not so much the destruction that the hurricane left as the sullen quietness it dropped upon the whole island, as if the big wind had spoken the last word, allowing nothing more to be said and leaving glum denizens quietly groping around among bent tin, torn doors, and tumbled bedsprings.

More miraculous than finding the Great Quartz was the survival of the van.

The Admiral was stiffening. His arm hanging by my side had lost its easy sway and moved inflexibly like a pendulum from the socket of his shoulder.

I put my thumbs in his arm pits and set him on the back seat, closing his shirt and spreading the collars so that they matched his bristling eyebrows and flaring mustache. To my surprise his body was malleable like soft clay or like a gaunt mannequin with yielding wires set deep inside so that I could fix his limbs in lifelike posture. And so, with the back seatbelt, I fixed him upright, and Jo Anne put the Great Quartz in his lap.

"He's still smiling," Jo Anne said.

Miracle upon miracle, the van started, though it was no easy route through the tangled debris to the Merrimac. I had no doubt that such a sturdy structure as The Admiral had conceived had shielded Claude and Gloria from the storm. But if the hurricane had spoken the last word, my Aunt Gloria had not heard it.

"Mother is going to be furious," Jo Anne reminded me.

Which was no poor prophecy.

Gloria spied us at the turn-in and met me with a verbal tornado of her own. She did not ask us where we had been but put her anger in direct assault.

"You'd squeeze blood from the palms of Jesus just to indulge yourself," she wailed at me. Her eyes were red from crying. Claude had opened the rear door and was looking at his dead father. Zip hopped in.

"Who under God's glorious sun do you think you are?" Gloria fired into me again.

Frankly—at that moment or even today—I'm not sure I could answer such a question, though I know in fact that, like the stranger at the funeral, I indeed do now have graying hair and I do now wear wire-rim glasses.

Could Jo Anne be right? I wondered.

Gloria touched her finger to the pink seam on Jo Anne's forehead and drew her breath for another blast at me—

"The Admiral's dead," Claude said.

Gloria retreated and put a hand to her breast.

"He went out to meet the hurricane and we brought him in," Jo Anne said.

"He lit his lantern for her," Claude said of his departed mother. The Admiral's smile had frozen. Zip was sitting beside my grandfather on the back seat.

"He was smiling when he died," I said.

There was a collective silence.

"Poor soul," Gloria softened. "He was a forgetful old sailor in love with the impossible."

They all walked away a distance, leaving The Admiral to Zip and me.

The impossible I wondered. *Had not Jo Anne and I just arrived from the impossible? Had I not already been there and, like an orphaned meteorite, crashed through some nebulous membrane to find myself exactly where I am?*

"Ha! Just perhaps!" arose the ant's familiar voice, "but a bit flaky and scorched in your descent, yet retaining a hopeful trace of density—enough to be weighed but not of a refinement to be desired."

Spencer was huddled under the rear shank of the Great Quartz on The Admiral's lap. So small and withdrawn was he in the sunlight that I, for a fleeting second, felt sorry for the precocious insect—not that he would tolerate my sentiments! Nor could I help but recall the pitiful hermit crab, arrived in darkness, that the infuriated Spencer with his hat-pin rapier had driven from my bed and out into uncertain space. Yet here was my familiar Spencer crouched under his adopted stone—a mere symbolic grain of sand—but by mischance large enough at any time to crush him and spill his rare juices on the sidewalks of our world. In spite of myself I could not stop a teardrop from my eye.

"Enough! Enough of this mushy swillistic sentimentality!" Spencer complained. "The Admiral! The Admiral!" he implored.

I had almost forgotten . . . *The cremation*, I remembered.

Yes. The Admiral had said to me, "See to my conclusion and with your own eyes *see* my ashes sown in the Gulf of Mexico."

It is amazing and yet bewildering now to recall my last days on Hurricane: how quickly nature rejoins herself—mends, blends, coheres again as if millions of nimble fingers were busy underneath the ruins knitting without reason or remorse to revive what she had so generously destroyed.

The seagulls had returned on their easy wings.

Without budge or bobble the shore-bound Merrimac had borne the storm. Inn Lafayette survived. Uncle Claude described to me in mournful detail how Zip had howled the night away, not *at* the storm but *with* the storm. The irreverent winds had forced the Church of the Holy Sepulcher to swallow both its entrance doors, but the hydrodynamics of the ancient fish had safely shaped the fatal gale around it. At the old fort Generals Lee and Grant were riding time again. Claude's shrimper was bashed around but still afloat. The stormy waters had driven my reclusive uncle from his vault below and back into the company of his long suffering

Venoria. After twenty years, they had at last seen each other. I wondered if they had kissed. And as I had clearly seen through the pane in the pilothouse, the big wooden letters S H O P and the ? mark were blown from Venoria's quaint place of shells, leaving the doubtful WHY NOT as sole identification.

No matter to me now that the lighthouse would, by decree, become property of the state; for the old tower and The Admiral himself had become immortal in my mind. The tropical property of our estate leased by Hollywood was torn and twisted, but the facade and wardrobe whence came The Admiral's fancy dress were flat and scattered. I disturbed nothing within the lighthouse save The Admiral's rock garden. These inspirited stones—freely and indisputably—were mine, including the enigmatic Donut Stone and its indwelling and inscrutable idea which to this day has remained a mystery. I placed the precious rocks carefully into a pillowcase to be reunited with the Great Quartz and with the relics of my own natural wonders. As surely as these stones were mine, so would the imperial Rolls Royce be Gloria's. Such grandeur suited her lofty disposition; Claude cared nothing for the vanities of appearance. "Stripped naked," he said, "you can't tell a duke from a dunce."

From the crown of the old tower Jo Anne rescued the inconspicuous lantern that had caught her attention during the eye of the storm. And so I—Jo Anne with her lantern and I with my imperishable stones—left the lighthouse for the last time.

I say the last time because with The Admiral gone and Jo Anne now astir in my soul, Hurricane could never be the same. Already I had decided to go to the clear, clean state of Arizona, the state of sun, sand, and sky to study the earth and stars! With The Admiral's money and my record at the academy no university would turn me away.

But it was leaving the island that baffled me. How profound and yet how sublimely silly it all seemed: the very idea of turning The Admiral into ashes and seeding his bones into the Gulf of Mexico!—of saying good-bye to Zip, a dog, my body buddy of old—but especially of wondering what now to do with Jo Anne and how to reckon with whatever endowment she had injected into my heart!—of fearing, even trembling now, that my ever independent Spencer might choose to desert me, to remain alone on Hurricane! Or was it I to be left alone on the mainland! See how profoundly and indecipherably silly it all was?

And Jo Anne! My pervading and mysterious Jo Anne! She was now *happening* constantly to me! If The Admiral had stones in which he had planted his cherished ideas—ideas that he could move, arrange, possess—what was I to do with my Jo Anne whose very existence now defied possession or arrangement and whose very breath and body transcended all idea?

Like a movie reel gone backwards and berserk, the pictures darted through my brain: poor innocent Rowdy . . . the cicada hull of Silent Sound . . . the withered leg of Uncle Minos . . . the old thrill of *Bull Bluegill* . . . Zip's colorful little turd . . . J/JA cut in the bark of the kissing tree—an ordinary beech of the species *Fagus*—and Jo Anne . . . my Jo Anne . . .

Was the jig-saw puzzle of my mind coming apart . . . ?

That night I came into Jo Anne's room and touched her awake. "Jo Anne," I whispered. I knelt beside her—she a mystery in the darkness. Without words we kissed until there were footsteps on the stairs.

Later that night I dreamt Jo Anne and I were in the Gulf alone, swimming toward the shore in the moonlight. We touched sand and walked naked upon the beach . . .

24

Spencer's Confession

I was surprised to learn that The Admiral was our only casualty on the island.

But if death did not exist for Spencer, why does it—like the returning gulls—keep repeating itself? How could its ominous shadow appear from nowhere or come from nothing?

And here again on the wharf was Woody the hearse man in the long, gray Cadillac as if he had arrived without appointment. And here was The Admiral as white and as dead as chalk. Women at the Holy Chapel had wrapped his body tightly in a sheet and brought him to the *Umbilicus*. He lay inert on a rolling latticework of stainless steel. Zip too, was present, sitting at attention. He knew my grandfather was dead. He watched Woody and his helper slide him into the hearse.

I would see The Admiral to Mobile and return his ashes that afternoon. Besides Woody, Zeorge, and Zip, I would make the short voyage alone.

"Sorry about The Admiral," said Captain Zeorge, as I walked aboard the *Umbilicus*. The third button on his coat was still missing.

"I hope you'll get that button put back on by tomorrow," I said.

"The Admiral wants you to hand me his ashes during the ceremony."

"Oh?" Captain Zeorge said. He was surprised.

"It's regulation," I improvised. "Reverend Millsap is going to read the scripture and I'm going to let The Admiral's ashes into the Gulf."

Zeorge straightened his cap and pulled in his belly. "I'm very much obliged," he agreed.

"Class A uniform," I instructed, hinting at the missing button.

"Right—and Sergeant Zip?" Zeorge inquired with a twinkle of merriment.

"Right," I returned. "Class A coat but no tails." Zeorge was pleased with our little military joke. He approached me, examining my ears carefully.

"Hardly any difference now," he said and turned to walk away.

"The button," I reminded.

"Right," he said. He cut me a neat salute and walked away.

My grandfather had written down in elaborate detail how his interment at sea was to be set for sunrise on a Sunday. Captain Zeorge and Reverend Millsap were to officiate. A cannon from the old fort would fire, at which signal—The Admiral was exacting about this—Jo Anne and I were to join hands, and I would pour The Admiral's ashes upon the deep. At the same time atop the old fort Generals Lee and Grant would be halted for a moment, for what I could not determine. A pre-opt prayer for The Admiral himself? I thought not. A thanksgiving for our deliverance from the hurricane? A reverence for his reunion with his dearest love? Perhaps. A timely pause for the generals? The horses? I could not tell.

Woody was starboard smoking a cigarette.

Larger questions were revolving in my head:

Would my Uncle Minos appear—to see and be seen—at the commitment of his father's ashes?

Would I reveal The Admiral's secret gift of the Leviathan sanctuary, the Church of the Holy Sepulcher?

Could I face my shame in hating the homely and lonely Millsap whose only sin had been in loving my mother, of falling to the enchantment of her voice that had drawn him toward his bliss but short of his grasp?

Would Spencer choose to follow me to the mainland? To Arizona? To the stars?

A larger question was Jo Anne. At the sound of the cannon when Jo Anne and I were to join hands and I—at the close of this calamity—would commit The Admiral's ashes to the sea, would what started at our willing lips still be happening to Jo Anne? To me?

I dared not yet call it *love* out loud lest I should stop its pull, lest I should impede such a purity by thinking I had touched it all or that in merely speaking the word I might frighten its fragile joy away beyond all hope of recall or utterance; for I could imagine nothing sweeter now than the mystery of Jo Anne's presence, the fragrance of her breath, her abundant hair, and the warm communion of her lips.

Zeorge sounded his barge horn. Across the Gulf was the gray skyline of Mobile. I opened the rear door of the hearse so I might see the last of my grandfather.

"Dear comrade, you can see neither the last nor the start of anything unless, of course, you can find yourself in the center of everything and then find the sides of the big bowl you're in."

I was in no mood for the ant's riddles. His voice was clear and crisp but carried a note of anxiety. He was sitting boldly—perhaps too boldly—on The Admiral's chest, The Admiral now strapped down and wrapped tightly in his desert-sheet of white.

"'Tis no desert I assure you," Spencer said. "I know the living sand when I see it. Speaking of sand, have you secured the Great Quartz so that its essence be preserved?" he asked.

I had. I had placed the stone upon my table of natural wonders beside Secret Silence and the disc of Mr. Grumps.

"And," Spencer continued, "pray you not murder The Admiral's secret of the Leviathan sanctuary, but leave it alive, a mystery in the old fish. Will you carry the Quartz with you to the mainland so its noble meaning be not forgot in your new and bewildered atmosphere?"

I was struck with the seriousness of the question. But it was more of a request.

"Yes," I said, "yes I will."

I had not noticed that Spencer was wearing a waistcoat open at the front to show his shining thorax—and a sleek pair of velvet slippers. For all his impertinence I was glad to see the redundant ant. With the imponderable questions tumbling in my mind, I fear I was becoming a bit too bold myself, extravagant, in fact intoxicated to find myself facing an airy future, cocked on a rocky crag somewhere from which I must fly or fall.

To keep my balance with the ant I would rattle his riddle.

"I don't give a doodler's damn about you or *the big bowl I'm in,*" I blurted.

"And neither do your crinkly cornflakes," said Spencer. "But, if the powers please, I must hope you to be more than a cornflake loosed in a roving bowl."

To the note of anxiety in Spencer's voice there was added a quarter note of anguish. I was sorry I had spoken so rudely to the ant and was deeply fearful that this might be the last I'd see of Spencer. I felt as if—in his new waistcoat and in his abrupt presence on The Admiral's corpse—that this was his civil way of bidding me farewell forever. So—mustering all my reserves and forsaking any attitude of modesty—I raised my voice without restraint.

"Was Jo Anne right?" I asked forthwith as if I were stripping myself naked before the insect. "Was *I* the stranger at my mother's funeral who saw myself in him? Will I be gray and wear wire-rim glasses? Am I already out there?—" I said, pointing into the future. "Am I yet to be?" My soul was filling to the brim. "Will Jo Anne and I marry? Will we roll and tumble naked in the dark, wallow in delicious secrets yet undisclosed and suffocate ourselves in rambunctious love and have lots and lots of babies?"

My lungs were empty. There was a slow relaxation in the ant's features. It was the first time I had seen a genuine human smile on Spencer's face.

"Of course, of course," he chuckled. "But shan't you have to wait and see?"

But something was troubling Spencer. Something deep inside was nibbling at his soul.

"In all my ages," he said, "I have tantalized the minds of princes and paupers, warriors and saints, but have always remained aloof and steadfast to the cosmosis of my nature. But," he confessed, "of late I have become a little bit of thee." He looked at me wistfully. "And so," he said, "I detect a weary future for myself alone, shifting from fallen kingdom to kingdom, from time to uncertain time."

A teardrop fell from his eye.

"I have lied," he admitted sadly. "I have said I do not cry. But, alas, tears are a habit of yours I have caught and cannot now deny—no fault of yours! But think not," he said with renewed vigor, "that I shall reprove myself or grubble in self pity or remorse. I am still of an ancient race, a *Formicidae* ever enraged to hold my own against the ravages of deceit and the vomitous insipidity of soft-bellied sloth and spinelessness!"

Spencer stood up on The Admiral's corpse, straightened his prim waistcoat and said with dignity—

"Oft-times I may have missed the mark but ever was my aim an honest one!"

I could not help but be taken by Spencer's bombast, for it was always the ant's brazen honesty that impressed me and that, in my moments of timidity, inclined me toward him. But mainly I was relieved. For if it were true that I might be a loss to Spencer, how much more a loss for me if I should lose him?

And yet a snag remained. Should I not be honest too?

Spencer was making his way away from me toward the foot of The Admiral. I was mindful of Spencer's obliviousness of death and his constant chiding of time—

"If you come with me," I warned, thinking only of the ant, "I may sometime die, like The Admiral here, and you with me!"

The comment stopped Spencer in his tracks. He turned, and a broad smile made his face almost human.

"Ha!" he blurted—then "Ha haaaaa ha," he returned with great gusto. "Me? Die? A gross supposition!" and added gleefully, "A hippopotamus hypothesis!"

"It could happen!" I insisted with real concern for the ant.

"Well," Spencer said, "that's just the chance I'll have to take."

"I'll bring the Great Quartz with me. Are you are coming?" I pursued.

Captain Zeorge sounded his barge horn. We were entering the port of Mobile.

That night in the secret of her room Jo Anne and I embraced and kissed and let our hearts run free.

Later in a dream we walked naked on the beach, our backs to the moon. Before us in the misty glare on the ramparts of a child's abandoned sand castle was Spencer, holding his hat-pin rapier to the stars and defying the relentless tide that rolled and broke, dissolving castle and all in the lunar light. In rescue Jo Anne rushed to the ruins and ran her fingers through the empty sand . . .

"Who was he?" she asked.

Suddenly I awoke.

25

A Commitment to the Sea

At sunrise on Sunday, Captain Zeorge cut the droning of the *Umbilicus* and we were quietly afloat in the Gulf of Mexico.

In the early light we were all shadows: my angular Uncle Claude and his petite and explosive Gloria; my reclusive Uncle Minos hunched forward in his mighty shoulders, Venoria holding to his arm; the Lincolnesque Millsap gazing out to sea; I, starboard, facing him; and Jo Anne standing next to me.

No, I would not divulge the secret of the Church of the Holy Sepulcher. "Leave the mystery alive in the belly of Leviathan," Spencer had pled.

The sun was emerging from the Gulf . . .

The silent cannon fired, the flame following itself—then the boom . . .

Captain Zeorge popped to attention and marched smartly from centerdeck up the left flank of our clan, executed a sharp right-oblique, halted, and handed me the open urn. I marveled at Zeorge's military adroitness. He stood at strict attention with his cap bill pulled parallel across his brow . . .

I knelt down on one knee with The Admiral's ashes . . .

Millsap crossed his chest, took a breath, held up his head, and read from the Book of Job such lines as The Admiral had prescribed:

> Where were you when I laid
> the foundations of the earth . . .
> or who shut in the sea with
> doors . . . Have you entered into
> the springs of the sea or
> walked in the recesses of the deep?

Millsap cleared his throat and turned a clump of pages. Then amazingly:

> I am a rose . . . a lily of the
> valleys . . . Arise my love, my fair one
> and come away, for lo, the winter
> is past, the rain over and gone . . .
> and flowers appear . . .

I had no doubt what had inspired these verses in The Admiral or that at this moment an echo of my mother's voice was sent ringing through The Reverend's brain. Nor did I fail to catch a tremor of this fearful bliss with Jo Anne kneeling by my side.

With a nod from Millsap, Jo Anne took my hand, and I released The Admiral's ashes to the sea.

It was all too large a moment to recall in full. Only fragments now remain: Millsap's lonely voice trailing off across the Gulf—my Uncle Minos, alive, now released from his salty vault, leaning on his withered leg and looking at the wholesome Venoria with her wispy smile—my gawky Uncle Claude, his lobster arms folded across his chest and his snippy Gloria with her lips tight-pressed.

Then came an instant image: The generals' horses halted for a pause. And there was Jo Anne kneeling with me, hand in hand, before the limpid waters, watching The Admiral's ashes strike the wavelets like diamonds, then descend . . .

The cannon fired again.

I could not see but knew the bronze horses were back in stride. And, facing tomorrow . . . and tomorrow . . . here was I.

26

From This Day Forward

I said goodbyes to all at the Merrimac and took Jo Anne to the wharf with me. She was nurturing a brown sack package. She touched her fingers to my lips.

"Is it still happening?" she asked me softly. I held her masterpiece *Bull Bluegill* under my arm.

"Yes," I said.

I kissed her hair.

"Between us?" she whispered.

"Yes," I said.

Zeorge bumped his barge horn.

Jo Anne put her head on my chest.

"A Likeness," she said and handed me the brown sack package.

It was The Admiral's lighthouse lantern. The old lamp was smudgy, empty, and smelled of burnt wick. Jo Anne put a penny pack of matches and a shiny twenty-five cent piece in my hand.

"Kerosene," she smiled.

She kissed her finger and touched it to my lips.

I put the lantern and *Bull Bluegill* in the van and drove across the landing ramp and onto the *Umbilicus*.

"It's the first time I ever seen your hermit uncle," Zeorge said of

The Admiral's sunrise service. He was wearing his blouse with the new button. "Thought you ought to have this," he said.

It was The Admiral's empty urn.

Zeorge's mate bumped the barge horn and we were underway.

Jo Anne was waving. I laid the urn on the back seat with the Great Quartz and got out of the van. I had not forgotten the keystone to The Admiral's rock garden.

"I most definitely would not have come without it," echoed a voice from the urn.

"What? What?" I said. "Spencer?" I said, putting my head and shoulders inside the van.

"This clay," came the voice with clinical detachment, "tho' crudely glazed, is of the finest extraction, perhaps from the Lower Paleolithic Epoch—quite a tick-tock before your time."

"Spencer," I said again to reassure myself of the ant's presence.

There was a small movement inside the urn, and then—

"Our old lighthouse Admiral has well imbued his thoughtful stones, but I fear it is I who know best the soul of this pregnant globe."

Spencer swept his forearm across the bounding horizon, then strolled forth from the mouth of the urn and hastened to the top corner of the Great Quartz. He was wearing the trim waistcoat and a white shoestring scarf. Then with cool certainty, "I know a great deal about clay," the ant said.

"Are you all right?" Captain Zeorge asked, laying a hand on my shoulder.

"All right," I said and lifted my head into the open air.

Jo Anne had moved to the end of the wharf. She was raising her hand. Zeorge was blocking my view.

"I hear it's off with you to Arizona," Zeorge said.

"I reckon," I said, trying to see around the large Captain.

"And Sergeant Zip?"

"He chose to stay," I said impatiently.

"Deserter!" said Zeorge, with a flavor of fun.

"Retired," I said, seeking a shortcut to our conversation. I raised a hand to catch Jo Anne's eye.

"No pension for our bobtail veteran?" asked the inquisitive Zeorge.

"Of course. Venoria feeds Zip every day his goody-bits."

"Ah, our hefty golden gal who swims bare-ass 'cross the bay."

Jo Anne's red hair was ablaze in the morning sun.

"Right," I said, "and thanks for doing The Admiral's ashes yesterday."

"Obliged," he said.

"And for the new button on your blouse," I said.

"Right," he said.

"May I?" I asked, indicating Zeorge's binoculars. He handed me the glasses and joined his mate in the pilot house.

I put the binoculars to my eyes to bring Jo Anne in closer view. Making no adjustments on the glasses, I took wide aim at Hurricane but first saw only Spencer's globed antennae bobbing on the horizon. The ant was sitting squarely on the axle of the instrument. Then, sighting through the tubes, I could see the ant's left leg swaying idly in the topmost arc of the right lens. Even in the ocular blur, I could tell this was Spencer's crooked foot.

"Oh great Zeus and Zanzibar!" Spencer cried. "Of course my dear silliness it is my crooked foot, but ne'er try I to hide it. And may I ask how you can see anything looking straight at *me*? Have you these brief summers learned nothing?"

I recalled our first meeting summers ago when I caught a glimpse of the Wholeworld Ocean through the ant's belly.

"These polished knobs," Spencer continued, shaking his antennae, "may for me catch the essence of infinity, but in your view they are, alas, as dumb-bells, as useless to you as dugs on a boar hog. Henceforth, heedless of me, I do indeed fear you and your careless kind may be washed astray in future distances. But—hear me!—you have inherited, at least from me, a residue of reason which, in fact, is a treasure left quite unmined."

This was all too big a gush for me to swallow.

I put my eyes back to the binoculars, making finer adjustments to bring the island back in view.

"Please align your eye in the proper azimuth if you wish to *see* what you are looking *at*," Spencer said.

Zeorge blew his barge horn.

A quick twist on the binoculars zoomed the island in. To the left, on the old fort, riding in slow pursuit, were the brassy Grant and Lee. In the middle was Johnny Revelation's Ark anchored in the sand. On the right was The Admiral's lighthouse leaning out to sea.

On the wharf, standing tiptoe under a new WELCOME TO HURRICANE SIGN, was Jo Anne, waving, speaking silent words to me . . .

The drone of *Umbilicus* was stretching me out while time and distance were rapidly crowding in, drawing me away but into a zany immensity too huge to miss, too rare to touch, too far to see.

"Ah ha! That's it!" Spencer avowed, "you see we really need no sack, no trunk, no wordy bundles to pack our mystery in, but, large or small, carry it lightly, anywhere, in no space at all." But I had not abandoned *Bull Bluegill.*

I looked up briefly at the ant, careful not to disturb his seat on the binoculars. He was pointing forward, or was it back, to Jo Anne. He gave his scarf a little flip so that it floated back to me.

"See?" he said.

I was not sure.

Through the glasses I could read Jo Anne's lips, the shape of her words.

She was saying *Is-it-still-happening-between-us?*

"Yes," I answered.

Made unstable by the vibrating barge, I held the binoculars as steady as I could.

"What is *it*?" Spencer wanted to know.

I could not answer.

Zeorge bumped the barge horn again.

Is-it-still-happening-between-us? Jo Anne's lips repeated.

"Yes, yes," I answered, receiving her words as warmly as they were sent.

Both of Spencer's feet were now fidgeting excitedly in the right lens. I dared not look at them lest I lose sight of Jo Anne. Her lips were shaping words to me, more slowly but with greater deliberation and expression.

"*Be-tween-us?*" she was asking.

"Yes," I said.

Under me I could feel the motion of the *Umbilicus* and the ever-expanding gulf.

"*Be-tween-US?*" she urged.

"Yes, yes," I said to Jo Anne, feeling between us a growing closeness while getting ever farther out of reach.

Her words were getting past me . . . I could catch only their direction, their inclination . . .

"Yes, yes, yes," I said, letting out my whole soul to bridge the distance . . .

"Oh excellent!" Spencer sang out. "Excellent well! For without such happy confidence, such sure connection, I fear you might ever have been poor company—detached, unfocused, perhaps deranged, a motherless calf bawling at the inconstant moon."

Jo Anne was fading now—her lips sending words that sailed over my head.

I held the binoculars firmly.

"What's she saying, what's she saying?" I inquired of the ant.

Zeorge's barge horn again . . .

I could feel Spencer walking lightly across my knuckles and up to the socket of my ear.

"Are you listening?" Spencer whispered.

"Yes," I said.

"She is saying 'Love . . . love . . . love . . . Can you hear me? Are we here now and ever yet to be?' . . ."

Yet to be, I thought. *Shall I grow gray? Wear wire-rim glasses? Am I, after all, traveling a million miles an hour backwards into the future?*

"Jo Anne . . . Jo Anne . . ." I whispered to her through the breeze. "Will we sometime tumble naked in the darkness, ignite our souls, engulf all distances, and make delicious love together?"

When I looked away from the tubes I could see, from the corner of my eye, Spencer resting calmly on my shoulder.

"Are we," I asked the ant pointblank, "are we—you, Jo Anne, I—are we here now and also yet to be?"

"But of course, of course," said Spencer quite leisurely, "but shan't we have to wait and see?"

About the Author

OXFORD STROUD grew up in Camden, Alabama. He left Wilcox County to serve in the Eighth Air Force in England during World War II, and studied some at Oxford University. After the war, he worked for a time with a logging company in the state of Washington. For thirty years he taught English Literature at Auburn University. Afterwards he and his wife Mary Anne continued to live in Auburn where they had reared a family of three sons and two daughters. Harcourt Brace Jovanovich published his first novel, *Marbles*, in 1991 and later selected it for reissue in paperback as the inaugural novel in their Harvest American series. He died in March 2002.